TWO MOONS OF EARTH:

BEYOND DESOLATION

N. Mil...

NORMAN COUSE

Published by Norman Couse
Publishing partner: Paragon Publishing, Rothersthorpe
First published 2014
© Norman Couse 2014
All characters and stories created by Norman Couse

ISBN 978-1-78222-352-8

Book design, layout and production management by Into Print
www.intoprint.net
01604 832149

Printed and bound in UK and USA by Lightning Source

Once again, I would like to thank my wife and best friend Elaine. Also Aimee, for another great cover illustration.

And last but not least Liz (Hettie) Hodgson, for pushing me to finish the story.

Also by Norman Couse

Two Moons of Earth: Beyond Voreda
ISBN: 978-1-78222-058-9

THESE ARE the further adventures of John Fox, a humble man travelling through a strange and marvellous world, but not his own.

How he got there is still the biggest mystery of all. A one he hopes to unravel, as he continues his journey with his new found family and friends. They move through lands never seen by either him or his friends. Facing wonders, marvels and dangers, none of which any of them could ever have imagined, changing them all and their ideas and outlook forever.

As they journey on, sharing in all the tears and laughter as they go, they face a tyrant whose very mention brings fear to all, even the bravest of men...

Two Moons of Earth: Where Am I?

ISBN: 978-1-78222-352-8

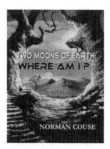

THIS IS the story of John, an average man in an average town, somewhere in England, but the events that unfold, just happened to happen to John, who is cursed with the knowledge that there is more to life. Knowledge for some is a blessing, but for others, with no hope of change, stuck in a meaningless existence, it's a curse. After all, ignorance is bliss... isn't it?

Until one winter's morning, he wakes up for another early morning shift. Thinking he's late, he rushes down stairs and out the door, but this is where his adventure begins. For instead of stepping out into a cold winter's morning, he finds himself waking to the sun beating down hard on his back. He is in the middle of a desert, how he got there, he has no idea, and where here is, is the biggest mystery of all. Which will take him on an adventure, across strange lands and places, seeing even stranger animals, and making friends with people and creatures, he couldn't have imagined. Some of which would travel with him, showing and sharing some of the wonders along the way, in these strange yet sometimes dark and marvellous lands, as he searches for answers.

1

THE NEXT MORNING everyone slowly starts to wake with Cin being the first to stir. He lies there with eyes yet to open, and hearing a giggling decides to listen a moment. He hears some of the very young greenem whispering beside him. "Do you think he's awake yet?" one whispers.

"Well he was stirring," giggles another.

"Poke him," giggles another.

"No I'm not poking him, you poke him, open one of his eyelids," sniggers another young greenem. "We can't do that."

"Let's just stand on him. Yeah let's," they all giggle together.

Cin can't help himself, try as he might, he can't help but smile. "Look he must be awake," whispers one excitedly. "He's smiling."

"No," replies another. "Sometimes they do that, it's wind I think."

Cin suddenly shoots bolt upright as fast as he can shouting, "*Boo*."

The young greenem are so startled they fall backwards giggling terribly. They then giggle even harder on seeing Big Dan, John, Billie and the others shoot up also, after being woken so suddenly by Cin's shout. Max yawns, stretches and wiping the sleep from her eyes turns to see Woodnut sitting patiently beside her cross legged. "Have a nice sleep?" he asks.

"Yes thanks," she answers.

But then a sudden terror grips her as she calls out, "Maxie."

"She's absolutely fine," Woodnut reassures her. "Everything went perfectly."

Max heaves a sigh of relief and asks, "So where is she?"

"She's on her way," replies Woodnut. "But she will have a patch over her eye, but it's only for a few hours, it's nothing to get alarmed about."

Max nods. "Oh I see yes," she says. Nods. "I can understand that."

Woodnut waves across the clearing and out of the trees towards them walks Maxie. As she gets closer her mum gets up and runs towards her arms outstretched. "Oh Maxie, I was so worried about you," she tells her, holding her tightly.

"I'm ok Mum, you shouldn't fuss so," sighs Maxie.

Max leans back scowling at her. "You never told me you would be knocked out, and it would be done by a fly, I mean come on."

Maxie shrugs. "Oh sorry Mum. Are you sure? I definitely remember saying about help from the xeazen."

"Hmm, right," answers Max glaring out of one eye. "Xeazen aye, and I'm meant to know what that is aye, hmm."

"Hey little lady," greets John as she approaches. "How are you?"

She smiles and replies, "Fine thanks Dad."

"So when's the grand unveiling then?" he asks.

Maxie smiles. "Not for a few while yet."

Breakfast is already laid out for them, and as they tuck in Max and Maxie are told about the previous evening and having to go to Tain province. Maxie sighs deeply on seeing her friend Little Billie getting so upset about them leaving.

Then soon breakfast is over and after a fond farewell to the greenem, which as always seems to take a while, as each and every one wants to either shake their hands or touch them as they say good bye. Finally they are on their way to the stronghold with Woodnut, Maxie, Little Billie and Spring Peeper leading the way. Fluff plods alongside John, "So where are you going?" John asks the jackerbell. "Do you not want to stop in the wood, I thought you would be more at home there?"

Fluff makes a sudden snarling noise making the two greenem giggle. John sighs. "Go on then," he says. "What is it?"

Woodnut shouts back, "He's just said he's coming with you, there's nothing for him here now anyway." John looks down frowning at Fluff who nudges him with his head then bends down and licks his hand.

John then cracks into a smile. "Oh I suppose," he grins patting his head. "How could I say no to that cute face?"

"Cute," mutters Big Dan nudging Cin.

"I know," whispers Cin. "That thing's enough to give anyone nightmares. Fluff indeed, Spike would have been a better name if you ask me."

Half way back and everyone is chatting when Big Dan turns to John and asks, "So are you going to tell us what all that was about last night then or not?"

Hearing this everyone falls silent and John shrugs. "Oh err, you noticed then, nothing really."

"Nothing," gasps Big Dan.

"Are you joking?" he cackles "We thought you'd gone insane. It must have been something, I've never seen anyone get as mad."

John sighs. "Oh ok then I suppose. It was those Suelan Tain people's excuse for destroying the greenem's home, and the unique forest and fauna, so called progress."

"But John, surely progress is a good thing?" asks Dan.

"I'm not sure to be honest," John answers. "I used to think so when I was young and knew no better, but these days a little older and a little wiser, I'm not so sure it is. You see it seems to me, by what I've seen on my own earth, in the name of progress is only a phrase used by either greedy uncaring unscrupulous governments, to line their pockets and those of their friends. Or by rich and powerful people to become even more rich and powerful, and it is always at the expense of some poor individuals or their land, who they hope are too stupid or too powerless to realise, or do anything about it anyway. Sometimes even having the cheek to say, it's for their benefit really, or the old classic, it will benefit you as well in the long run. We used to have great forests like you have here, the lungs of the earth they called them. As the trees take poisons out of the air and produce oxygen, and keeps the climate as it should be, and producing clean air for us all to breath. But even knowing that hasn't stopped them cutting down and destroying them, all for the sake of, guess what, yep you got it, progress, to make the land a richer one for all there. But as a matter of fact, all it really meant was the rich got richer, the poor got poorer, and the earth is choking, and the weather is changing everywhere, and the people's of the forests who lived there in relative peace and harmony, now have no home and no way of life, and once truly remarkable cultures are dead or dying. But that is just one example my friends, there are many others, different cultures, different countries different environments. But always the same excuse for destroying people's lives, or their homes, by the people above them, progress. So I hope you can all understand and forgive me for my outburst last night. But when you've seen what I've seen, you would not want it to happen again, you have a marvellous earth here, please do not ruin it. If you try and teach harmony not progress you won't go far wrong."

Big Dan shakes his head in disbelief. "John my friend," he says. "That was amazing, yet a little scary, but tell me, is that the function of trees, is that what they do. Why would your people destroy them knowing that?"

John shrugs. "Greed, plain and simple, greed."

Woodnut and Spring Peeper just stare at Big Dan as if he's an idiot. "What is it?" asks Dan a little puzzled. "What else do you think trees are for?" shout the two greenem. "Just to look good and make houses out of." "Well actually yes," stutters Big Dan slightly embarrassed.

"Well they're not," answer the two greenem in unison.

Woodnut then turns to John, "You know I could never work out why you have always looked at everything with such fascination, both in your eyes and heart, now I understand."

No one says much, instead contemplating what John's just told them, but as they pass the last handful of trees John stops and turns to Fluff and tells him, "Maybe you should head back to the trees pal, stay there for the night. I can't imagine you'd like to go back into that stronghold again in a hurry, we'll see you tomorrow." Fluff makes a strange noise and heads back to the trees.

Now nearly at the stronghold gate Tif quietly whispers to John, "May I ask you something?"

"Yes of course," answers John.

Tif sighs. "It's just there's been something praying on my mind since you said it," he says. "You want us to be friends with the two provinces you've just come from, and invite the two lords here to talk and trade. But what if they see this as weakness and one of them tries to take over or invade. How do we know they'll be telling the truth?"

John nods. "Hmm ok I see. And I'm pleased you asked rather than worry. These two lords are good men who want change themselves, and I mean no offence here, but lying and twisting is something only your people do. Be in no doubt if either of these men have a problem with anything, or anyone they will not hesitate to tell you, to lie or twist the truth, would not even enter their heads. And besides if any leader of any province breaks the peace and I have to come back and sort it out, be in no doubt once again, they know it and now you know it, I will rip through that province like a tornado and I will show no mercy. Now I hope that has put your mind at rest, but if there's anything else do not hesitate to ask ok."

Tif pats him on the shoulder. "Thanks John. That will do, I trust your word."

After a rest in the main hall they all gather their things and meet back outside. Billie gives Max and Maxie a kiss and a hug, as does Little Billie, but she still cannot help it and sheds a few tears. "Remember," Maxie tells her. "You now have a forest full of friends, and we can keep in contact as often as you like."

Tif, Hinata and Nia, are also there to wish them good bye and good luck, with lots of arm shaking and back slapping.

"So," asks John picking Maxie up. "When do we get to see this new and improved eye of yours then little lady?"

Maxie looks over to Woodnut who nods and Maxie wriggles back down. "Is everybody ready?" she asks nervously.

She then carefully takes hold of the patch and lifts it up, she then closes her normal eye and starts to look around with her new one. "What's it like?" asks her mother.

"It's weird," she mutters. "Everything looks so different, even you, all the colours, it's like nothing I could have ever imagined."

"Is this how you see everything and everyone?" she asks the two greenem.

Spring Peeper scratches his head. "I've no idea I just see things. To know that, I'd have to see through your eyes also."

John kneels down. "Give me a look then."

Maxie keeps her head still. "So what does it look like?" she asks.

"It's just the pupil of your eye at first glance, it doesn't look black anymore, it kind of has a purple hue about it," John replies. "Gees Louise, when you look really close, behind the hue it looks as if your pupil has been divided into lots of different segments, a bit like a xeazen's eye."

Then as everyone else takes a closer look Maxie's eye starts to water a little and she has to close it. "What's the matter?" gasps Max rather alarmed.

"Nothing Mum," Maxie reassures her. "It's a little bright that's all."

"Yes it will be for a few days," Woodnut tells her. "You will have to keep putting the patch back on, just until your eye and your brain gets use to the light difference."

John mutters ratching through his pockets. "Maybe I can help there, here put these on."

"What are they?" asks Maxie.

John smiles. "Sun glasses, put them on."

"What are they for?" she asks.

John smiles. "A couple of reasons," he says. "If it's a bright sunny day, maybe a little too bright they protect your eyes, just take the glare off."

He winks. "And secondly, they look cool."

"Oh my yes, that's much better, thanks Dad," announces Maxie.

"Where on earth did you get such an item?" asks Nia.

Shrugging John replies, "E-bay."

Then with a last farewell and a see you soon Max and the three boys set off for Tain led by Spring Peeper.

John and Woodnut then follow Billie, Tif and the others back inside and up to the big hall. By now most warriors are up and having breakfast when they walk in and a cheer goes up as they enter. John and the others give a wave as they sit down. One of the warriors stands up and shouts over, "My Lord we are going to have a game of battle down after breakfast if you would like to join us."

"Yes thanks I would like that," replies John. "But first I would like your undivided attention for a while, I have something important to tell you all."

He then goes on to tell the stunned people his intentions and why. Some are sad, some are pleased Tif is one of their new leaders, and a few aren't bothered either way, but all want to send him off with a great celebration that evening, and true to their word that evening is full of laughter merryment and happiness, the like of which had never been seen in that place before, with a new freedom enjoyed by all. With Tif even teaching them a couple of songs he remembered from the night before, which like everything else goes down a storm.

At the end of the evening John says his farewells to the men just before retiring, as he plans to get up just after day brake and set of before most of them have even woken. Every man woman and boy there stands up and bows as he leaves the hall. Early the next morning just before dawn he starts to stir, when to his surprise there is a knock at the door and a head pops round. "Are you decent?" comes the call.

"Yes come in," shouts John.

In walks Billie and her daughter. She walks up to the bed carrying a tray as John sits up a little more before the tray is placed on his lap. To his utter delight he sees the tray is full of bacon sausage and eggs from their farm. "Well slap me backwards," he gasps. "This is fantastic. How did you know?"

Billie grins. "That's easy, I've never seen anyone eat thin back and sausage with as much relish as you."

Little Billie goes over to Woodnut. "Don't think we've forgotten about you," she tells him carrying a large tub.

"Thank you," he replies. "But I don't eat the same food as you."

The little girl smiles and places the tub down in front of him. "Yes I know."

Woodnut then sees the tub is filled with fresh clean damp earth and smiling broadly he slides his feet into the tub nearly squealing with delight. "This is amazing," he shouts. "How did you know? I mean, where did you get this please? You must tell me."

"Good stuff is it pal?" asks John.

Woodnut nods excitedly. Little Billie giggles then taps the side of her nose, "You have your secrets and I have mine."

Then after breakfast John gets dressed and packs his bag, but not before taking Spot out, who is curled up fast asleep.

The dawn has just raised its first fingers, and it's still quite dark as he and Woodnut make their way through the narrow passageways and down to the main door. He gives a sigh as he opens the large door and steps outside, but as he does, to his utter shock and surprise a loud cheer rings out. The courtyard is full and everyone is there to wish him farewell, with his two personal guards and maids first to greet him. "My Lord please this is a tragedy," the two guards' cry. "If you have to go, may we come with you?"

"What all four of you?" asks John.

"Yes of course," answers one of the maids.

"Please call me John, I am your lord no longer. And if it were any other time, as long as you wanted to travel with me as friends and not servants I would say yes of course. But I have to catch up with the others, and I will be travelling faster than you could ever keep up with. But more than that, I do not know what we have to face when we get to our destination, and I would not want to put you in danger."

"As you wish my Lord," sigh the two men. John shakes his head.

Billie and her daughter are next to come up, with Billie giving him a kiss and Little Billie hands him a neatly wrapped package. "I'll put it in your bag," she tells him.

"What is it?" asks John.

Billie smiles back. "Cured thin back and sausage," she tells him. "We keep it for the winter months, it tastes just as good, but will not go off."

John's eyes light up like lanterns. "Thank you very much, you have just made me the happiest man alive." Billie gives out a little chuckle, "If only everyone were as easy to please."

Tif and Nia approach next and Tif says, "We have a little something for you John."

Nia hangs a chain around his neck. "This is the official chain of office for the lord of this land, and the crest is the crest of Taraten."

"Should one of you three not have this?" asks John.

Tif grins. "Nah we'd only argue over it. And besides, we are just keeping the seat warm for you so to say. Or perhaps that daughter of yours one day, a rather remarkable young lady."

John bows. "I'm honoured and privileged, not just by this gesture but to have known you all, until we meet again my friends."

As John and Woodnut set off, Hinata leads the way through the honour guard that has formed an arch of swords all the way to the gate. John pauses in the gateway and turns. "I want to thank you all for this honour my friends. You are a people reborn, for the better, and for the wiser, the future is now in your own hands, guide it wisely. And finally you Hinata, goodbye my friend, you have proven to me more than all, that there is still a chance for anyone to make a change for the better, if they so wish."

Hinata bows smiling proudly. "And you have shown me my Lord, err John, there can be good in all."

He then grins. "And to never go on looks."

John smiles and bows once more then turns and walks away, with Woodnut leading the way. Even as they go over the crest and down the hill John and Woodnut can still hear the men cheer and call their farewells to them.

2

JOHN LOOKS DOWN at Woodnut. "Do you know, I can't believe it, but that was actually quite emotional, only a few days ago they were going to torture and kill us, how bizarre? Now, how about I put you on my shoulders and we have a little run."

"Not yet," answers Woodnut pointing ahead to some trees.

"Why what's over there?" asks John a little confused.

"Your friend Fluff," giggles Woodnut.

John sighs. "Oh yes I forgot about him. I never thought, he should have went with the others, he'll never keep up."

"It wouldn't have made a difference," Woodnut tells him. "They are just people to him, he sees you as his friend and saviour, and you will have a hard time telling him otherwise. But do not worry they are excellent trackers, as are all species of jackerbell, you may out run it, but you will not lose it."

As they get closer to the trees the jackerbell comes bounding out towards them. It screeches to a halt at their feet wagging its strange tail. John gives it a rub under the chin. "Nice to see you dude, I thought you might have went with the others. I should have told you, I'll be running very fast, you will not keep up with me."

Fluff starts to make the oddest noise. John cannot help but smirk as he turns to Woodnut, "What's he saying?"

"He's not," answers Woodnut. "He's laughing at you, he doesn't believe anything can out run him, let alone an ooman."

John still a little amused chuckles, "I had no idea they could laugh."

"Most animals can laugh John," Woodnut tells him. "It's only oomans that are arrogant enough to think they're the only ones. Take the time to listen and learn, and you'll start to hear it all around you."

"All around me aye," replies John looking at him suspiciously.

Woodnut starts to giggle, "No I didn't mean it like that."

"Which way are we going now anyway?" asks John, taking off his bag and ratching inside it.

"The far side of the open ground," answers Woodnut. "Where that big tree is, near that house."

John nods as he waves a large piece of cured sausage under Fluff's nose. "I see. Smell good pal."

Drooling, the jackerbell gives out a loud grunt. "I tell you what then," John says winking. "You beat me and Woodnut to that tree and it's yours, ok."

The excited Fluff takes off immediately. "Hey that's cheating," shouts John throwing his bag on his back and popping Woodnut on his shoulders. "Hold on tight dude."

"To what," yelps Woodnut grabbing John's ears out of desperation.

John then takes off running with Woodnut screaming like a siren, but he is soon squealing with delight as John gets into a rhythm picking up speed, and running at full pelt it's not long before he's hurtling past Fluff.

John and Woodnut are waiting leant against the tree when Fluff finally gets there. John grins pulling the cured sausage out of his pocket. "Not laughing now. Guess this is mine then," he says taking a nibble off the end. "Hum lovely." He then winks and hands half to Fluff, who gulps it down then licks his hand. He then picks Woodnut back up and puts him on his shoulders. "Right pal," he says turning to Fluff. "I won't be running that fast but, you may struggle to keep up. Would you like me to stop and wait now and again?"

Fluff makes a few strange noises and gestures. Woodnut nods turning to John, "He says he knows you're scent, he doesn't have to see you. It doesn't matter how far ahead you are, he will find you with ease."

"Well I'm impressed," replies John nodding to Fluff. "Which way now Woodnut?"

Woodnut points to a tiny village in the distance. "Head straight towards that village until we cross the big river, then off to the left and follow that line of trees until you're just past the village."

John sets off slowly running settling into a steady pace. "How can you run so fast for so long?" asks Woodnut in a shaky voice and giggling with every bounce.

"I'm not sure to be honest," answers John. "I guess it's something to do with the gravity on this earth, or I'm eating better and exercising more, a combination of both maybe. I'm not sure, all I know is back on my earth, I couldn't run a hundred yards without panting like a dog."

After jogging for an hour or so they come to the banks of a large river, John puts Woodnut down and the two walk along the bank for a while, taking in the sights and sounds of the river while heading towards the bridge a mile or so ahead. "Your directions were a degree or so out my friend," says John.

"Just a little," giggles Woodnut. "I thought you'd like to walk by the river."

John nods grinning back. "Yeah I could do with a rest."

"At this rate we should catch up with the others by evening," says Woodnut.

John nods. "Excellent," he says. "But it is a pity we couldn't spend more time looking around this place. I bet it's quite interesting, unmoving and unchanged when you think about it, the people of this province have never even met someone from outside it, it would be good for them also I think."

He then starts to chuckle to himself. "What is it?" asks Woodnut.

"I've just thought," answers John still chuckling. "I bet there's some strange ones amongst them."

"You mean even stranger than the rest of you oomans," giggles Woodnut.

John winks. "Well I don't know if they'll be that strange."

They then hear a loud panting behind them and turn to see Fluff running towards them, but instead of stopping it runs straight past them and down to the river for a drink. "Come on," says John. "We'll have a sit down by the river for five."

John and his two friends sit down together and watch the river flow slowly by. As the minutes pass Woodnut gives John a nudge and points up the river a little away, he then turns to see a mother flurry slowly wadding into the water followed by a dozen young all in line impatiently waiting their turn, and chirping noisily as they try to catch up with their mum. John smiles to himself muttering softly, "This is the weirdest place, spiders that think they're ducks, what next worms that eat fish." He then starts to feel his bag move and Spot appears on his shoulder, he lifts it down and onto his knee and gives it a stroke, but it's not there long before it also goes down to the water for a drink, before slowly sliding in and under.

John reaches around and gets out a couple of pieces bacon, eating one himself and giving the other to Fluff. "Do you think Spot would like a piece of this?" he asks Woodnut.

Woodnut giggles and points back over towards the flurry and its young swimming behind her. As they watch, the smallest one at the back suddenly disappears under with barely a ripple. Woodnut giggles again and John thinks nothing more of it, until Spot appears back out the water again, walking towards him with the last leg of the young flurry disappearing down its throat.

"That answers that question," shrugs John rather bemused. "You should have told me, I'd have stopped it, and give it some bacon or something."

Woodnut just shrugs. "It's just part of life John, everything eats, or is eaten by something else."

"I can't argue with that I suppose," replies John frowning. "But I bet you wouldn't say that if there was something that eats greenem walking towards us."

"I might," giggles Woodnut.

Spot climbs back onto John's knee, curls around, closes its eyes and making a soft wittering noise falls asleep, now quite content. John feels awful about moving it so sits for another five minutes. "Right I think we'll walk the next mile to the bridge and run from there." He puts Spot down on the bank beside him. "That includes you young lady, you can walk your duck off." They then slowly walk down to the bridge which stands just behind a large willow tree overhanging the river. Then as they get onto the bridge they see a young boy fishing, sitting in a small dip between the tree and the bridge. John stops leaning over the rail and watches the lad for a minute or two, then shouts, "Caught anything yet?"

"No not yet Sir," answers the boy a little startled. "I haven't been here long. I've never seen you around here before Sir, are you from the stronghold?"

John nods. "I was there for a while. But I'm not from this province."

"Y, Y, Y you're not," stutters the boy. "I've never met anyone from another province before, you're not going to hurt me are you Sir?"

John laughs. "No, why would I do that?"

The boy heaves a sigh of relief, then suddenly drops his pole and starts to scramble backwards terrified until he finds himself backed against the tree.

"What's the matter?" asks John rather shocked himself at the boy's reaction.

The boy points behind John who looks round at Fluff and Woodnut.

"What is it?" asks John.

"Me and Fluff I think," giggles Woodnut.

"Oh I see," replies John turning back round.

Fluff steps forward and puts his head over the rails as John pats him on the back. "It's ok," shouts John. "They won't hurt you, they're with me."

The boy calms down slightly and shuffles back to where he was, grabbing his pole. "Th, that's a jackerbell Sir. Are you not scared?"

"He's my friend," answers John. "You should never be scared of a friend, or it isn't really a friend."

"There are rumours Sir, that the new Lord Taraten has a pet jackerbell, and he walks with a thousand greenem. Do you know him Sir, is that where you got yours?"

John gives out a wry laugh, "A thousand greenem aye, surely there wouldn't be enough room to move in the stronghold if there were that many there, but you could say I know him I suppose, yes."

The young lad now quite excited starts to chatter away, "They say he was the one that moved the moon stone, and that he brings peace to all. Is that true Sir?"

"Let's hope so," smiles John. "Now I have to be going young man, good luck with the fishing."

"Yes Sir," answers the lad. "I hope so too, or we don't eat tonight, my father isn't well enough to work at the moment."

"Oh that is sad, we can't have that now can we?" sighs John, now ratching in his bag before he pulls out his bag of money.

He then bends down and whispers to Woodnut, "I don't know how much this stuff is wortt. What do you think I should give him?"

Woodnut rubs his chin then answers, "Several of them big brown ones and a few of them little shiney ones."

"Sounds good to me," nods John standing back up.

He then shouts to the boy, "Hold out your hands young man, here just in case you don't catch anything."

He then drops the coins into the boy's hands. "Thank you Sir," gasps the boy. "But, but, are you sure Sir, this is an awful lot of money."

"Does that mean you don't want it then?" grins John winking to the boy.

"What's your name anyway lad?" he asks as he starts to walk away.

"Rea Sir", shouts the boy. "And yours Sir?"

"Just call me John, nice to meet you again young man, now I've got to go."

"John," mumbles the boy, as he watches them crosses the bridge and out of sight.

"I don't believe it," he gasps flopping down. "It's him that was really him."

Just over the bridge and Spot is allowed to get back in the bag, and John puts Woodnut back on his shoulders. "Is everyone ready? Which way now?" he asks.

Woodnut points to the left slightly to some trees a short distance from the village, three or four miles ahead. "Hold on tight," shouts John as he starts jogging making Woodnut giggle with delight again, but he runs a little slower this time to let Fluff keep up. Then it's not long before they reach the line of trees and John slows down to a walk. "What's the matter?" asks Woodnut as John puts him down.

John shrugs. "Nothing, I just thought you'd get a good view of the village from here. We may not have time to explore this land, but we can stop and look a while. It's like a picture postcard of life a few hundred years ago, from back where I come, like a snap shot from history."

Woodnut just scratches his head. "All these places just look the same to me John, and I never understand why oomans want to live in a box made out of dead trees, locking themselves away from nature."

John grins. "Could it be to keep us safe and warm?"

Woodnut just shrugs again. "If oomans didn't spend most of their lives fighting and killing each other, over who owns what, then maybe they wouldn't have to."

John nods. "Fair point, as always my friend you are very wise."

Beside them Fluff is making a strange noise. "What's the matter with him?" asks John. "Don't tell me, he's laughing at us again isn't he."

"Yes," giggles Woodnut.

They walk along together chatting until the little village peters out and apart from a small farmhouse near the woods some distance ahead the way is clear. "Well shall we carry on chaps?" says John in a funny voice. The jackerbell gives out a grunt and takes off as John bends down and picks Woodnut up when something catches his eye just in the trees. He stands back up and makes his way over. "Where are you going?" shouts Woodnut running to catch up with him.

"Nowhere," answers John. "I'm just going to see what this thing is."

Then just ahead is a creature about seven inches long and five inches tall slowly sliding along on one foot like a snail, leaving a fine silk like substance in its wake, on top of the foot there is no shell but a relatively round blob resembling a melted scoop of ice cream, with the whole thing being a creamy white colour. And the whole thing being topped by a little brown dome on top. John kneels down beside it, running one of his fingers across the hair like substance behind it. "You must be some sort of snail," thinks John aloud.

"John what are you doing," gasps Woodnut. "Leave that thing, that, that, horrible creature alone."

John looks at Woodnut rather surprised. "Why is it poisonous?"

"No not really not unless you try and eat it," answers Woodnut.

"So what is it?" asks John, "Some sort of snail or slug."

Woodnut bursts into fits of laughter, "Yeah its nothing but a big stinky slimy slug."

Then calming down a little he says, "It's a boing boing, now let's go and catch up with Fluff."

John smiles. "A boing boing aye. A rather unusual name."

Then as John watches, its large foot retracts into its body mass, and two long arm like appendages start to appear out the sides. John sits speechless watching in fascination, and to his further surprise, two other appendages start to appear underneath it, but like neither arms nor legs more like two finally coiled springs about two to three inches long, it then proceeds to hop away making a boing boing noise as it goes. John puts his hand out in front of it to stop it, it then turns and tries to hop the other way, but he stops it with the other hand. "Well its obvious now how they got theire name," he says to himself.

"Come on John, leave that horrible thing alone, lets go," begs Woodnut.

"You know," says John. "It wasn't that long ago people thought you were horrible creatures."

"That's different," snaps Woodnut. "We try to be kind, they're nothing but pompous snobs."

John slowly turns his head towards Woodnut in total disbelief. "What the heck do you mean by that?" he asks. "How on earth can these things be either pompous or snobs?"

"They just are," snaps Woodnut angrily. "They think they're so much better than everybody else."

John just stares at Woodnut, unsure if he's winding him up or not. "Go on," says Woodnut. "Poke that brown dome on the top of its head."

John a little unsure gently pokes it, then a moment later a loud shout rings out, "Leave me alone."

John looks all around. "Who shouted that?" he gasps.

"He did," says Woodnut pointing to the boing boing.

"But, But, how," exclaims John. "I can't even see a mouth."

"He can talk in your head if you touch the silk behind it," Woodnut tells him.

"Well slap my face and call me Susan," gasps John. "You can speak telepathically."

"You poked me in the eye," comes a loud voice in John's head.

"Then," it snaps arrogantly. "You expect me to talk to you."

"Well I've news for you oh great one," it says sarcastically. "We don't speak to lower life forms, now let me go, now."

John is utterly gob smacked, and stutters, "My, my name is John, nice to meet you, sorry for the eye, I didn't realise what it was."

"Oh, I know who you are," snaps the creature. "And my name is only for my people. And as I told you, we don't normally speak to lower life forms. So you should think yourself, very very lucky, now let me go monkey."

John stunned moves his hands out the way and the creature hops away. He then stands back up still stunned and walks back. "Sorry Woodnut," he says. "I guess you were right about them things, what an arrogant creature. Now we'd better get a move on."

He pops Woodnut on his shoulders. "Fluff must be either miles ahead or wondering where we are," says John.

But they barely get up to speed, when less than half a mile ahead the jackerbell is stopped, snarling and growling ferociously at a small farm house a few hundred yards away.

John stops putting Woodnut back down and sighs. "I tell you what. I can see why people are so scared of these things, it's not just large and mean looking, but when it does that, it does look truly terrifying."

3

"WHAT'S THE MATTER pal?" asks John, but Fluff's eyes are fixed ahead at some children with sticks playing in the yard.

"Stand back a little John," says Woodnut. "I'll find out what the problem is."

Woodnut finally gets its attention and listens to Fluffs snarls moans and growls. "What is it then?" asks John.

"You see that large cage in the yard," answers Woodnut. "And the kids poking sticks in it, and hitting something."

John shrugs. "Yeah so, it's a farm."

"Maybe to you," answers Woodnut. "But all our friend here knows is, some poor animal is trapped and caged in there, and being tortured and tormented. He said if he was not with us he would have gone down there and savaged them. You have to remember John, he was trapped, tormented, and starved himself for an awful long time. He's an intelligent beast John, and his pain is deep, and his emotions still high."

John sighs. "Yes of course, sorry. And I can understand totally, but I can't really go around releasing farm animals everywhere I go now can I."

"I'm not sure it is John," answers Woodnut.

"You must have good eyes," gasps John. "I can just about make out the back wall and a few bars on the side. What's in it then?"

"I've no idea," answers Woodnut. "I can't see from here either. It's our friend here Fluff, he can smell its fear, but surprisingly he can't make out what it is either."

John nods. "Now that is impressive. He can smell its fear from here, no wonder he has no problem finding us. Ok, I tell you what then, you two wait here and I'll go down and have a look, see what it is. Tell the children off for being cruel if it's a domestic animal. And if it's a trapped wild animal then I'll release it. Does that sound fair?"

Fluff gives a nod, than as John sets off he gives out a large snarl. "John," giggles Woodnut. "A message from Fluff, he says he'll be watching from here and if you need help, he'll be straight there."

John turns slightly giving a wave as he goes.

He gets to the open yard, where the four children are so engrossed in what they are doing, and the names they are calling, they do not notice him beside them until he shouts, "What are you lot up to?"

The children nearly jump out of their skin. "Who are you?" asks one of the children.

"My names John, and do you not know hitting things with sticks is cruel, would you like it?"

"What's it got to do with you," shouts another of the children. "It's our pet."

"And you think that gives you the right to beat it do you," snaps John.

"Yeah, we can do what we want it's ours, we're going to tell our Dad," shout the children as they run off.

"That's good," mumbles John. "Saves me looking for him, now let's see what we have here then."

He then looks through the wooden bars to see huddled in the corner a relatively small creature not more than four feet tall. And although humanoid in appearance quite obviously not human, totally devoid of hair and with olive green coloured skin. John stands there stunned. "Twice in one day," he thinks to himself.

"Now who, or more appropriately, what are you?" he mutters aloud.

The creature turns and straightens up a little; "Gees Louise," gasps John. "You're just a child, a boy, I think."

"Are you going to poke me now?" comes a trembling voice.

"Well knock me down with a feather," gasps a stunned John. "Stand up child, I promise I'm not here to hurt you."

Cautiously and carefully the strange looking child stands up. "What's your name son?" John asks.

The boy just shrugs and in his croaky shaky voice answers, "They call me allsorts Sir, it depends on what mood they're in."

"No, you don't understand," answers John. "You are obviously an intelligent creature, capable of speech and conversation. What did your mother and father call you?"

"I don't know Sir," he answers. "I don't remember them."

John nods. "What species are you? Where are you from?"

The boy just shrugs again. "I don't know Sir. They found me in a wood Sir after hearing me crying, and they brought me here. I don't really remember much before it."

John shakes his head in disbelief. "And how long ago was that then?"

"Two summers and one winter Sir," he answers.

"You what," shouts John. "Are you telling me you've been in there, this whole time?"

"No Sir they put me in the barn in the winter."

"How could people do that?" snaps John. "That's awful, would you like to get out of there?"

"Yes of course Sir," answers the boy.

"But where would I go," he says starting to cry.

"You'd better go now Sir," sobs the boy. "Before the farmer gets here, he can get very angry."

John frowns, "You let me worry about him."

"Hey you there, what are you doing, this is my property," comes a loud angry voice behind him.

John smiles kindly at the boy and winks. "Don't worry. Remember where there's life, there's hope. And I'm here to bring hope back into your life young man."

The little creature just cowers back in the corner. "Hey you I won't tell you again," shouts the man grabbing a pitch fork.

John turns around and marches towards him smiling politely, and trying to keep his temper. "Good morning," he says. "This your farm is it."

"Yes of course," answers the man. "And you're trespassing on it stranger."

"Please," replies John. "My name's John, now let's start again, we seem to have got off on the wrong foot."

"You'll get off on the end of my fork in a minute, if you don't tell me your reason for being here," shouts the farmer.

John starts to frown clenching his fists. "Ok, if you want to be like that," he says. "My friend saw your children being cruel to this creature, hitting and poking it with sticks and the like, and he asked me to come and have a look."

"So," grumps the man pointing his fork towards John again. "What's that have to do with you or your friend? This is my farm and I'll do as I please. Who cares anyway? It's just some freak, some weird greenem cross."

"This is a living speaking sentient child," snarls John. "Even if it were a greenem, what gives you the right to do this? Have you not heard of the new law? Cruelty is outlawed, to all people and creatures."

"Pah," laughs the man. "Yes I have heard this, and of this new Lord. But this is my farm and I will do as I please. And I have also heard he has a pet spiked jackerbell, and travels with a thousand greenem, and that's how he won the previous Lord."

"Now listen and listen good," snaps John. "You are the second obnoxious thing I've came across today, and my patience's is wearing very, very thin."

He then starts to pull the chain out from under his shirt. "You see this, recognise it do you."

The man stands there speechless, eyes transfixed on the chain. "Good," growls John. "I see you do, this means your land, your farm, your children, even you. Your life belongs to me, and that jackerbell you mentioned is not a pet, he is a friend, and I travel with only one greenem usually. And if you don't damn well believe me you can ask them yourself, they're waiting for me over there by the wood, look."

The farmer slowly turns his head and looks over. He gasps with terror discarding his pitchfork instantly and drops to his knees and starts to beg and plead, "Please my Lord, I, I didn't know, I had no idea, how could I. Please do not harm my family, if you have to kill someone, please just me I beg you."

With that the man breaks down crying. "Stop crying and get up man," snaps John. "Do you always treat people so nastily? Why, what was the point? And if you knew about the new law and not being cruel, why did you still do it."

The farmer still sobbing gets to his feet. "I don't know why," he says. "I'm sorry my Lord, it won't happen again. Please, I'll, I'll, let the freak go if you wish, take him with you. Yeah that's it, take him with you, if you wish my Lord."

"Just please spare my family and me," panics the farmer.

"Wow," John thinks to himself. "What type of place is this when people are so scared of their ruler, even for their whole family's lives, when they've done nothing?

"Right quieten down," John tells him. "No one's going to be hurt or punished, this time. But from now on you will be nicer, you and your family, to all. People, greenem, whatever ok, and no cruelty to any animal, is that understood?"

"Y, yes my Lord. Th, thank you," whimpers the man. "W, we heard you were a good man, we just never really dared to believe it, if you were in our position you wouldn't either."

John sighs. "No, I suppose not, he was a cruel and sadistic man, and those trials were nothing but murder, no ordinary person could have ever survived them."

"But you did my Lord," replies the man.

John winks cheekily. "Yes, but I'm no ordinary person. Now tell me, the child, where did you get him. Tell me all you know."

"There's not much to tell my Lord. We came across it coming up for about two and a half years ago now. We were visiting relatives near the border and happened to be passing the edge of an ancient woodland. When my eldest girl heard this strange croaky crying coming from just inside the wood, child like but not quite, if that makes sense Sire. She insisted we take a look, and there a little way in, partly obscured under a bush was where we found it. But we did not take it then, I wouldn't let my daughter touch it. It was the next morning on our way back home, we heard it again, and went for another look. It had crawled nearly out of the wood, but had obviously been abandoned, and my daughter asked if she could take it home and keep it as a pet. I thought, well it was going to die anyway, why not. It seemed to grow very quickly and then started to talk a little. And that's all there is to know my Lord, I promise you of that."

John stands nodding until the farmer stops then asks, "So do you have any idea what species it is? Or where it may have come from?"

"No my Lord," he answers. "Would you like me to unlock the cage it's quite tame."

"No it's ok," answers John. "I'll sort it."

He then walks over to the large cage and sees the child still cowering in the corner. He pauses a moment shaking his head, then grabs the thick wooden bars of the locked cage door, and with a sudden sharp yank rips the door clean off breaking the lock at the same time. He then smiles to himself as he hears the farmer and his four children gasp behind him. He then turns and throws the door towards the farmer, and the man goes white as it lands at his feet. The young boy in the corner of the cage squeals with shock turning sharply to see what's going on. John then smiles kindly at him putting out his hand. "Come on little one," he says. "It's time to go, let's see if we can't find your parents."

The child's large black and orange bulbous eyes fill with tears as he cautiously gives John his hand. "Are you sure Sir?" he croaks. "I don't want you to get in trouble."

"Hey trust me," says John softly. "It's all sorted, no one will hurt you now, you have my word."

The boy stands up straight and slowly walks out. As they start to walk away the child looks over towards the farmer and his children, but quickly turns his head away and stares at the ground. John seeing this whispers, "Stand up tall, put your shoulders back and hold your head up high. You have done nothing wrong, you are the victim here not the criminal." The boy raises his head and nearly smiles.

As they get further away and out of earshot John asks, "Now tell me young man, what is your name?"

The boy just shrugs. "Whatever you want Sir, they usually call me allsorts."

John smiles kindly. "My name is not Sir, it is John ok. I can't believe you haven't got a name, that's awful. What name would you like then?"

"I'm, I'm not sure Sir," stutters the boy.

John smiles. "What did I say?"

The boy smiles back. "I'm not sure John. They called me Froggy a lot, but I'm not sure what that means."

John sighs deeply. "That's not a name son. It's an insult, and we will not call you that. I tell you what, you take your time, we'll think of something. Now tell me, do you remember anything about your past, your parents, where you're from. Anything, anything at all."

"No not really," the boy replies. "Being very happy. I'm not sure why, but it is a memory I used to cling on to, to keep me alive. The oldest girl told me once my mother was a person like them who was raped by a greenem. And when I was born she could not bare the sight of me and dumped me in the wood to die, and that I should think myself lucky that they came along."

John is speechless for a moment then gasps, "That's awful. I can't believe someone could say something so cruel to anybody, let alone to a child."

"Does that mean its not true Sir, err John."

"No, it's not true," answers John. "You should wipe those horrible words and thoughts from your mind. But tell me, have you ever seen or met a greenem before."

"No never," he answers. "I haven't seen anything."

"So do you know anything about greenem?" asks John.

"No nothing," he answers.

John nods. "Well I do, and I'll share a little with you. Greenem are living walking intelligent creatures, who evolved from plants, and they do not mate like us. So even if they wanted to, they could not do that awful thing to a lady."

"Now correct me if I'm wrong," he continues. "You are not a plant are you?"

The boy smiles. "No."

"Something else you should know about greenem," John tells him. "They are the most peaceful caring creatures you will ever meet, who love life and laughter, and would never hurt anyone or anything. Ok?"

The boy smiles. "Ok."

John smiles back. "Now that's better. You have a nice smile, you should do it more."

This makes the child smile even more. "I have it," the boy then says excitedly.

"What's that young man?" asks John.

"When I first saw you back there," croaks the boy sheepishly. "You told me, where there is life there is hope. I would like my name to be Hope, because I have lived in it for so long. I just never thought it was possible, or do you think that's a silly name."

"No," replies John in a soft kind voice. "I think it's a wonderful name, Hope it is."

"Where are we going now?" asks the boy.

John smiles. "Over to the trees, to meet up with my two friends, one whom will know exactly what species you are, and where you hale from. I see you wear no clothes, is this intentional, or did they simply not give you any."

"A bit of both," answers Hope. "I was found in clothes but I grew out of them. But the new ones they gave me just absorbed the moisture from the surface of my skin, leaving me dry, sore and thirsty, and felling very ill."

"Oh right yes," stutters John. "I noticed your hand was moist, I just thought it was nerves. So your whole body is like that."

"Yes John feel," Hope says letting go of John's hand but as he does so there is a faint popping sound.

John smiles. "What was that?"

"Sorry," apologises Hope. "It sometimes happens when I grip too hard."

John looks at his hand and sees four circular suction marks on his hand, a little confused he takes the boys hand and turns it over. "Now that is interesting," he mutters. "You only have three fingers and a thumb on each hand, yet you have five toes on each foot."

Then as he takes a closer look at the boy's hands he notices a little circular indentation at the end of each finger, like little suction cups. "What are those for?" he asks.

The boy gives him an odd look. "They help me grip things, I tense them and push the air out, and they hold things tight, do yours not."

John shows him his hands. "I don't have them," he says. "I see your toes, they seem very long, and are slightly webbed. Do you have them on the end of your toes also?"

"Yes," answers the boy. "But they're not as strong. Why what does all this mean?"

John then touches the boys back and head. "You do have a moist secretion on your skin. I'm maybe wrong, but my first thought is that you are evolved from some sort of amphibian species. But my friend Woodnut should know better, nearly there now."

As they reach the wood, Woodnut jumps to his feet, but Fluff just lies there flat out sleeping. Woodnut just stares at the child rubbing his chin deep in thought. John smiles. "These are my friends. May I introduce you to my best friend and travelling companion, Mr Woodnut Greenfern. Woodnut this is Hope."

"Nice to meet you Sir" replies Hope.

"It's nice to meet you to," giggles Woodnut.

"Why is he laughing at me?" asks Hope with a quiver in his voice.

"He's not giggling at you," John reassures him. "It's just not often he gets called Sir. You'll have to get used to giggling I'm afraid, it's a greenem's favourite thing to do."

Woodnut then bows low. "Please call me Woodnut, all my friends do."

The child's eyes nearly pop out of his head. "You're, you're a greenem," he splutters. "You are nothing like I expected."

"Don't tell me," giggles Woodnut. "Much more handsome."

The young boy suddenly blurts out a little giggle, then throws his hands over his mouth in shock.

"What's the matter?" asks John.

The boy's eyes fill up. "I didn't know I could do that," he says.

Woodnut's mouth falls open hearing this, and he stares up at John in disbelief.

"My friend," says John staring back. "You have no idea, I'll tell you all in a minute." John then winks. "Now young man, I'm afraid that's something else you'll have to get used to doing, it happens when you're happy. And I see a lot of happiness in your future. Now let me introduce you to this sleeping beauty. Are you getting up Fluff?" he shouts.

Fluff jumps to his feet instantly. But the sight of this large scary imposing beast taller than he is makes the boy squeal and rush behind John's legs.

"It's ok," John tells him. "He won't hurt you, will you pal?"

The jackerbell gives out a strange bark. John smiles taking the lads hand and leading him back around. "You see. Hope this is Fluff, Fluff this is Hope."

"Nice to meet you Sir," greets Hope.

Fluff starts to make a strange noise. "What's he doing?" asks Hope.

John grins. "He's laughing. I guess he's not used to being called Sir either. You have a lot to thank Fluff for as it was him that noticed your cage and insisted I go over and release whatever was in there. He was caged himself for a long time, and now he can't bare the sight of them."

The young boy suddenly rushes forwards and throws his arms around Fluff's large powerful neck and hugs him, thanking him over and over again. Finally he let's go and turning back to John asks sheepishly, "If you don't mind, please could I rest a while, that was an awful long walk." He then bursts into tears, "Please don't get cross with me."

John picks him up and gives him a cuddle. "Hey it's ok, calm down, I thought we were friends, aye." Woodnut stares in disbelief as John calms the boy down then puts him down. "Right you sit down there little man. I'll take my bag off and maybe we could have something to eat. Perhaps our friend here Woodnut, could check you over, and make sure you're fit and healthy ok."

Still sobbing the boy sits down. "John, what did they do to this child?" gasps Woodnut despairingly.

John takes a xentham fruit from his bag and hands it to Hope and asks him, "What is your favourite food in the world?"

"I'm not sure what it's called," he answers.

John smiles. "That doesn't matter," he says. "Just close your eyes and picture it in your mind ok. Can you do that for me?"

The boy nods. "Yes."

John smiles. "Good, now you bite that xentham fruit I gave you, it will taste just like that."

The child does as he is told, eating the fruit with relish. "Hmm it even wriggles," he sniggers.

As he sits there eating John proceeds to tell Woodnut and Fluff all he knows about the boy and his life so far, and his treatment by the farmer and his children. The boy sits there quietly resting as John finishes his tale. "Shall we go now?" he asks.

"No not yet," answers John. "You sit there quiet a moment longer. So what do you think Woodnut, what species is he, any idea? Where could we find his people or parents?"

Woodnut simply stands in front of the child with his hand on his chin deep in thought studying the boy closely.

The child's eyes light up as John hands him another xentham. "Wriggly in the mouth," he giggles again.

Curiosity getting the better of him John asks, "What is this favourite food? And what did they feed you anyway?"

"Scraps of meat," he answers. "That's what they gave me mostly, they made me try vegetables, I think that's what they called them, but they just made me ill. But my favourite food was the things I caught myself. Sometimes I used to catch these large colourful flies, they were very nice, but my favourite things were these little brown furry things that used to scuttle around the yard at night."

"Mice maybe?" asks John.

"Yes that's them," shouts Hope excitedly. "Do you like them too?"

"That's not bad is it?" he then asks suddenly looking a little worried.

"No not at all," John reassures him. "If that's what you like to eat, so be it. Our friend Fluff here is not vegetarian either you know. In fact the way he's snarling towards that farmhouse, and after hearing the way you were treated, he would quite happily go down there and eat everyone down there I think."

Fluff suddenly looks round excitedly. "No," exclaims John. "That doesn't mean you can."

Fluff gives out a loud grump then sits back down. Making Hope snigger again.

"So what's the score then Woodnut?" asks John.

"This child is a mystery," announces Woodnut. "I have never seen his like, I never thought I'd see the day. I will have to tell the old ones about this, but first his health. Could you lay him down flat for me please?"

The boy lies down on the grass, and Woodnut starts his examination, poking him, prodding him, and listening to his chest, even tasting the secretion on his skin. "Are you a doctor?" asks the child, but Woodnut is too busy and does not reply.

John stares at the boy and tells him, "You could say all greenem are doctors. But tell me, how do you know this word? The word doctor is a word I thought only I knew. I have never heard anyone else use it in these lands."

"I'm not sure Sir, err John," answers the boy. "It just seemed right, I must have heard it somewhere."

"Sit up child," asks Woodnut. "Open your eyes as wide as you can please. Uh hum, now put out your tongue please, as far as you can."

But to their surprise the child's tongue doesn't just come out towards Woodnut, it shoots clean past him. "Wow," shouts John. "Well I'll be gob smacked, your tongue must be three foot long at least."

Then with a big smile on his face John starts to clap. "John please," snaps Woodnut. "I'm doing an examination here."

"Oops sorry," apologises John.

"Ok that'll do" says Woodnut.

"What's the matter with my tongue?" asks Hope sheepishly staring at John.

John smiles. "Nothing little dude. Most impressive, wouldn't mind one like that myself."

Woodnut just stares at him. "What?" shrugs John. "There's got to be a thousand handy uses for a tongue that size surely? Err, I could clean my ears without having to take my hands out of my pockets for a start." Woodnut just shakes his head, but Hope laughs terribly. "Well what's the prognosis then?" John then asks.

"John this child is a true mystery," replies Woodnut. "His species appears to have evolved from amphibians. But I have never heard of such an evolved species as his anywhere, unless it's from a part of the world my people have never been to or heard of, that is always a possibility I suppose. So it's a little hard to tell his health with a hundred percent certainty. But he seems to be in quite good condition, a little malnourished and dehydrated, and we should try to build his muscles up when he gets stronger. But first plenty of food and fresh water. I think there's a small stream not to far ahead, he should paddle or bathe in it. If I'm right he should absorb the water directly through his skin."

The child starts to look very worried. "What does all that mean, you're not going to hurt me are you." Woodnut sits down beside him, and try's to explain to him slowly and carefully everything he has just said, making the boy feel a little better, but is still a little nervous, having never seen a river, or even bathed.

As they stand up to leave John tells the boy, "Right as soon as you start to feel tired, you tell us, and we'll stop immediately, ok. We won't get mad, it's what we want you to do alright."

Hope smiles nodding. "Yes ok. May I ask where are we going?"

"Our friends and family are up ahead," John replies. "We are going to catch up with them, then on to the next province where we have a problem to solve for some friends."

Hope suddenly starts to look worried again. "Do, do, you think your family will like me?" he says. "Will they mind me being there?"

John smiles kindly. "Hey trust me," he says. "Of course they'll like you. I think you're going to be very popular."

Ten minutes of walking and Hope starts to tire. "Are you alright?" asks Woodnut.

The boy nods nervously, then gives out a loud scream that nearly deafens them from a suddenly inflated throat pouch. As John turns round holding his ears, he sees Fluff has come up behind the boy, put his head between the boy's legs and thrown him on to his back. And the child is now riding on Fluffs back like a horse, with a smile that now nearly meets around the back literally. "I see someone has a new best friend," says John winking to the boy.

The child leans forward and puts his hands around Fluff's neck and gives him a kiss. John grins. "Are you up for a bit of fun?" he asks.

"What do you mean?" replies Hope.

"Do you think you could stay like that?" asks John. "And hold on tight with both your hands and feet."

"Yes of course," answers Hope.

John grins. "Excellent. If you start to struggle just ask him to slow down or stop."

"Right pal," says John winking to Fluff. "I have five bits of cured bacon in my pocket, the first to the river gets three bits the loser gets two."

But he doesn't get the chance to finish his sentence before Fluff has taken off with Hope squealing and laughing on his back. John picks up Woodnut and starts to run. It's only a twenty minute jog till they reach the bank of the small river with John letting Fluff just pip him to the post. Fluff stands there excitedly waging his strange tail, and licking his lips as John gives him the bacon. John and Woodnut sit down on the river bank and dip their feet in the water as a little encouragement. Hope climbs down off Fluff's back and stands beside them sniffing the air loudly. "I know this smell," he tells them.

"Why don't you put your feet in?" asks John. "You'll be ok, we're watching you."

Cautiously Hope dips one foot in, then quickly puts the other in. The feeling of joy and relief that comes over the child is so great it leaves him breathless and speechless, as he proceeds to lie down in the cool water. "I guess he likes it then," sniggers Woodnut.

The boy starts to swim around the river like he'd spent his whole life there, disappearing down in the deep part, and popping back up again in the shallows again giggling and laughing. After a short time he shoots out of the water landing beside them chewing something like there's no tomorrow, and in a muffled voice with bits of food flying out he tells them, "You have got to try this."

"It's the nicest thing in the world, honest," he tells them excitedly, holding out half a fish.

John and Woodnut just smile. "You eat it," John tells him. "I've just had something."

"Mr Woodnut," Hope asks excitedly. "Would you like to try some?"

Woodnut giggles and points down at his feet buried deep in the ground. "I am eating thank you," he says.

The young boy just smiles then takes another bite, he then sees Fluff licking his lips. "Would you like one?" he asks.

Fluff gives out a loud bark. "Brilliant," shouts Hope diving back into the water. "I'll go and get you one, there are loads down there."

"I tell you what," says John quietly to Woodnut. "Do you think you could get a message to the others?"

"Yes of course. What do you want to tell them?" whispers Woodnut.

"Tell them," continues John. "We'll be a little later than expected, and tell them that the child will be with us, and not to look too surprised. And a little care and kind words towards him when we first meet would go along way I think."

Woodnut nods. "That sounds an excellent idea. I'll get word to them as soon as possible."

Hope pops back out the water with a large wriggling fish and gives it to Fluff, who excitedly proceeds to kill and eat it. "Are you having fun?" asks Woodnut.

"Oh yes," answers Hope. "This is the most wonderful thing I have ever done. Honest, this is the best day of my life."

He then dives back into the water and John sighs. "How sad," he says.

Woodnut nods. "Yes I know what you mean. When a splash in the river is the most wonderful thing you have ever done."

"It's going to take some getting him out of there," says John.

"Another hour or two wont matter John," replies Woodnut.

John smiles. "Nah guess not. But he's definitely some sort of amphibian, that's for sure, he's in there like it's his second home. I tell you what though, I don't know how I got here as you know. All I remember is rushing out my door then bright light, and next thing I know is wakening up in the desert on what turns out to be a different world. And for all we know, something similar has happened to him, but he was just too young to remember."

"Before I met you John," answers Woodnut. "If someone had suggested that to me, I would have laughed so hard it would have split my bark. But now, well, it would answer a few questions, but we will not tell the child John, he's been through enough without them theories to worry about."

Hope then jumps back out the water with a full belly and stretches out beside them in the sun. "We'll be moving on soon," John tells him. "If your feeling up to it that is."

"Oh yes," answers Hope happily. "I've never felt this good before, in my whole life. Honest, I feel as if I could do anything."

"I tell you what Woodnut," says John. "You were right about him being dehydrated, he hasn't half filled out, and he looks at least a stone heavier."

"Are you feeling better after that?" asks John.

"Yes Sir, err John," replies Hope. "I feel much better, hmm, new yes that's it."

"Am I just imagining it?" asks John a little confused. "But wasn't he a darker shade of green earlier, he seems very light now, a pale lime green in fact."

"Yes I probably was," answers Hope. "My colour changes depending on my mood, and how I'm feeling, and how hot or cold I am. I can go from this very light colour to nearly dark brown, but I think this is the lightest I've ever been. But it's also the best I've ever felt."

"Well knock me down with a feather," exclaims John.

"Well I would say that confirms it John," says Woodnut. "I don't know about your earth, but some of the amphibians here have those exact same characteristics."

"Yes there are on mine also," agrees John.

"Shall we go now?" asks Hope in his croaky voice.

John puts Woodnut on his shoulders, goes back away runs and jumps clean over the small river. Hope and Fluff swim over together. The four then walk along together with John and Woodnut chatting as they go, when pausing for a moment Hope says rather timidly, "May I ask you something John?"

John smiles. "Yes of course young man, anything, fire away."

"Back on the farm," continues Hope. "I was too scared to watch, I thought you were going to be hurt, as was I. What did you say to that angry farmer to let me go? He's not a nice man, especially since his wife died." John gives him a cheeky grin. "Let's just say I introduced myself, and then made him an offer he and his children daren't refuse."

"But how?" asks Hope. "Were you not frightened, he was very big and very loud."

John gives out a little chuckle. "He was only a little bigger than me, that's not big, wait until you meet our friends Big Dan and Cin, now that's big. Sometimes people make a lot of noise because they can do nothing else but, and it's their way of either bluffing their opponents or avoiding conflict altogether you see."

"Yes kind of," answers Hope. "It's maybe just because I'm small."

Woodnut starts to giggle, "I don't know, you look pretty big to me."

John chuckles too as Hope stares down at Woodnut a little confused, then realising what he means starts laughing himself. "Just because you are small does not mean you are not brave," John tells him. "Take Woodnut and the other greenem for example. He and his people stood against the Lord of this province, and all his men the Tosh warriors, the most feared warriors of any land anywhere. At their own stronghold, to rescue me and the others, and won. And there are a lot smaller than you or I, and they are fully grown, you are still growing young man."

The young lad smiles broadly. "I understand now yes."

"That sounds very exciting," he says turning to Woodnut. "Would you, could you, well tell me about it please."

Woodnut takes his hand as excited to tell it, as the child is to hear it. And as the next few hours pass Woodnut tells the spellbound child every step he and Maxie had taken, from the moment they entered that province, and he listens to every word enthralled.

They then walk along but don't notice the ground underfoot getting increasingly wetter and boggier, until they find themselves up to their ankles in mud. Woodnut tells them to stop a moment and asks if he can stand on John's shoulders for a quick lay of the land. "Hum," he mutters. "We must get up onto higher ground, to that line of trees on the ridge there. This is getting dangerous here, and we should not have come this way."

"Hey silly man," comes a loud shout behind them, making even Fluff jump. John smiles. "Hi cutie."

Lilly milk giggles and blushes. "Stop it," she tells him. "From this point on John, you must all walk in single file and follow me carefully. This area you are in is very treacherous, and many people and creatures have died here."

"But first," she gasps noticing Hope staring at her. "Who are you child?"

"My name is Hope Miss, nice to meet you."

Lilly Milk is so surprised by the child she doesn't even giggle at being called Miss. "Where did you find this child?" she asks Woodnut. "I have never seen his like."

"Nor I," replies Woodnut. "We found him caged in a farmyard, John rescued him."

"Where are you from child?" asks Lilly.

"I'm not sure Miss," answers Hope.

"Hmm right," says Lilly suddenly snapping out of it. "We must go before the light starts to fade."

"Quickly follow me," she tells them.

The little mossy then leads the way with John taking the back, to keep an eye on everyone. She leads them twisting and turning, sometimes seeming to loop back round, and its nearly two hours until they are finally at the edge of the marsh land, and at the bottom of the ridge.

"I will leave you now," she tells them. "Now be careful where you are going next time."

The light is now starting to dim as Woodnut turns to John. "We should make our way to that large tree up there," he tells him. "Its hollow I can see the mark of my people on it, it will be a good place to shelter tonight."

"That's a good hike up there," replies John. "Woodnut you get on my shoulders and maybe Hope you could ride on Fluff's back. It won't take long that way."

And just as he said it's not long before they reach their destination and are standing beside the old large tree. "Is this where we are staying tonight?" asks Hope climbing down off Fluff.

Woodnut nods while fiddling with a knot on the tree. "Yes."

Then with a loud crack a piece of the tree bark starts to open. "Follow me," says Woodnut going in. "Oh and mind the steps, there are three going down."

Hope follows first followed with a very tight squeeze by Fluff and John, who closes the door after him. The four friends sit down and stare up at the dimming sky above. John nods. "Well this is cosy."

"The others stayed here last night," Woodnut tells them.

"Did they?" gasps John. "They did make good time, or have we taken our time."

"They made very good time," Woodnut replies. "But I don't think they stopped until very late, it won't take us long to catch up in the morning."

Hope gives out a loud yawn and John smiles. "Somebody's tired."

"Yes very," answers Hope. "It has been the best day of my life, but also the most tiring. Although it does feel strange, I'm normally just starting to wake up at this time."

Then with another loud yawn he curls up tucking his arms and legs under his body and falls asleep. John gets a drink, and some food out of his bag and splits it with Fluff, then after talking with Woodnut for an hour or so, he falls asleep himself.

John wakes up early the next day with only a little dim light filtering down to the bottom of the hollow tree. As he lays there he hears a gentle humming somewhere beside him. He sits up and looks round, and straining his eyes he sees its coming from a nearly invisible Hope. Who has gone a pale brown colour in the dim light, blending into the surrounding tree nearly perfectly. Hope sees John staring at him and stops instantly. "I'm sorry, did I wake you."

John smiles. "No not at all. Please carry on, the only other person I've heard humming like that is my daughter. Who taught you?"

"No one, it's just something I learned to do myself at night, when I was alone," he answers.

"Are you nocturnal by nature?" asks John. "Is it going to be a problem for you travelling through the day?"

"When they first put me in that cage, when I was small," sighs Hope. "I used to be awake all day and sleep all night, but they used to play with me back then. But it wasn't long before the novelty wore off, and there was nothing to do all day but sleep. I then realised I could see really well at night, it felt kind of, err, more natural to me, yes. I could watch the night creatures, and eat the ones that came close enough, otherwise I would have probably starved. But I really don't mind being awake during the day, not now I have friends like you. It might just take a few days to get used to it, that's all."

John nods. "If you're sure. If we can help in any way, you only have to ask ok."

Hope smiles. "Thank you I will."

Woodnut goes to the secret door and opens it, and they make their way out into the cool morning air. In the dim light of dawn John opens his bag and takes out some cured meats. He gives the drooling Fluff a few pieces first, then turns to Hope. "Would you like to try some?"

"Yes please," answers Hope excitedly so John gives him a couple of pieces of each meat, and then taking some himself puts the parcel back into his bag.

The child sniffs a piece of bacon first, then tentatively takes a nibble, his eyes suddenly light up and he crams the rest in. "This is wonderful, it's nearly as good as the fish yesterday, honest," he says in a muffled voice.

John grins. "I'm pleased you like it. Now if everyone's ready, we'll get an early start."

"Could I have another piece of meat first please?" asks Hope with his head bowed.

John nods. "Yes of course young man. Help yourself."

He smiles excitedly. "Thank you."

He is about to put his hand in John's bag when Woodnut shouts, "Stop."

"What's the matter?" asks Hope with a tear in his eye.

"Don't worry it's ok," answers Woodnut. "You haven't done anything wrong."

"But John," he continues. "Spot's in there."

"Oh yes," gasps John. "That was lucky, I forgot about her. I'm sorry young man, but until Spot gets used to you, you can't just put your hand in my bag. You see that's her home. And if she doesn't know you, she can be a very dangerous animal, and we don't want her biting you now do we."

He then gets a piece of meat out and hands it to the boy and winks. "There you go."

"I'm sorry, I just thought your pet was tame," answers Hope.

John picks his bag up and puts it on his back and sets off. "She's not really a pet," John tells him. "She's more of a, err, hem, how can I put it, err, a wild animal that happens to live in my bag. She can leave anytime she likes, she just chooses to stay."

"Yes mummy," sniggers Woodnut.

Johns frowns at Woodnut and says, "I tell you what. Why don't you take Woodnut's hand and he can tell you the story behind it. Would you like that?"

The boy nods excitedly. "Yes please."

They make good time with Hope now looking and feeling more invigorated than he ever has. As the sun starts to rise and warm the earth, the child's skin starts to get lighter and lighter. As they continue they start to find themselves travelling under a canopy of very large tall trees and although spaced a good distance apart, the foliage at the top stretches from one tree to another. Sending down broken shafts of light and illuminating parts of the ground like natural spotlights, and with barely a breath of air it starts to get a little sticky. "How are you doing young man?" asks John. "Would you like to stop a moment?"

"No it's alright thank you," answers the boy politely. "I don't know whether it's the trees, the heat or the stickiness, but I just feel wonderful. I could happily stay here."

John smiles. "If you like it here then, I think you're going to love it where we are heading for, a rain forest."

"I'm not sure what that is," replies Hope excitedly. "But it sounds wonderful."

It's nearly dinnertime and the line of trees they are now following are oak trees when John asks, "Shall we stop and have a little dinner?"

Woodnut and Hope agree and are about to sit down when Fluff starts to get very excited, running ahead and running back. "What is it?" asks John.

Fluff just gets more excited. "Woodnut could you do the honours please?" asks John.

Woodnut talks to Fluff. "It appears the others are not far ahead," he tells him. "And he says if we run it should only take another ten, fifteen minutes to reach them."

John smiles. "Excellent. Who's up for a little jog?"

They set off and are only jogging for a few minutes when they come across a large dip in the land and pause for a moment. They then find themselves looking down across the tops of the woodland ahead. A wood consisting of mainly oak and other broadleaf trees, but beyond the wood to the right is a small village and on the opposite side to the left is a similar village, more or less an identical distance and size from the wood as the other, with just the woodland itself separating them. "We should maybe walk down this bank John?" says Woodnut.

John winks. "Yeah, but where's the fun in that, hold on tight dude."

He takes off with Woodnut squealing wildly, and John not running, but jumping and skiing down, hotly pursued by Fluff. Woodnut does not stop squealing until John stops at the bottom. "Are you alright up there?" chuckles John.

Panting heavily Woodnut stutters, "That's the scariest most fun thing I've ever done. If we had time I'd ask to do it again."

But before John can reply they hear a skidding through the leaf littler behind them and are nearly ploughed down by Fluff trying to skid to a halt. "Are you alright Hope?" asks John. "You're nearly white, I didn't know you could go that light."

"No," pants the young boy. "Neither did I, that was terrifying."

"So you wouldn't want to do it again then?" asks John.

"Oh yes please," giggles Hope as John pats Fluff on the head. "Back up to the top and back down again, the winner gets a piece of sausage."

Fluff takes off making Hope yell with shock. "He does that every time," sighs John. "That's got to be cheating, right hold on pal."

"Yippee," squeals Woodnut as John bounds off.

It's not long before they're back down and John lets Fluff and Hope pip them to the post, and after splitting the sausage they set off walking. It's another ten minutes walk through the defused light of the trees until they see bright light splintering towards them from a small clearing ahead. Getting closer still they start to hear the sound of raised voices and shouting. "Sounds like trouble ahead John," says Woodnut.

"Isn't there always," sighs John, "It seems to haunt us wherever we go."

"We could always go around John," says Woodnut.

Fluff then gives out a loud snarl and points ahead. John shrugs. "I guess not. It must be the others, let's take a closer look."

They walk up a little further and stop behind a large bush and carefully peer through. What they see is not a small clearing but a track running through the forest, and there in the middle are Max, Cin, Big Dan and Lane and the others. Max, Maxie and Spring Peeper are tending to the wounds of a badly beaten man, while Cin, Big Dan and Lane are standing around four men kneeling in front of them.

John sighs. "Better see what's going on then. You three stay here."

Fluff gives him a nudge and growls. "He wants to come and help," giggles Woodnut.

"I tell you what pal," winks John. "You stay here and if I need you I'll give a whistle ok. Then you can terrify the life out of someone if they cause trouble. How's that?"

Fluff gives out a strange growl that makes Woodnut laugh. "What is it?" asks John.

"I can't repeat what he said in front of the child," sniggers Woodnut. "But he begrudgingly promises not to hurt anyone.

"But," he giggles again. "He will try and scare them to death."

John shakes his head, gives Fluff a suspicious look and pats him on the head and says, "Be good."

4

JOHN THEN PROCEEDS out onto the path. No one sees him at first until he shouts, "Everyone having fun."

"Daddy," shouts Maxie running over and jumping into his arms.

John gives her a kiss and puts her back down. "You see these four men Dad," shouts Maxie. "We caught them beating this poor man up, just to take his money, and they even threatened us."

"Not for long I'll bet," grins John.

"No," giggles Maxie. "The boys sorted them out. I'll have to go now, I'm treating the poor man's wounds."

John takes another few steps forwards towards the others. "Ah, nice to see you John my friend," greets Big Dan. "You're just in time, we were just discussing what to do with these curs. According to the poor fellow they were beating up, they do this on a regular basis, and they are well known and much feared in this area."

"To be honest John," nods Lane. "If you hadn't come along when you did, we were probably just going to kill them, it's the only way of guaranteeing they stop their evil ways."

"Sounds fair," shrugs John.

The four men start to beg for their lives. "Stand up," John tells them. "Now tell me boys how many times have people begged you to spare them, either their lives or their last bit of money."

The men stand there with their heads bowed until one answers, "We don't normally kill people, just rough them up a bit."

"Oh that's alright then," replies John loudly.

"Is it?" asks one of the men hopefully.

"No you fool," snaps John.

Lane and Cin cannot help but laugh. "So why do you do this?" asks John. "Can you not just get a job like decent folk? Or do you just like bullying and hurting people.

"This is our job," one of the men tells him now getting quite brazen.

"What do you mean," growls Cin. "This is your job?"

"Err well everyone knows," stutters the man. "This is our wood, and if you cross it you run the risk of having to pay the toll. That's why they try to cross in different places."

"Tut, tut, tut," goes John. "Now it does seem we have a problem now doesn't it? You say this is your wood, I say this wood belongs to my friends, and they've been here an awful lot longer than you."

"Who do you think you are little man?" shouts the leader "You wouldn't be so brave if your large friends weren't here."

Cin, Lane and Big Dan grimace and look away fearing the worse.

John sighs lowering his head and shaking it. "Everywhere I go," he mutters to himself. "It's not as if I'm small." Then staring the man dead in the eye he replies, "Yes that's right, now what ya gonna do about it?"

Big Dan gives out a loud booming laugh. "Err well nothing really," stutters the man.

One of the other men now looking very nervous suddenly bolts making a run for it down the track. "Do you want me to go after him John?" asks Lane.

John puts his hand up and shakes his head, he then turns slightly and gives a little whistle. Out of the wood snarling and screaming bounds Fluff, like some fearsome beast from the lowest pits of hell. He pounces on the man, flattening him to the ground, and holds him down with his mighty paws. He is drooling and snarling with teeth longer than a man's fingers, and no more than an inch from the man's face. It is such a shock and fearsome sight that every man there jumps back and gasps with shock. "Right," asks John calmly. "Anyone else want to run?"

The three men shake their heads, as does Cin. "Not you, you fool," whispers Lane elbowing him.

"Oh yes sorry," stutters Cin snapping out of it. "I'm just pleased that things on our side though."

"Yeah, right with you there," whispers Lane.

"Fluff come here pal," shouts John.

Fluff stops snarling and runs over to John sitting down by his side. John smiles giving him a rub under the chin. "Now, you back over here," shouts John.

But the man doesn't move. Big Dan gives a wry chuckle, "I think he's either passed out or dead John."

"Nearly did myself," he mutters.

"Now," says John staring at the leader. "When I say this wood belongs to my friends, I didn't mean my human friends. I meant the greenem and other creatures of the forest, from creeper to jackerbell. Do you understand?"

John then notices out the corner of his eye behind the others two little eyes, and a hand signalling to him, and realises its Lilly Milk. It takes him a few moments to realise what she means before she disappears again. "Right sorry yes, where was I," he stutters. "Lost my concentration for a moment there, sorry."

"From creepers to jackerbells," prompts Lane.

"Oh yes that's right thanks," nods John. "Right boys I'm going to cut to the chase here."

"Get on with it," shouts the leader. "If you're going to kill us, just kill us, or let us go."

John looks to Fluff. "Do me a favour, hold him pal, and if he says another word rip something off ok."

Fluff bounds forward, the man puts his hands out instinctively to stop it, but to no avail. The large powerful beast just pushes his head between them and grabs the man by the privates, making every one, including John grimace. "I meant an arm or leg or something," sighs John.

The man's mouth falls open and he is too frightened to even breathe deeply. "Just nod slowly if I ask you something ok," John tells him.

The man slowly nods. "Good," grins John. "Now from this moment on you four will mend your evil ways, you will get jobs and you will never rob or hurt anyone again. And if you are ever in this wood, or any other wood for that matter, you will show it, and the creatures in it the proper reverence ok. Do you understand?" All the men slowly nod. "Good because if you don't," continues John. "It is not me you need to fear, if you are ever seen robbing or hurting again, you will simply disappear, either devoured by an animal like my friend here, or perhaps the earth it's self. Be in no doubt where ever you are, you will simply disappear as the earth its self now knows who you are."

Then to everyone's surprise and shock two of the men are pulled down into the earth nearly up to the waist. The two men scream in terror. "You can let him go now dude," says John patting Fluff.

Fluff lets him go and sits back down beside him, much to the man's relief. The man then turns in horror to see his friends half buried. "How, how did you do that?" he stutters.

"I didn't," answers John. "As I said, the earth itself now knows of your evil deeds, now be good. You are now marked men, now and for always. And next time you will not be this lucky."

The two men are suddenly raised back out the ground, as quickly as they sank, and all three drop to their knees. "We will," they beg. "Please let us go now."

John nods and the men get back to their feet. They then go and pick their friend up and are about to leave when John shouts, "Haven't you forgotten something."

The men shrug. "Don't you owe this man some money," frowns John. "Those are mighty full purses you have there gentlemen."

He winks. "Give."

Four large pouches are then handed to him. "You have a cheek," shouts one of the men. "You're as bad as we are."

Fluff starts to snarl, and the man quickly covers his private parts and steps behind his friend. John does not answer but simply throws the pouches down beside the injured man still having his wounds treated. "Do you know others they have robbed?" asks John.

"Yes Sir, lots," answers the man.

John nods. "Good, take what is yours and hand the rest out fairly to the others. Could you do that for me please?"

"Yes Sir, thank you my Lord," answers the man with a quiver in his voice.

"You can go now boys," shouts John turning back around.

The four men slowly make their way down the track, until one is pulled down nearly to the knees. "Something's got me," screams the man.

His friends quickly try to pull him up, and all four take off running. Lane, Cin and Big Dan turn to John in disbelief. "John of all the things you have ever done that is the scariest," booms Big Dan heaving out a large sigh.

"You have control over the earth," gasps Cin.

John winks. "Hey trust me."

"Hmm yeah," mumbles Dan suspiciously.

John then walks over and bends down by the bruised man, "Are you ok now."

"Yes my Lord," answers the man. "After what I've seen you do to them hoodlums, I've never felt better. May I go now my Lord?"

"My name is John, not my Lord, and yes you may. Share that money out fairly now, and if you have anymore trouble, go to the stronghold and ask for Billie. Tell her I sent you, she'll sort everything out for you ok."

The man smiles and he starts to walk away, but then pausing for a moment turns back around and says, "Yes John but there are rumours and legends of a man, a man of the forest, who looks out for all that are in it. Are you he?"

"Yes that's him," shouts Maxie sniggering.

"I knew it," answers the man walking away.

John just frowns at Maxie, then ruffles her hair. Max leans in and whispers to John, "How did you control the earth."

John winks. "I didn't, it was Lilly."

Max giggles, "Now that makes more sense."

John feels a nudge and sees Fluff has placed his head under his hand. "And you," he grins. "Have a wicked sense of humour, I nearly felt sorry for that man."

Fluff starts to laugh. "What's it doing?" asks Max, "Is it upset?"

John smiles. "No he's laughing." smiles John.

Hearing this sets them all off laughing.

"Where's Woodnut?" asks Maxie.

"Oh yes," replies John. "I nearly forgot."

"Where's this child we've been hearing about?" asks Big Dan.

"I'll go and get them," answers John. "A little kindness and a few nice words guys ok."

He then walks back over to where Woodnut and Hope are hiding. "Are you alright?" he asks.

"Yes thank you," answers Hope. "But I'm a little nervous."

John smiles kindly. "Here take my hand." smiles John kindly.

Hope smiles back and takes his hand, and with Woodnut taking his other they walk out together and over to the others. "I'd like to introduce you all to Hope," bows John. "Hope, this is Max my wife and our daughter Maxie, and this little fellow with them is Spring Peeper, then we have, Big Dan, Lane and Cin."

The young boy suddenly goes very shy and lowering his head mumbles, "Nice to meet you."

"Awe you poor thing," sighs Max as she picks him up and gives him a cuddle. "Don't be shy, you're with friends now dear."

"Nice to meet you little man," says Big Dan putting his arm out. Hope stares unsure what to do next.

Dan carefully takes his arm and gently shakes it. "Friends" he tells him.

The young boy breaks out into a smile replying, "Friends."

Cin then takes his arm and does the same as does Lane.

Woodnut is whispering to Maxie as Max puts the child down. "That's awful," she exclaims before she grabs the boy's hand.

"Come with me," she tells him, and runs off with him into the woods followed by Woodnut.

"Just carry on," Woodnut shouts back. "Well catch you up later."

"Where is she taking him?" asks Cin.

"I could be wrong," answers John. "But I think it's to get him some clothes."

"You mean he's not meant to be naked," gasps Max.

"No we don't think so," sighs John. "But normal clothes tend to dry his skin out, so the people that had him just didn't bother."

As they continue walking John tells them all he knows about the child, much to their shock, surprise and fascination. Another few hours walking and John asks, "Would you mind if we stopped and had something to eat, I'm starved?"

Max nods. "That's a good idea I'm getting hungry myself."

They stop beside a large tree and lean against it when the top of John's bag shoots open as Spot jumps out and proceeds to run up the tree. "Someone's keen today," chuckles John.

"That's got to be the fastest I've ever seen that lazy thing move," laughs Lane.

All then becomes clear when they hear a loud crunching noise above, and look up to see Spot eating a large creeper freshly plucked from its web.

After a bite to eat and drink they are about to set off again when Woodnut and Maxie turn up, still holding Hope's hands. The young boy stands there now wearing a pair of shorts made out of woven leaves. "I was expecting a little more somehow," remarks Cin.

The others nod in agreement. "No silly," laughs Maxie, "These are just temporary until tomorrow, when the greenem have finished making his new clothes."

"Oh I see," nods Cin.

"Come and sit down here beside me little one, and we'll have something to eat aye" he says smiling to Hope who then sits down beside him and Cin hands him a couple of xanthem fruit from his bag.

"That's a nasty scar on the top of your arm there," says Big Dan. "How did you do that?"

Hope looks at the scar at the top of his left arm then shrugs. "I don't know, I think it must have happened when I was a baby. It's always been there."

"Does it hurt at all?" asks Lane.

"No Sir" answers Hope. "I never feel it."

"To my friends my name is Lane, little one, not Sir, ok."

Hope smiles. "Ok."

They then set off once more walking all day, stopping occasionally to rest or eat, with Hope getting the occasional ride on Fluff's back. It's nearly dark before they decide to make camp under the last few trees at the base of a large and imposing grassy hill, which seems to just go on and on. A small fire is made from some dead wood and dried animal dung, gathered from around the area. They all sit around staring into it, all but Woodut and Spring Peeper who are sat back a little just in case. "I tell you what," splutters Lane taking a mouthful of beelack juice then handing it round. "I'm not looking forward to walking up there tomorrow. I know it's only grass, and there's no climbing, but that is a hike and a half for anyone, man or beast."

"Yes and that's just the first," answers Spring Peeper.

"You what?" come the gasps.

"How many are there?" asks Big Dan.

"That's the first of the five founders," the little greenem tells them.

Woodnut cannot help but fall about laughing at their reactions. "What are you laughing at?" asks Cin. "You have to go up there as well."

Woodnut just shrugs and carries on chuckling. "What are the five founders?" asks Max.

"It's just the name of the five hills we will have to cross," answers Spring Peeper. "Don't worry there's only one really big one."

"Oh well," sighs Lane. "At least we get it out the way first."

"No silly," replies Spring Peeper. "It's the middle one."

"No please, tell me you're joking," gasps Lane.

"No sorry," replies the little greenem sheepishly. "But Tain province is on the other side of them."

Lane grabs the beelack juice and takes another swig.

"This is a journey and a half," says Big Dan. "And it's got me thinking. How is it, it may take us ten days or so to get your home. Yet when Maxie sent for you, it only took you a day or two to get to Taraten."

Spring Peeper looks at him oddly before he replies, "Well we didn't walk, if that's what you think. We rode the air and let the wind take us."

"You did what," gasps Big Dan suddenly sitting up a bit more.

"Mid morning," answers the little greenem. "When the sun warms the air, it causes some to rise up, and if you go to the right place and it's strong enough, we can rise up with it. We do circles until we are high enough to hit the quick slip, which is a small but very, very fast wind that blows around the earth. And when needed helps us travel vast distances in a very short time. And when we get to roughly where we are wanting to go, you slip out and float back down to the ground see. But it's usually only done in emergencies, as it can be quite dangerous. But I do know some others asked, and were brought by flurry."

"By grimlocks three rotting flaps," exclaims Cin. "That's incredible."

"By what?" asks John. "Come on, I'm not having that, no way, admit it, you just made that one up."

"No not at all. It's an old saying." grins Cin.

"Ok then," says John suspiciously. "Anyone else heard of this saying. No, see I knew it."

"Well it's an old Voreda saying," winks Cin.

"I bet it is," mutters John.

"You can fly?" asks Hope excitedly.

"No not really fly," answers Woodnut. "We are very light, and just know how to use the wind and air."

"That sounds absolutely amazing," replies Hope clapping his hands excitedly.

Soon yawns start to go round the camp and one by one they all start to fall asleep, all but the two greenem, who spend hours telling the child stories and trying to answer all his questions.

After their late night everyone wakes a little later than normal. John, Woodnut and Spring Peeper are first up, shortly followed by the others, and it's Spring Peeper that spots a neatly folded pile of clothes sitting beside a small neat, well made back pack

"Hope," he shouts excitedly. "I think your new clothes are here."

Hope runs over excitedly and picks them up for a closer look, and then proceeds to hug them. "They feel wonderful," he shouts.

The others watch smiling, and a little excited for him themselves. "What should I do now?" he asks.

"Put them on silly," shouts Maxie.

The child stares at them a little unsure what to do first so Max walks over to him and kneels down. "You lot turn around while I help get him dressed," she says.

"Come on dear," she continues smiling to him kindly, and with Max's help he is soon dressed.

"Well," he whispers to Max nervously.

"Very handsome," she whispers giving him a peck on the cheek "Now let's see what the others think."

"Right," she shouts. "You lot can turn round now."

They all do so and give a loud cheer and clap with calls of, "Very smart," and "Very handsome."

Suddenly the child bursts into floods of tears throwing his arms around Max so she kneels back down beside him. "What's the matter dear?" she asks. "Do you not like your new clothes? You can take them back off you know, or we can get you some more."

"N, n, n, no," sobs the child. "I think they're wonderful, that's all. You have all been so kind to me."

"I, I, I, just can't help it," he sobs. "Its like my best dream ever but better, and I'm just scared I'm going to wake up any moment and be back in my cage."

"Shush now," whispers Max cuddling him. "It's not a dream and you are awake, and I promise you, you will never have to go back there ever again. Now give me a kiss and dry your eyes dear. Look they've made you a bag as well, shall we have a little look."

Still sobbing he nods his head. Max picks the bag up and hands it to him. "It's so light," she tells him. "And what a wonderful pattern. Now why don't you open it dear, see if there's anything inside it."

Carefully he opens the bag and gasps. "It has, it has got something in it," he shouts excitedly.

"Let's have a look shall we," says Max before she peeks in and takes out first a neatly wrapped package, and carefully opens the corner for a peek.

"It's a pack lunch," she tells him wrapping it back up.

"What else?" he asks excitedly.

"It's a spare set of clothes," smiling she replies, carefully putting everything back in.

She then helps him on with his new bag. "Feel better now," she whispers.

"Yes thank you," he whispers back.

She smiles. "Ok then, now why don't you take Maxie's hand and lead the way for us then. Woodnut and Spring Peeper will help."

He lets go of Max and runs over to Maxie, who has heard everything and grabs his hand, then each of them grab one of the greenem's hands and all set off skipping ahead.

Max walks back over to the others. "What was all that about?" asks John.

"He was just a little overwhelmed, that's all," she answers "The poor little mite."

Lane heaves a big sigh. "It's a sad day when a child that size gets upset over his first set of clothes."

Cin sighs also. "Yes indeed my friend."

The going is quite slow up the large hillside and several stops are made before they are even half way up. The sun is slowly starting to set by the time they reach the large rounded bowl like top. John gives a shiver as a cool breeze brushes past them, and they look ahead to the peaks in front of them, with the orange glow of the setting sun sinking ahead of them. Cin sighs. "Now there's a view that was worth the climb."

Big Dan nods. "Yes I know what you mean. But I think it's going to be a rather cold night on the top of here, it's a pity we couldn't have made it down to the bottom."

Cin looks down the hill with his hands on his hips and says, "It'll be dark soon, and it would be just too dangerous to walk down there in the dark.

John gives out a loud, "Hmm" as he crouches down looking to the bottom of the hill.

"What are you thinking?" scowls Big Dan.

"Maybe, well, hmm," goes John again.

"What?" shouts the others.

"You're so impatient," replies John. "Now Spring Peeper my little friend, is this side as smooth and grassy as the one we just hiked up."

"Yes John," answers the little greenem. "There all like this, why."

"Hmm, so no rocks or stones jutting out," mutters John.

"Yes it looks as smooth and flat as a woobles foolanger," says Cin nodding.

"A what?" stutters John. "Come on, you just made that one up, you must have."

Cin just grins. "Come on John what are you thinking."

John just grins back. "Hey trust me."

Then without warning he takes his pack off. He throws it on the ground, grabs Hope, and shouts, "Hold on tight dude."

Jumping onto his bag he uses it as a sled and sets of down the hill, with Hope squealing and laughing all the way hotly pursued by Fluff.

"The man's insane," laughs Lane. "He's going to die, it took us all day to get up here, can you imagine the speed he'll be doing by the time he hits the bottom, he's going to end up shooting clean up the next hill."

"Yippee," comes another shout.

They quickly turn to see Maxie and the two greenem setting off on Maxie's bag. "No stop," shouts Max, but it's too late, and they are well on their way down screaming and laughing as they go.

"I don't believe it," gasps Lane. "That kids as bad as he is."

"I tell you what," laughs Big Dan. "I hope he's got some very special treats for Spot, she's going to be mighty upset by the time he gets to the bottom."

"Oh yes," laughs Lane. "I bet he's forgot about her."

Max takes her bag off and sits on it. "Go on then, someone give me a push," she huffs.

"What are you doing woman?" shouts Cin.

"Well," she says sighing. "If we are going to die, we might as well do it together."

"And besides," she giggles. "It does look fun."

Lane shrugs then takes his bag off, jumps on it and shouts, "Oh well, who wants to live forever anyway."

Big Dan stares at Cin who stares back. "I guess we don't have much choice then," stammers Dan.

Cin with eyes like bin lids cannot speak and just nods in agreement and they take their bags off in unison, and are soon shooting down the hillside also.

John is nearly at the bottom, and thinks to himself as he slides down, "This isn't too bad at all, we don't seem to be going as fast as I thought we might." But to the others it feels as if they are travelling at a tremendous speed. John and Hope finally come to a stop at the base of the next slope. Hope jumps off his knee panting profusely his eyes bulging like tennis balls, and with his pupils fully dilated it makes his large eyes look completely black and rather ominous. "Are you alright?" asks John.

The child just nods still trying to catch his breath. John smiles. "Did you like that?"

Hope still trying to catch his breath just nods excitedly as Fluff skids to a halt beside them. They stand up and turn to watch the others come down. Maxie with the two greenem arrive first, waving madly to them as they speed down the last part and come to a halt a short distance away. "Do you think we've got time to go back up there again?" asks Maxie as the greenem jump up and down excitedly.

John gives out a loud chuckle, "You enjoyed it then."

They nod excitedly. "I'm sorry," answers John. "It may have taken only thirty minutes or so to come down, but it took all day to get up there. But don't worry, there will be another tomorrow."

"Aw," sighs Maxie.

They all then stand and cheer as Max slides to a halt. John takes her hand and helps her up. "Are you alright darling?"

"I don't know," she stutters. "Am I."

She then pats herself all over a little dazed as Lane slides to a halt next and jumps straight up before he grabs John's arm and shakes it. "John my friend I think you've just found the best reason in the world to climb a hill."

Big Dan and Cin arrive more or less together squealing like school girls until they think they're in ear shot and try to stop. The others cheer wildly as they stop, and composing themselves they take a bow. "Well that saved a day's walk," pants Cin.

"Hey John," shouts Big Dan. "Have you apologised to Spot yet, or is it dead."

John gasps. "Oh my god."

Then panicking he runs back over to his bag. Cautiously his heart racing, he carefully peeks into the bag with one eye open and the other shut, then opening both he exclaims, "I don't believe it."

"What is it?" gasp the others. "Is it alright?"

"You won't believe it," says John shaking his head. "Its, its, fast asleep."

"Impossible," barks Big Dan grabbing the bag. "Here give me a look."

" HU that is the laziest animal I have ever known," he grunts. Spot gives a yawn and curls up a little tighter.

They sort themselves out for the evening, getting a little food and drink and sitting in a circle to talk. "It's definitely a lot warmer down here," says Max. "I think it would have got rather cold indeed up there."

Hope sits tucking into his pack lunch given to him by the greenem, with Fluff curled up around him fast asleep, being a little more tired than the others due to half running and half sliding down on his paws. Cin smiles at Hope. "Well someone's going to be nice and warm tonight, that's for sure, have you had a good day little man."

"Yes thank you," answers Hope politely.

"That is a mighty fine set of clothes you have there," Cin says. "May I touch them?"

"Yes certainly," replies Hope.

Cin feels the fabric between his thumb and forefinger. "This is extraordinary," he exclaims. "It's so thin yet seems so soft and warm. What does it feel like to wear?"

"Lovely," answers the boy. "It's so light I feel as if I still have no clothes on, but I'm nice and warm all the time now. It's such a nice feeling, and it doesn't stick to my skin either."

Cin nods. "Truly, there are lords that will never have this quality of clothing. Tell me Woodnut, how did your people make such a garment?"

"They must have worked all day and night on them," answers Woodnut. "I have never seen their equal, it's comprised of woven together strands of creeper silk, weaved and interwoven with strands of flurry hair and creeper feathers. Similar to the blankets and pillows you had at the party, but with a little more care, and also made to be stronger. It may look very delicate, but I can assure you it would take an awful lot to ever damage them."

The little boy sits there listening, his eyes filling up again. Big Dan sitting on his other side leans over and puts his arm around him. "It's ok little one, get yourself some sleep now, it's another big climb tomorrow." The young boy smiles and nods, then curls up tightly, putting his hands and feet under his body, with Fluff then curling up around him a little tighter. He falls asleep as Lane watches and smiles. "That jackerbell seems to have taken a real shine to the boy."

John nods. "Yes it does seem that way. It was Fluff that wanted him rescued."

Big Dan chuckles, "One things for sure, no ones going to bother that child in a hurry now."

Max turns to Maxie and the greenem. "It's time you lot turned in for the night also," she tells them.

But after their long days hike it's not long before they are all fast asleep. Everyone is up with the sun the next day, and excluding Cin and Big Dan are keen to get underway and to the top of the next hill, in anticipation of sliding down the other side. And by the end of the day that is exactly what they are doing, with Cin and Big Dan squealing all the way down once again, and stopping once more when they think they are in earshot. They make camp for the night at the base of the next hill, which is the third and largest hill of the group. As they sit there having something to eat and staring up at the evening light Big Dan tells them, "There is no way we will make it up there in one day, it is half the size again."

Lane nods. "Agreed, but if we can make it three quarters of the way up and camp for the night, I think we will be doing well. We can make camp early on the other side the next day and recuperate a bit before we carry on. There are two more after that one I think, that's right isn't it, Spring Peeper."

"Yes exactly," answers the little greenem. "I also think it's a good thing it will be the middle of the next day when we reach the top of the large hill."

"Why's that?" asks Max.

"Wait until you see the view from the top of there," he giggles. "It will take your breath away, a perfect panoramic view of both provinces. It would have been such a pity if we'd missed it."

John smiles. "Well, now that does sound like something to look forwards to."

Everything goes as planned and they reach the top of the tallest hill the day after the next at around mid day. Once there they throw their bags down, and take in the awe inspiring views of both provinces. "I tell you what," sighs Big Dan staring ahead. "This view really does take my breath away, even more than them suicide slides you make us do down the sides of these hills. I never thought in my wildest dreams, that I would be here standing at the top of the tallest hill about to enter Tain province, staring out upon views I never thought possible. I do so wish my father could have been here to see this, he would have been in his element, I think he would have been so proud."

John puts his hand on Dan's shoulder and replies, "I think as long as you keep his memory alive my friend, he will always be here with you, in that I'm sure."

Big Dan starts to choke and cough as tears fill his eyes. "We should move on soon," he says with a quiver in his voice. "This cold wind is starting to hurt my eyes."

"If you say so my friend," replies John in a kind voice.

"I tell you what," shouts Lane. "Is it me or are these five hills perfectly in line."

They all stare intently swivelling their heads backwards and forwards, some with fingers outstretched and one eye closed trying to eye them up. "Hmm, how strange," says Max. "Do you know I think you're right, they do look nearly perfectly in line?"

"What do you think John?" asks Cin.

John scratches his head. "I've no idea to be perfectly honest, and it does seem rather unusual.

"Have you any ideas guys?" he asks the two greenem. "Is there something under these hills perhaps, could it be a fault line or something."

The two greenem just shrug. "We've no idea," answers Woodnut. "They're just hills as far as we are aware, they've always been here."

Cin laughs, "One things for sure, there will be no sliding down this one, not even John's that mad. It would take close to an hour or so to slide down it, that's if you lived to see the bottom."

But suddenly there is a loud shout,"Wahoo."

So they all turn to see Lane sitting on his bag and sliding down the large hillside. "Gees Louise," gasps John. "And he says I'm mad."

"Oh well," he continues. "In for a penny in for a pound."

Then grabbing Hope he jumps on his bag and takes off down the hillside closely followed by Maxie and the greenem, then Max. Big Dan and Cin stare at each other and in unison say, "No way."

They then pick up their bags and set off walking down, with Fluff walking beside them. "You not fancy it either aye," asks Cin.

Fluff gives out a loud snarl. "I guess that means no," chuckles Dan.

After a few hours walk they get to where they feel is a safer distance, and proceed to slide down the rest of the way. The others have been waiting down the bottom for hours, when they finally reach the bottom, and all stand and cheer their arrival.

5

THE NEXT FEW days go better than planned and its mid afternoon when they reach the top of the last hill, and they stare down at the province ahead. The green grass of the rolling hillside below slowly cascades down fading into a sea of golden yellow, which just seems to go on and on, until reaching a forest of flame red trees in the distance. "Wow," gasps John and Lane simultaneously.

Even Woodnut is speechless for a moment. Cin silently shakes his head then turns to Big Dan, "Have you ever seen such a land Dan."

Big Dan shakes his head. "No truly never," he mutters.

"That sea of yellow is shadow grass," says Spring Peeper rather nonchalantly.

"Why do they call it that?" asks Max.

"Sit, sit everyone," the little greenem tells them. "Let's watch, it will become clear in a moment, sometimes it can be quite wonderful to watch. Not many people ever get the chance to appreciate it properly, as it is best viewed from high above, like where we are."

So they all sit watching, not really sure what they are looking for. But suddenly a shadow starts to form in the yellow grass below, which starts to spread out across the land like a Mexican wave. They look up towards the sky to see if it's a cloud drifting over, but the sky is clear and blue, with not a cloud in sight. Spring Peeper giggles. "No silly," he tells them. "It's the grass itself, it can change colour from light to dark, keep watching."

"Is no one bothered about the wood in the distance?" asks John.

"What do you mean?" shrugs Maxie.

"That wood in the distance," he panics. "Its on fire, should we not be trying to do something about it."

"John your eyesight," laughs Big Dan.

John sighs. "There's nothing wrong with my eyesight, it's you lot, it's not natural to see that far I tell you." They all start to laugh. "Well," answers Lane through the chuckles. "If you did have our not natural eyesight, you would see that wood isn't on fire. It's just the colour of the trees themselves, and quite amazing they are too.

"I must admit," sighs Woodnut. "I have heard of these trees and this wood, but I have never seen them. I'm so looking forwards to going there, the greenem are red to match the forest, they are found nowhere else on earth."

"Look everyone," then shouts Cin.

They all look to the land below to see another shadow form in the grass. And as it spreads across the land instead of a wave, it breaks off into patterns of rolling curves, which slowly break off themselves forming hundreds of curls, spirals, spikes and waves. They sit there for over an hour watching show after show of patterns, roll slowly across the land, with no two being the same. Finally Lane stands up. "I'm sorry everybody, but we are on a mission, and I think it's only proper we now make hast."

"Tell me Spring Peeper," asks John, as he gets to his feet. "Why does the grass do that?"

The little greenem just shrugs. "Nobody really knows."

"There are all sorts of myths about it," continues Woodnut. "Amongst my people anyway as most of your people don't even realise it does that. But there are some old greenem that have studied it their whole lives, and they still aren't sure. But what I can tell you is, there are more different types of grass on earth than anything else, it's the only thing that's been here longer than we have."

"So what are some of the myths?" asks John.

Woodnut shrugs. "There are so many, hmm, let me think, ah yes, there's those that say it's the shadow grass trying to communicate, but no one has worked out the language yet. There are others that say it's just the wind rolling down the hills forming patterns in the grass. Others say it's the grass blushing at the gentle and tender embrace of the breeze. Some even say it has a grain of intelligence, and it is simply to relieve its boredom as it waits to evolve a little more. But there are too many silly myths about shadow grass to mention. I personally think if there was anything to any of these myths, the elders would have worked it out centuries ago. But it does make for good stories on an evening for the younger greenem."

"Wahoo," comes a shout, and they turn to see Lane sliding down the hill side.

Cin frowns, shaking his head. "That's just not right. I can understand John liking it, I mean he's a little insane, and that speed is nothing to him. But Lane, no that's just not right."

John frowns in return. "Oh thanks very much."

Big Dan pats Cin on the shoulder, "I know exactly what you mean," he says. "I think it's the exhilaration, he misses fighting for something I think."

Cin nods. "Yes I can understand that, I must admit sometimes I do myself."

"Yippee," comes another squeal as Maxie and the greenem set off, shortly followed by John and the others, and last but not least as always Big Dan and Cin.

As the laughter and banter subsides, they put their bags back on and set off, now leaving the lush green grass of the hillside, which begrudgingly gives way to the golden yellow of the shadow grass. But as they take their first tentative steps into it, the shadow grass reacts instantly, sending out an explosion of shadows across the land in every direction. But instead of forming waves or pattern, it seems to form a cascade of symbols. Making all but John and the greenem stop instantly dead in their tracks. Woodnut tugs on John's trouser leg. "What?" asks John.

Woodnut shrugs and points to the others behind. "What's the matter?" asks Woodnut.

But no one answers, Big Dan simply points to the shadow grass ahead. "What?" asks John again.

"John," gasps Cin. "I thought you were joking when you said you couldn't read."

John gives a loud sigh and slumping his shoulders moans, "I've told you, I can, oh what's the point."

Then he mutters, "Hang on, what do you mean anyway?"

"John," shouts Woodnut. "Lift me up quickly."

He stands Woodnut on his shoulder and supports his legs. "I don't believe it," gasps Woodnut.

Spring Peeper climbs up on to his other shoulder and John then supports him with his other hand. "Oh my," mutters Spring Peeper. "I think, I think I'm hallucinating."

"If you are," replies Woodnut. "Then so am I."

"For god's sake," moans John. "Can somebody please tell me what's going on?"

"It's the shadow grass John," stutters Woodnut. "It has filled the land as far as the eye can see with two words. Welcome friends."

"Oh that's nice," answers John nodding.

"That's nice, that's nice," shouts Woodnut. "This is momentous, its, its, well, I never thought, well I mean, we never, who could, the old ones tried."

"Woodnut," shouts John. "You're rambling."

"Oh, yes sorry," he replies snapping out of it. "But John you have to understand. This is, well I just don't have the words to describe it. There are elders who have studied this, as I told you. And after all this time it does this, we thought it was just grass, it's made, it's made, err."

"First contact," nods John nonchalantly.

"Yes, yes exactly," replies Woodnut excitedly. "That is an excellent description."

John nods. "That's cool then aye."

Woodnut still on his shoulder stares down at him in disbelief; "I really don't think you understand John," he gasps. "Are you not surprised, even a little, or did you know already, or suspect it."

"Nope," answers John rather blasé. "And I mean this with the greatest respect. But I'm standing here with two walking talking articulate and intelligent plants on my shoulder, who are also friends with a species of intelligent fly. Behind me is a boy who appears to have evolved from some sort of frog, who is sitting on the back of the biggest meanest looking canine creature I've ever seen in my life, who also understands every word I say, and has a wicked sense of humour. So what I'm trying to say is, no nothing surprises me anymore."

Woodnut looks a little puzzled for a moment, then turning to Spring Peeper starts to giggle, "Suppose so when you put it like that."

"Yeah," giggles Spring Peeper.

"Quick let us down," shouts Woodnut frantically.

"Why?" asks John.

"Please," insists Woodnut.

So John lifts them down, and they both immediately bury both their hands and feet deep into the ground. Then they all stand there silently watching the two greenem for over half an hour, but to no avail, the two greenem take their hands and feet from the ground, and stand back up both looking very disappointed. John kneels down beside them. "Well guys," he says. "What's the verdict, did you make contact."

Woodnut silently shakes his head as Spring Peeper mutters, "Maybe the elders might have more luck."

John reassures them, "Don't be sad guys, you have just witnessed something no one has. Not even your wisest elder, this is something to be very proud of. But not only did you witness it, it spoke to us, and called us friends, that means you two also you know. And I think the elders will have so many things to ask you, they won't know where to start, you will give them new inspiration. But do you know what I think really? I think if your people don't make contact, or don't work it out, it's not a bad thing. I think some things should stay a mystery, don't you? After all, where would the fun in life be, if you knew everything my little friends? I bet the old fellows that have studied the shadow grass for so long have enjoyed doing so. If they'd made contact, or worked it out straight away, where would the fun have been in that now? Now how about we find these old greenem, and you can tell them all about your exciting news. I think they have the right to know before anyone else, don't you."

"Yes, yes of course," they answer in unison.

"Quick, quick, we must go," says Spring Peeper excitedly. "We are going that way, that's where we'll find them."

John smiles. "Calm down dude," he says. "Which way would you like us to go?"

"Oh yes," giggles Spring Peeper. "Sorry, towards the forest of the fire trees."

"Let's go everybody," calls John.

As they walk along the same two words irradiate out across the land from each of their footsteps, this goes on sporadically for hours until they reach the edge of the forest. They pause a moment, to stare into the bright red fauna ahead illuminated perfectly by the diffused sunlight reflected from the large red leaves from the trees high above. Then the two greenem and Maxie start waving madly towards the trees as giggles and laughter is heard coming from the trees and little scarlet faces start to appear through the undergrowth, all waving their little scarlet hands. "By the dancing flames of the black fire," gasps Cin.

John turns and stares at him, with one eye closed and the other open. Cin grins. "OK, ok, I'll give you that one. But it's no worse than some of yours."

Just then an old deep dark red greenem steps out of the forest, walks over to them and bows. They all bow in return. "My friends call me Old Red," greets the old greenem. "I never thought we would ever get the pleasure, and honour of meeting you all."

John steps forwards and bows again, "No my new friend, I can assure you the honour is all ours."

He then proceeds to introduce the others and himself, much to the broad smiles of the old greenem. Who then signals to the wood, letting the other excited greenem rush forward as custom has it on first meeting. They all sit down as the young greenem crowd around them. "This is amazing," says Max. "They're all scarlet. I know you told us earlier but, wow, what a beautiful colour."

"Oh thank you," giggles one of the young scarlet greenem.

"It must be impossible to tell if they're embarrassed," giggles Maxie turning to Woodnut and Spring Peeper. "No, no you can," sniggers Spring Peeper. "It's actually quite easy, their cheeks go darker, and if they are really, really embarrassed they can go nearly black."

"Hey Woodnut," shouts Lane. "Tell me, if you're a Greenem, does that mean these are Redems."

"No," replies Woodnut a little puzzled.

All the little red greenem start to giggle terribly on hearing this, with Woodnut now going a little scarlet himself after realising he didn't get the joke. John seeing this starts laughing, making Woodnut go even redder, and pulls a face back at him.

Hope sits there a little nervous with his arm around Fluff. "And who my child are you?" asks Old Red.

"My name is Hope Sir."

The old greenem sits down beside him. "Please Old Red to my friends, or Red, which ever you prefer my lad. Now tell me young man, what species would you be, I've never seen your like."

The boy just shrugs. "I don't know," he says. "John and Woodnut think I'm some sort of err, hmm."

"It's ok," Red reassures him. "Woodnut my boy, could you come here a moment please."

Woodnut comes over and bows. "Ah yes the child."

"Do not be nervous Hope," he continues. "You are with friends."

"Yes I know," Hope answers. "I'm just not used to seeing such a large group, it's a little scary."

"Would you like me to tell some to go?" asks Red.

"No it's ok," he answers. "I have to learn."

"How was your trip across the hills Woodnut?" asks Red. "Did you stop at the top of the last one and watch the patterns?"

Woodnut's eyes light up. "Oh yes, oh my gosh," he stutters excitedly. "Are the old ones still here?"

Red nods. "If you mean the old greenem who studied the shadow grass, yes. But there are only two left now, and they are very old, and resting a little deeper in the forest. They would have liked to have met you, but they don't travel far or even fast these days. Why?"

"Could you take Spring Peeper and I to them immediately please?" asks Woodnut. "We have news that will bring new meaning to their lives."

Red stands up straight. "What is it?" he asks excitedly.

"I will tell you when I tell the old ones," answers Woodnut. "I mean no disrespect, but what I have to tell, they deserve to hear first."

Red bows. "Yes, yes of course. If it's what I think, it's only right."

He then turns to Hope, "But you child, this may sound a little strange, but please tell me. Are you always that colour?"

"No Sir," answers Hope. "My colour depends on my mood, light and temperature."

Old Red then turns back to Woodnut. "Let us go immediately, but this child must come with us."

"Why?" asks Woodnut.

"There is an old legend," continues Red. "Known only to a few, told to me by the old ones, but come we must go."

The old greenem then takes hold of the boy's hand, and after shouting on Spring Peeper the four set off into the forest, with Fluff following slowly behind.

"Where are you going?" shouts Maxie.

"We won't be long," shouts Old Red. "You can just stay there if you like."

Maxie looks to her mum. "Just stay here dear," Max tells her. "Look at all these lovely young greenem that have come out just to meet you. They're so excited, you don't want to disappoint them now do you."

Maxie smiles sitting back down. "No of course not."

"How far do you think we're off our destination?" asks Lane.

The others just shrug. "You'll have to ask Spring Peeper when he comes back," replies Big Dan.

"Three days Sir," comes a little voice beside Lane.

Lane looks down to see a young scarlet greenem smiling up at him. "Three days aye," he says still smiling. "That's not too bad."

The little greenem shrugs. "Oh yes it is Sir," he answers now looking very sad. "We all know why you're here, and where you are going, but you are going to be too late. We have just had word from the old greenem from that rainforest, Evening Thunder his name. And he has word they will start felling in two days, he said if you wish you need not continue."

"Is that so?" replies Lane, now looking very serious. "You see that leaves me with a serious problem. Because you see, I gave my word we would come and help, and I never break my word. So that is exactly what we are going to do, and if that means we have to travel all night, then so be it. Even if we do not get there in time, I do not believe for a moment they will cut down the whole forest, they won't even make a dent."

"No Sir," answers the little greenem. "Not unless they burn it I suppose."

Lane stares back horrified. "They wouldn't do that surely, would they?"

The little greenem shrugs. "They have been known to in the past."

"Then that settles it," replies Lane. "We will set off as soon as Woodnut and the others return, if that's alright with the rest of you."

"Yes of course," answers John and the others.

The little greenem smiles broadly and turns looking up to the branches of a nearby tree, and gives a little wave. And fluttering down onto the little greenen's arm comes a long wing. Lane leans forwards staring closely at the fly. "Bzzt is that you?" he asks. "It is isn't it? May I ask, was it you who brought this news from the old rainforest greenem. Hmm, Evening Thunder wasn't it."

The long wing stands up tall on its back legs and proceeds to bow politely. Lane smiles kindly at the little greenem and says, "Would you mind if I talked to your friend Bzzt myself."

"No of course not," answers the greenem.

Bzzt flies over on to Lane's outstretched hand. "I know you are probably very tired after your long flight," asks Lane. "But do you think it's possible you could relay a message back to Evening Thunder for me please?"

The little prince then flies up onto his shoulder and shouts in his ear, "Yes I will try my best, but I may not reach him much earlier than you, maybe a day at best."

"Can you hear what he's saying?" interrupts John.

"I could," frowns Lane. "Until you butted in."

"Oops sorry," apologises John.

"Honestly John your hearing," snaps Lane. "It's as bad as your eyesight."

John just sighs. "Now my little friend," continues Lane. "Where was I? Ah yes, tell the old greenem we are coming and nothing, but nothing will stop us? Although if he can stall them some how, keep them talking perhaps, if he can. We are led to believe the people of this land do engage in talks with greenem sometimes, then all the better. But as I heard John say once, come hell or high water we will be there, ok."

The little long wing flies back onto Lane's hand, only to pause for a moment, to stand proudly and bow before taking off with his message.

"Well," laughs Big Dan. "I think it's time for a good meal, it looks as if we are going to need the energy."

Deep in the wood Spring Peeper, Woodnut and Hope are all following Old Red who is skipping through the wood bubbling with excitement, until finally they come to the foot of a large ancient old tree, with many large roots and hollows. Old Red stops between the foot of two large roots. "Woodnut if you could come with me please, and could you two just wait here until I call you."

Red and Woodnut walk up to the base of the tree, Old Red kneels down and in a slight dip, were he sees the two old greenem they've been looking for. They are lent back, side by side fast asleep and out for the count. Old Red gently shakes one of the ancient them. "Diddler," he says softly. "Wake up Diddler, there's someone here to see you."

After another gentle shake the ancient greenem slowly opens one eye. "Oh young Red it's you," he yawns. "How are you doing young greenem? What do you want my boy?"

Woodunt gives a little giggle. "And who's this?" asks Diddler.

"This is Woodnut Greenfern," Red tells him.

"Greenfern, Greenfern," mumbles the ancient greenem. "You wouldn't be the young greenem travelling with the oomans would you?"

Woodnut smiles bowing slightly. "Yes that's me."

The old greenem sits up and bows back. "It's an honour to meet you young greenem. I've heard all about your adventures, very interesting, and most amusing."

"No I can assure you," answers Woodnut. "The honour is most defintely all mine. I grew up with stories of you and your studies of the shadow grass, fascinating, which brings me to the point of me being here in front of you now."

"I thought you were on your way to the rainforest," replies Diddler yawning and finding it hard not to nod off again.

"I'm sorry my boy," he apologises. "But when you get to my age, even being awake is an effort."

Woodnut smiles. "That's ok. If you would like to wake up your partner, I have something amazing to tell you both."

The ancient greenem smiles politely and turns to his friend. "Knock Knock, wake up, there's someone here to see us."

The other ancient greenem gives out a loud snore and just rolls around. "Knock Knock, wake up," he shouts again giving him a shake.

"I'm sorry," shrugs Diddler. "Why don't you tell me young Woodnut? And if I can ever wake him up, I'll tell him what you said."

Woodnut bows politely. "As you wish, as you know we came across the five hills, and when my friends and I reached the top of the last one, we sat and watched the shadow grass from the top. And it was marvellous sight, with patterns and waves rippling across the land in all directions. But when my friends and I reached the bottom and stepped onto the shadow grass, instead of patterns and waves in front of us, the grass spelt out two words, and sent them out right across the land as far as the eye could see, thousands and thousands of times, over and over again."

The ancient greenem is speechless and sits bolt upright. "I am, very very old, and it's nearly time for me to return to the earth, if this is some sort of joke young greenem, it is in very poor taste."

Old Red takes his hand. "No my friend," he reassures him. "This is no joke."

"Spring Peeper," he shouts. "Could you come here please?"

Spring Peeper comes over and bows. "Yes it's true, I saw them also."

Tears come to the ancient greenem's eyes. "And that's not the only thing," Red tells him.

"Could you step forward please young man?" he asks Hope.

Hope steps forward smiles and bows politely. "Now who are you?" asks Diddler. "Or may I ask, what are you?"

Old Red whispers in Hope's ear opening. "Could you please if possible change colour."

"Yes sir, if you like," replies Hope a little puzzled.

As Red steps back Hope starts to change from nearly white to a pale green and then to dark brown. Then from out of nowhere comes Fluff, who seeing his friend change colour so rapidly sits down beside him, just to make sure he's in no trouble. Diddler the ancient greenem is so overcome and excited he nearly passes out, and collapses down. "Oh no," gasps Woodnut. "We've killed him."

Old Red kneels down and takes Diddler's hand and gently taps the back of it. "Diddler, Diddler, wake up Diddler."

The ancient greenem slowly opens one eye and smiles broadly at Old Red. "Ah it's you young greenem," says Diddler softly as nearly all greenem are young compared to these old fellas.

"I had the most amazing dream, there were two young greenem here, and the old prophecy was coming true, it was wonderful," he continues.

"But you woke me up at the best bit," he grumps.

Old Red smiles kindly, and says softly, "It was no dream old friend, look behind me."

The ancient greenem then jumps to his feet muttering excitedly, and starts to run this way and that. "We must learn more, we must see for ourselves," he mutters. "No. no, no. You must tell us first."

Red stops him. "Calm down old friend, don't you think someone else might want to know what you've just learned."

"Hum no," says Diddler a little confused.

"Oh, oh, wait yes of course, what a silly old greenem I am," he says excitedly running back to his friend. "Knock Knock, wake up," he shouts.

But the other ancient Greenem just makes a funny noise. Diddler grabs him again shaking him violently this time. "Hu who's there?" shouts Knock Knock, in a rather alarmed voice.

Diddler shakes his head and shouts, "That stopped being funny centuries ago you old fool, now sit up old friend and prepare yourself. For we have been waiting our whole lives for this moment."

Woodnut and Spring Pepper then tell the two ancient greenem all they know. Knock Knock sits there dumbfounded not saying a word, open mouthed and staring at a rather uncomfortable Hope.

Then after being made to repeat everything several times Woodnut bows to the two ancient greenem and says, "May I ask you both something."

"Yes of course," they both reply. "What is it?"

"Well earlier," answers Woodnut. "I heard the mention of an ancient prophecy, could you please tell me what it is, and perhaps it's origins."

"Yes, yes of course," replies Diddler. "It's the least we can do."

"I love this story," interrupts Knock Knock. "It's so old, and I'll be honest with you after all these centuries, a story is all I thought it was."

"If you're quite finished," grumps Diddler.

This makes the two young greenem, Hope and Fluff giggle terribly. "Now where was I," continues Diddler. "Ah yes the prophecies. Now it's said that when oomans and greenem walk together, there will come friends following the five founders, accompanied by a child of many colours riding the untameable beast. Then on that day the earth itself shall announce their arrival."

They all sit there speechless for a few moments on hearing this, all but Fluff who after giving a snarl turns around in protest at being called an untameable beast, making them all giggle again. "It's just an old saying" Hope reassures him, "They didn't mean it."

"No of course not," says Knock Knock loudly. "We are all friends here. Come now, turn back round, you travel with good people, and have shown your worth."

"What is the origin of this story?" asks Woodnut.

"That's a good question," answers Diddler. "I think maybe Knock Knock knows more about this than I, if you would old friend."

"Ah yes," continues Knock Knock excitedly, "This story is nearly as old as time, they say it was told to the first desert people, by a greenem that travelled with them. And this was before they had even reached the desert, and that greenem then spent the rest of his days travelling and telling this prophecy and many, many others. In fact nearly every prophecy and legend told was by this one greenem."

"Ah yes," replies Woodnut excitedly. "I remember being told all about this greenem and his stories as a youngster. In fact I was named after him you know, I've always been proud of that."

"And so you should," nods Diddler. "You know I've heard he's still alive somewhere, waiting, refusing to die."

"Waiting for what?" asks Spring Peeper.

"No one knows," replies Knock Knock. "He refuses to say."

Woodnut suddenly gets a puzzled look on his face as he turns to the two ancient greenem. "But tell me, a few things do puzzle me though," he asks. "How can the first desert people, actually be desert people, when they hadn't even reached the desert yet? And where were they travelling from in the first place, if not the desert, and what were they before it?"

Knock Knock stares back at him, now with a puzzled look on his face. "You know," he answers. "I never thought of that. I'm, I'm not sure, Diddler do you know?"

"No I must admit," chuckles Diddler scratching his head. "I like the way you think young greenem. Now may I ask you something?"

"Yes of course anything," answers Woodnut.

"Marvellous," continues Diddler. "Could you perhaps take us to meet your friends, and then accompany us back to the heart of the shadow grass?"

Glowing with pride Woodnut bows. "It would be an honour."

"Excellent," shout the two ancient greenem in unison.

"I tell you what Diddler old friend," says Knock Knock, as they follow the others back. "After all these years of trying to work out the shadow grass, and the meanings behind the patterns, it had left me so looking forward to returning to the earth and finally resting, I can't tell you. But now, it must be all this excitement I feel invigorated, it makes me feel eight hundred again."

"Yes I know what you mean old friend," agrees Diddler. "After all this time, to think it has intelligence, it gives me a new lease of life also."

Light breaks through the fire red trees as they reach the edge of the wood and they start to hear the laughter and conversation wafting towards them from the friends ahead. Woodnut and Spring Peeper walk out first shortly followed by Hope and Fluff. "Excellent timing," shouts Lane on seeing them. "We are just about to eat. Then I'm afraid we will have to set off, I'm sorry my little friends, but we have had grave news." Woodnut just smiles graciously and nods. Spring Peeper rushes over to ask just what the grave news is.

Hope and Fluff sit down with Max and Maxie.

Woodnut walks over to his friends and bows. "I would like to introduce you to, two very important and ancient greenem, legends among all my people." Old Red then walks out shortly followed by the two ancient greenem, who after hearing Woodnut's build up are smiling from side to side. On seeing the two greenem John stands up and bows followed by the others. The two old greenem are delighted at this and bow in return. Woodnut introduces his friends, he then turns to the two ancient greenem, "And it is my honour and privilege to introduce you to firstly Diddler."

"And last but definitely not least," continues Woodnut. "Knock Knock."

Both the old greenem bow again. "Who's there?" blurts out John chuckling.

Woodnut and the others just glare at him, Diddler shakes his head and puts his hands over his eyes. Knock Knock bursts into fits of laughter. "Excellent," he cries, "Someone with a sense of humour, you know we weren't sure you oomans had one."

"Are you joking," gasps John sitting down beside him. "It's a classic, I know hundreds of knock knock jokes."

"I bet I know more than you," chortles Knock Knock.

Still shaking his head Diddler mutters, "You've started something now; there'll be no stopping him now."

John and the old greenem then sit there together telling each other knock knock jokes. One after another and roaring with laughter after each one, as everyone else just sits there watching them rather bemused, not really knowing what to make of it. "Stop, stop," cries John. "I think I'm going to pee myself."

The two of them laugh harder as Cin nudges Lane and Big Dan and whispers, "What's a knock knock joke?" Lane and Dan just shrug. "Hey Max," asks Lane. "Do you know?"

"No, I've no idea," she answers. "But whatever it is, it must be very funny."

John and Knock Knock hearing this fall about laughing again. "Woodnut my lad," says Diddler. "This ooman of yours is as bad as this old fool."

Knock Knock winks. "You're just jealous, just because you haven't got a sense of humour."

"No sense of humour," laughs Diddler. "Now I know you're joking, to have put up with you for all this time, you silly old plant. I must have a sense of humour second to none."

Hearing this makes them all laugh, all but Spring Peeper. "Please Lane what is this grave news?" begs the little greenem.

On hearing this the two old greenem fall silent, and Lane tells them all he has just learned and their plan to travel day and night. Spring Peeper is still looking very sad. "Don't worry little one," Big Dan reassures him. "As Lane told you, we will get there, and we will stop this." The little greenem just nods.

Meanwhile the two ancient greenem are quietly deep in conversation, and after a few moments stop, turning back to the others. "Maybe we can help you a little," says Diddler.

"Yes," says Knock Knock. "But you must do as we say, or all hope for your future is lost,"

"Yes," continues Diddler, "There is a plant, a weed, but when you are at your most tired, when travelling by day and night, if you eat one of these leafs, one and no more mind."

"Yes," continues Knock Knock. "It will give you strength and energy, it will make you feel as if you are at the start of a new day."

"Yes yes," says Diddler. "You will be able to travel none stop to the rain forest."

"That's excellent," they all reply but Lane gives them a suspicious look. "What do you mean, our future is lost."

"Ah yes good question," answers Knock Knock. "This plant is very common, found everywhere, but if taken too much, or for any length of time it is very addictive."

"Yes," sighs Diddler. "Then all hope is lost, as it will consume your mind and destroy your body."

"Please do not look alarmed," says Knock Knock. "Taken very occasionally over just a couple of days, the effects should be minimal."

"Yes," nods Diddler excitedly. "When desperate, just take one leaf."

"Stop," shouts John.

"What is it my boy?" asks Diddler rather alarmed.

"Where I come from," John tells them. "There are also plants with similar effects, and with the best intentions in the world, they destroy lives and kill millions. So I think we should not take them, but if we have to, we should not know what they are. Tell only one, Woodnut perhaps, and he should give them out if necessary."

"Those are wise words," replies Knock Knock nodding.

"Yes indeed," continues Diddler "That is how it will be."

Knock Knock then whispers to Woodnut, whose face turns to surprise as he gasps, "Really, well I never knew that."

As they all start to eat Woodnut tells them, "I will rejoin you before you reach the forest, but our paths must part for a short time. I will be accompanying my two ancient friends back to the shadow grass first, but I will pass the knowledge on about the plant to Spring Peeper."

Woodnut then whispers to Spring Peeper, who in turn looks as surprised as Woodnut did when he was told.

It's not to long before they are all ready to set off once more, and after saying goodbye to what felt like every greenem in the forest they are on their way, but not before John stops turns back and asks Old Red, "When all this is over, may we come back to visit, and perhaps stay a few nights, as this fire red forest is a truly ore inspiring sight, and with such good company it would be such a pity not to?"

Old Red smiles broadly and nods as a mighty cheer goes up from all the scarlet greenem. John bows to them politely and turns back to catch up with the others. Woodnut and the ancient greenem also set off back towards the shadow grass, accompanied by Old Red.

With Spring Peeper leading the way the friends make good time, but their decision to keep going and not stopping, soon takes its toll on all but John. As to him, it still seems as if he's only walking at just over half speed, and several hours at this slow pace, takes barely any effort at all. "Are you lot ok?" he asks, but no one answers, too tired to waste the effort on speech.

"Well I think we should stop for a short rest," he tells them. "You all look as if you're dead on your feet."

"If you insist," come the muffled replies, but all are actually relieved, collapsing to the ground.

They then sit panting and sighing taking a quick drink and a bite to eat. John whispers to Spring Peeper, who looks equally shattered, "I think it's time you gave them a leaf each."

Spring Peeper quietly slips away as the others lay there flat out. He isn't away long and goes around each of them, popping a small leaf in each of their mouths, all but John. "Maybe later," he answers.

"Are you sure?" asks Spring Peeper.

"Yes thanks," answers John. "I don't feel that bad, and besides, I'm not sure what effect it may have on me."

"Oh yes," gasps Spring Peeper nodding. "That is a very good point, and it may even be poisonous to you for all we know."

Another ten minutes rest and they all start to get to their feet. "Come on John stop slacking," jokes Cin, now feeling fresh and relaxed.

But Spring Peeper still looks very tired; not being able to take one of the leaves himself so John gently picks him up and puts him on his shoulders. "Here little friend," he says. "Why don't you guide us from up there? You should be able to see better."

Yawning loudly the little greenem thanks him and they set off again. All goes well even when travelling by night, guided by the light of the two moons until the next morning, when all the travelling and no sleep starts to get the better of John. "Sorry guys," mumbles John, with barely the energy to speak himself now. "I'm going to have to rest a while."

"Yes of course," replies Lane. "Why don't you have one of them leaves while you rest, they work really well. They just make you feel, well err, hmm, refreshed, yes that's it refreshed."

"Yeah maybe," sighs John. "But I'm really not sure, I should be alright after a short rest."

"Why not try just half a leaf then," Spring Peeper tells him. "It may help."

"Ok then I suppose," yawns John. "If you think it'll help. I'm bushed."

Spring Peeper hands him a small peace of leaf, and John pops it in his mouth and swallows. "So how long will it take to work?" he asks.

"I'm not sure," answers Spring Peeper. "The others started to feel less tired within a few minutes."

"Oh that's good," nods John. "Because I don't know how much longer I can."

Then as he suddenly falls silent a loud snoring noise is heard. "I guess he really was tired," laughs Big Dan.

"Don't worry," chuckles Cin. "He'll wake up in a moment when that leaf kicks in."

They sit down and rest themselves, waiting for John to wake up but the minutes pass and starting to get a little impatient Max leans over and gives him a shake. "Wake up dear," she says softly, but to no avail.

"Wake up," she shouts loudly shaking him violently this time.

"He can't be that tired," she says frustratedly.

"Don't worry," giggles Maxie as she then pulls her water bottle out of her bag. "I'll wake him."

"You can't do that," giggles her mum.

Maxie drips a few drops of water on his face, but there's no response, so now frustrated herself Maxie proceeds to pour the full bottle over him, but John doesn't even give a grunt, he just gives out the odd snore. "Well," sighs Lane scratching his head. "I guess we know what effect that leaf has on him, good job you didn't give him a full one. How long do you think it will last?"

Spring Peeper bends down examining John's face and breathing. "Hem, I don't know, an hour, a day, it's impossible to tell."

Big Dan sighs heavily. "It seems all our travelling through the night has been for nothing, we are going to lose the time waiting for John to wake up."

"No," shouts Max. "We should carry on but one of us should stay here with him, it's what he would want, we all know that. We could have done with Woodnut here, he could have watched over him, and when awake it wouldn't have taken them long to catch up, with Woodnut on his shoulders."

"I'll stay with him," croaks Hope. "I don't mind honest."

Max kindly smiles. "That's very kind of you dear, but I think it would be best if you continued with us."

"I'll do it," comes a little voice.

They all look round trying to work out who said it. "I must be imagining things," says Big Dan running his fingers through his beard.

"Down here you big oaf," comes a little voice.

They all look down to see Lilly milk's bright little eyes starring back up at them from just above the ground.

"I should have known," frowns Big Dan. "Oaf aye."

Lilly pops out of the ground, bows then flops to the ground yawning. "I'm sorry," she apologises. "But I'm very tired, trying to keep up with you all, it has taken it out of me also, and I to need to rest."

"So am I to understand," asks Lane, "that you also travel with us, all be it under ground?"

The little mossy just shrugs. Cin shakes his head. "If you'd told me I would have carried you."

The little mossy leans back against John using him as a pillow and closing her eyes mutters, "Go, we'll catch you up later."

Lane grinning then asks, "And tell me little one, if you are asleep also. How are you going to keep John safe?"

Then with a loud grump Lilly suddenly disappears back down into the earth, only to reappear again a moment later. Lane turns to the others and shrugs, but as he does so Max gasps, "Look."

Maxie and Spring Peeper giggle away together as eyes start to appear from the ground all around them, hundreds of them, then with no sound or warning they all pop up out the ground and stand there both male and female mossy. Then after a small bow, and a wave of giggles they disappear down as quickly and silently as they had appeared. Lilly settles back down again, getting comfortable and closing her eyes once more she mutters, "Nothing, but nothing goes over or under the ground without us knowing, now can I please get some sleep."

With a look of utter shock on his face Lane turns to the others and stutters, "Well, it works for me."

Then with a look of equal shock themselves the others nod in agreement, and all set off leaving John and Lilly Milk fast asleep. "I tell you what," says Big Dan, as they all walk along. "That was one of the most impressive sights I've ever seen."

"I can't argue with you there," the others reply.

"You know," sighs Max. "John tells me he's from another earth, and all this is new to him, but it has just dawned on me, how little I actually know about this earth, our home myself. It wasn't until I met him and started to travel, I realised this planet is nearly as alien to me, as it is to him. There are so many wonderous things and marvellous creatures, more than I could ever have imagined."

"I think," answers Big Dan. "In that we are all in agreement."

"Hu!" huffs Spring Peeper just ahead. "Mossy, nothing but show offs."

Hearing this Max runs up behind him picks him up and whispers, "But greenem will always be my favourites."

Then winking she gives him a kiss on the cheek before putting him back down. The little greenem goes as red as a berry, and runs ahead giggling as he does so, with Maxie now chasing him, threatening to give him another if she catches him.

John slowly starts to wake, and feeling pretty good he rolls over, just too hear muffled cries of. "Get off me you silly man."

A little shocked he sits up. "Lilly Milk," he gasps. "What are you doing here?"

"Keeping an eye on you, until you nearly crushed me," she snaps.

"I tell you what guys," yawns John. "That leaf definitely works. I feel wonderfully refreshed. Guys."

Then after looking around and seeing there's no one there he asks Lilly, "What's happened? Where is everyone?"

"You were very tired," she tells him. "And that piece of leaf you took, just had the opposite effect, knocking you out. So it was decided to leave you, and being tired myself I volunteered to stop with you."

John nods. "Sounds reasonable."

"You are fast and will catch up," continues Lilly. "Are you not bothered I was asleep too?"

John winks. "Nah, I trust you, and besides unless you knew it was going to be one hundred percent safe, there's no way you'd stop out in the open, let alone sleep."

"Not bad for a silly ooman," she giggles cheekily.

John then stands up putting his bag back on. "How are you feeling now?" he asks.

"Still a little tired," she yawns. "But I'll be ok. Do you see that rise in the distance ahead, and the tip of that tall tree, they have just stopped there for a rest."

"How do you know that?" asks John in surprise. "Err doesn't matter."

"I'll maybe see you later silly man," she yawns.

"Before you go," shouts John.

"What now?" replies Lilly impatiently

John smiles. "I'm not as fast as you, you know."

"Yes I know," she replies.

Then quick as a flash he grabs the little mossy pops her on his shoulders and starts to take off. "Hold on tight now," he tells her. "Grab my ears if you like."

For the first five minutes Lilly does nothing but scream and squeal, demanding to be let down. "Hey trust me," shouts John. "Just relax and enjoy the ride, you can go in my bag and sleep if you like."

Then as he runs along he hears giggles and laughter coming from the ground all around him, with the occasional flash of eyes just peaking out. He grins. "Your friends seem to like you being up there."

Lilly puts her tongue out at every set of eyes she sees. "Hu," she grumps.

"Ok then," says John slowing down from a run to a slow jog. "I'll let you down; you can make your own way."

"Hmm, err, n, no it's ok," she stutters, now secretly enjoying herself. "Maybe it would be faster this way, I can't let you get too far ahead, there's no telling what trouble you'd get into.

I'll just have to just put up with it I suppose, if you insist," she says sheepishly.

John smiles to himself replying, "Yes, I insist."

John speeds up again and is soon in a rhythm again travelling a good distance between each stride, much to the muffled giggles and delight of Lilly behind him. At this pace it's only a few hours before they see their friends in the distance and John gives out a loud whistle. Max and Maxie turn around instantly. "Dad," shouts Maxie waving her arms.

"Amazing," gasps Max. "How by all the stars can he run so fast?"

They all stop and wait for him to catch up. "I still say it's not natural to run that speed," grunts Cin shaking his head. "How does he manage to still breathe, surely the air must just rush past him."

"What's that on his shoulders?" asks Big Dan.

"It's Lilly Milk, I think," answers Max.

Spring Peeper starts to chuckle, "I bet she's not up there voluntarily, they hate being off the ground."

Then he suddenly stops laughing muttering, "Yes now that is surprising."

"Hi guys," shouts John skidding to a halt.

Lane smiles. "Nice to see you John."

Lilly's eyes are nearly as wide as plates and lit up like lanterns. Seeing them all staring at her she then tries to hide her delight and shouts, "You can let me down now silly man. Making me stay up there, you should be ashamed of yourself."

"I'm sorry," apologises John, putting her down and winking.

Lilly gives him a little smile and wave, then seeing everyone still grinning at her, she squeals with embarrassment and disappears down into the ground instantly, making them all laugh. "Well shall we continue?" laughs Lane. "We are making good time and should be there sometime tomorrow morning, according to Spring Peeper."

John nods and they set off once more.

6

IT'S A WARM damp morning on the far side of the rainforest they are heading for and the old greenem of that forest, Evening Thunder, is standing at the forests' edge. The young greenem are hiding in the trees and bushes a short distance behind him as the old greenem then marches out of the forest and akes a firm stance just in front of the trees. He stands tall and fearless as close to twenty men, some warriors and some not approach, some on horse back, and some in wagons. Seeing the old greenem the men are ordered to stop some distance away by the official looking man leading the way. He dismounts his horse and proceeds slowly over towards the old greenem. He turns ordering the men to stay where they are, as all the other greenem show themselves forming a line along the forests edge. But they then merge silently back into the wood after hearing the man's order to his men.

The man stops several feet short of the old greenem and bows politely. "Evening Thunder I presume."

The greenem nods and bows in return as the man continues, "My name is Elandra. And I am here as an official representative of Lord Tain, to negotiate an amicable agreement on the proceedings to follow."

"Pah nonsense," exclaims the old greenem. "You're only here to try and ease your lords, and your own conscience. Before you destroy our home, and a wonderful and unique forest with plants and creatures found nowhere else. And you have the gaul and cheek to call yourselves the civilised people. Well if being civilised means death and destruction, then I choose not to be civilised."

"Please, you don't understand," replies Elandra. "Let me explain it to you. In a way you may understand more easily."

"Do not patronise me Sir," snaps the old greenem. "In your years I am several centuries older than your eldest person, and I know more of life than you could ever imagine."

The man gives out a wry laugh. "Centuries old," he scoffs irately. "Do you think I'm a fool?"

At this the old greenem smiles broadly. "No," shouts the man. "You are nothing more than a verminous weed, with your lies and untruths, with just enough intelligence to enable you to speak. Spending your lives with your roots buried in the shit from whence you came. My Lord Tain may think you are deserving of life, but I think you are nothing more than a blight on this earth, and as such should be exterminated."

The old greenem's smile starts to fade as anger sweeps across it. Until just at that very moment a fly lands on the old greenem's shoulder. And to Elandra simply that, nothing more nothing less, not even worth the effort of a mention. But to the old greenem, it is a long and trusted friend, Bzzt the long wing with his return message from Lane and the others fast approaching. It only takes Bzzt a brief moment to pass on his message and he flies off again. The old greenem can hardly contain his sudden joy. Then remembering what Bzzt had just told him, he pulls himself together and trying hard to look sombre, he looks back over to Elandra and asks, "Please let us stop this before anymore harsh words are spoken. You said yourself you are civilised people, let us sit down together now, and talk as such and as you said. Tell me in simple terms and I may understand more about your lord's generous offer."

Elandra smiles broadly, bows and proceeds to sit down. "Now this is much better isn't it? See you can be quite civilised yourself sometimes. And if you try really hard, you never know, with practice and a bit of tuition, who knows, you could be just like us."

Evening Thunder sits there staring at him, unsure whether to burst out laughing or just tell him exactly what he thinks of him, and his so called civilised ways.

In the background amongst the trees, talking and giggling is suddenly heard coming from the greenem there, and just the faintest of cheers, either unheard or ignored by the old greenem sitting with his back to them, but Elandra sitting opposite notices a single greenem walk silently out from the woods towards them. Stopping just behind Evening Thunder it proceeds to stand there silently just staring at him. "Well," asks the old greenem. "Are you going to tell me your lords' offer or not?"

"And who would you be greenem?" asks Elandra.

"I told you my name," replies Evening Thunder.

"Not you, you old fool," snaps the man.

"You may call me Mr Greenfern, Ooman."

The old greenem can hardly believe his hearing and tears of joy come to his old eyes as he slowly turns his head. Then smiling kindly at the old greenem

Woodnut says softly, "But you may call me Woodnut my old friend. Now if this man will excuse you for just a moment, I would like a word with you please, if I may."

The old greenem trying hard to hide his happiness at seeing Woodnut turns back to Elandra, "Would you mind?" he asks. "I won't be long."

"No please, by all means," replies Elandra. "And whilst you're at it, maybe you should teach that young greenem some respect when he's around people, it might help him live longer."

"Some of my best friends are people," answers Woodnut. "And as for respect, is not a right or privilege exclusive to man. It is a gift, to be earned, by all those of good deed and good intent, now if you'll excuse me."

"Some of your best friends are people," laughs Elandra. "You're as big a liar as that old greenem beside you."

Woodnut glares at him. "We'll see."

The old greenem takes his hand. "Come my boy."

They then walk a short distance and speak in a way only greenem would hear or understand. "Woodnut Greenfern aye," sighs Evening Thunder proudly. "It's an honour to meet you young greenem, I never thought I'd have the pleasure. I wish it was under better circumstances."

"No the pleasure is all mine," replies Woodnut. "Now do not worry, my friends will sort this all out, one way or another."

"Are they here now?" asks the old greenem excitedly.

"No not yet old friend," answers Woodnut. "I was meant to catch them up after staying a while with Knock Knock and Diddler. But as fortune would have it, I was offered the chance to get ahead of them and be here, and took it. But I'm led to believe they are making their way through the forest as we speak. And with luck they should be here by early afternoon. So if you can keep this arrogant ooman busy until then, all the better. Now you'd better return before he starts to get impatient."

"Yes of course," says a smiling Evening Thunder. "My word, you are a sight for sore eyes young Greenfern, when all this is over you must tell me of all your adventures."

"Yes of course," replies a smiling Woodnut kindly. "It would be my pleasure."

With that Woodnut turns and walks back to the forest, much to the delight of all the greenem waiting there.

Evening Thunder goes back over and sits down with Elandra. "Now where were we?" he asks.

"Oh yes that's right," he says smiling. "You were going to tell me your proposition."

"Good news?" asks Elandra fishing hopefully.

"Just news of friends," answers Evening Thunder nonchalantly.

"Now," continues Elandra. "I am authorised to offer you a few options, and using my own discretion, perhaps a combination of a couple."

So the old greenem sits there cross legged with his hand on his chin, listening intently and nodding as the man explains. "My lord is a fair man," says Elandra. "And as long as you don't upset me, I think we can come to a good arrangement. Now the first option is, we will build you new homes just outside the main town. There you can all live together like normal civilised people, or try to anyway. You would have access to the town and most of its amenities, like the local tavern. I bet you'd like that aye. And we could perhaps get someone to teach you, and school your young in our ways; make it a little easier to forget their own."

"Yes, yes I see," replies Evening Thunder rather sarcastically. "We could sit around all day getting drunk and fighting. We could maybe even become mini warriors, and fight and kill greenem from other areas."

"Yes that's it," answers Elandra excitedly. "That's the spirit, you see, your sounding more civilised already."

The old greenem shakes his head in disbelief, then speechless for a moment pulls himself together and asks, "Now please tell me the other options you mentioned."

"Yes of course, by all means," continues the man smiling, believing he is doing really well. "Now if you don't wish to live in houses or near town, we could escort you, guaranteeing your protection and safety mind you, to any other forest or wood in the province. And we will also supply crates for you to take some of the animals with you, if you so wish. And if where you are wanting to go is too far for your little legs, or to carry crates, we could maybe even transport you in the wagons. Well?"

The old greenem leans back deep in thought for a moment then asks, "What if we have adapted to the soil requirements of this forest, and could not live anywhere else? And as for the animals, there would be no point in taking them with us. As this is the only environment in the world that we know of, where they can live. Most of these animals you will never see in another forest anywhere, which is the reason I've been imploring your people to spare it."

"Oh," nods Elandra. "Well I don't see a problem here, you may take as much soil with you as you wish. In fact if when you think about it, if you don't take any animals with you, you can carry more soil with you anyway. We could even put some on the carts for you, see, what a good idea. Now that's fair isn't it?"

The old greenem can hardly believe his hearing, and thinks to himself, "I cannot take anymore of this self righteous buffoon." Then getting to his feet he bows politely and turns to head back to the forest. "Well?" shouts Elandra. "Have we an accord? What are your thoughts?"

The old greenem stops and slowly turns back. "So you want to know my thoughts do you," he says. "Then I will share some with you. I think there is change coming to this land, and it will start right here. And just like the changing of a season, it cannot be stopped or halted, but it can embraced if you have the foresight. And just like the wind itself, it can come as gently as an evening breeze, or like the mightiest storm destroying all in its path, the choice is yours. For what will happen here, has happened before and will again, and it can never be stopped."

The man sits there totally confused and stammers, "What, what does all that mean? What by the moons are you talking about? Have we an accord or not?"

The old greenem bows once more. "If it's alright by you I will go now and tell the other greenem what has been said here. It may take me to mid afternoon to prepare them for the events to follow, if that is alright by you obviously."

"Yes, yes of course," replies Elandra still a little confused.

"Take as long as you need," he answers, pleased in the belief his plans have gone better than expected, getting back up and walking back over to his men. "Well Sir?" asks one of the men.

"They're even more stupid than I thought," he cackles. "I was hoping for a little resistance, it would have given me the excuse to kill a few. The lies them two greenem were coming out with was unbelievable."

"Perhaps we could still kill a few Sir," shouts another warrior.

"No I'm afraid not," answers Elandra. "I have strict orders from Lord Tain, only if they resist. And you know the consequences if you disobey Lord Tain."

The old greenem reaches the forest and is met by Woodnut. "How did it go?" he asks.

The old greenem nods his head. "Perfectly we have plenty of time for your friends to get here."

"What did he offer you?" asks Woodnut.

Hearing this all the other young greenem crowd in close to listen. "You won't believe it," gasps Evening Thunder. "I didn't know whether to laugh or cry, the offers he made were too stupid to comprehend. Sit, sit everyone, and I will tell you."

They then all listen as the old greenem tells them all the man Elandra had said until mid-day when a young greenem runs excitedly up to Evening Thunder and Woodnut shouting, "They're here, they're here."

The old greenem gets up and goes to greet them. "I'd just like to thank you all for coming," he says. "Please sit a while, you must all be very tired."

Lane who is leading the way with Spring Peeper stops and bows in return. "No need for thanks old one. You would have done no less for us."

They all then take their bags off and sit down before Lane then proceeds to introduce them all. The old greenem stands back up beaming with delight, then after bowing once more introduces himself. "And my name is Evening Thunder.

"Wow," shouts John. "Now if that isn't the coolest name I've ever heard in my life."

Big Dan frowning whispers to Cin, "He said a similar thing to me once you know."

Nodding Cin replies, "Yeah me too, although I must admit, that is one cool name."

"Oh no," gasps Cin.

"What's the matter?" asks Big Dan.

"I think I'm starting to sound like him," Cin gasps again.

Big Dan starts to laugh, making the others turn. "Oops sorry," apologises Big Dan now going a little red.

Woodnut starts to snigger. "Their leader out there has been in talks with Evening Thunder," he tells them.

"And he's made, err, hem, let's say some rather interesting offers," he says still sniggering terribly. "Tell them his offers Evening Thunder, if you don't mind repeating it again."

"Yes, please do," asks Lane.

"Certainly, I'd be happy to," answers the old greenem.

They all then sit there silently as he goes on to explain all that was said. John yawning terribly nudges Woodnut, "I can see why you were laughing pal. Is this guy for real or what?"

Lane sits there white with anger before he explodes, "The arrogance of this cur. As much dirt as you can carry, and to call you a liar, and not just you but Woodnut also. When I was younger I've killed men for less. And as long as you don't upset him aye, oh I'll show him upset alright, and there's no time like the present. If everyone's ready, let's get this party started."

"Now how would you like to proceed?" he asks the old greenem. "Would you like us to go straight out and speak to him now, or perhaps?"

"No, no," interrupts Evening Thunder. "If you could all stay just out of sight. I will go out and tell him we are not interested in his offers. And maybe give him another chance first, and if rejected, then please do as you see fit."

"Would you like one of us to come out with you? Just to make sure you are ok?" asks Big Dan.

"No thank you my lad," smiling Evening Thunder replies. "It should be ok."

He then proceeds to get up and walk to the edge of the wood. "Well I don't trust that Ooman," says Woodnut. "I think I'll go with him."

John grins. "No, I've got a better idea. Lilly. Oh Lilly Milk are you there?"

Two little eyes then pop up just in front of him and he winks and says, "Hi cutie. Could you be so kind as to go with the old greenem please? And if that man tries anything funny, or goes to hurt him, could you stop him. Bury him perhaps, just up to the knees or waist maybe. Put the frighteners on him a bit you know." Lilly Milk nods and giggles as she disappears again. "That's how you did it," shouts Cin.

"I should have known," laughs Big Dan.

"What?" asks John.

"In the forest with those robbers," shouts Cin.

"Yes John," replies Dan. "We thought you were commanding the earth its self."

John laughs shaking his head. "Sometimes things are not always as they seem."

"Commanding the earth indeed," he laughs. "As if – what do you think I am?"

Lane gets up followed by the others. "What about the two children?" asks Cin.

"Well I'm going out, you're not leaving me here," announces Maxie.

Hope sits there quietly beside Fluff, not knowing what to say. "Well I think she's more than earned the right to come out and face them with us," Lane tells them. "What do you think Max."

"Yes I agree," sighs Max. "As long as she's careful that is, and does as she's told mind."

Max then kneels down beside Hope and tells him, "I'd like you to stay here my dear, you look very tired. Fluff will stay here with you and the greenem will look after you. Just while we sort this out ok."

"If you think that is best," answers Hope sheepishly.

Max smiles and gently rubs his cheek. "I do dear yes."

Evening Thunder slowly walks from the forest stopping roughly half the distance from Elandra and his men. "Sir, over there, that old greenem's back," shouts one of the warriors.

"Excellent," replies Elandra rubbing his hands together.

"Do you think they've agreed Sir" asks one of the men.

"Yes of course," he answers. "What choice do they have? And if they don't, I'll just have to make an example of that old greenem. I think that'll get their attention nicely, and get the point across at the same time."

He then makes his way over to Evening Thunder and stopping just in front of him he bows politely smiling from ear to ear. The old greenem bows in return and clearing his throat says, "I'd just like to thank you for your kind offers. But after careful thought and deliberation, I'm afraid we'll have to decline them. For you see this rainforest is unique, amazing and wonderful, and we have lived here longer than your people have lived on this earth. But I have an offer for you and your Lord, if you would like to go and get him. I will personally show him the sights, sounds and wonders of this amazing environment. And I think you will both then realise just what an important place it is, and what a mistake you are making."

"My Lord never makes mistakes," shouts Elandra.

"Then your Lord is truly unique," replies Evening Thunder. "I will give you some time to think about it."

And with that the old greenem turns and walks away. "I need no time to think," shouts Elandra. "How dare you have the cheek to make me an offer?"

The old greenem turns back round. "Then it appears our talks are over."

And with a last bow he proceeds back to the forest. "No," shouts Elandra. "I have a final message to your people."

Then drawing his sword he charges forward towards the old greenem who turns back around, and for a moment he's frozen with terror. With sword raised high Elandra is then nearly upon him as the old greenem raises his hands in a vain attempt to protect himself. But suddenly Elandra is pulled down and finds himself buried up to his knees in the earth below. He flails his arms with the sudden shock and surprise, loosing grip of his sword and dropping it. Panicking he tries to re grab it, but before his hand reaches it, the sword is also swallowed up by the earth. Struggle as he might Elandra is now stuck fast. "You'll pay for this," he stutters.

A little bewildered himself Evening Thunder composes himself once more and walks back over, stopping just out of arms reach and stands there silently. "You'll pay for this, this witchcraft," shouts Elandra. "I'll burn you all."

But as he shouts this out, he finds himself pulled down even more and yells with fright as the old greenem stares at him solemnly. "Now I think you should learn when to keep quiet, before you disappear completely. You call yourselves civilised and honourable; who do you think you're fooling by stating this time and time again. Me, my people, other oomans, no, I'm afraid only yourselves. But tell me, is this what civilized people do when they can't get their own way is it, attack from behind with a large weapon. I'm only a fraction of your size, peace loving and unarmed, do you see me as a threat, or scary perhaps. No Sir, I say you are the savages, you are the blight. You are blind to the beauty and diversity of life, by the false assumption that the gain of wealth and material objects will bring you happiness. Well it does not Sir, it is nothing more than greed you follow, a self destructive and deadly force which seems to affect your people like a plague. And I am no fool Sir, did you honestly expect me to agree to any of those insulting offers you made. We have lived here longer than your people can imagine. And will continue to do so long after you have gone, and are nothing more than a vague memory. Oh and one last thing, I am no liar Sir, only oomans lie, we have no need."

The old greenem then turns to walk away. "You can't leave me here," shouts Elandra. "Use your witchcraft and get me out of here now."

Evening Thunder turns back round chuckling, "Only oomans believe in such stupidity, witchcraft indeed."

"How else did you do this?" shouts Elandra. "Well we have a witch also, and she is much more powerful than you will ever be."

"You really don't understand do you," the old greenem tells him. "It was not I that did this to you. I have no knowledge of how it occurred. But I will tell you something, you have now started something you can never stop, and we have nature itself on our side."

He then turns and heads back to the forest. A cheer goes up from the other greenem as he enters the forest again. "How did it go?" asks John, now seriously struggling to stay awake.

"This is worse than twelve hour night shift," he mumbles to himself.

"Than what?" asks Max sitting next to him.

"Err doesn't matter," he answers. "I'm too tired to explain."

"I don't know how you did it my boy," says Evening Thunder. "But you saved my life, that ooman was going to kill me."

John winks. "It wasn't me, it was our friend Lilly Milk you have to thank."

"Lilly Milk?" replies the old greenem scratching his head and looking round. "If I didn't know better I would say that was a mossy name."

"It is," giggles Maxie.

"Lilly," she shouts.

Lilly Milk then pops up just beside Evening Thunder. "Well I never," he exclaims. "Thank you very much my dear, it was very kind of you. But I didn't know you could do that. And I'll be honest, when that ooman was pulled down I nearly got a bigger shock than he did."

"You're welcome," she giggles.

The old greenem then leans forwards and whispers, "This is very unusual for a mossy, they are normally."

"Normally what?" snaps Lilly. "I'm standing right here beside you, you stupid old greenem."

"See what I mean," huffs Evening Thunder.

A big smile comes across John's face as he sits there watching them argue, and the absurdity of it all hits home. He can't help but think to himself, "I wonder if all this is a dream, maybe the alarm will go off soon. Gees I hope not, how could you face another dull day at work after all this. Or perhaps I won't remember any of it, maybe we dream like this every night, transported to magical lands somewhere, only to fade into a distant memory as a new day dawns and we awake." Then as his thoughts slowly fade, he finds himself still confronted by the little mossy and the old greenem still trading insults, and he bursts out laughing, stopping the argument dead. "What are you laughing at silly man?" snaps Lilly.

John shrugging replies, "It just come to me, I'm sitting at the edge of a forest watching two plants argue."

"Yeah so," grumps Lilly. "What's so funny about that? Where do you expect us to argue, the middle of town."

"No," shrugs John. "But come on, two plants arguing."

"I'm not sure what you mean my boy," says Evening Thunder a little puzzled.

"No me neither," agrees Cin, closely followed by the others.

John yawns rubbing his eyes. "Err doesn't matter, just me I suppose."

"Anyway," he says trying to quickly change the subject. "Did you just leave that man buried out there?"

"Yes of course why," Lily answers.

"Leave him there I say," growls Big Dan. "Let his men dig him out, teach him a lesson."

"Yes I agree," nods Cin.

"Well I suppose," yawns John. "But can you imagine the shock he'll get if he is suddenly thrust back up and expelled from the earth that would be better than when he was first pulled down."

"Oh yes," shouts Lilly excitedly. "That does sound fun."

"Why don't you go to the edge of the forest and let him see you there," she then tells Evening Thunder. "Then I'll push him up, he'll think you did it."

"Yes," laughs Evening Thunder. "That does sound fun, let's go my dear."

The old greenem then makes a stand just out of the trees, and stares silently at Elandra struggling to free himself. Spotting the old greenem he shakes his fist furiously, to which the old greenem simply bows. But as sheer coincidence and luck would have it, it coincides with Lilly Milk shoving him back up and out. Making the man shout louder than when he was first pulled down. Elandra now free and panicking scrambles to his feet and runs back over towards his men, shouting as he gets closer, "Kill them, burn them, kill them all now."

The men unsure what has just happened stand there a little bewildered, just staring at one another. "What are you waiting for?" screams Elandra as he gets there. "Charge now, kill them, kill everything, I'll show them."

"Yes Sir," shouts an excited warrior, and the charge begins, some preferring to be on foot and some charging past them on horse back.

Max stands up. "It's time to go out, they're charging."

So they make their way to the edge of the forest led by Lane but Big Dan turns round and asks, "Hey where's John?"

"I'll get him," sighs Max. "I can hear him snoring, I think he's fallen asleep."

Cin just grumps, "Typical, the one time we could do with him at his best, and he can't keep his eyes open."

"I'm here ya big lug," calls John walking over yawning. "I was just resting my eyes for a moment, you try being up for days with no sleep."

"I have been," Cin answers.

"When you two are finished," bellows Big Dan. "We should really get out there."

So with the charging warriors now half way to the trees Lane steps out, and marching forward he draws his sword and makes a stand, followed by Big Dan, Cin and Max, with Maxie and John standing just behind them. Woodnut and Evening Thunder then also walk out and stand firmly by Lane's side. The horsemen leading the charge are suddenly filled with confusion at the sight of the warriors standing side by side with the greenem and pull their horses to a halt. Max heaves a deep breath. "Well that went better than expected." "Stand tall my dear," whispers Big Dan. "It's not over yet."

"I say kill them all," bellows Cin. "Teach all in this province this forest is off limits."

Lane turns to him frowning and shakes his head. "What?" cries Cin. "It's only four each."

"No my friend," answers Big Dan. "That leaves two if you include that cowardly leader back there."

Cin shrugs. "Yes I know, but I thought we could leave one each for the girls."

John standing behind starts to laugh. "What do you say John?" asks Cin.

"Yeah," yawns John. "I agree with you, let's kill them all as quickly as possible."

"John," shouts Max. "You're just saying that because you want to go to sleep."

"Maybe not," he yawns again.

The two girls just glare at him. "Ok, ok," he stutters. "Maybe I am."

Back at the other side of the of the clearing Elandra sees the friends march from the trees and take a stand. "What the," he says to himself, unsure of what he's seeing himself. The horseman turn around in their saddles for instructions from him. "There's only five and a kid," he shouts to his men. "If they want to stand with the greenem, then let them die with the greenem."

Then kicking their horses they continue the charge. "Lane," shouts Woodnut.

"Yes my friend," he answers.

Woodnut smiles up at him. "Put your hand out towards the horses and show them the mark on your palm."

"Why what will that do?" asks Lane.

Woodnut giggles, "Maybe nothing."

A little closer and Lane puts his hand out as if to halt, and as soon as he does the horses seeing the mark skid to a halt, throwing their riders head over tail off in front of them. Seeing this the two greenem and Maxie laugh that hard they nearly fall over. Lane looks down to the nearly doubled up Woodnut. "Nice one."

The men get to their feet dazed and confused, rubbing their various bumps and bruises. "What the heck happened there?" shouts one of the men.

"I've no idea," shouts another.

Then seeing the friends still standing there they draw their swords and start to run, but after only a few steps they seem to stop. "What's the matter?" asks a warrior.

"I'm not sure," answers another. "I seem to be stuck."

Then in one sudden jerk the man is pulled down to his waist. "Help, help," he screams panicking and clawing at the ground. "Something's got me, I can feel it."

His friends grab his arms and after some tugging and pulling manage to get him out. "This isn't right," shouts the man scrambling backwards. "This is witchcraft, I'm out of here."

Then fear gripping the rest, they all retreat back towards Elandra. Big Dan gives Max a nudge and a wink. "Now you can breathe a bit easier, they will not fight now, they will try and talk."

As the men reach Elandra he starts to shout, "What are you doing you cowards, turn and fight, there's only five of them."

He them grabs the spear off a warrior just in front of him and raises it high to run him through. "Please Sir," begs the warrior. "There is witchcraft at work here, y, y, you retreated Sir."

Then out of sheer frustration Elandra pulls his arm right back and throws the spear as hard as he can towards the friends. The spear slowly but surely whistles high through the air towards them. "You know that's not a bad throw," says Cin. "Maybe we should move back a little."

"No don't move," Lane tells them.

"He's right Lane," says Big Dan. "It's going to be awful close."

"Yes I know," Lane answers. "But I have an idea. John do you think?"

"JOHN," he continues annoyed. "Can somebody please wake him up?"

Max turns and slaps John. "Corr blimey," he gasps rubbing his cheek. "What was that for?"

"Wake up," she snaps.

"I'm awake," grumps John. "I was just checking my eyelids for holes. Ok, damn woman."

"JOHN," shouts Lane. "Do you think you could catch that spear?"

"At that speed," shrugs John yawning. "With one hand, it looks as if it's been thrown by a child."

Lane and Big Dan then part as John steps forward in front of them, and prepares to catch it.

"What are they doing Sir?" one of the warriors asks Elandra. "They aren't even trying to move."

Elandra stands there proud as he watches his spear gliding towards them but he then see them part and John step forward. "What are they doing?" he gasps.

"I don't believe it" he then shouts.

"What is it Sir?" asks one of his men.

"I think," he stutters. "They're going to sacrifice their servant, that little fellow. The barbarians. They are obviously trying to show us that life has little meaning for them, or their servants."

They then stand there transfixed watching the spear get closer and closer, some even taking pity on what they think is John's sacrifice, and shout, "Get out of the way you fool."

Then breathing a sigh of relief they see the spear is about to come down just short of him. But to their utter shock and bewilderment, they see him step forward raise his right arm and catch the spear with one hand, stopping it only a foot from his face. "D, do my eyes deceive me?" gasps Elandra. "Did anyone else see that?"

"Yes Sir," come the gasps.

"How could anyone do that?" shouts one of the men.

"What are those other four warriors capable of, if their servant can do that," shouts another.

John turns to Lane. "What do you want me to do with it now?" he asks.

"Throw it back," shouts Lane. "Aim for a wagon, there's no point in hurting anyone at this stage."

So John spins the spear around and throws it back hard and fast. Some of the men yell in shock as they see it hurtling towards them, others in panic just trying to find out what's going on. Cin nudges Lane. "I tell you what, if that thing does hit someone they won't feel much that's for sure."

"Truly," nods Lane.

The spear then whistles past Elandra and several other men, and hits the side of the wagon barely slowing down. It then crashes through the other side and stops after lodging in the corner joint of the next wagon, but not before pinning a warrior to it by the collar. A cold sweat forms on the brow of the pinned man, as he realises just how close he has come, and promptly faints.

"Oh shit," gasps John. "I think I've killed someone."

"JOHN language," shouts Max. "And no he's not dead, I think he's just fainted."

"Oh thank god for that," he sighs somewhat relieved.

"Well if that didn't get the point across nothing will," laughs Big Dan.

"Point across," giggles Woodnut. "Good one."

"Hum, what," replies Dan.

"Oh yes that was quite good wasn't it," he chuckles.

"Elandra Sir," calls one of his men. "I don't think these are ordinary warriors, maybe you should talk to them Sir."

"What ME," stutters Elandra. "Err hem, yes of course, I, I suppose. Do you think I should?"

"You're not frightened are you Sir?" asks a warrior.

"N, n, no of course not," he stammers. "I'll go right now, maybe I should take one of you with me. Drew, you're the head warrior here, you can come, a show of strength perhaps."

"As you wish Sir," Drew answers. "But I don't think it will be much of a show. Two of them warriors are massive, even that third, mean looking warrior is bigger than I Sir."

"Nonsense," shouts Elandra with a sudden rush of bravery. "Let us go now and meet with these, these greenem mercenaries. They must obviously be simple of mind, or easy bought."

So he marches out with Drew beside him; hands raised high in a sign of peace.

"Surprise surprise," laughs Cin.

"It seems they now want to talk, maybe I should go and talk with them," he growls.

"No I think I'll go," interrupts Lane. "You stay here my hot headed friend. But if you don't mind John, your ear and worldly knowledge may come in handy I think. And perhaps Evening Thunder, you may want to come also, and represent your people and your interests."

The old greenem bows. "Thank you my lad, but I would rather Woodnut went. It is he who truly represents our people, and he knows oomans better than I ever will. No offence, but they still make me nervous, that's if you don't mind Woodnut my lad."

"Yes I'd be happy to," answers Woodnut. "That man owes me an apology anyway."

"Why what did he do?" asks Cin.

"He called me a liar," answers Woodnut.

"He did WHAT," bellows Cin. "Are you sure I shouldn't go Lane."

Lane shakes his head. "No not this time my friend, now let's go and see what he wants."

The two men and Woodnut walk away but stop when Max shouts over to John, "Try not to yawn dear, it doesn't look good. Well not on a first meeting."

John barely gives half a nod and with a slight wave of the hand he and the rest carry on.

They stop when they meet Elandra who says, "Greetings strangers, my name is Elandra, and this is my head warrior Drew."

Lane bows his head slightly. "And greetings to you also, my name is Elaine, and this is my friend John, and my other friend Woodnut."

Elandra bows his head. "I see by your leathers, you are a warrior of Luguvalio, and your friend is a desert man. I have heard of the desert people, but have never met one. I always expected them to be taller somehow. No matter, he is your servant, err slave, I presume."

"He is my friend," growls Lane. "And you would be wise to keep a civil tongue in your head, or this will be the shortest bloodiest meeting of your life."

"Err, yes sorry," stutters Elandra. "I meant no disrespect."

"Let's sit," interrupts John.

"Sit," exclaims Elandra.

"Yes sit," says John smiling politely. "It just makes it a bit fairer setting for my best friend here, Mr Woodnut Greenfern. Who is here as a representative of his people."

"Is this some sort of joke," exclaims Elandra. "This greenem is your friend."

"You got a problem with that," snarls Lane eyeballing the man.

"N, n, n, no of course not," stutters Elandra sitting down.

"Haven't you got something to say to me?" scowls Woodnut in a serious voice.

"I'm sorry," mumbles Elandra.

"What was that?" asks Woodnut. "Come now, you were loud enough earlier, when calling me a liar."

"Ok ok, I'm sorry," shouts the man irately.

"Thank you" smiles Woodnut.

"Now let's get down to it," frowns Elandra. "Why are you defending these greenem? How much are they paying you? They can't have much wealth to offer, or perhaps they have offered land, whatever it is we will double it."

"We are not here for money, land or glory," answers Lane. "We are here to help friends."

"Help friends," laughs Elandra. "Save some stupid forest for a few greenem, ridiculous."

"This is their home," Lane tells him gruffly. "And no less important to them than yours is to you. More so probably, their home is also home to creatures and plants found nowhere else."

Elandra gives out a wry chuckle. "So a few animals die in the name of progress, it's not exactly going to change our lives forever now is it."

"Huh progress," growls John trying to keep calm. "Well that's where you're wrong. This rainforest here, you seem so desperate to destroy, will change your life. And it will change the lives of all the people around here forever if destroyed."

"What do you mean?" asks Elandra.

"This isn't just a few trees, or a small wood," John tells them. "This is one large living breathing rainforest, and it isn't called a rainforest for nothing. This place generates its own weather system for goodness sake, and feeding many rivers and tributaries I'll bet. And if you destroy that, you may find to your expense just how fragile a balance nature can be. It's an old analogy, but if you break the link, you destroy the chain, and you may find your whole weather system changed forever. And not just here everywhere to some extent, and unfortunately I've seen it before. In some places it will be subtle, with some seasons starting early, some late, other places it'll be more dramatic, floods drought, who knows, there's no telling to be honest. But one thing is certain, you destroy that place, it will happen."

"Pah," exclaims Elandra. "I've never heard such nonsense in all my life, you must think me a fool."

John and Lane turn to each other and smile broadly then turn back to Elandra and nod. Woodnut who up until now has tried to be serious cannot help but snigger. "Is this some sort of joke?" shouts Elandra angrily.

Lane turning serious stares Elandra dead in the eye and tells him, "I am as ignorant as you of what my friend has just told you, but be in no doubt as I'm not. For what he has told you will be true, and you would be a fool to ignore it."

He then turns to Woodnut. "Excuse me my friend," he says." But forgetting the greenem for a moment. Do this for yourself and your people if nothing else."

"Whether true or not," answers Elandra. "I have no choice, I am under orders from my Lord, and I have to follow his orders to the letter."

John sighs. "Well I'm sorry to hear that, I would rather be someone's friend than their enemy any day. But if you insist on carrying on with this madness, and using your lord as an excuse, we will defend our friends, and you will not win. Now come on, your lord must be a reasonable man to some extent, or he wouldn't be where he is now."

Elandra starts laughing, "I have the warriors of an entire province at my disposal. What chance do you honestly think you have?"

"Well if you want to be like that," growls Lane. "We have the armies of three provinces and the desert people at our disposal."

Elandra is speechless for a moment, and looks over to Cin and the others before he replies, "I see two Luguvalio men and that large Voreda warrior, and there's your little desert friend here. Not that I believe you, but that is only two provinces. And the desert people would never leave the desert."

"We have just come from the province of Taraten," says Lane proudly. "And every warrior there would not hesitate to help us if asked."

Elandra and Drew look at each other then fall into fits of laughter. Through the laughter Elandra splutters, "Now that has brightened my day up no end, at least you have a sense of humour. No one enters Taraten, or should I say, no one leaves Taraten, you should perhaps learn a little about the places you are going to lie about. The Tosh warriors there have a poison that cripples any man, and their Lord Taraten is an evil savage man, who rules with fear and brutality."

Suddenly filled with rage Lane jumps to his feet drawing his sword. "You call me a liar you cur."

Elandra and Drew quickly get to their feet with Drew also drawing his sword. "What do you expect, with so many tall tales" shouts Elandra.

Drew then steps forward raising his sword to protect Elandra. Lane now as mad as mad can be and seeing it as a challenge swings his sword at Drew's. He hits the sword that hard it knocks Drew off balance and stumbling backwards he falls to the ground. Lane then raises his sword once more to finish him off but John quickly grabs the sword, and now getting mad himself shouts, "Jesus, does everything on this damn planet have to end in violence. Can no one just sit down and work things out like decent civilised people."

Shaken by what has just happened Elandra stutters, "But, but, we are Tain, we are the civilised people."

"So why don't you damn well act like it?" growls John stepping forward and leaning right into Elandra's face.

"John, can you let go of my sword please," interrupts Lane. "You're bending it."

"Oops sorry," apologises John. "Pass it here a moment, it's not an heirloom or something is it."

Then grabbing it tight in both hands he gently manipulates the kink between his thumbs and bends it back, He then holds it up to his eye and looks down the blade, and after another little tweak he hands it back to Lane and tells him, "Here try that."

Elandra stands there open mouthed, not quite believing what he has just seen, and Drew still on the ground sits there equally stunned. Lane swings his sword to one side then the other, then swings it high above his head and is about to bring it down. John sighs. "No, I didn't mean try it that way."

Lane grins and winks. "Oh sorry John, I was only joking."

Elandra suddenly goes white with shock and fear. "Please," he shouts. "Let us talk more, as you say, like civilised people."

"Could we not have just done that in the first place?" asks John.

"Well, well," stutters Elandra. "We did try."

"Try," snaps John. "You just tried to bribe us, then you threatened us, then you called us liars, how was that talking like civilised people."

"May I speak openly?" asks Drew.

"Yes of course man," barks Lane. "Say what you think, no harm will come to you."

Drew nods cautiously. "Thank you, it's just some of the things you told us, were a little hard to believe, to say the least. And no offence, but around here everyone knows of Taraten province and their Lord, and no one in their right mind goes there."

"Is that so," answers John reaching into his shirt to pull out the chain given to him by his friends in Taraten.

"Do you believe us now?" he asks

Elandra and Drew gasp with shock. "But, but," stutters Elandra. "I, think that's. Hem, am I seeing correctly, it can't be, it looks like a lords chain of office. In fact if I see those marks correctly, no this cannot be, that would mean you are Lord Taraten himself."

John gives a cheeky grin and winks. "But, but," stammers Elandra. "I thought Lord Taraten was a gangly man, an aging man, full of bitterness and cruelty."

John leans forwards and growls in a menacing voice, "Yeah he used to be, before a tragedy befell him."

"Tragedy, what tragedy?" asks Elandra.

John leans forwards and snarls, "Me."

Both Drew and Elandra suddenly look away. "Please forgive us my Lord," begs Elandra. "We did not know, we overt our eyes in respect my Lord. This puts a whole new light on things."

John a little puzzled looks to Lane, who a little bewildered himself simply shrugs, and shakes his head.

"Why are you looking away?" asks John.

"Respect my Lord," answers Elandra. "We can't look you in the eye without permission."

"Huh, what," gasps John.

"It must be their way John," answers Lane. "Strange as it seems."

John shakes his head muttering, "What a load of. Turn back round please, I never trust anyone who can't look me in the eye."

"Thank you my Lord," reply the two men.

"Not again," mumbles John rubbing his eyes. "Right let's get a couple of things straight ok. Firstly, tell the rest of your men not to overt their eyes, there is no need for it. You can show respect to a person without doing that, ok. And secondly my name is John, not my Lord or Lord Taraten or otherwise."

"John," interrupts Lane. "It might be prudent to use your title for a while, its more impressive, might give us a little more leverage."

"No," grumps John. "It just makes me feel uncomfortable. We are all born the same, and we all die the same. And all men are equal when the memory fades."

Elandra and Drew sit there in total confusion. "But this isn't right," says Elandra. "We have a strict etiquette to follow my Lord. We cannot just call you this, this woman's name, it shows total disrespect."

"Now listen," snaps John. "I am very, very tired, and in no mood to argue."

"I'm normally a very placid man, but if you're not careful I'll show you how I became Lord Taraten," he barks.

"Please everyone, let me explain," shouts Lane.

Then turning to Elandra he explains, "You have different customs, different ways of showing respect. Your people are different than ours, this isn't a bad thing, it's just the way it is. And as we hope to respect your ways and etiquette, we hope you can respect ours. Does this make sense to you?"

Elandra bows. "Now you put it like that, yes it does, we will try our best."

Lane smiles. "Excellent, as will we, won't we John."

"Yeah I suppose," grumps John, finding it hard not to yawn.

"This is an historic day," says Elandra proudly. "To be the first person to talk with Lord Taraten. Many of my people have been sent there as peace envoys, but only one has ever returned, and he told tales so ghastly, I dare not repeat them. But I must go now, I must tell my Lord, we must prepare for your visit. You do want to speak to my Lord Tain I take it."

"Yes please," answers John. "It would be an honour, but I would prefer it be a low key visit, if you know what I mean."

He winks and Elandra bows. "Yes my Lord, if that is what you wish," he answers a little confused. "We will depart straight away if that is alright by you my Lord."

John nods. "Yes, we look forward to it."

Elandra bows. "Until tomorrow."

John yawns sarcastically. "Yeah fantastic. Time for a little over due sleep me thinks."

Bowing once more Elandra and Drew leave and return to their men. "What's happening now Sir?" asks one of his men.

"We must return home as quickly as possible," he tells them.

"I have to tell Lord Tain of the good news," he blusters excitedly.

"What news Sir?" the men shout.

"You won't believe it," Drew tells them. "But that little man over there. The one we thought was their servant, he's actually Lord Taraten."

A gasp of shock and bewilderment goes through the men, as they stare across in amazement.

John, Lane and Woodnut get back to their friends in the wood. "Well," asks Max excitedly. "How did it go?"

John nods yawning. "It seemed to go quite well. What do you think guys?"

"Yes it ended up going very well I would say," answers Lane. "And tomorrow we are to be guests of Lord Tain himself."

"Well Woodnut my boy?" asks Evening Thunder.

Woodnut smiles broadly. "The forest is saved for the moment. And when we talk to the lord of this province, I am sure it will be saved for all time."

A loud cheer goes up from all the greenem, who then rush forward picking up Woodnut, and proudly carry him around on their shoulders, much to Woodnut's giggles. Spring Peeper steps forward and with a tear in his eye bows as low as he can to Lane. "I want to thank you once again for saving my home."

Lane kneels down. "There's no need to bow so low. It's always a good feeling to help a friend, a reward in itself, you came to save us, did you not."

Spring Peeper nods smiling from ear to ear. "Yes."

"Now," says Lane standing back up. "How about you take us to a nice part of the forest and we will celebrate. Then an early night I think, we all may need it, it's another big day tomorrow aye."

"Yes, yes," replies Spring Peeper excitedly. "Follow me everybody, we have the perfect place, Hope and Fluff are there already."

They all then follow the troop of greenem marching proudly along in front of them. John is at the back trailing behind, his head spinning like a top trying to take in all the sights and sounds of the rainforest. The old greenem Evening Thunder stays back with him, just to keep an eye on him. "Anything in particular catching your eye my boy?" asks the old greenem. "I've never seen anyone as keen to look around."

"Are you joking," answers John. "It's amazing, the sights, sounds, the smells, even the dampness and humidity, it's the whole experience. This is a dream come true for me. Where I come from there are rainforests like this, but I've only seen them on TV. I never dreamt I would ever get the chance to explore one."

"TV," replies Evening Thunder with a puzzled look.

John nods scratching his head. "Oh, err, yes, it's like a box that shows you moving pictures, from wherever people have taken them from I suppose. Err it doesn't matter."

"Here hang on a minute, what's that," he then gasps darting over to a small carpet of flowers.

The old greenem quickly follows him over. "Well I never," gasps John proudly. "It's a tortoise."

Then as he kneels down beside it, the tortoises head and legs shoot in and the front of its shell closes up like a drawbridge. John grins. "Well I'll be gob smacked, it's a box turtle."

The old greenem looks at him a little bewildered. "Well, yes my boy," he says. "What else would it be, you have obviously seen them before."

John nods. "Yes, but back on my earth, never on this one. I used to have one as a pet when I was young." The old greenem scratches his head and laughs, "Your parents' idea was it, slow you down a bit my boy. I bet taking that for a walk took you forever did it."

"Hang on," gasps John picking it up and inspecting it.

"The front of the shell is clear, I mean I can see through it, honest," he shouts. "I can see its little head, and its eyes. How bizarre it's watching me watching it."

"Well yes of course it is," chuckles the old greenem again. "How else would it know when it's safe to come back out?"

John nods and shrugs. "Do you know, that does make sense to me? But the box turtles where I come from do not have a see through front, it is as dark as the rest of the shell."

Confused again the old greenem asks, "So how do they know when it's safe to come out?"

John shrugs. "They don't I suppose, they just take a careful peek I guess."

"Come on you two," comes a voice.

They both look around to see Maxie standing there. "Everyone else has started to eat," she tells them.

John smiles and puts the turtle back down and they follow her to a large clearing. He is met first by a very excited Hope. "This is wonderful," he exclaims excitedly. "This whole environment, the air, the dampness. I think this is where I came from you know. I didn't know anything could make you feel so good."

John puts his hand on the boys shoulder and smiles. "I'm pleased you like it young man, so you wouldn't mind staying here a while then. Just while we go and see this Lord Tain fellow."

"No I don't mind at all," he replies smiling happily.

"John come and sit down," shouts Cin. "You have to try some of this fruit, it's wonderful."

John sits down beside his friends on a specially prepared cushion. But after several yawns and only a mouthful of food he can no longer keep his eyes open any more, and is soon fast asleep. "The poor thing," says Max softly stroking his cheek. "Sleep well my dear."

The others talk and party until nearly dark, with only Lane and a handful of greenem left up. A little worse for wear due to, too much beelack juice he lies there staring up at the dusky sky trying to get comfortable. "It's no good," he announces sitting back up. "I just can't seem to settle."

"I know," says Spring Peeper. "Do you see that creep vine tree just past the first line of trees there?"

Lane nods. "Yes."

"The air under that tree will be a lot cooler and dryer," the little greenem tells him. "The top of the tree draws all the heat and moisture from below it."

Lane jumps to his feet. "Excellent," he shouts smiling and grabbing his stuff.

He then makes his way over and leans back against the cool bark of the tree. "Oh yes this is much better" he mutters aloud.

But as his eyes start to flicker he sees something flutter down towards him, and as it gets closer he sees it's Bzzt, and he puts his hand out for it to land on. "Hello my little friend, it's nice to see you again. And what do I owe the pleasure."

The little fly bows and proceeds to tell him, that this type of tree is his favourite place to sleep, for the same reason as his, and with another bow and a fond goodnight, Bzzt flies off to a branch just above him to sleep.

7

It's the early hours of the morning when Lane is awoken by a bright light and searing pain. He opens his eyes but nothing more; unable to either scream with pain, or move from it. Fear grips his heart and his mind, as he sees the earth around him, and the tree above him, slowly start to dissolve and disappear, then he starts to choke as he looks on at his own body now doing the same. With the last thing to go being his eyes, staring desperately out towards an equally terrified Spring Peeper, now franticly racing towards him.

Spring Peeper is under a large tree opposite Lane, where it is a little warmer and more humid than the tree Lane's under, and just how he likes it. And he also is fast asleep, until the early hours, when by chance he happens to open one eye. Something all greenem have a tendency to do, just to make sure nothing is creeping up on them. His eye automatically closes again as it would normally. But something being not quite right triggers him to wake up automatically, and he sits up rubbing his eyes. And as they start to focus on the large tree ahead, he sees it is enveloped in a strange light. A perfect circle of light all around the tree, he stands up and steps forward for a closer look, unsure of what he's actually looking at. But seeing the terror on Lane's face, he realises instantly something is seriously wrong. The little greenem looks up to see if he can see where the light is coming from, but to no avail. Above the circle of light is only darkness. He then looks back down towards Lane, and sees to his horror, the tree and soil around it slowly starting to dissolve into nothing.

The little greenem screams with terror, as he then sees his friend Lane also start to slowly dissolve away. He dashes forwards to the light terrified, but compelled to help his friend, but unsure how. As he gets closer to the light, he stares deep into Lane's soulfully pleading agonising eyes, and tears start to form in his own, as he then notices there is nothing more left of him. And he hits the edge of the light as he sees Lanes eyes finally fade into nothing. But hitting the edge of the light, is the last thing Spring Peeper remembers until he is awoken by the voices of several frantic greenem calling his name.

"Spring Peeper, Spring Peeper, are you alive?" calls one.

"Wake up please," calls another.

The little greenem slowly opens his eyes, but can barely move and his body is suddenly racked with pain right down the front from head to toe. "What happened?" he cries.

"We, we were going to ask you the same thing," another greenem replies.

"We heard your screams and came straight away," they sob. "But when we got here we found you just lying here.

"Yeah," cries another. "We thought you were dead."

"W, why would you think that," moans a disorientated Spring Peeper.

"Do, do you not know?" gasps one.

"How can he not," gasps another.

"What is it?" cries Spring Peeper.

One of his friends then carefully takes his hand and shows him. "Look at your hand," he cries softly. "It is burned terribly, as is most of your body. But, but it's strange, I have never seen anything like it."

Spring Peeper screams again as what actually happened to him suddenly comes flooding back. "Lane, Lane, Lane," he cries. "Is he ok?"

"I've no idea," answers one of his friends. "He's not here, he will be over sleeping with the others."

"No, no," cries Spring Peeper. "He was over there, under the creep vine tree."

"What tree?" gasps one of the greenem. "He's babbling. There's no creep vine tree here."

"Get me up," demands Spring Peeper. "Get me to my feet."

So the others carefully get him up and he stares over to where the large tree once stood. "G, get me to John and Evening Thunder as quickly as possible," he moans through the pain.

Four greenem then carefully carry him over to the middle of the clearing where the others are still fast asleep. But each step they take sends pain shooting up and down his little body, the like of which is nearly unbearable.

Once there one of the other greenem gently shakes the old greenem Evening Thunder. "Wake up old one, please, it's an emergency."

"What, what," splutters the old greenem.

"Can it not wait till morning?" he yawns.

Then seeing Spring Peeper having to be held up he quickly jumps to his feet. "Spring Peeper is, is that you," he gasps.

"Lie him down quickly," he continues. "What happened my lad, you look as if you've been struck by lightning?"

"It's Lane, he's gone," cries Spring Peeper.

"What do you mean?" asks the old greenem. "Did he do this to you?"

"No," moans the little greenem, now racked with pain. "He's gone, I, I, I think he's dead."

A look of horror comes across Evening Thunder's face. "What do you mean, he's dead?"

"It's my fault, it's all my fault," sobs the little greenem.

"Nonsense," the old greenem tells him. "Now just you lie there quiet a moment, I will wake the others."

Evening Thunder then rushes over to the others, "John, Max, Cin, Dan, wake up quickly, everyone wake up."

"What is it?" yawns Maxie.

"Something terrible has happened," he replies.

Seeing the look on the old greenem's face Maxie quickly wakes the others. "What is it?" asks John.

"I don't know," she replies. "I just know something bad has happened."

"Oh my god," shouts John suddenly catching sight of Spring Peeper lying there. "What the hell has happened to him?"

The others hearing John's alarm jump to their feet. "Oh my word the poor thing," gasps Max.

"What happened?" asks Cin.

"We don't know," answers Evening Thunder. "They found him just inside the forest there. They thought he was dead. Then he awoke and just started babbling incoherently."

"If this is the work of them Tain men," growls Big Dan. "I promise you now, I will hunt each and every one of them down."

Hearing their voices Spring Peeper tries to sit up, but has to be helped by his friends. "It's all my fault," he cries.

John sits carefully down beside him. "What is my little friend?" he asks.

"Lane's dead," cries the little greenem.

"He's what," gasps the others.

The little greenem starts to cry, partly with guilt and partly with pain. Maxie sits down on his other side, "Here put your hands on mine," she tells him.

"I can't, it'll hurt," he cries.

"Please," says Maxie softly. "Trust me, I will ease your pain."

So the little greenem carefully places his hands on hers and in a moment or two, the relief on his face is plain for all to see. "Now tell us everything," she tells him kindly.

So the little greenem goes on to tell them all that he saw, even to the point where he was taken to them. "So you see," cries the little greenem. "If I hadn't made him sleep under that creeper tree he would still be here."

"Don't blame yourself," Maxie tells him. "If you had known what was going to happen, you would have kept him away would you not."

"Yes, yes of course," sobs Spring Peeper. "But, but."

Maxie then whispers softly, "Shush now, rest." And as she places her hand on his forehead he slowly lays his head down again falling fast asleep.

"Right lets get organised," shouts John standing back up. "Can someone take us to where they found Spring Peeper?"

"Yes of course," answers one of the greenem quickly leading the way.

"Maxie could you stay here and help look after Spring Peeper please," asks John. "And if someone could go and get your best healer to help also."

"That would be me," answers Evening Thunder.

"Right lets go," shouts John following the greenem. But he is quickly overtaken by a very worried Big Dan. Woodnut also shoots past, desperate to find out just what has happened.

Once in to the trees and the little greenem leading the way stops, points and says, "Here this is where we found him."

"Stay back please," shouts Woodnut. "Let me look before the area is trampled."

Big Dan and the others do as asked, as Woodnut crouches down with hand on chin. After a moment or two he stands back up and looks around. "Anything?" asks John.

"Yes this is where he landed," answers Woodnut.

"He was flung from over this direction," he continues as he points to a large gap in front of him some twenty feet away. He then marches over to the gap, stopping and crouching down once more. The moments pass and he waves the others over. "What is it?" asks Big Dan.

Woodnut stands back up. "Look," he shouts.

They stare down in front of them at a perfectly circular dip in the ground. "What are we looking at?" asks Cin.

"I'm not sure," replies Woodnut. "But this is the spot where Spring Peeper was flung from. And in the centre that was where Lane was resting, under a large creep vine tree."

"That is impossible," shouts Big Dan choking slightly. "Trees or people don't just disappear, perhaps it was a flash fire. Or, or, maybe this isn't the right spot, he, he seemed awful confused you know."

"No look at the ground," stutters Max. "There are no burn marks; in fact the ground is perfectly clear."

"Yeah too clear," answers John. "It looks like the top layer has been perfectly extracted."

"But what does all this mean John," stutters Big Dan desperately.

John sighs. "I'm sorry, I'm not sure, err, I've really no idea. Woodnut could you investigate here a little more please. And I'll go back and question Spring Peeper some more. If he's feeling up to it, that is?"

"I'll stay here also," stammers Big Dan. "You never know it's maybe a joke, yes that's it, a joke, you know what he's like. I'll have a look around, he's maybe just wandered off and got lost."

As they wander back to the clearing Max sighs and says, "Poor Dan, I've never seen him so upset."

John sighs deeply and replies, "Perfectly understandable, they've been friends their whole lives. This is awful. I really do hope this is just him mucking about, although if I find out it is, I'll have his guts for garters."

Cin sighs. "As do I, but after seeing that poor greenem, I fear the worst."

John slowly shakes his head. A few minutes later and they reach the clearing. Maxie and Evening Thunder are knelt down beside the little greenem who is now sitting up. John kneels down in front of him. "How are you feeling now my little dude?" he asks.

"Much better thank you," answers Spring Peeper.

"Alas this only temporary," whispers the old greenem. "We are going to bury him soon."

"You're going to what," exclaims John. "Oh my god that's awful."

"No silly," interrupts Maxie. "He will be buried in a special place, which will soothe and heal him."

"Oh, ok, that's alright then," stutters John.

Evening Thunder and Spring Peeper both start to laugh, but Spring Peeper stops instantly. "Ooh, ooh, not funny, not funny."

John sighs. "Right, could you tell me again, just exactly what you saw and did please."

The little greenem then goes through it all again, and at the end asks hopefully, "Did you find anything?"

"No I'm sorry," answers John. "Did you see anything else? Anything at all, err, something before it perhaps, was he acting strange at all, was he talking to anyone. Did you see anything? Anything overhead, something flying above, unusual lights anything at all."

"Oh, oh yes," answers the little greenem excitedly, then his excitement fades as a sudden realisation dawns on him, and he falls silent and solemn once more.

"What is it little one?" asks Cin.

"He was talking to someone before he went to sleep," mutters Spring Peeper. "He was talking to Bzzt, and when I went to sleep they were still talking."

"So once again," asks Cin. "What does this mean?"

Evening Thunder sighs. I'm afraid to say, whatever happened to Lane will also have happened to prince Bzzt. You see creep vine tree is their favourite place to rest the night, and being so late, he will almost certainly have been sleeping there also. I will have to inform his people."

"Please," begs John. "Is there anything else, anything at all?"

"No, no, I'm sorry I just wish there was," replies the little greenem sadly. "If only I hadn't got him to sleep there."

"Why what difference would that have made?" asks John.

"What do you mean?" asks Spring Peeper.

"Well," continues John. "What the heck would someone want to destroy a tree for? But, if someone or something was after Lane, it would not have made a difference where he slept now would it. In fact if he had not slept there, and was still amongst us, we may have all been faced with the same fate. You probably saved us all, you see. And there's one thing I do know about our friend Lane, whatever happened, he would not have blamed you or anyone else, not for one moment. Now you just concentrate on healing, and let us do all the worrying, ok."

The little greenem nearly raises a smile, but as the pain shoots through him he lies back down again before he is then carefully picked up by his friends, and taken away.

Woodnut and Big Dan make their way back into the clearing. "Did you learn anymore?" asks Woodnut.

"Only one thing," replies John with a heavy sighs. "He wasn't the only one sleeping there."

"Oh no," cries Woodnut. "Creep vine, it wasn't, it wasn't, Bzzt was it."

John just nods solemnly. "This is a double tragedy," gasps Woodnut.

"Did you learn anything?" asks Max.

Woodnut sighs. "No nothing of worth. But what I can tell you is, whatever did this, must have been more powerful than I can imagine."

"What do you mean?" asks John.

Woodnut shakes his head. "Well, it destroyed everything inside that circle, even below the ground. There isn't even a root left, not a worm, not a beetle, not even a piece of fungus, all life within that circle has gone."

"What the hell could do something like that?" shouts John.

"To be so specific," he continues. "Why Lane? He's bothered no one, well no more than any one else."

Max sighs. "Perhaps John, they weren't after him. Maybe they thought it was you, and just got the wrong person."

John slumps down. "No not again, I thought we had left all that back at Luguvalio."

"Surly not," shouts Big Dan. "If someone has that sort of power and knowledge, they would not make such a simple mistake. No offence John, but even at first glance, you are quite distinct."

"He has a point John," agrees Cin. "I'm not sure they were after you, in fact, why take the chance. Surely they would have just killed us all, they obviously have the power."

John sitting back up replies, "Do you know, you both have a good point there? This is just getting stranger and stranger?"

"I've sent word out," says Maxie. "I've asked every greenem in this forest and beyond if they can look for Lane, or report anything unusual back to us."

Big Dan sighs. "That is an excellent idea, thank you. He was my best friend, my oldest friend, even as a small child we were best friends."

Starting to choke he stops bows his head and wipes his eye. "When I find out who did this," he mutters. "Man, woman or beast, I will kill them all, even if it means dying myself."

Seeing him so upset John nudges Max nodding his head towards Dan. She smiles in return and puts her arms around Big Dan. "As will we all," she tells him softly.

"So what now?" asks Cin.

John shrugs. "I'm not sure, wait here and see if any of the greenem come back with news. Then we'll take it from there."

"That shouldn't be long," replies Evening Thunder. "If he is anywhere in this forest we should hear about it by no more than mid morning."

Everyone sits there in silence until day break, with the minutes passing like hours until the first greenem reports from his part of the forest. But with no more news to report their hearts sink once again. And as the next few hours pass, more and more report in, but all with the same lack of news. "This is torture," shouts a frustrated Big Dan. "I would have rather found his body. At least we could have some closure and have been able to bury my friend, with the dignity and honour he deserves."

Finally the last greenem from the furthest part of the forest reports in, and looking very sad he simply shakes his head. "So what do we do now John?" asks Max.

John shrugs. "I'm at a loss. Dan have you any ideas? Is there anything more you think we could be doing?" Big Dan shakes his head. "Sorry John, I am at a loss like you. But I do know, if he was lost hurt or injured anywhere in this forest, our greenem friends here would have certainly found him. Now we have made arrangements to meet the lord of this land, and I think we should go, or it would show great disrespect, and sitting moping will do no good."

Evening Thunder then bows to Big Dan. "If I hear anything, anything at all, however insignificant, I'll get word to you, you have my word on that."

Dan bows in return. "I know you will."

The friends then gather their things, and with a sombre farewell they set off to the main town and stronghold of Tain. The going is slow with no one speaking a word, even Maxie and Woodnut are walking silently along together. They walk most of the morning but only get a fraction of the distance they would normally. Finally a lack of food and water on top of a heavy heart force them to stop. Up ahead standing like a lone centre is a large coornut tree shading the ground around it with its large canopy. Cin sighs. "We shall rest there a spell and take some refreshment. I think we need it."

Reaching the shade of the tree they all sit down taking their packs off and force themselves to eat. Spot suddenly rushes out of John's bag, for what reason no one knows. But she runs around and around with great excitement, before running over to Maxie and doing the same to her. Then she bolts up the tree and disappears into the canopy. For one fleeting moment it nearly raises a smile, before the darkness descends on them once more. "Why is everyone so sad?" comes a voice.

They look around to see a greenem standing there by the tree so Woodnut stands back up and bows instantly. "Meadow Spirit, it's an honour."

The strange greenem smiles politely and bows in return. "I ask again, why so sad?"

"We lost our friend earlier, he was killed in the forest somehow," answers John.

Slowly nodding Meadow Spirit answers, "And you know this for definite do you?"

John shrugs sadly. "Well no, not really,"

"Your friend was not killed," interrupts the strange greenem. "He was taken, all be it unintentionally."

"He, he was what," gasps Big Dan. "By who, does this mean he is still alive."

"Who or what has taken your friend," answers Meadow Spirit. "Nobody knows, not even I. But what I do know is, this has happened for centuries, not very often, but it does. Usually very carefully, and very subtly, as not to harm whatever taken. It has been noted things taken can be as small as the most delicate flower, or as you now know, as large as the largest tree. But just as it takes, sometimes it gives, plants, animals, insects even oomans."

"How do you think your people got here?" he asks them. "John you of all people should know this?"

They all sit there silently listening utterly dumbfounded until Max is the first to speak, "So what does all this mean, will our friend be returned, or do we have to go somewhere to look for him."

Meadow Spirit shakes his head. "The stories, legends, and prophecies tell us your friend will be taken. But unfortunately they never mention his return. For all we know he did die, or perhaps he walks another path now, just as you do John."

"Hang on," growls Big Dan. "So you knew something was going to happen to my friend, and you did nothing."

"You don't understand," replies Meadow Spirit. "These legends and prophecies have been passed down for hundreds of years, over a thousand in fact, by only one original ancient greenem. And just as time passes, sometimes so does their interpretation, sometimes they come true, sometimes they don't. It is not an exact science. There are legends about all of you, most still to be written, or still to pass. Even you young Lilly Milk, silently listening, but never seen, and always watching. But do you honestly want to know them. Perhaps it will change the events to follow, but perhaps not knowing them would change them also, the conundrum is yours."

"Please?" asks John. "Could you possibly do me a favour?"

"Favour, I do not do favours," interrupts Meadow Spirit. "But you may ask I suppose."

John pauses a moment, then asks, "The little greenem, Spring Peeper, he blames himself terribly for what happened. Could you please tell him just what you told us, and put his mind at rest please."

The strange greenem smiles broadly and bows graciously. "This I will do, now I must go."

He then turns to Woodnut bowing once more, and with only the slightest of grins and the cheekiest twinkle in his eye tells him, "And when you come to write the legends and prophecies this time young greenem. Perhaps you will describe them a little clearer, as to cause less confusion."

He then walks off behind the tree. "What?" gasps Woodnut. "Me, but, but, how, but that's impossible. Please come back, I must ask you."

Woodnut then runs off behind the tree after the other greenem, but is back within a moment. "Well?" asks Cin.

Woodnut scratches his head. "He's gone."

"What do you mean, he's gone?" shouts Big Dan. "That's impossible; he must be hiding in the tree somewhere."

Woodnut shrugs. "No it's not that type of tree, he's just gone."

"How?" asks Maxie.

Woodnut gives a bewildered shrug. "He's Meadow Spirit, he comes and goes as he pleases, he answers to no one."

"Hey Woodnut what did he mean?" asks John. "When you write the legends this time. I thought you said, in fact he also said, they were wrote hundreds of years ago."

Woodnut flops to the ground. "I, I, do not know what he meant, but they were."

Then he suddenly starts to smile. "It is very rare, but on occasion he has been known to joke, yes, this must be one of them times, oh I feel very honoured."

John grins broadly then whispers, "Yes of course, but didn't he say there are legends about all of us, maybe your journey is about to take a different path."

Woodnut scowls at him. "Don't say that, that's just not funny."

John winks. "Hey who says I'm joking."

"Stop it," cries Woodnut.

"John seriously," asks Cin. "What do we make of all this? I don't mind telling you, it creeps me out."

"Yes me too," agrees Big Dan with a nod and running his fingers through his beard now deep in thought. "I now don't know whether to be pleased, or afraid."

"Yes, and what did he mean by me also," comes Lilly Milk's little voice.

"What the heck are you all asking me for," shouts John. "How the hell am I meant to know, I'm as confused as you are. It seems to me we should all be asking Woodnut here. Oh mighty king of legends and prophecies."

"Don't look at me," stutters Woodnut. "I'm as confused as the rest of you."

Cin sighs. "That's it, it's official, I don't think I'm ever going to sleep again."

"Yes I know what you mean," moans Big Dan. "If I do, I think it will be like greenem, with one eye open."

"Right everyone quiet now," shouts Max. "I've had enough of this, and its bad enough we lost our friend today, without everyone getting freaked out over some ridiculous mumbo jumbo, spouted by some weird greenem. I'm sorry Woodnut, but he is, he talks gibberish, there are always prophecies and legends amongst people, ours as well as yours. And yes through different interpretation, some will at sometime or another sound similar to an event or person, but that is all. And even if it were true, there's nothing you can do about it, and as you have said in the past John, we should just be the best person we can be. Now let's put all this stupid talk behind us, we should not forget our friend, but we should also take solace in the fact that he may not be dead. And I do not personally believe for one moment, the future of one person can be told whole heartedly, by a several hundred year old prophecy. But what I do know is, until I met you John I never believed it, but now I do, there is always hope, and I will take that hope, and hold it tightly until I find our friend alive, or bury him with honour. Now is everyone clear on this."

"Yes Max," come the answers in a slightly relieved tone.

"Now let us carry on as we were," she tells them. "Lane knows where we are going, it's what he would want. For all we know he's already there waiting for us."

They set off once more their hearts lifted just a little, with even the odd conversation now and again."

8

THE GOING IS now a little faster and its mid afternoon when they see in the distance, a large sprawling city surrounding a large official looking building. "My gosh," gasps Max. "This is the biggest settlement I've ever seen."

Big Dan nods. "Truly. I take it we are heading for that large building in the middle."

"Why would this many people want to live together?" asks Woodnut.

Cin sighs. "Truly my friend, I understand the feeling of security in a large community. But surely, you must lose that sense of community in somewhere so large. What do you think John?"

John nods. "Well I must admit, it's the largest most modern looking place I've seen in all the time I've been here. But where I come from, this place wouldn't be considered large, err, more of a big village, or perhaps a small town, err maybe. But you are absolutely right, the larger towns and cities become, ironically the more distant and isolated the people in them become. And some of the loneliest people can often come from the largest cities, where I come from anyway."

"How awful," puffs Max. "I would hate to live like that."

"It's not deliberate,"John replies shrugging. "Sometimes people come into large communities looking for work, or perhaps just a new start and the possibility of a better life, it just often doesn't end up that way. Everyone together but no one talking and even less listening, you of all people should know that Max."

Max smiles at him lovingly. "Yes of course, but sometimes I forget, it seems like a lifetime ago now my love." John gives her a squeeze.

It's another hour before they reach the outskirts of town. Passing the first few homes Max whispers to the others, "Look at the way these people are living."

Big Dan sighs. "Yes these are more like shacks than homes; the people in this area must be either very poor or very desperate."

"Or both," agrees Cin.

"Hu," grumps Woodnut. "And to think they wanted my people to leave their home in the forest, just to live here like this. How insulting, we would rather burn in the forest. This is an existence, but it isn't life, I would not wish this on any greenem, or even ooman. I bet you've never seen anything like this John."

John heaves a heavy sigh. "Actually, yes I have, and to be totally honest I've seen a lot worse. On TV that is, from various parts of the globe. And compared to some of them, it really isn't that bad, it's obviously a ghetto where the poor and most desperate are forced to live. By circumstance or otherwise, but I was quite surprised and pleased by your reactions to be honest."

"What do you mean?" asks Big Dan. "I don't understand."

Shrugging John answers, "It tells me this type of thing isn't common. And if this is the worst you've all seen, that is a good thing."

Big Dan nods. "Oh I see. The more I learn about your earth John, the less I like it, and I'm not sure whether to pity or resent the fools that reside over it."

Woodnut nods in agreement. "Yes John, your people seem to know so much, but actually understand so little."

A little further on and the streets of the small ghetto are filled with people. And on seeing the friends approach all stop what they are doing instantly, and turning towards them stand silently with their heads bowed until they pass, not daring to look up at them for a moment. "Well this feels just more than a little awkward," mumbles John out the corner of his mouth. "I don't know about the rest of you."

"Yes very strange behaviour," agrees Max.

Cin simply shrugs. "It must be their way of showing respect to their peers in this province."

"Not to be allowed to look at someone," growls Big Dan. "I would stop this nonsense in a heartbeat if I had my way."

"That's it, I've had enough of this," shouts Maxie. "Stop and cover your ears."

But they barely get their hands to their ears as Maxie lets out the loudest whistle she can, bringing most of the crowds to their knees. "Now listen up everyone," she shouts. "You do not have to look down, you should overt your eyes to no one. We are merely travellers passing through your land, please hold your heads high with pride, and know you are as good as anyone. Now go about your business in peace, and if you wish to watch us, then you may, or if you would like to talk, then we will listen also."

On hearing her speak some of the people start to slowly raise their heads, but seeing Cin and Big Dan watching they quickly bow them down again.

Then realising they are not going to be punished they raise their heads once again, and like the opening of a floodgate everyone around them follows suit. Most bow and go about their business, but some just stand and stare. "Now we can carry on," grunts Maxie.

Her mother smiles. "Well spoken my dear."

As they continue along the road, the homes and houses start to get noticeably better, with the odd shop intermingled here and there. "What's that?" shouts Maxie running over to a shop window.

They all follow her over, and in the window in the front of the shop, are dozens of small containers. All are filled with small brightly coloured objects of various size and shape. "What are they?" she asks excitedly. "They look lovely."

"I'm not sure dear," answers her mum.

"Food of some sort I presume," replies Cin.

"They're sweets," answers John. "Unless I'm mistaken, yes it's a sweet shop."

"A what shop?" asks Big Dan.

"A sweet shop," with a shrug John replies. "Err, sweets you know, sweets, aimed usually at kids. Treats to be given now and again, they're normally made from boiled sugar, flavoured and coloured with different things, very sweet hence the name. Good as a treat, but you shouldn't eat them all the time, they can be bad for your teeth. Although I don't suppose that's a problem for you lot."

"Damn bunch of sharks," he mutters to himself.

"I still don't know what a shark is," Max says frowning. "But when I do, it better be something nice and not them sand ones we saw once."

John sighs. "How does she do that? Damn woman."

She frowns, but slyly breaking into a grin. "What was that?"

John winks and says. "Err, nothing dear. It's a beautiful creature with marvellous teeth, just like yours darling."

"Anyway, he continues. "Maxie would you like to go in and try some aye."

"Yes please," she answers excitedly.

John then leads them all in and they are then there for over half an hour trying nearly every sweet in the shop, much to the amusement of the owner. Finally they leave with pockets bulging, all but John. "Hey John," splutters Big Dan through a mouthful of sweets. "These sweets of yours, fantastic, if I'd known about these things earlier. I would have happily fought my way here long ago."

"Yeah me too," splutters Cin, having to tilt his head back to stop from dribbling.

"Why didn't you get some dear?" asks Max.

John shakes his head. "As I told you, where I come from they're basically boiled sugar. These things you're eating taste as if they're made from dung, I don't know how you can eat them."

Cin and Big Dan just look at each other and shrug. "Tastes good to me," they splutter in unison.

Max sighs. "Come on John, there must have been one in there you liked."

"I couldn't stomach anymore without being ill," he answers.

A little further on and they are in the heart of the city. "Well if this isn't the finest place you've ever seen," exclaims Big Dan.

Cin nods. "Yes truly."

Max gasps in awe looking round. "You must have to be rich to live in this part," she mutters.

John nods. "It seems that way. The closer you get to the centre, the more prestige there must be, which is often the way."

"How odd," exclaims Big Dan. "This is the first major city I've ever been in, where I don't know where anything is?"

"On yes, how unusual," agrees Cin.

John shrugs. "Only for you lot. Where I come from all cities are laid out differently, and it would be more unusual to find even two the same. Hey Woodnut do you want on my shoulders pal, it seems awful busy around here, you don't want trampled."

"No thank you," answers Woodnut. "I'll just walk behind you with Maxie, they'll all move for you."

Soon they get through the town square and come upon the large imposing building and stronghold of Lord Tain, ruler of the province. Cin nods. "Very impressive. But no surrounding wall, not very secure."

Big Dan agrees, "Maybe they think they don't need it. After all it looks completely made of stone, I can't imagine how long it must have taken to build."

They then see just in front of them a large wooden gate guarded by two warriors with spears. "I take it that's the entrance then," says Cin. "Let's not keep the nice man waiting then.

As they reach the gate the two guards stand to attention. "We are here to see Lord Tain," John says smiling.

"Could I have your name Sir?" asks one of the guards.

"Yes certainly," replies John. "John Fox, we are expected."

The guard looks to his companion and shrugs. Cin losing his temper bellows, "This is Lord Taraten you fools, you dare to keep us waiting."

The two guards go instantly white and lower their heads. "I'm, I'm sorry my Lord," stutters one of the guards. "Please forgive me, the chancellor awaits you just inside with an honour guard, I meant no disrespect my Lord."

And with that the two men bow and open the gates, and the friends proceed through. John turns to Cin, "Did you have to? You nearly frightened them to men to death." Cin just grins and shrugs.

As they get through the gate they hear a clash of spears behind them, Cin and Big Dan instantly draw their swords, and in a flash have the two guards pinned to the wall by their throats, swords pressed firmly against their wind pipes. "Please," gasps one of the guards.

"What are you doing?" shouts John.

"N, n, nothing my Lord," stammer the two men.

"Come on spit it out man," booms Big Dan sternly.

"There was a greenem following you Sir," stutters the other guard. "W, w we were just barring the entrance. Th, that's all Sire."

"That's our friend," replies John. "Either of you got a problem with that."

"N, n no my Lord," stammer the men.

John nods. "Good, let them down boys."

He then turns to Woodnut and asks, "You alright dude?"

Woodnut brushes himself down. "Yes thank you, let us proceed."

"After you my friend," replies John beckoning him forward.

They continue through the gates, then through another set. Just ahead into a neatly paved courtyard adorned with all sorts of colourful plants where they see a very official looking man waiting for them, with two rows of honour guard standing just behind him. They all bow instantly on seeing John and the others. The friends pause a moment and bow in return, before carrying on. The official looking man steps forward and bows again. "I am one of my Lords chancellors," he tells them. "My name is Glendra, and may I say it is my honour and privilege to greet you here today. I will show you to your rooms, and help you in any way you may need. But first my Lord, would you and your company like to inspect the guard."

John a little unsure looks to Dan, who nods in return. "Yes thank you," answers John.

The guard stand to attention proud and tall, but with their heads down and their faces pointed to the ground. John then walks along first nodding as he goes. "Yes very smart, but I'm no expert. My two friends here are both heads of their respective armies. What do you think guys?"

"Terrible," bellows Big Dan. "When standing to attention, guard or warrior, the head should be held high, and the eyes should be fixed firmly forward. If one of my men stood in front of me like that, I would beat him for being a coward. What happens if they are attacked, by the time they look up they be dead."

Cin nods. "Yes I wholeheartedly agree. If one of my men was that sloppy in front of me, be in no doubt, he would never do it again."

John turns to Glendra and shrugs. "Sorry, they look alright to me, but they're the professionals. But I must admit I can't get my head round all this averting the eyes rubbish. What do you think Woodnut?"

Glendra looks a little shocked but says nothing. Woodnut giggles, "I wondered why they were looking down. I just thought they found me really interesting."

"Hmm, yeah right," answers John. "We don't even find you that interesting."

The two girl's start to giggle. Woodnut huffs, then grins himself. "But no, seriously John I like you find it very bizarre, I just don't understand it. To be frightened to look at each other, what an awful way to live your lives."

Maxie nods in agreement. "I hope they don't expect me to do it, I don't care who they are."

"Well," interrupts Glendra sheepishly. "I must inform you all, my Lord Tain is most adamant on this, and many people have been severely punished for not showing the proper etiquette or respect."

Big Dan leans forward and stares him dead in the eye and bellows, "Are you threatening me little man. I lost my best friend today. Be warned I'm in no mood for fools or threats, and I never trust anyone who can't look me dead in the eye."

"N, no Sir, it's just the way it is," he stutters. "I'm just doing my job please."

"And the rest of you so called warriors," booms Dan. "When you stand to attention when I'm there, you stand with your heads held high, or you will be showing me disrespect. I will not tell you twice, you have been warned."

"Now you man," he continues. "Show us to our quarters, and send us maids as we wish to freshen up first, and be sharp about it man."

Glendra bows nervously. "Y, yes Sir, as you wish Sir,"

He then leads them through the courtyard shuffling along nervously, with Big Dan breathing heavily just behind him. "Poor Dan," Max whispers to John. "He's taking Lanes' loss very badly."

John nods. "It's to be expected, to lose a life long friend is bad enough, but under such strange circumstances, with no body to even mourn. It must be very hard indeed. We'll have to keep a close eye on the big fella I think, or someone's going to bare the brunt of it. And I wouldn't like to be in their shoes."

"Yes I agree," whispers Max. "I'll try and stay close to him, keep his mind off things if possible."

They are led through beautifully decorated hallways with elaborately patterned floors and walls. And after climbing up a steep set of stairs are shown into a large room. The room is luxuriously furnished with the finest of things, from the seating to the tables, and adorned with a plethora of foods and drinks. Glendra bows. "My Lords and Lady, this is our finest suite for visiting dignitaries. And this as you can see is the communal area, where you may all relax spend time and such.

"There are four doors as you can also see," he tells them pointing around the room. "These lead to your bed chambers. They are all furnished the same, you may decide yourselves which you want. There are provisions in each room for any need that may occur, and each room also has its own personal maid. They will tend to your every need, use them as you see fit. Now with your permission my Lords, I'll take my leave, and return for you in an hour. But before I go my Lords. I was led to believe there was another member in your group. Will he be joining us later, or not."

They all bow their heads in sadness. "No I'm sorry," answers Max. "We don't think so, something happened to our friend in the forest."

Glendra bows politely. "Oh I do apologise, I'll take my leave."

Sadness and silence fills the room and John is the first to speak, "How posh is this place, who's for a peek in the bedrooms."

"Me, me, me," shouts Maxie excitedly.

Cin sighs. "I must admit, this is the most luxurious place I've ever seen."

Big Dan nods. "Yes the stone floors and mouldings on the walls, they must have been working on this place forever."

Max goes over to the nearest bed chamber door, and once inside she is met by a maid. A lady of ageing years, a little shorter than most with short scruffy grey hair, and just a little chubby. She smiles broadly on seeing Max, and curtsies, Max likewise bows in return. "It's nice to meet you my Lady," greets the woman. "I'll see to all your needs for the duration of your stay."

John follows her in and the others crowd around the doorway. The jolly woman smiles. "Oh my, you're not all staying in this room are you?"

John nods. "Yes, yes we are."

The maid stands there a little shocked until Max slaps Johns arm and smiles. "No my dear were not. My husband's only joking with you, it will just be him and I that are in this room."

"Oh, oh I see," chuckles the maid bowing. "You had me for a moment there Sire."

Maxie grabs Woodnut's hand. "Let's go and look in our room," she shouts excitedly.

The pair of them then run to the next door, knock and rush in, where they are also met by a maid, another lady of ageing years, and of similar appearance. The lady bows, as does Maxie and Woodnut in return. The maid stands back up and looks down at Maxie and smiles. Then noticing Woodnut she scratches her head. "I'm not sure how I may serve you little Sir, but I will try my best."

Woodnut giggles terribly setting Maxie off also.

They all settle into their rooms with the help of their maids, and after a wash and change meet back out in the main room. Cin smiles broadly. "I could get used to this. Luxury room and personal maid."

John sighs. "Ooh I don't know about that. It just makes me feel awkward, maids and servants. I just can't get used to it, it just doesn't seem right somehow."

Big Dan and Cin just look at each other and shrug. They then jump as there is a knock at the door and in enters Glendra. "My Lords and Ladies," he says. "If you are ready, my Lord will see you now."

Big Dan smiles and gestures ahead. "After you my Lord."

John frowns muttering to himself. "One minute," shouts Maxie running back to her room and franticly ratching through her bag.

"Right," she shouts running back and slipping on her sun glasses.

John puts his thumb up. "Looking cool."

Cin looks down at her. "Any particular reason."

"Yes I don't want people staring at my special eye," she answers.

Cin shrugs. "Fair enough."

Maxie smiles cheekily. "And they look good."

They are taken along more luxurious hallways, and through even more luxurious rooms, until Glendra stops outside some large double doors guarded by two warriors. The warriors stand to attention as they stop, and stand silently with their heads down. Big Dan growls. Max links arms with him. "Hey be good," she whispers softly. "Remember why we are here. I know it's hard my dear, but getting mad may be very counter productive. Let's try and focus, and help our friends in the forest, it's the reason Lane was leading us here after all."

Big Dan sighs. "Yes you're right. But I must admit, I'm finding it so hard. Please if I forget or lapse."

"It's ok," she whispers. "I'll be here if you need me, as will we all. Now let's go and meet this Lord, and perhaps keep an eye on John."

Big Dan breaks into a wry chuckle, "Yes, I think this is going to be very interesting."

Max frowns. "Hmm."

The two guards open the doors and Glendra proudly walks through and stops to announce them, "My Lords, ladies, gentlemen and warriors. May I have your attention please, it is my privilege and honour to introduce, my Lord and Lady Taraten and their daughter Max. It is also my further pleasure and honour to introduce, their friends, and representatives from two other great and noble provinces. Firstly from the province of Luguvalio, and the head of all Lord Luguvalio's army is the mighty Danielle, and next to him, representing Voreda province, and also the head of all Lord Voreda's army is the equally mighty Cinthia."

Each of the men bows in turn but John taps Glendra on the shoulder and asks him, "Are you not forgetting someone?"

"No my Lord, I don't think so," he replies scratching his head.

John gestures down towards Woodnut. "How about my best friend here, Mr Woodnut Greenfern."

Glendra bows graciously. "Yes of course my Lord, my mistake, please do forgive me."

He clears his throat once again. "My greatest apologies," he announces to all there. "May I also introduce, my Lord Taraten's other friend, and representative of his people, Mr Woodnut Greenfurn." Woodnut smiles and bows politely.

Glendra then leads them all across the large elaborately decorated hall, filled either side with people, all bowing their heads and looking to their feet as they pass by. Big Dan growls, and is promptly frowned at by Max. Dan just shrugs. Ahead they see a line of official looking people standing either side of two large luxurious seats. And between them a large elaborately carved wooden throne, with a stern looking man residing upon it. He is a clean shaven man with long hair swept back and tied, and adorned with a crown of elaborately twisted metal. They all stop a few yards in front, and Glendra bows to his Lord, then to John and proceeds to introduce them. They all bow their heads. Lord Tain staring John dead in the eye bows in return.

"This is indeed truly a great hour. I never thought I'd live to see the day when we would be paid a visit by the infamous Lord Taraten. You and your land have been feared for as long as anyone can remember. And because this is such a momentous occasion, I will overlook your friend's impertinence and insults in front of their betters."

John's eyes start to squint as he tries to fight loosing his temper. Lord Tain then tells them, "There is a rhyme your friends may wish to remember. It is taught to our children when very young, it goes overt the eyes to show respect, until your betters tell you, you may look direct."

John nods. "Yes of course, and there is also a rhyme where I come from, which you also may wish to learn. It goes you can kiss my hairy arse, ya pompous git, who the hell do you think you are."

John then clears his throat. "I'm sorry," he apologises. It's rather long I know, you may want to practice it a bit."

Big Dan starts to laugh; Cin just shakes his head and whispers to Max, "If we have to fight our way out, stay close behind me."

"Is this how you greet me in my own land?" bellows Lord Tain. "Just because you are a Lord does not give you the right to come here and insult me in my own hall."

"Exactly," shouts John. "Now you think about that yourselves, we came here in peace, and we have shown respect, and will continue to do so. But it doesn't seem to me that its respect you require, you want my friends to overt there eyes. What, to make you feel that you are better than they are, well I'm afraid you're not. But likewise my friends and I are no better than you or your people, we are all born the same and we all die the same, and remember this, all men are equal when the memory fades."

"Pah nonsense," shouts Tain. "So are you honestly trying to tell me a lowly surf or peasant, is as good as myself, or my head warrior here, or my advisers and wise men."

"Yes of course," argues John. "Just because someone may have been born to a less privileged life, does not mean they are any less important than you or I, or anyone else."

"You are deluded," laughs Lord Tain. "Yes of course it does, we are all well educated and taught in all matters, so are you saying if we went out and picked some peasant at random, he would do better than I."

"So the key to this is education," answers John. "That's what you are telling me."

"Well err, yes I suppose," replies Lord Tain.

John shrugs. "Oh ok, so this peasant, if I educate him to a much higher standard than all of you, that would make them better than all of you, even yourself. Would you then happily overt your eyes from him until told otherwise."

"N, n, no of course not," stutters Tain. "We, err, I, I would still be better than them."

"Oh of course," interrupts John. "Now we're getting down to it. It's all about snobbery, that's right isn't it, you think you are born to better people. So automatically that makes you better than everyone else, it's actually got nothing to do with knowledge or education, like you were just trying to argue has it."

Some of the Tain warriors start to slowly draw their swords. Big Dan nudges Cin. "Get ready my friend, looks like a short visit."

But a voice is suddenly heard shouting from behind the warriors, "How dare you argue with my Lord Tain, you curs, you lovers of greenem, kill them, kill them all."

The warriors draw their swords, as does Cin and Big Dan. "Stop this now," screams Lord Tain. "Who dares to shout such a thing, these are my guests."

The warriors part to show a very nervous Elandra standing there. "You man, come here, come here now," hollers Lord Tain absolutely seething with anger.

Elandra slowly and nervously steps forward. "How dare you interrupt?" screams Lord Tain. "I was having the best argument I've had in years, not since my late father. How dare you order someone's death, in this of all places? And not only without my permission, but to the Lord and Lady of another province. You could have started war you fool, you will pay for this humiliation in front of our guests."

"Please my Lord," begs Elandra, "I, I, I."

"You will be executed in the morning," barks Lord Tain.

Woodnut starts to giggle. "Please my Lord," interrupts John bowing. "Let not our first meeting be tarnished by the blood of a fool. Spare him, demote him, give him a job belonging such a fool, so he may never forget this lesson, and be an example to others."

"Tain smiles broadly. "Yes, yes of course, that is an excellent idea."

"Thank you my Lord," cries Elandra dropping to his knees.

"It is not I you should be thanking," hollers Lord Tain.

Elandra begrudgingly turns and thanks John. "From this moment on," announces Lord Tain. "You will lose all rights and privileges, and you will live in the servant's quarters and will answer to Mistress Bertram, head of all servants. And you will do as she tells you from this point on."

Lord Tain then gestures across the room to a tall thin faced mean looking woman, who promptly marches and bows. "Yes my Lord."

"Mistress Bertram," says Lord Tain. "Could you take this servant away, get him the right attire, and put him to work straight away please."

The woman curtsies grinning broadly. "It will be my pleasure, now come with me surf."

And as they walk away together the woman is heard muttering to him, "So who's the lowest cur now, scum was I."

Cin chuckles and nudges Big Dan. "Guess he wasn't that nice to her in the past then."

"Yes," chuckles Dan. "Humility can be a hard lesson to learn, well for him anyway."

"Should have let them execute him," grumps Woodnut.

"Hey," says Maxie nipping his arm.

Lord Tain then stands up and bows. "Please let us start again."

He then looks to either side of him. "Give your seats to Lord and Lady Taraten," he tells them.

The men then get up instantly bow and step away. John and Max step forward and sit down, Maxie runs forwards and sits on her mothers' knee. Cin whispers to Big Dan, "How do you think John knew their Lord would love a good argument."

Big Dan shrugs shaking his head replying, "I don't think he did, sheer luck I would say. I think he was expecting to have to fight his way out of this place as much as we did."

Lord Tain then raises his hands. "More seats for our other honoured guests, and the best of drinks. We should raise a toast."

Seats and drinks are given; even Woodnut is given a seat, but can hardly be seen on sitting in it. "Wait I have an idea," says Lord Tain, waving to a servant girl. "At the back of the hall there is a child's high chair, fetch it would you girl."

She rushes off and is soon back. Cin lifts Woodnut into the chair. "How's that my friend?"

"Much better thanks," giggles Woodnut.

"Now has everyone got a drink?" asks Tain. "Good, to a brighter future between our two lands."

Everybody raises their mugs and cheers. He then turns to John. "I'm sorry about earlier, maybe we could have another argument later?" he asks enthusiastically.

John stares at him silently for a moment just a little bewildered, then snapping out of it answers, "Of course not, no."

"But why not?" asks Tain despairingly.

John shakes his head. "I don't think that's possible, you can't just argue for the sake of it, that's impossible."

"Yes of course you can," shouts Lord Tain.

"Oh no you can't," shouts John in return.

"Yes of course you can," yells Lord Tain again. "It's not that hard."

John winks points and smiles. Tain nods, with a smile broader than a child on Christmas morning. "Oh you're good. You know, we have several mood trees in full blossom in the orchard out the back, perhaps we could go out there and take a little afternoon refreshment."

"That sounds an excellent idea," agrees John.

A large warrior walks up and bows. "My Lord, may I and a couple of my men accompany you."

"No, no, it'll be ok," answers Lord Tain. "These are good people, I can see that."

"No my Lord I must insist," replies the warrior. "I mean no disrespect to my Lord Taraten, or his friends, but the people of Taraten aren't exactly known to be the most honourable of people. In fact they are well known for twisting and lying."

"How dare you insult our guests," shouts Lord Tain.

"No please," interrupts John. "He only told the truth, he didn't lie. The people of Taraten were like that but no longer. It was not just encouraged by the previous Lord, it was law, but no longer."

"What do you think?" he asks turning to Cin and Big Dan.

"I think," booms Big Dan. "If he had not insisted on coming, he wouldn't be much of a head warrior. His Lords protection should always come first."

Cin nods in agreement. "Oh as you wish," grumps Tain. "I suppose I better introduce you then, this fuss pot is my long time friend and head warrior Trace."

The warrior smiles and bows so Cin stands up, unclips his sword, and lays it on the table. "As a gesture of good will," he says.

Big Dan rises and does the same, even Max and they then make their way out the hall following Lord Tain.

"What are mood trees?" asks Cin.

They all shrug, except Maxie. "It does what it says," she answers. "When in blossom, the smell and pollen from one of these trees when under one, affects your mood. And depending on the type, the blossom, strength and smell, can make you feel happy, sad, angry, mad, all sorts really. But the effects fade the moment you move away."

Lord Tain hearing this turns around. "My word little one that was very clever of you, you know of these trees then."

Maxie nods. "I've been told about them, but I've never seen one."

"May I ask you little one. Why do you wear those covers on your eyes? Are you blind?" asks Tain.

"No Sir, They're just shades," she answers.

"Shades," asks Tain a little confused. "What is their purpose? And how do you see where you are going?"

"Is it much further until we get outside Sir?" she asks.

"No little one, just around the corner," he answers.

"Then I'll show you when we get outside," she tells him.

Once outside the sun is shining brightly and they are taken to a large table with benches, surrounded by a dozen or so large blossoming trees. Big Dan keeps quietly chuckling to himself, and muttering, "This should be good."

"What are you up to?" whispers Max.

Dan grins. "Me, nothing."

She frowns. "Hem, I'm watching you boy."

"Here," says Maxie taking off her sun glasses and handing them to Lord Tain.

Tain cautiously slips them on and suddenly gives a loud shout, making his three warriors jump. "This is amazing," he hollers. "Shades you call them, yes,

yes, I can see they do. They actually shade your eyes from the sun. But, but, I can still see perfectly, I have never seen their like. What are they made of? How do they work?"

"I'm not sure Sir, you'll have to ask my Dad," answers Maxie. "Can I have them back now please?"

"Yes of course my child here," he says before he carefully takes them off and hands them back, but then gasps loudly pulling back. "Your eye child. Are you ok? Does it hurt? Are you blind in that eye?"

Maxie takes the glasses from him and slips them back on. "No don't worry, I'm ok," she tells him.

He sighs. "If you're sure child. But if you change your mind, we have many excellent physicians, who could look at that for you."

Maxie bows. "No thank you Sir, everything is as it should be."

Lord Tain shakes his head. "Yes of course."

"Please now everyone sit," he continues. "Isn't it a wonderful afternoon?"

John shrugs. "No not really, the suns too bright, and the winds too cooling."

"Surly not," answers Lord Tain. "Does it not feel warm on your skin, with the wind complementing the sun perfectly?"

"No of course not," snaps John. "It's burning me."

"Oh you talk rubbish," shouts Tain. "Is this all you're going to do, complain."

"I'm not complaining," shouts John.

"Yes you are," argues Tain.

"You asked me," argues John. "And I'm telling you."

"Oh this is ridiculous," complains Lord Tain.

John smiles. "I'm sorry, I thought you wanted to come outside and argue."

Lord Tain smiles broadly and wages his finger. "You are good," he replies. "I didn't even see that one coming, you're as good as my father was." Max, Cin and Big Dan just look at each other and shrug.

After a few drinks everyone is sitting happily chatting away together. "My Lord Taraten, may I ask you something a little more serious?" asks Trace.

John nods. "Please, and call me John."

Trace bows slightly bemused. "Hem yes John. In the past my Lord Tain and his father, the previous Lord Tain, have sent peace envoys to your land. Yet all were murdered, only one ever came back. Anilis was his name, and he has never been the same since. They tortured him, mentally and physically before letting him go, he talked of trials, and being made to watch his friends face them. And after every one they told him he would be next, he said it was ghastly. He was even made to watch his best friend face a spiked jackerbell, the screams of this poor soul as he was eaten alive, still haunts his dreams to this day. So why after all this time, do you suddenly want peace?"

Everyone falls silent and Tain nods. "That is a fair question."

John sighs deeply nodding also. "That was the previous Lord Taraten," he tells them. "As I told your man Elandra, back in the forest."

"Here hang on a minute," he asks, a thought suddenly popping into his head. "How did that mans' friend manage to get to the third trial?"

"He was carried up a ladder and thrown directly in," answers Trace.

"One moment," interrupts Lord Tain. "Did you say you told Elandra?"

John simply nods. "We were not informed of that," answers Tain angrily. "May I ask, was there an accident, or did you beat him."

John sighs deeply. "Yes I beat him, we were just passing through, we did not want trouble, but we were captured, and I was also made to face the trials. This Lord was the cruellest man I've ever known. And I am truly sorry for your friend and your other people's loss, but it was not I, and the first thing I did on winning him was have that area torn down. And you have my solemn word, no one will ever be treated like that again, all torture has been outlawed. And I left the province being run by three truly good people."

"That makes a lot of sense," answers Trace. "No disrespect my Lord, but you are nothing like we expected, and are still not. You said you were just passing through, so I take it you did not wish to become Lord of that province."

John shrugs. "No not at all."

"So how by the two moons above did you manage to complete these trials?" asks Trace. "I'm led to believe it was impossible."

John shrugs again. "It wasn't easy, it took the help of friends."

Lord Tain shakes his head. "Remarkable, did he then just relinquish power."

John sighs shaking his head. "No not at all, he then had us tortured, well tried. We escaped, he then challenged me to a sword fight, and the rest as they say is history."

After a little more to eat and drink Lord Tain gets up. "Come let us sit under the turquoise blossoms of the first few trees here, the effects of this should create a feeling of great happiness."

Big Dan smirks. "Yes lets."

Max shoves him and says, "Come on what is it."

"Err, nothing Max honest," he answers trying to hide his grin.

They all then sit there chatting and it's not long before the soft perfumed sent of the blossom fills their lungs. Maxie smiles. "That smells wonderful."

"Hem, yes wonderful," agrees her mother.

Then within a few moments of sitting there all are filled with an overwhelming feeling of happiness and joy. "Well John," asks Big Dan hopefully. "How do you feel?"

John shrugs. "I don't, err. I feel normal."

"You don't feel anything?" asks Dan disappointedly.

"Happy, mad, angry," he emphasises.

John shakes his head and shrugs. "No more than I did before. I don't think these mood tree things work on me."

Big Dan sighs deeply. "Oh well."

"Ooo," shouts Max trying hard to frown at Dan, but being overcome by the happiness. "I know what you were up to now my boy."

"Don't think I don't, I'll sort you out later," she tells him.

Big Dan just smirks. "I don't know what you mean. I just wanted him to be happy."

Max sighs happily. "No, don't let this smile fool you. You were hoping this stuff was going to have the opposite effect weren't you."

Big Dan starts to smile and chuckle, "It's just the blossom Max, honest."

Woodnut sits there roaring with laughter on seeing them overcome with happiness from the trees. "We should plant these trees everywhere," he sniggers. "Keep you ooman's quiet, and stop you fighting for a while."

"John," he whispers hopefully. "Do you think we should talk about saving the forest now, while they are feeling so happy under these trees?"

"No," whispers John. "They may come to their senses later, and think we've tricked them in a moment of weakness. Let's learn a little more about them first, and hopefully become friends, don't worry my friend, one way or another, we'll sort it all out."

Woodnut nods but smiles nervously. "As you wish, you know best."

So they spend the afternoon sitting under various mood trees, feeling everything from euphoria, to sadness, all but John and Woodnut on whom they have no effect. But both still thoroughly enjoy themselves, watching the others and making fun of them. Finally they all make their way back into the stronghold where Tain sighs. "Well I must say, that was the best afternoon I've had in a long time. Now there is to be a celebration tonight in your honour, then tomorrow perhaps we can talk about the reason for your being here."

John nods. "That sounds good to me."

Tain then bows to them. "If you'll excuse me, I have things to organise," he apologises. "You may look around anywhere you see fit, or retire to your rooms, the choice is yours. I'll see you in an hour or so."

Two of the guards then follow Lord Tain, but Trace stops with them. He smiles. "If you like I can show you around the stronghold or town if you like."

Cin nods. "Yes we'd like that."

"What do you lot think?" he asks and everyone agrees.

The time passes far too quickly before they are approached by another warrior. "I've been sent by my Lord," he announces. "If you would like to make your way to the big hall, the celebrations will commence."

"Thank you," answers Trace just before they reach the double doors of the big hall where two guards are standing to attention, but instead of looking down they look straight ahead.

"Much better, excellent work men," booms Big Dan.

The men beam broadly and Dan pats one on the back on passing, nearly sending him flying. Trace chuckles as the doors are flung open. Glendra stands there waiting for them and bows. "Would you all be standing please, as I introduce Lord and Lady Taraten and their party?"

Lord Tain stands and says, "May I also add, as a mark of respect to our guests, please do not overt your eyes."

They are then led over to Lord Tain's table and seated before John stands back up and calls out, "I hope this isn't too early for a toast. Because, I'd just like to raise my mug and thank you all for your kindness, on making us feel so welcome. And may our provinces live in peace and harmony from now, until the end of time." A cheer goes up from all as drinks are raised high.

The food and drink flow freely with everyone deep in conversation. "My Lord Tain," asks Max. "Have you no wife? I seem to be sitting in the chair of a lady, it's well worn and can't have just been placed here for me."

"Yes my Lady," answers Tain. "I am happily married, but alas my wife had to rush away. I fear her mother is gravely ill."

John nudges Big Dan and whispers, "Why is everyone staring at me, have I got something on my chin."

"No," chuckles Big Dan. "Nothing on your chin. You are Lord Taraten remember, a figure and province that has struck fear into the hearts of all that has heard of it."

"Well I don't like it," grumps John.

"You could always have them stare at their feet again," says Big Dan grinning, but John just sighs deeply.

Maxie is sitting by her mother with Woodnut, and as normal both are giggling away together. "Mum," she asks. "Why are there no tables in front of us? Why is it so open?"

"Some halls and taverns are dear," replies Max. "It's for entertainment purposes usually. I presume that is the reason here also."

"Yes my Lady that is exactly right," answers Trace sitting a little further along.

"What type of entertainment do you have?" asks John.

"All sorts my Lord," answers Trace. "From great story tellers to clowns, fools and jugglers."

He winks. "Even scantily clad ladies jigging about."

"Would you care to see them?" he asks hopefully. "Unless it would show disfavour with my Lady here that is."

Max gives out a sudden squirt of laughter, then composing herself replies, "No fine by me. What about you John."

"Yeah why not, should be good for a giggle," he chuckles.

"Yes go on John," shouts Cin, promptly backed up by Big Dan.

"Excellent," shouts Lord Tain. "My wife doesn't care for them, so we don't get to see them much."

"But if you insist," he says excitedly.

John winks. "Ok I insist, dancing girls it is."

"What girls?" asks Trace.

"Err jigging girls," sighs John. "Where I come from, err doesn't matter."

A moment later a side door is flung open and the whole room falls silent, and gasps come from around the hall. As a small thin wild haired old woman comes dancing in, muttering as she goes, and dressed in a long baggy hemp like skirt and top. Big Dan nudges Cin, "I don't think much of their jigging women."

"No," sniggers Cin. "More John's style there I think."

"What was that?" shouts Max.

"Err, hem, nothing Max," stutters Cin.

"It'd better be," she snaps. "I now owe the both of you."

Cin thumps the table. "Damn woman."

"What was that?" she asks again.

"Oh nothing," stammers Cin. "There was a bug on the table."

John turns to Lord Tain and says, "Is she not rather old for a dancing girl, although it's nice to see another woman with hair apart from my wife, all be it a bit wild."

Tain sighs with despair. "I'm afraid this is no jigging girl, she is the very thing I didn't want here tonight. I don't know how she found out. I should have known, you can't keep secrets from her, I just hope she's here for a good reason."

"Why, who is she?" asks John. "Can you not just send her away?"

Tain sighs. "I wish it were that simple. She is feared by all, no one dares stop her. She comes and goes as she pleases, but she can be very good council at times, and knows things no one knows. But there are other times she's as mad as they come. Some know her as witch, others as mad woman, she doesn't mind either." John gives out a wry laugh. "You mean she likes to be called witch and mad woman."

"Yes," whispers Lord Tain.

"Oh come on," laughs John. "Witch my eye, you can't really be frightened of some old woman. What's the worst she can do to you?"

"No you really don't understand," whispers Tain. "She can put spells on a person, she's been known to make people go mad and think there anything from a hairy hog rooting about in the mud, to creepers scurrying across the floor. This I have seen many times with my own eyes. She has even been known to disappear in a blinding flash of smoke, and when she starts to repeat her magic words, they can get in your head and stay there for days."

Maxie and Woodnut getting a little bored start to quietly hum a song together. "There you see," shouts Lord Tain panicking slightly. "She's bewitched your child and her pet, it's always the simple of mind it affects first."

"What did you call my daughter?" shouts Max.

"Max quiet please, "shouts John. "You'll have to excuse me my Lord, but my daughter is simply humming. And be in no doubt, Woodnut and my daughter are the two most remarkable people you will ever meet. And as for that old crone, well I'll believe it when I see it."

The old woman stops the other side of the hall in front of a large table, and gently sways back and forward with her back to the others. The people on the table slowly start to sway with her. "There you see," cries Lord Tain. "She's bewitched them."

She stops suddenly turns and comes over to their table, skipping, dancing and even singing as she does so. "Ninginy nanginy noo."

She then stops in front of John and Lord Tain. "Quickly," whispers Tain. "Cover your ears, she's putting those words in your mind."

"Ninginy nanginy noo," laughs John. "You've got to be taking the."

"John," shouts Max.

He sighs. "I wasn't going to say it."

The old woman points to John, and in a scary voice shouts, "You people come from far away, and you fight for greenem, this the spirits have told me."

Gasps come from around the hall, with whispers of, "How did she know that."

John just sits there smirking from ear to ear. "This is some sort of wind up isn't it? It doesn't exactly take a mathematician to work that one out. Come on you old crone, you'll have to do much better than that."

"Unbeliever, unbeliever," shouts the old woman.

"John," whispers Max. "Are you sure you should be upsetting her?"

John just turns and glares at her so Max goes bright red and turns away. The old woman then points to Lord Tain. "You should have invited me here, and asked for my council, instead of letting the spirits tell me."

"I'm s, sorry," stutters Tain. "A simple slip of the mind."

"I'll slip your mind," she tells him. "In fact; I'll slip all your minds."

She then starts dancing and swaying, backwards and forwards, humming as she does so. She then takes a necklace out from under her top. "Do you like it?" she says softly. "Doesn't it sparkle, watch it closely, and it will sparkle even brighter."

Lord Tain's eyes start to glaze over as does Max's and the others. However John jumps up leans over the table and quick as a flash grabs her necklace, snapping the chain as he sits back down. He opens his hand for a closer look. "Nice necklace, now please, don't let me stop you bewitching people. Oh, and sorry for the interruption."

"Give me that back now," shouts the old woman.

"What, what happened there?" asks Max and the others a little disorientated.

"Yes," asks John sarcastically. "Tell me old woman, what did happen there? Are you not carrying on with your mind control?"

"No I shan't, I've changed my mind," she replies putting her tongue out.

John nods. "Yes, I thought you might."

"Please give me back my necklace," she asks, her attitude suddenly changing. "It's all I have of my mother's, in fact, it's all I remember of her."

"Now that's better," smiles John handing it back.

"Oh no," she sighs. "Look, you've broken the chain."

John waves his hand beckoning the necklace back. So fighting back the tears she hands it back. "This is a fine chain," says John. "I've never seen its like, in these lands anyway."

He then throws it to Woodnut. "Do you think you could fix that dude?" he asks.

Woodnut studies it closely. "Yes I think so," he answers.

John winks. "Come on then you old goat. Are you going to show us some more witchcraft then?"

"Maybe I will, and maybe I won't, maybe I will and maybe I won't," she sings over and over again as she dances away around the hall.

"You're lucky," whispers Lord Tain. "She seems to like you. I've seen her do this many times before, she just seems to slip from witch to mad woman at the drop of a hat, here watch this."

"Oh witch, witch could you come here please," he shouts then takes two coins from his pocket as she dances back over. In one hand he holds up one large coin, and in the other a tiny silver coloured one. "Now," he asks. "Would you like this large dull coin, or this small shiny one?"

She points excitedly to the small shiny coin, still singing and dancing as she does so, "Ninginy, nanginy noo."

"There told you, see, "chuckles Tain. "Mad as they come, any sane person would have taken the rueland." John totally confused looks to Max. "The rueland is the larger one dear, and worth several times that of the smaller one."

John nods. "Oh ok."

Several calls then come from around the room, as other people also offer the old woman her choice of coins. The old woman dances, skips and even cartwheels from person to person, each time excitedly taking the small shiny coin. "That settles it for me," laughs Cin. "Mad as they come, she could have made a fortune if she'd accepted the rueland."

John grins. "And tell me, is this a new thing she's doing."

"No not at all," laughs Trace. "She's done this for years, she disappears now and again. But she's done this for as long as anyone can remember, and you know, never once has she been known to take the larger coin."

John looks to Woodnut and the pair of them burst into fits of laughter. "Why are you laughing?" asks Trace. "All I have told you is true my Lord, honest ask anyone."

"Yes," replies John wiping a tear from his eye. "In that I have no doubt."

"Why are you laughing?" whispers Big Dan.

"She's not mad," he whispers back. "She's an old con woman, sly as a fox I'd say."

"Really," gasps Dan. "Sly as a fox, now are you sure you mean fox, John."

John sighs. "No I don't want to know, and yes I mean fox, a fox from my world, ok."

Big Dan smiles. "Yes, yes of course, I'm sure it's very clever. Anyway why do you say she's sly?"

"Think about it," whispers John. "Everyone thinks it's really funny as she accepts the lesser amount from them yes, and they've been doing it for years."

"Well yes," shrugs Big Dan. "It was quite funny. I was tempted to do it myself, the way she giggles at the same time, quite comical."

John nods. "Ok, I can see that. But what if she'd accepted the larger coin from Lord Tain. Would you or anyone else still want to do it?"

"No of course not," answers Dan.

"Exactly my friend," smirks John. "Think about it, she's been fleecing these suckers for years."

Max with her excellent hearing starts to chuckle, "Oh yes, the sly old thing, she must have made a small fortune over the years."

The old woman skips back over to there table, wiggling her fingers, and waving her arms at John and his friends. "I'm not going to put a spell on you this time," she cackles.

So John slowly stands up and leans right over the table, beckoning her to do the same and then whispers in her ear, "You may fool these people you old fraud, but be in no doubt, you don't fool me, not for an instant." The old woman steps back and smiles. "Ninginy nanginy noo. Do you know what those words mean? Do you know where they're from?"

John shakes his head. "Yes they're gibberish. Please, enlighten me."

She sighs deeply. "It's been so long, I can't even remember them properly myself. But you, you are different, different from these other people, and even your friends. And if you had known these words, I would have said you were the one they'd tried to stop."

A serious look comes upon John's face and asks, "What do you mean *they'd tried to stop?*"

The old woman doesn't answer but cackles and with a "Ninginy nanginy noo," she cartwheels away, then pauses for a moment and does a handstand. Her baggy skirt falls down over her head revealing her bare bottom.

"No god please," shouts John. "Stand back up you old crone."

"I don't care what you say John," gasps Cin. "She's as mad as they come. That's just not natural behaviour from an old woman."

The two girls and Woodnut just giggle. "Old crone," mutters the old woman standing back up. "Ooh yes, I like that, you may call me old crone from now on."

"Sly or not," John thinks to himself. "She's definitely a few rows short of an allotment."

"Now understand this," she cackles pointing directly at John. "I leave you with this proof of my powers. And think of this when I disappear. I could do the same to all of you, and you would never be seen again."

Then as she cackles there is a bright flash of light, and a large puff of smoke, as a small explosion comes from just in front of her. Chaos then ensues as people fall back off their chairs, holding their eyes, temporarily blinded by the bright flash, and a little disorientated by the sudden bang. Maxie lifts her sunglasses up and looks to John and asks, "Dad, what was that?"

"A diversion," replies John jumping to his feet as he has seen the old woman making for the doorway.

Then jumping over the table he sprints to cut her off. The old woman is so pleased with herself she does not notice him beating her to the doorway and she runs right into him and squeals with shock. "How did you get here?" she stutters.

John winks. "Maybe I can do magic to aye."

"Impossible," she shouts.

John nods and asks her, "So tell me, where did you get the gunpowder to make that flash?"

"It's magic," she cackles.

"Less of the crap now," snaps John getting very serious. "You must tell me as the people of these lands can't be allowed to get their hands on it. It would mean the end of their innocence. And death and war on a scale you couldn't begin to imagine."

"I shoot it out of my fingers," she cackles. "Now stand aside, or I'll do it to you."

But quick as a flash John picks her up and throws her over his shoulder. "Let's go."

"Let me down," she squeals thumping his back.

Then realising the futility of her position, she says softly, "Put me down, and I'll tell you."

As everyone comes back to their sense's they see John and the old witch standing together, and all sit silently. "Tell me quietly then old woman," says John.

"That's crone to you," she huffs.

He sighs. "Ok, ok, tell me what you know please, old crone."

"Many years ago," she tells him. "When I was very, very young, I was taken in by an old man who took pity on me. He was thought of as very strange also, but he didn't mind, he said it suited his purpose and people left him alone. He was always collecting things, heating them up, boiling, burning and mixing things together, exploriments he called them."

"You mean experiments," says John.

"Yes, yes that's it," she nods excitedly. "He taught me so much as I grew up. Then one day he called me in, and very excited he was. He had been working on something for quite a while, but it didn't work out, and in a fit of madness threw his mixture in the fire. That was how he invented the flash bang, by accident. Flash bang, that's what he called it, not this gong powder you call it. Only I have the recipe, no one else even knows it exists, it's wrote on a piece of parchment. But he like you must have realised what he'd done, and told me to tell no one of it, under any circumstances."

"He was obviously a very intelligent man," nods John. "Where is he now?"

Her head bows as she sighs. "He was very old, and illness took him many years ago."

"I'm sorry to here that," he says softly. "I would have liked to have met him."

The old woman then places a pouch in his hand. "The recipes in here," she tells him. "But please, give me a little time to collect some of my possessions."

"A little head start, please," she begs.

John smiles and slips the pouch in his pocket. "Thank you," she sighs trying hard to raise a smile.

She then turns to go when suddenly making her jump, John shouts loudly to everyone. "Did you see that? It's a miracle, witchcraft I tell you, she transported me from my table in a blinding flash of light, she is a witch."

"Please forgive me," he shouts turning back to the old woman and dropping to his knees.

The old crone stares at him in disbelief, as he gives her a sly wink. "Well," he whispers. "If they're stupid enough to believe you, who am I to spoil it."

Her eyes light up and she smiles broadly. "Thank you," she whispers.

"Yes I forgive you, unbeliever," she shouts loudly. "You may stand, and now I must go."

"No please," shouts John. "Stay with us, take a little food and drink, if you please, mighty witch."

"Are you sure?" she whispers.

He winks. "Yeah, and besides my friend Woodnut still has your necklace. Nice bit of hypnosis by the way, has no one ever clicked you for that yet."

"I don't know what you mean," she snaps, "It's magic."

John just frowns at her. "Ok, ok," she sighs putting her tongue out at him. "You're the first person it hasn't worked on; these people seem very susceptible to it." She then starts to skip dance and cartwheel around the room, singing the same three words over and over again, "Ninginy nanginy noo," until she gets to the table.

"We've fixed your necklace," says Maxie. "Would you like to sit here with us?"

"Yes I would like that," she answers wiggling her fingers at Maxie. "Ninginy, nanginy noo."

"You're very silly," says Maxie.

The old woman a little shocked asks, "You can see me?"

"Yes of course," answers Maxie. "Please sit."

The old woman is given a chair. "I just thought with these covers on your eyes, you were blind."

"Maxie smiles. "No, not everything is always as it seems. You of all people should know that."

As John sits back down Lord Tain whispers to him, "I told you she was powerful."

John grins and shrugs then Max whispers in his ear, "Are you sure Maxie's safe sitting with her."

John just turns and scowls at her. "Ok, ok," she mutters, "I get it."

A few drinks later and everyone is back talking and laughing again.

"I tell you what," mutters Trace leaning over to Lord Tain. "I'd love to know how the witch really knew to come here tonight, tonight of all nights."

"Yes I agree," nods Tain. "Her sprits or something she said, whatever they are."

The old woman hearing this gives out a wry chuckle. Maxie looks at her suspiciously, then turns to Lord Tain and Trace. "Would you really like to know?" she asks.

The two men look to the old woman, and nod cautiously. "Why do you know Maxie?" asks Big Dan.

"No not yet," she answers. "But I will in a moment."

"Be careful child," cackles the old woman. "It was the dark spirits that told me. If you're not careful, I will have them take your soul."

Maxie turns to her. "Please, I like you, Woodnut and I think you're very funny, but never threaten me, I don't like it. And you really don't want to get on my bad side."

"Now please Sir," she asks turning back to lord Tain. "Could you tell everyone to be quiet please, and then simply ask who was it that informed her. I've been dying to try this out anyway."

"Err hem, I'm not sure," stutters Tain still staring at the crone.

Big Dan then throws his chair back and stands up. "Everybody quiet," he booms. "I have a question for you all, who told the witch we were here?"

Maxie then stands up, slips her glasses up onto her head, closes her old eye, cocks her head and slowly stares around the room with her new eye. "Ask again," she tells him.

Once again Big Dan booms the same question but no one says a word. Maxie's head still cocked and one eye closed then stares at a man standing with a tray the other side of the room. She slips her glasses back down and points to the man. "He did it," she shouts.

"Are you sure Maxie?" asks Big Dan.

Maxie nods. "Ah, ha."

"You there servant," shouts Trace standing up.

The man suddenly makes a bolt for the door, but is stopped by the two guards and brought over. "How did you do that child?" gasps the old woman.

Maxie giggles and cheekily replies, "Why don't you ask some of your dark spirit friends, I'm sure they'll tell you."

The old crone stamps her foot with frustration. "You are your father's daughter, that is for certain," she grumps.

Maxie smiles broadly. "Thank you, I think that's the nicest thing anyone has ever said to me."

"It wasn't meant to be a compliment," she grumps again.

"It wasn't me my Lord," cries the servant. "You can't believe this child, she lies."

Max flies off her seat and plants the man clean on the chin knocking him to he ground. "My daughter never lies," she shouts.

"Max sit down dear," John tells her.

"Please little one," asks Lord Tain. "How did you know it was him? Did the mad woman tell you?"

"No Sir," she answers. "I will tell you, but you alone."

Lord Tain nods waving her over. "It's my eye," she whispers. "The one you thought was blind, it's a special eye, it doesn't see like my other, or anyone else's for that matter. And when I look through it alone, people's faces look, well, different. They kind of glow different colours, depending on what they're doing and what they're feeling. But when someone lies or feels really guilty, like he did, their faces glow even brighter, and err, how can I describe it. Err yes, sparks, flashes, like little needles of light shoot out of their cheeks and head. They can't help it, they don't even know they're doing it, but I see it, and that's how I know he was lying."

"That is remarkable," gasps Lord Tain. "Really?"

"Yes Sir," nods Maxie.

Lord Tain then turns back to the servant. "Yes it was he who told me," comes a shout from the old woman. "He paid me to come here, he said he wanted payback."

"Now who's getting payback aye," she cackles madly.

"Stand him up," shouts Lord Tain angrily.

"Elandra," he gasps. "I spared you earlier today, and you repay me like this."

"Life of a servant," shouts Elandra. "What life is that, I would rather be dead?"

Tain then bows his head. "Then death it is."

"No stop," shouts Woodnut running along the table giggling as he goes.

"Yes err?" asks Lord Tain.

"Woodnut Sir," he answers.

"Yes Woodnut, what have you to say?" asks Tain.

"If it's death he wants rather than being a servant," giggles Woodnut. "Let him live, and give him a job that will make him wish he was a servant."

"Oh yes, oh I like that, that's good," smiles Lord Tain his eyes lighting up. "An excellent idea, now let me think. Ah yes I have it, from this moment on you will no longer be known as Elandra, but as Dung Hill. And you will spend your days in the stables mucking out the horses, and on an evening when your duties are over, there you shall reside. Now be gone Dung Hill, you will never see the inside of this building again. Guards, take him away," he continues.

Woodnut is so delighted he bows his lowest bow to Lord Tain, then turns back to Elandra. "Oh Dung Hill," he shouts. "And this is what happens when you try and stab my old friend Evening Thunder in the back. That which you sow, so shall you reap."

John winks to Woodnut putting his thumb up. "He did what?" asks Lord Tain.

"Please my Lord," bows Woodnut. "This is a celebration, could we possibly talk of this tomorrow."

"Yes, yes, of course," answers Tain. "Very wise of you."

"What happened to the jigging girls?" shouts Dan.

"Oh yes excellent idea," shouts Trace as he claps his hands and waves to a servant.

A few moments later and some scantily clad rather large ladies come jigging out. "Hu," grumps the old witch. "I dance better than that."

Cin, Big Dan and John roar with laughter, but only them, as everyone else is too scared of her to do so. A few hours later and Lord Tain yawns, "Well this has been the most remarkable and fun evening I've had in a long time. Now if you'll all excuse me, I will retire for the night. I'll see you outside in the orchard for breakfast perhaps."

John bows as Lord Tain leaves the room. "That sounds good yes thank you."

"Hey crone," shouts John. "How about a few tricks, err, I mean show us some more magic. How about a spell on someone, perhaps make them think there a, greenem perhaps."

So the old woman jumps to her feet cackling excitedly, cart wheeling and doing handstands and singing, "Ninginy nanginy noo."

Woodnut walks over and sits down beside John. "What are you up to?" he asks.

John shrugs. "Nothing, it's just a bit of fun."

"Can she really put spells on them?" asks Woodnut. "Can she really make them think they're greenem?" "Kind of," whispers John. "But it's not magic or witchcraft, just a cheap party trick."

The old crone then stops at a table across the room, and soon has the people there running around the floor on their knees, talking in funny voices, and pretending to be greenem. "We don't do that," grumps Woodnut. "And we definitely don't sound like that."

John gives him a nudge. "Come on, it's just a bit of fun, it's just their interpretation of you."

Woodnut starts to snigger, "I suppose, it is a little bit funny." Most of the others there just sit and stare in disbelief and fear.

"No sing root tonight John," asks Big Dan.

John shakes his head. "No just ale, I thought it might be more prudent to keep a clear head tonight."

Max puts her hand over her mouth to try and hide her yawns but John sees her and stands up and takes her hand. "I'm tired myself, come on Maxie bed time."

Everyone stands as they leave the hall. And as they walk back to the room Max asks, "Did she really magic you across the room?"

"No don't be silly," laughs John. "I ran over."

"You ran," repeats Max. "But I didn't see you, there was a flash of light and smoke, and you just seemed to appear over by the door."

John grins like a cheshire cat. "And you keep telling me how bad my eyesight is. Paid off this time didn't it. Your people's eyesight being a lot more sensitive, meant you were temporarily blinded, and a little disoriented, giving her, and me, time to run out, or would have in her case. By the time you all pulled yourselves together, low and behold, so called magic."

Max nods. "Oh I see."

"Yes that's right Mum," says Maxie. "I saw it all as my eyes were shielded somewhat by the glasses."

John puts his arms around them both. "Bed now ladies, it's been a long day."

The next morning John wakes up early and goes through into the large communal room. Cin is next to rise and enters the room. "Morning John," he says.

Maxie is next. "Morning Dad," she greets him on entering.

"Morning guys," replies John.

They then sit there chatting until the others rise and come through. A short time later and there is a knock at the door. "Enter," shouts Cin.

Glendra comes in and bows, "My Lord is in the orchard if you wish to join him for breakfast."

"Yes thank you," answers Max. "We will follow you down."

In the orchard the sun is just starting to warm the ground forming a slight dew. Woodnut instantly buries his feet in the ground, and raises his hands to the sky. As the rest gather around the table Lord Tain asks, "What's your friend Woodnut doing?"

"Like you having breakfast," answers Maxie.

"Oh yes of course," replies Tain scratching his head.

They then all sit enjoying the early morning sun and eating a little breakfast, apart from Maxie and Woodnut, who are now chasing each other around the trees giggling and singing, "Ninginy nanginy noo," as they do so. Lord Tain a little unsettled asks, "Do you think they should be saying that?"

"Oh it's ok," shouts Maxie. "Harry told us they're magic words anyone can sing."

"Harry," asks Tain. "Who's Harry?"

"The old woman," shrugs Maxie. "You know the witch."

Lord Tain and Trace both gasp in unison. "You mean she has a name,"

Maxie giggles, "Yes of course you silly things. But don't go telling anyone, I don't think she'd like that."

Tain sighs in shock. "No, no, of course."

"Come on," laughs John. "What did you think she was called?"

"Did you think she was named baby witch or baby mad woman as a baby," jokes John.

"You know," says Cin. "I half expected her to have a man's name for some reason." Maxie and Woodnut just giggle and go back to chasing and singing.

John's mind starts to wander as the others chat away, and he finds himself humming along to the song, not even realising he's doing it. "What was that dear?" asks Max.

"Hu, what?" asks John snapping out of it.

"You were saying something," replies Max.

"No, no, I don't think so," he answers.

"Yes you were," answers Max.

"Yes I heard you also," says Trace. "Something about putting them together, and what have you got, you kept repeating it."

John's eyes suddenly light up. "I did. Hang on, no can't be, surely."

"What is it?" they ask.

"The old crones so called magic words," he replies. "Unless I'm mistaken, I know what they are, but, but, surely not. I mean, that would mean."

"John what is it," barks Cin. "I thought you said it was just gibberish."

John nods. "It is."

"John you're not making sense," says Big Dan.

"Err, it doesn't matter," shrugs John. "I'm probably wrong anyway, sorry just ignore me." Big Dan frowns at him as he sits running his fingers through his beard.

They all finish eating and Lord Tain waves to servants to clear the table. "Now shall we talk about the reason you are here?" he asks.

"Yes please," answers John. "But first, Woodnut time to talk."

Woodnut comes over climbs up, and sits now looking deadly serious. "You want a greenem to be part of the talks?" asks a bewildered Lord Tain.

"Yes of course," nods John. "And I mean this with no disrespect, but please, don't take my friend, or his people for fools. If you are ever lucky enough to get to know them, as we have, you will find there is no one wiser anywhere."

Lord Tain bows his head. "I am led to believe the greenem are the reason you are here. Although when I was first told this, I must admit, I thought it was some kind of taraten trick or joke."

"No my Lord," answers John. "No trick, no joke."

"So," asks Tain. "You honestly want me to put a forest and a few talking plants, over the expansion and progress of my people?"

John's head sinks to his chest, and his breathing gets deeper, until suddenly raising up again, he starts to shout angrily, slamming his fist on the round bench. "What is it with this progress crap, and expansion rubbish," he growls.

There is then a loud deep thud, as his fist hitting the centre of the table, cracks it clean across, making them all jump in the process. With a look of shock and horror Lord Tain stutters, "Surely that is a sign of a truly honourable and civilised people, wanting to advance, to do better, not for oneself, but for your people."

"So," growls John. "You're honestly doing this for your people are you, to make it better for them aye. You mean like those poor souls who live in the slums on the edge of your town. Oh, how they've benefited, too terrified to look up as they beg in the streets. And living in, what, huts, dilapidated sheds, I wouldn't treat animals as badly as you treat them. Hey but that's ok, because that's progress, isn't it, and there's always got to be some who have to suffer in the name of it, isn't that right."

"Well," stutters Tain.

"Yes exactly," continues John cutting him off. "It's only the poor and oppressed, they're used to hardship anyway, aren't they. A bit more won't make any difference will it, no they won't mind. Hey, and if they do, there's nothing they can do about it anyway. We'll just tell them it's for their own good, and bamboozle them with a few fancy words. They're too stupid to understand, aye, and by the time they do, it's too late anyway, isn't that right. Now if you want to prove to me you really are civilised and honourable, you'll help your poor and underprivileged, feed and educate them, make it a good place for everybody to live. Not just a place where the rich get richer, off the backs or at the expense of the poor, or by raping the forests and earth, in the so called name of progress. Oh but let's all not forget the classic. For the long term progress and future of all. Yeah right, lining the nests of their families and friends, for their future in other words. Please look after what you already have, if you do honestly want to look civilised, intelligent and honourable, try to live in peace and harmony with nature, or at least along side of it. Be a shining example to all, of how good people should be, and act. I've seen the effects of so called progress, and in the long term it's not pretty, and unfortunately very self destructive for all, people, nature, even the earth itself."

Lord Tain and Trace sit there open mouthed and silent, unsure whether to be, happy, angry, or even declare war. Cin nudges Big Dan muttering, "Well I thought he handled that quite well, don't you."

Trace hearing this leans over. "You are joking aren't you?"

Big Dan whispers back, "No, you should have seen him the last time someone mentioned progress to him." Trace simply shakes his head.

Woodnut stands up and bows. "Please Sir may I speak, before something is said in haste."

Still not saying a word Lord Tain nods. "Thank you," answers Woodnut. "Oomans do not think much of my people, and we are usually persecuted and victimised, at best, tolerated or ignored. But you Sir have shown great wisdom and honour. As my people tell me you do not do these things, and on occasion even talked and entered in dialog with them. This alone stands you out above all other leaders, in this you should be proud. My people like all living things are part of this world, and as such we try to live in harmony with it. This does not mean we are any less intelligent, or have any less right to live, but oomans seem to see the world so narrowly. But on rare occasion, there comes a person who can see just a little broader, and a little clearer. And with a bit of guidance can start to see the world and life for what it is, sacred marvellous and wonderful. And if you would show a little more of that same bravery and courage you've shown already, I would like to invite you both to come back with us to the forest, in which you seem so keen to destroy. As honoured guests of course, and there you can talk with, and meet my people, and then I think you will see, we are not as you think. Please, help us to help you, we can show you cures for diseases and illnesses you thought impossible. We can show you new foods easy to grow and harvest, for even your poorest people. We can show you how to work with the forests and land, to sustain it, not just destroy it and move on to the next bit. A legacy for your children and your children's children, please do not destroy what you have, what we all have, before you even know it exists. If you do you will lose more than you could ever imagine. So once again I say, please let us show you the beauty and complexity of our forest, and all that live there."

Woodnut then bows his lowest bow and sits back down. Lord Tain puts his hand over his mouth and sits silent, deep in thought.

Trace leans back a little shocked and blurts out, "How do I, we, know this just isn't some trick to get us alone and do away with us."

"If that were our intention," answers Woodnut politely. "We would not be speaking now, my friends here would have seen to that, or one day you would have simply disappeared."

Trace stares at the little greenem oddly. John gives Woodnut a sly wink, then Woodnut jumps off his seat. "Please could you stand a moment," he asks Trace. "Don't worry, no harm will come to you."

Now smiling broadly Trace stands up and takes a few steps back. Woodnut just stands there emotionless not saying a word while Trace stands there smiling down at him. "Well what now," chuckles Trace."

But as the words leave his lips he is suddenly and sharply pulled down into the earth, not buried completely, just past the waist. He shouts and squeals with shock, then as quickly as he was pulled down he is pushed back up.

Lord Tain is still just sitting there silent, but his eyes are now wide as wide can be. Woodnut climbs back up and sits back down. Trace shaking a little sits back down stammering, "Some of my men told me this had happened back at the forest."

"But I never thought, I mean how could I," he rambles.

Then pulling himself together he bows his head to Woodnut. "You have made your point little friend."

"What are your thoughts my Lord?" he asks, a tremble still in his voice.

Lord Tain takes his hand from his mouth and shrugging his shoulders slowly shakes his head. "My Lord Taraten, John, everything you said, you answered before I even got a chance to think of the question you had asked. But every answer you gave for me, to those questions is what I would have said, it is as if you could read my mind, I truly do not know how you did it."

"No tricks," shrugs John. "I've just heard these same ridiculous arguments before unfortunately."

"And you young greenem," smiles Tain. "Mr Greenfern, how you did that to my friend here, I don't even want to think about. But may I say, your people chose wisely in you I think, for your words are wise, and I sit here astounded by their complexity. And if proven to be true by your people, I think only a fool would turn down such a generous offer, and we shall prepare this evening, and go at first light tomorrow."

"Yes," shouts Maxie clapping her hands and jumping up and down.

Lord Tain smiles again. "Well I seem to have made somebody very happy," he chuckles.

"No you've made us all very happy," smiles Max.

Lord Tain then starts to laugh to himself. "What is it?" asks John.

"I just find it funny," he answers. "It's the first argument I've ever had where I answered without ever saying a word."

They all laugh and then sit there most of the morning laughing, joking and generally just shooting the breeze. "Shall we go in and have a bit of lunch?" asks Lord Tain. "And then maybe I could introduce you to some of the people, especially you Mr Greenfern, see what you think of my physicians, and their remedies."

9

THEY ALL GET up to go in, and as they walk along Lord Tain asks, "I was originally told there was another in your party, a warrior also, but Glendra informs me he's been delayed, by some sort of accident. Will he be joining us tomorrow at the forest?"

The smiles and laughter stop instantly. "I'm sorry," answers Cin. "You'll have to excuse us my Lord, something happened to our friend deep in the forest the other night, and we fear the worst."

"That's terrible," sighs Lord Tain. "What happened? Did he wander off and get lost, these forests can be very dangerous places. They don't call that forest, the wretched forest for nothing you know."

"No, not for us," sighs Cin. "Not when you're friends with the greenem, nothing bothers you, nothing in nature anyway, they see to that."

Lord Tain stops instantly. "What do you mean?"

"Well," continues Cin. "When you are in the forest, any forest, and under their protection, no animal would ever deliberately hurt you. They respect the word of the greenem too much to do so."

Lord Tain stands there a little shocked. "Really," he gasps. "So what does this mean for your friend?"

"We honestly don't know," sighs Cin. "All we know is it had something to do with light, it took him, melted him, killed him, we honestly do not know."

Lord Tain nods, his mind deep in thought. "Maybe it was the sky gods," he answers.

"The what?" gasps Cin.

"You know," answers Tain pointing up. "The gods that live in the sky."

John hearing this shoots forward. "You have heard of God?" he asks.

"What is it John?" asks Cin.

"Yes," nods Big Dan. "I have heard you use this word before, many times."

"As have I," agrees Max. "Usually when you're shocked, or angry."

"And on occasion when you're happy," she giggles then blushing. "I just thought it was general word, to be used at such times."

John doesn't answer, he just stares at Lord Tain and asks, "Please tell me. How do you know of these gods, and what do you know? I thought the peoples of this earth did not know of such things, as you can see my friends don't."

Trace then shrugs. "Just what the old witch told us, isn't that right my Lord."

"Yes, yes, that's correct," answers Tain. "If you believe her that is. She tells us the sky gods live in the clouds, and are all seeing and all powerful. She also told us they take things to amuse themselves, or destroy things that don't. So maybe they were displeased with your friend for some reason."

"John," gasps Max. "Do you remember when Maxie was kidnapped? Their leader said something similar, he knows everything, maybe it's true, and maybe it's the same person, this god thing or, something."

John starts to frown. "Now the only problem with that is, and I mean no disrespect here, but I personally think it's all a load of rubbish. God my eye, if there was such a thing he'd have more to answer for than us, certainly on my world anyway."

Trace whispers in Lord Tain's ear. "Excellent idea my friend," replies Tain. "Would you like proof? Would that help perhaps?"

John's mouth falls open, and utterly gobsmacked he stutters, "You, you have proof, you, you've met, err, seen, believe."

"John pull yourself together," snaps Max. "You're rambling."

"Oh, yes, sorry," he apologises.

"To be honest," answers Tain. "I thought it was just the ranting of an old mad woman, well, until recently that is, when down by Desolation Border my men were given a gift by them."

"Desolation Border," mutters Big Dan. "Sounds a nice place."

"What do you mean, given a gift?" asks John.

Lord Tain then turns to Trace, "Maybe you should tell them my friend you were there."

"Yes of course my Lord," answers Trace. "Every few months or so I take a handful of men and we patrol our borders, and it was there we were camping one night. Not far from the border with Desolation, not my favourite place as you can imagine. I remember we stayed up late talking around the fire, I mean, who could sleep there. But finally we did, and when we awoke the next morning just a short distance away, it was there, it filled us all with both terror and marvel. No one has ever seen such a thing, it has a terrifying beauty to it."

"So what is it?" asks John. "Did you see someone leave it? Or perhaps you just never noticed it in the first place."

Trace gives out a wry laugh. "You haven't seen it, trust me, we'd have noticed it, it wasn't there the night before, and no one, but no one, could move that on their own. There was no marks leading up to it or away from it, and when we came to move it, we had to sure it up either side, and it took a team of six horses to pull it."

Nodding John answers, "And this is why you think this god left it for you I presume."

Trace just shrugs. "How else could it have got there? That's what the old witch told us when she first saw it, she also told us in the wrong hands it was an instrument of death."

"Perhaps you would all care to see it," says Lord Tain nonchalantly.

"You have it here," replies John excitedly.

"Yes," shrugs Tain. "It's housed in a large room at the front of the building, under guard."

"Could we go now?" John asks excitedly again.

"Yes of course," smiles Lord Tain. "I don't see why not. Trace could you go and get the wise men, and meet us down there please."

Trace nods then heads off. "John are you sure about this?" asks Max. "We will be safe won't we?"

"I presume so," he shrugs.

"Has it ever caused injury?" he asks.

"No not at all," answers Lord Tain. "It doesn't move, it's just a thing. No one touches it anyway, they're too scared. It's very beautiful if you ask me, but it has filled the hearts of some with terror. My wise men think it's some sort of torture device, they just haven't worked out how yet."

"Can we go right now then?" asks Maxie now very excited herself.

"Yes of course my dear," smiles the lord.

Big Dan and Cin just look down at her and frown. Maxie just puts her tongue out at them and skips ahead with Woodnut. "That child seems to have no fear," chuckles Tain.

"You have no idea," mutters Big Dan.

They get to a set of large double doors which open immediately and on entering the room the twenty odd people inside bow instantly. "As you were," shouts Tain.

On the far side of the room, they see two warriors standing guard in front of a large curtained area. Lord Tain claps his hands. "Right who's for a drink to calm the nerves aye."

Big Dan and Cin smile broadly and drinks are brought. "You know," nods Cin. "This is really good ale, much different from the ale in my province."

"Would you not prefer some sing root John?" Dan asks.

Lord Tain just looks at him oddly but doesn't say anything as Trace is approaching him followed by two official looking men. "My Lord the wise men you asked for," says Trace bowing.

"Ah yes, thank you," nods Tain turning to the wise men. "My Lord Taraten and our other noble guests, are here to see the verum. Now you two have studied it more than anyone, they may wish to ask questions."

"Yes my Lord," answers one of the men.

"It would be our honour," says the other.

They then turn and bow to John and the others and tell them, "Anything you wish to know, please do not hesitate to ask."

"Why is it called a verum?" asks Maxie.

"I was just going to ask that," says John.

"That's just what the old mad woman called it," replies one of the men.

"Actually," says the other. "She calls it a verum verum."

"So do we get to see this thing or not?" asks John sarcastically.

"Err yes, yes of course," stutters Lord Tain gesturing to the guards who bow and taking a piece of curtain each proceed to pull it back.

"Well I'm impressed," gasps Cin.

Big Dan says nothing just stares ahead nodding. Max steps back slightly. "What the heck is that?" she stutters. "It's like, I mean, well it's like nothing I've ever seen."

Big Dan nods. "I agree, it's a little scary, but I can't seem to take my eyes of it."

"Can Woodnut and I go and sit on it please?" asks Maxie excitedly.

They all turn and just stare at her. "What?" she shouts. "It has a seat."

"No, no," stutters her mother a little flabbergasted.

"John dear, what do you make of it?" she asks.

John does not answer as his mug of ale slips from his hand crashing to the floor. "John, John, what's the matter?" shouts Max.

But John still does not answer, his eyes transfixed. "John," asks Big Dan. "Are you ok?"

But still no answer. "I wasn't expecting this from your Lord," sighs one of the wise men.

"This has happened before," he tells them. "But normally to the weak of mind, he'll be alright if we take him outside. At first we thought that was its purpose, to bewitch."

Cin nudges Big Dan. "What do you think's wrong with him?"

Dan shakes his head. "I'm not sure," he answers. "The only other time I've seen him this bothered about something, was that time on top of that mountain when he first noticed the two moons above. But this, this is something completely different."

"So what do you think we should do?" asks Cin.

Big Dan just shrugs. "When he's ready we'll know."

"John," shouts Max again slapping him, but still no response.

"This is bad," sighs the other wise man. "I fear your Lord has lost his mind to this beast of torture."

"What did you say?" snaps Max. "You insult my husband again, and I'll beast you alright."

"I'm, I'm sorry my Lady," stutters the wise man. "But you can see the state of him, we must remove him at once, before the verum takes his mind forever."

"Yes, yes of course," agrees Max still a little bewildered.

"Come my Lord," says the wise man, but John's eyes are still glued ahead as the man takes his arm. However he instantly grabs the man's hand to pull it off his arm. But still transfixed he forgets to let go, and the man drops to his knees more or less instantly, pleading, "Please my Lord you're hurting me."

John still doesn't speak. "My Lord you're breaking my hand," shouts the wise man.

"John," shouts Big Dan.

"Hem, what, yes, right sorry," apologises John letting go.

"Now tell me wise man," he asks sarcastically. "How is it I know what that is and you don't, oh wise one?"

There is a gasp from some, and a unison surprised, "You do" from the rest.

"Well yeah," answers John still a little bewildered himself. "You see that's mine, err, I mean, it belongs to me."

"It does," comes the gasps.

"Yep, that's what I said didn't I," shrugs John.

"You lie," shouts the wise man.

"That's impossible," shouts the other. "You've never seen it before, you could tell by your reaction, you just want to take it back to Taraten with you."

Maxie rushes over. *Don't you dare call my father a liar!"* she screams at the men.

John suddenly smiles broadly. "Ok then, how is it that I know what it is, and what it does, and you don't."

"Huh, I'd like to see that," sarcastically replies one of the men.

John grins. "Ok then, let's go. And please gentlemen, lead the way."

"But, but," stutter the men.

"No, no," interrupts Lord Tain. "You two will go up there with Lord Taraten, how dare you call him a liar." "He would be quite within his rights to ask for your heads, if he's telling the truth that is," he says staring at John.

The two men then cautiously make their way forward as John bends down and cupping his hands whispers in Maxie's ear, "Have you still got them things to put in your ears for blocking the sound?"

Maxie nods. "Good," he whispers. "Put them in, and make sure your mum and the boys have something too and Lord Tain I suppose. Now watch closely, and when I give you a nod. Ok?"

Maxie's mouth falls open as she turns and asks, "What on earth are you going to do?"

John just gives her a wink as he walks away replying, "Just what I said, show them what it does."

Big Dan nudges Cin. "Did you see that, I don't know what he's up to, but that is the first time I've ever seen Maxie look shocked."

"Hey John what are you going to do?" he shouts.

John doesn't turn back round, but clapping his hands together shouts back, "Hey trust me, this is my baby." Big Dan grumps, "I hate it when he says that, it always means he's up to something."

"What did he say to you dear?" asks Max.

Maxie still a little alarmed replies, "Gather round quickly, you as well my Lord."

The two wise men stop standing either side of the verum, and start to look more and more nervous as John approaches. John smiles a cheeky smile at them. "Hey don't look so worried boys, what's the worst that could happen. Seriously, you have my word this is no instrument of torture, and it doesn't posses the mind of the weak, or whatever."

He then takes a small object from his pocket and holds it up to show them. "What's that?" asks one of the wise men.

Winking John replies, "This awakens the beast."

The two men are too shocked to answer. "Nah only joking," John continues with a cheeky grin. "It's the key, without it my bike wouldn't work. This switches it on because this is a mode of transport."

He then jumps on the bike lifts it up and takes it off its stand. "What are you doing?" squeals one of the men. "Get of it now before you hurt yourself, if it falls it'll kill you."

"Hey trust me," says John slipping the key in the ignition.

"It fits," gasps the other wise man. "But how, just who are you."

John smiles to them kindly. "Whether there is a god or not is not for me to say," he tells them. "As I simply do not know. But what I can tell you for definite is, this was built by the hand of man. Now if you would kindly have those double doors opened, I'll show you exactly what it does."

One of the men then bows turns to the doors and shouts to have them opened. John looks over to Maxie and the others and winking gives a sly nod. They put their hands over their ears as John starts the bike, and with a twist of the throttle the engine growls loudly into life. Screams and hollers of fear and pain come from around the large room, as people fall to their knees holding their ears in terror. He gives it another rev, and sees the only people now standing are his friends, Lord Tain and Trace, with their hands clamped firmly over their ears. He takes his hand of the throttle for a moment and strokes the tank. "First time baby, I knew you could do it," he says aloud. "Now let's show them what you do."

He flicks into gear and after another quick rev takes off across the room and out the doors. He drives it down the hall until he comes to a wider part and doughnuts it clean around, and drives it back into the room stopping by his friends. He then switches it off. "What do ya think guys?" he asks excitedly. "Isn't it a beauty, this is my baby, 650 cc. Come on, say something then."

They all stand there speechless, even Woodnut can't raise a chuckle, until they hear Maxie shout, "Can I have a go next."

"No," they shout in unison.

"What is this?" asks John. "All shout together day, that's all you lot have done, are you practicing for a chorus line or something, its quite comical to be honest."

"What do you expect?" replies a flustered Max. "Are you sure that things safe, it doesn't look natural to me. You've never mentioned it before, and how did it get here anyway."

John puts the motorbike's stand down and gets off. "Now that's what I'd like to know," he says. "I never thought I'd see it again, it was stolen from outside my house about a year ago. I told the police, but nothing, I even got the insurance pay out for it, but how the hell did it get here."

"I hope you don't think it was someone from Tain that stole your verum," interrupts one of the wise men now standing by Trace.

"Be quiet you gonk," snaps John.

The man bows. "Oh thank you my Lord."

John shakes his head. "Why do I bother? No of course I don't you fool, you people don't even know where I'm from, wise man indeed, hu."

"Once again, you leave me speechless," sighs Lord Tain trying not to look too overwhelmed. "Truly I don't know what to think."

John jumps back on. "Come on then," he says with a wink to Tain. "Get on the back, I'll take you for a spin."

"But, but, I but," stutters Tain.

John laughs. "Come on don't be scared, you sound like a farmyard flurry clucking away."

"Well can you blame me," stutters Lord Tain. "I don't even know how it works. I mean how does it work? What makes it move? Why don't you fall over when it does?"

"Hey trust me," grins John. "You'll be ok I promise."

"Well maybe," he stammers. "Let me think about it a moment."

However he suddenly feels the bike get heavier on the back, and a little voice shouts, "You snooze you lose, me first, let's go Dad."

"Maxie get of that now," squeals Max.

"Hold on," shouts John quickly starting the bike and flicking it into gear.

Then with a screech of tyres they take off and out the room, shooting down the hallway with Maxie hollering with delight all the way.

"Oh wait till I get my hands on you two," shouts Max stamping her foot.

Trace taking his hands from his ears shakes his head in disbelief. "That kids as bad as he is."

"Yes we know," replies both Cin and Dan.

John and Maxie are now at the bottom of the hall, and stop at the large doors leading outside. "What do ya think?" he asks giving a wink.

Maxie doesn't answer but jumps off and flings the doors open and then jumps back on. A quick rev and they take off across the yard, much to the screams of horror from all the terrified warriors and others outside. "This is the best thing ever," squeals Maxie at the top of her voice.

John then turns around at the front gate, much to the relief of the two guards standing either side of it.

The others have now come out to watch and John pulls up beside them. He switches the engine off and Maxie gets off and stands there jumping up and down with excitement. "Right who's next," grins John.

"By all the stars," exclaims Lord Tain. "That thing moves as fast as a horse."

John gives out a wry laugh. "My friend if I'd went much slower I would have fallen over, this can go faster than you people can imagine."

Now Tain gives out a wry laugh and smiles. John just stares back and slowly nods. "You can't be serious John?" asks Cin frowning.

"Get on yu big lug, and I'll show ya," replies John winking again.

"You have got to be joking," puffs Cin. "I'd rather fight an army."

"Hu," says Max. "Call yourself fearless warriors."

"Come on then," she sighs climbing on the back. "Let's get it over with then."

"This will be alright wont it," she whispers.

"Yes of course," whispers John. "Now hold on tight my love." Max gives a squeal as they set off.

"Oh no," sighs Cin as Big Dan stands there shaking his head.

"What's the matter?" asks Trace.

"It looks as if we'll have to have a go now," announces Big Dan.

"Why's that?" asks Trace a little confused.

"Because," grumps Cin staring down at Maxie. "If we don't two certain females will make sure we never hear the last of it."

"Maybe not, you big scaredy flumps," giggles Maxie.

"See," frowns Cin.

"Well I think it looks marvellous fun," splutters Lord Tain. "My go next."

"My Lord," shouts Trace. "I do not think this is safe for you."

"Yes of course, how stupid of me," sighs Tain. "Obviously you want to go next and make sure it is safe for me, as you wish my friend."

"What?" exclaims Trace with a tremble in his voice.

"No, no, I insist," replies Lord Tain. "You were right as usual, I apologise, and it was very selfish of me to want to go first."

Trace shakes his head mumbling, "Me and my big mouth," much to the laughs of all.

John then returns and Trace reluctantly gets on the back, shaking like a leaf from the moment they set off until the moment he gets back the whole time screaming like a police siren, with everyone laughing once again. Max wipes tears from her eyes. "Come on, it wasn't that bad."

"You, you must be joking," stutters Trace.

Woodnut is laughing so hard he beats his fists on the ground, and between breaths gasps, "That's the first ooman, I've ever seen go away with yellow skin and come back with white."

"My Lord," says John. "Would you care to?"

"Would I ever," Tain gasps rushing over excitedly.

They are not away long and once back Lord Tain just sits there staring. "Sire, Sire, my Lord," shouts Trace. "Are you ok?"

Tain says nothing and Trace gives him a gentle shake. "My Lord."

"Ur bur, bur, bur, ur, b, b," is all that comes out of Lord Tain's mouth.

"What have you done to him?" shouts an alarmed Trace. "He's been bewitched."

Then snapping out of it Lord Tain pushes Trace away and starts to shout, "Again, again, please you must."

"As you wish," grins John. "But how about a bit further this time, through town perhaps, and maybe a bit faster if you're up for it."

"Am I," shouts Tain.

"John you be careful on that thing," shouts Max as they take off. They then fly out the main gate and up the main street, with people scattering in terror.

A few minutes later they reach the edge of the town and John pulls over. "Well, what do ya think?" asks John.

"Please, call me Suelan, and this is the most amazing thing I have ever done. I didn't know anything could go so fast."

"My friend," grins John. "You think that was fast, you have no idea, I'm barely in second gear. But unfortunately, I don't think there's anywhere around here long enough, or flat enough to really open it up. Lord Tain gulps loudly. "Really, but why do you need somewhere long and flat?"

John gives him an odd look replying, "If you hit a hole or a large rock, and come off at speed, or even slow for that matter, what do you think would happen."

"Oh yes I see," answers Tain. "How stupid of me, so this is quite a dangerous thing then, this, this, molar bike."

"That's motor bike," says John smiling. "And yes it can be, if you're not careful, and sometimes even then. So if you wish to walk back, I understand."

"Does this mean we can't go further?" asks Tain.

John grins. "Hang on."

"Marvellous," squeals Tain. "But don't go so fast, as a little further ahead you'll see a turning to the right, go down there and follow that track until we go right around the slope and past the farm. Then follow the small track down the rise to the left."

John then drives slowly along following the route he was told to follow and stops at the end of the small track. "Well John my friend," smiles Lord Tain. "Is this long and flat enough for you?"

John grins from ear to ear and replies, "Yep that'll do."

He then drives the bike onto a large carpet of purple and stops. Then getting off the bike he kneels down for a closer look at the small plants covering the large expanse of ground. The plants stand barely an inch and a half high, and are an iridescent purple in colour. "This is amazing stuff," he says.

Lord Tain shrugs. "It's only purple bud and it's cultivated by the farmer up there."

"Oh I see," nods John. "Are you sure we should be on it then?"

"Yes, yes, it's ok," nods Tain. "It was harvested weeks ago, it's just the plants that are left now, and they won't fruit again now until next year, don't worry it's very hardy stuff."

John then jumps back on the bike and starts it up, and with a quick rev takes off across the carpet of purple, getting faster and faster with Lord Tain screaming like a siren as they go. After a few lengths up and down the large expanse John pulls up. "Well," he chuckles. "Was that fast enough for you?"

Lord Tain can hardly speak, "I, I, thought I was going to die. I, I, thought at that speed, we wouldn't be able to breathe. Everything was a blur, how do you know where we are going, or, or, when to stop."

John just smiles, shrugs then climbs off pushing Tain forwards, and then climbs on the back. "What are you doing?" squeals Tain, more than just a little alarmed.

"I just thought you'd like to learn to drive it," shrugs John "It's not hard."

"But, but," stutters Lord Tain.

Morning then turns into afternoon and they see Max, Dan, Trace and the others walking down the track towards them, and they drive over to meet them. "M, m, my Lord," gasps Trace. "You're, you're steering that beast."

"Yes that's right," smiles Lord Tain now hardly able to contain his excitement and pride at his friend seeing him drive up.

"We thought something had happened to you," says Cin.

"Yes," nods Big Dan. "We thought you'd had an accident."

Max and Maxie just stand there scowling. "Oops sorry," apologises John. "I guess we just forgot the time. How did you find us anyway?"

"What do you think these things are for on the side of my head, decoration," frowns Max.

"This is a truly marvellous day," announces Lord Tain. "We must celebrate tonight, and maybe, we could do this again tomorrow John."

John nods. "Sounds good to me, with only a couple of minor problems."

"And what would they be my friend?" asks Tain.

"Well," continues John. "I promised my greenem friends in the rainforest, we would all go and talk with them."

"Hmm, yes of course," nods Tain. "But surely another day or so won't make a difference would it."

"What do you say young greenem?" he asks, looking down at Woodnut.

Woodnut unsure how to reply simply shrugs then tries to smile politely. "There you see," chuckles Tain. "I'm sure it's all going to work out for the best in the end."

John cocks his head to the side and replies, "And what if your home, your land, your entire province and its people, was hanging in the balance. And you didn't know whether everything and everyone you loved and cherished, were to be destroyed or not, would you like to be left waiting in limbo like that."

Lord Tain heaves a heavy sighs. "Now you put it like that, of course, we shall go after breakfast in the morning. You know, and this may sound silly, but I never realised the enormity of it all, until now, and you put it like that."

"Anyway," he then sighs snapping out of it. "What was the other problem you mentioned?"

"Oh yes," nods John. "It's the bike, it had a full tank when we started, and it's still about three quarters full, but."

"I'm sorry John," interrupts Tain. "But I'm not sure I follow."

John opens the petrol cap and rocks the bike a little. "You see that liquid in there, that's petrol and it's that, that the bike runs on, it powers it so to say, and when it's gone, I wouldn't know where to get anymore."

Lord Tain nods hand on chin. "Oh I see," he answers. "That would be a pity, but still, this is a truly magical beast, surely we could find an alternative somewhere."

"Well I suppose," shrugs John. "Nothing's impossible I guess, but it might take you a lifetime to work it out."

"Lift me up John," asks Woodnut. "Let me put my hand in that liquid."

"No sorry dude," replies John. "This stuff is quite poisonous."

"I'll just dip my fingertip in then," answers Woodnut.

"If you're sure," sighs John lifting him up.

Woodnut then dips his finger in then jumps back down. "This is very similar to a poison found in small pools in a place I know," he tells them. "Black as night it is, and a lot thicker, very rare though thankfully. And it's been the death of many a poor animal that has stumbled into it, ooman's also."

"That's oil," answers John. "It's actually refined from that, and is used itself to keep the engine lubricated."

"Excellent," shouts Lord Tain. "We can make some more of this fuel stuff then."

"Sorry," sighs John shaking his head. "That's way above my head, refining oil, I wouldn't have a clue. I wouldn't even know where to begin."

"Oh don't be such a pessimist John," replies Tain. "It's a start, and that's more than we had a moment ago, if you give up that easily on everything, I'm surprised you get anything done. We'll talk further about this later, but first I'm starting to get a little peckish, how about we all head back."

John doesn't reply to the question but points to the bike, winks and says, "My Lord, shall we."

"John my friend," smiles Tain broadly. "I've told you please call me Suelan. And that would be marvellous, but would you drive it up the path, and maybe I could drive it through the town, let my people see me driving it you know."

"Sounds good to me," replies John.

"I'll come back for you lot in turn if you like," he continues.

"No," comes the unanimous response, all but Maxie and Woodnut that is, who seem very excited at the prospect.

"No chance," says Max frowning at the pair of them. "You two can walk back with us."

"Aw but Mum please," pleads Maxie.

"Aw but nothing," answers Max. "I don't trust that thing; it's not natural to go that fast, now not another word from either of you."

John starts the bike much to the scowls from Max, and takes off with Tain on the back. "Did I hear right," stutters Trace. "My Lord asked your Lord to call him Suelan. I must say this is unheard of. I once saw a man executed for less, your friend must have made quite an impression."

"Yes," nods Big Dan. "He has that effect."

As Lord Tain drives slowly through the town John shouts in his ear, "Press that button there."

Lord Tain nods and proceeds to press the small button. Even from behind John can see him smile with delight, as the horn sounds, making the transfixed people jump and cower even more. Then Lord Tain shouts with delight as he pulls up outside the main door in his courtyard. A large group of guards and warriors have gathered, and he cannot resist one last press of the horn before switching the key off and handing it back to John. They get off and Lord Tain stands there admiring it. "This is such a great thing," he says in awe. "It's a miracle, a true marvel of man. I still can't believe it, it's like some sort of dream, and to think I rode it. This is a day I will remember with fondness, delight and pride for the rest of my life."

Some of the guards rush over shouting, "My Lord, My Lord, are you ok. We saw you on the front of that devilry. We weren't sure what was happening to you."

"Oh it was nothing," replies Tain nonchalantly now full of bravado. "I was simply driving it back. Lord Taraten taught me how to tame the beast and make it do my bidding, isn't that right John."

John smiles and nods. "Yes and may I say, I couldn't have done better myself."

"If you're ok then Sire," reply the men backing away nervously.

"Yes, yes, you may go," he tells them.

"It's a pity we will not get another go tomorrow," he then sighs. "It's an incredible feeling."

John nods. "Don't worry, there'll be plenty of other times in the future I'm sure."

"What do you mean?" asks Tain.

John just throws him the key, "It's yours, you can have it, call it, a gesture of good will."

"No, no, I couldn't," splutters Tain. "You have proven beyond any shadow of a doubt it's yours. We thought it was made by gods. It's such a thing, it is one of a kind, and its value must be immeasurable. I couldn't even begin to imagine its worth; it must be easily more than my province itself. I, I, couldn't."

He then stretches his hand out offering the key back. John smiles at him kindly and closes Tain's hand around the key replying, "I wouldn't say it's worth your whole province, but maybe, just maybe, a rainforest on the edge of it perhaps."

Lord Tain puts his hand on his chin and cocks his head to the side, and stands there silent for a few minutes deep in thought. "Well," he mutters aloud.

"To own such a thing, even without this fuel stuff. It would be a monument, a shining light, a monolith to the endless possibilities and creativity of man. It would show us all that nothing is impossible, and that progress is in our own hands."

"Hmm, yes, yes, I'll do it," he shouts excitedly. "You have a deal, I'll get the paperwork drawn up straight away, the forest is yours and everything in it and around it, to do with as you please, none shall enter without your permission."

"What's the matter John?" he then asks seeing John frowning. "Have you changed your mind?"

"No, no, not at all," answers John. "It's just that, all this progress you're striving for, you know it's not always a good thing. I've seen at first hand the effects of progress back in my own land, bikes like that, cars, millions of cars all running on oil. And I'm afraid, with the best intentions in the world, greed can take over to the determent of the people, places, animals, land, even the earth itself I'm afraid."

Lord Tain gives out a wry laugh. "Surely you jest, if there were such a place we would have heard of it."

"No," replies John shaking his head. "No you wouldn't. Now why don't we go somewhere private, for a sit down and I'll tell you a story."

Lord Tain then takes him to his private quarters and tells the guards on the door, they are not to be disturbed by anyone, under any circumstance. They are there for hours with John telling him all about himself, and his marvellous story, and the world in which he came from, and all its problems. Right up until the point he entered his province. Finally the door opens and they head down for something to eat. As they walk down Lord Tain whispers, "I, I, I'm speechless."

Then he stutters, "You are a revelation my friend, I knew there was something about you, as soon as I saw you. But you have my word, we will set laws in motion to make sure we don't make the mistakes of your people, or try anyway, but there has to be little progress John."

John nods. "Yes of course, you are very wise. But let it go at it's own pace, and just make sure it really is for the good of all, and not just for the greed of the few. We destroyed so much of our planet, especially the forests. Before we even realised just how important and significant they were. As I told you earlier, everything from cures and medicines, to new food sources. All gone before we even knew they existed, even the air we breathe, as it even controls the climate we live in. So please, I would still like to take you to visit the forest tomorrow."

"Yes, yes of course," agrees Lord Tain. "After what you've told me, I wouldn't miss it for the world. Trace and I shall accompany you in the morning as planned."

They then get to the hall where the others are all tucking into dinner. "Hey John, where've you been," splutters Cin. "We thought you'd disappeared, come and sit down, this food's great."

John and Lord Tain sit down. "Sorry guys," apologises John. "I guess we just got carried away gabbing."

"Now there's an under statement," mutters Tain under his breath.

"Well what's happening now John?" asks Max.

John shrugs and replies, "In the morning we head for the forest, nothing's changed that. Are you not having anything to eat Woodnut?"

Woodnut giggles, "There's nothing here that takes my fancy."

John winks. "So why don't you go out to the orchard and take a little something under the mood trees. Come on I'll keep you company, if that's all right with the rest of you that is."

Everybody nods politely, and John and Woodnut proceed outside. Big Dan leans over to Cin and whispers, "He's up to something."

"Isn't he always," Cin whispers back.

Outside John sits down under one of the mood trees and leans against it, as does Woodnut, who instantly buries his feet deep in the earth. "So John," asks Woodnut. "What do you want?"

"Ah pleased you asked," replies John smiling. "I know its short notice, but do you think you could get word to your people, back at the rainforest."

Woodnut shrugs. "Yes of course, there's a female long wing in the tree next to us, but it'll take it all day to get there."

"That's ok," answers John. "I would like to impress Lord Tain and Trace with your peoples' knowledge and wisdom, everything from medicine to science, but without giving too much away, know what I mean. Oh, and full formalities from your elders when we meet, they seem to like that type of thing. Oh, and you know Lord Tain loves a good argument, if you know any greenem that like to argue."

Woodnut starts to giggle uncontrollably, "Some of the elder greenem have been known to argue for centuries, literally, all in fun of course."

"Do you think you could organise that?" asks John.

Woodnut replies smiling, "Consider it done." He then continues, "But tell me truthfully John, do you think we can honestly change his mind."

"Oh yes, sorry," apologises John a little puzzled. "It doesn't matter now."

"Of course it matters John," snaps Woodnut. "That's why we're here."

John shrugs. "Oh, no, sorry pal, you don't understand. I should have explained better. It's sorted, it's mine, it belongs to me now."

"John stop it, please," snaps Woodnut. "That's just not funny."

"Who's joking?" says John winking. "Let's just say I've done a swap. The whole forest is now mine, everything in it and even around it, it now all belongs to me, cool eh?"

"R, really," squeals Woodnut. John just nods.

"Yippee," shouts Woodnut pulling his feet out of the ground. He then jumps on John throwing his little arms around him.

"But, but, how," he stutters. "What on earth could you have swapped? I mean, I can't even begin to imagine."

John gives him another wink. "Let's just say, he's now the proud new owner of a shiny new motorbike."

"John are you sure," gasps Woodnut. "That is a truly kingly gift; I've never seen its like."

"Yes now you put it like that, maybe you're right," smirks John. "Maybe I should take it bac. What do you think?"

Woodnut's face suddenly turns to horror. "N, no, I didn't mean it like that."

John starts to laugh and gives him a friendly shove and grins. "No I'm joking."

Woodnut sniggers a relieved snigger. A puzzled look then comes on his face and he asks, "So if the ancient forest is now yours, why do we still have to take them there?"

John looks to him a little more seriously now replying, "Well my friend the trouble is, people die and memories fade. We have to educate them, for the future protection of the forest, and your people."

"Oh, yes of course," nods Woodnut. "You are very wise as always."

They both turn on hearing a familiar giggle, and see Maxie coming towards them. "What are you two up to?" she shouts cheekily. "And don't tell me you're not."

John gets up. "I'll leave it with you then," he says to Woodnut.

"Excellent timing young lady," he says on passing Maxie. "Woodnut will fill you in, and you can give him a hand if needed."

John then goes back into the hall and sits back down with the others.

"Everything sorted?" asks Dan.

John grins. "Hum, I don't know what you mean. I was just chatting with Woodnut."

"Yes of course," frowns Big Dan.

"Now," says Lord Tain enthusiastically. "About tonight, I was thinking another party. Maybe in one of the smaller halls with just a handful of friends. How does that sound to everyone?"

They all smile and nod in agreement. "There's only one thing I'm not sure about," Tain continues nervously. "The witch, maybe I should ask her tonight. I upset her last night by not inviting her. I don't think it would be wise to upset her two days on the trot. After all, you saw what she did to you John."

John smiles. Suelan my friend, she's just some mad old lady, who can do a few tricks. She can't hurt anybody."

Cin shakes his head. "I don't know John that must have been mighty powerful magic last night, to move you across the room like that."

"Hmm yes I agree with Cin," nods Big Dan.

Woodnut and the girls now back at the table start to giggle, much to the frowns of Big Dan. "Do you know something?" he asks.

"No, no, not us," Maxie answers.

"Hmm," grumps Big Dan suspiciously running his fingers through his beard.

"Well I'll tell you what," sighs John. "If it'll make you feel better, you can invite her and we'll be happy to see her, I suppose. She was good entertainment anyway. But I still say she's just some senile old crone." Lord Tain claps his hand and replies, "Excellent, I'll send someone straight away."

"Does she live far?" asks John.

"No not really," answersTrace. "Why?"

John grins. "Why don't you play the old crone at her own game Suelan my friend? Surprise and shock her, show her the magic you've learned yourself."

"What do you mean John?" asks Tain.

John shrugs, winks and replies, "Why don't you go and invite her yourself?"

"Oh yes, I see what you mean now," says Tain excitedly. "I could go on the verum verum, err I mean molar bike."

John nonchalantly nods but then shouts, "Hang on, verum verum, and you say it was the old crone who called it that. Verum eh, hmm, I wonder. She can't have meant vroom vroom surely. Yes, maybe you should invite her."

"Yes, yes I will, I'll go right now," answers Lord Tain excitedly heading out the door.

"Oh and be careful on that thing," shouts John.

"Oh my god no," he then exclaims.

"What is it?" asks Max.

John gasps, "I think I've just turned into my parents." Everyone laughs.

"I had such apprehension about coming here originally," says Cin taking another mouthful of ale. "But now I'm so glad we did. It's such a good feeling going somewhere and meeting nice, honest, genuine people for a change. Especially after our experiences in the last province."

Trace gives out a wry laugh, "What were you expecting to find here? On the whole we are a civilised peaceful people."

"Well," continues Cin. "Lane, Dan and I were expecting to have to fight and kill, either all your men, or your Lord, in order to save our friends home in the forest."

Trace laughs again, "What four of you, a woman a child and a greenem. And I mean no disrespect there, but please."

Cin's face starts to change from smiles to anger but Big Dan pats him on the shoulder. "Calm down my friend, these are friends now. And it seems to me we won over twenty of your men back at the forest without even raising a sword, with the exception of Lane that is."

"Oh well, yes I suppose," stutters Trace.

John starts to laugh, "He's got you there."

"Well who knows," laughs Trace putting his hands up.

"But know this," growls Cin turning to Trace. "My whole life no man or army has ever bested me, bar one, and I now stand with him."

Trace leans back giving out a sigh and looking to Big Dan. Big Dan just nods his head.

"Yeah," shouts a little voice.

"It was me and Woodnut wasn't it," shouts Maxie.

"Yeah easy," giggles Woodnut.

"Oh it was, was it," frowns Cin getting up.

"Yeah," they shout again before taking off out the room hotly pursued by Cin.

Trace a little confused asks, "They will be alright won't they?"

"Yes of course," answers Max. "They won't hurt him too much."

"Oh, that's alright then," replies Trace still a little puzzled.

"Don't worry," bellows Big Dan. "They're just having a bit of fun. Do your children not play or tease you?"

"They are taught to respect their elders and betters," answers Trace.

"As are ours," nods Big Dan. "But there's nothing wrong with a bit of fun and games now and again aye." "Young or old," he chuckles loudly slapping Trace on the back, and nearly knocking him over the table.

"Oops sorry," he bellows again.

"Yes, yes of course," nods Trace grimacing slightly as he puts his shoulder back and straightens his back up. "Now if you'll excuse me, I have to organise things for this evening. I'll see you in a couple of hours then."

"So what were you and Woodnut up to out there?" Max asks John.

"Yes John, do tell please," says Dan.

John then tells them his agreement with Lord Tain, and their conversation in Lord Tain's private quarters. "Now this is excellent news," booms Big Dan. "Wait till I tell Cin, he'll be over the moons. Tonight there really will be cause to celebrate, I'll go and tell him the good news straight away."

A few hours later and they are taken to the small hall where they are greeted by Glendra. "My Lords and Ladies," he says and bows as they approach. "It's good to see you."

"And you," replies Max. "You will be joining us this evening won't you?"

"Hmm, err," stutters Glendra.

"Yes of course you will," says Max smiling as she links arms with him. Max then leads the way with a panicking Glendra still on her arm. Then on entering the room he turns nervously to Lord Tain shrugs and bows. Lord Tain stands up and says, "Excellent, come sit down your places are prepared."

They all sit down on the large table with Lord Tain and a couple of others.

"Get yourself a chair then," Max tells Glendra.

Glendra bows and looks to Lord Tain who waves his hand at him saying, "Do as she tells you man."

Lord Tain then stands back up. "May I introduce you to my wife Yarin. Yarin this is Lord and Lady Taraten. Also known as John and Max, and this is their beautiful daughter Maxie. And the little fellow giggling away beside her is Mr Woodnut Greenfurn, their friend, and representative of the greenem. And these other two large gentlemen are Big Dan, leader of the Luguvalio warriors and Cin, leader of the Voreda warriors."

Yarin smiles and bows to them all in turn. "A pleasure to meet you," says John bowing to her.

"And you my Lord," she answers. "I must admit, I was more than just a little intrigued, when I was told the news of your visit, and please I mean no disrespect, but you are nothing like I expected."

"None taken my Lady, and please call me John," says John. "And may I ask how your mother is? Your husband informed us she had taken ill."

Tears suddenly come to Yarin's eyes. "I'm afraid she is gravely ill with a terrible fever. My father and our best physician are looking after her as we speak. But they say they have done as much as they can. I'm just back tonight to pick up some fresh clothes and will be returning to her bedside in the morning. So you will have to excuse me if I don't seem very happy."

Max takes her hand. "That's awful, you poor thing," she says softly.

Maxie and Woodnut are whispering back and forward until finally Maxie turns to Yarin and says. "Please my Lady, if you like Woodnut and I could go with you tomorrow. I think maybe we could help your mum get better, or at least ease her suffering."

Yarin wipes a tear from her eye and smiles kindly and replies, "Thank you my dear, but I think my healer knows a little more than you and your pet."

Maxie just shrugs. "As you wish."

Hearing this Big Dan turns to Yarin and says, "My Lady, I would just like to tell you that that young lady there, and our friend Woodnut, have an understanding of medicines and cures, the like of which most physicians could only dream of. This is an offer you should grasp with both hands."

Yarin sits there stunned a little unsure what to reply. Max takes her hand again. "It is as he said," she tells her softly. "Trust them as they will help, and if she's as ill as you say, what harm could it do anyway."

"Don't worry," Maxie tells her. "Woodnut and I will have your mum feeling fine in no time at all." Yarin dries her eyes and simply nods then sees Maxie take something from her pocket before she leans over the table and hands it to herself. "Here swallow this," she tells her.

"Why what is it?" asks Yarin.

Maxie sits back down and replies, "It'll give you back the strength you've lost while caring for your mum."

Yarin cautiously pops it in her mouth and begrudgingly swallows it. "Well," asks Cin a few minutes later. "Do you feel anything?"

Maxie sighs, "It doesn't work that quickly silly, you've got to give it time to work. Huh men."

"Y, yes I knew that," stutters Cin.

"Ignore him my Lady," Maxie tells her. "Try and eat something, by the time you've finished your meal it'll have started to work, and you will start to feel better.

John looks around the small room and the dozen or so people and a little puzzled asks, "Did you invite the old lady, Suelan?"

"Yes," nods Lord Tain. "It was the first time I've ever seen her lost for words. You should have seen her face when I turned up outside her home on the verum verum."

"You did what," gasps Yarin. "I heard, I mean, someone told me, but I never thought for a moment it was true."

Then a look of horror comes across her face. "Oh no you haven't invited the witch have you, please tell me I heard wrong. She gives me the creeps, and I don't mind telling you."

"Yes my dear, I had to," answers Lord Tain. "She's here somewhere in the building, I don't know where. You now how she likes to make a dramatic entrance."

Yarin gives a shudder. "Some of the things that old witch does, the way she just appears in a flash of smoke. It's not natural I tell you, she'll be the death of someone one of these days, you mark my words."

Maxie giggles as she puts on her glasses. "Don't worry about her my Lady, she's harmless, she wouldn't harm anyone. She just likes to be silly and she'll be leaving soon anyway."

"What do you mean child?" asks Yarin. "And have you a problem with your eyes."

"No Miss," answers Maxie. "And the old woman's life is destined to take another path I feel. Now if you would all care to cover your eyes a moment she's about to come in, and is creeping up to the door as we speak."

Everybody then looks at them oddly as Max, Dan and Cin put their hands over their eyes as instructed. Then most giggle until with a blinding flash of light and a puff of smoke the door bursts open and the witch appears. There are also gasps and yells from around the room with some even falling backwards off their chairs. Max, Dan, Cin and John then uncover their eyes to see the old witch standing in the middle of the room cackling away. John frowns at her, "You just couldn't resist it could you."

The old woman just smirks. "I thought we had an agreement," frowns John. "You haven't got anymore of that mixture have you, some more you forgot to tell me about."

"No," she shouts putting her tongue out. "I had a little mix left and thought I might as well use it up."

"Hmm," grins John suspiciously. "Come and sit down."

"Don't you tell me what to do," she cackles. "Or I'll put a hex on you boy."

John sighs. "Ok, just stand over there then. I just thought you'd like to sit here with us that's all."

Yarin whispers to her husband, "What was all that about? Are you sure it's safe for him to talk to her like that?"

"My dear," whispers Tain. "I think the old witch has finally met her match. He is the only person I have ever seen her remotely scared of. I'm still not sure why myself though."

"Ok, you may have the pleasure of my company," the old witch cackles dancing from one foot to the other. However she then does a handstand baring her all, and then proceeds to walk over on her hands. "No please," shouts Cin.

"And that's not normal behaviour," shouts Big Dan.

"Please God no," gasps John turning away. Max, Maxie and Woodnut just start to giggle terribly at their reactions, with most of the other people there too scared to say anything and they simply turn their heads away. "Can you not just sit down properly, like normal people you old crone," bellows Cin as the witch flips back over and on to a chair at the table.

"Don't think I'm scared of you, you big oaf," she shouts. "You be careful or I'll turn you into something even more horrible than you already are."

Cin leans forward and growls at the old woman who promptly makes a face at him and tells him, "If you are half as fit as me at this age you would be lucky."

"And you," growls Cin. "Are a good advertisement for ignoring the old."

John, Woodnut and Maxie are curled up in fits of laughter. "Now how about a drink everyone," shouts Lord Tain nervously trying to settle things down.

Ale is served to all. "Can I have a hot sing root please?" asks John.

"Yes, yes of course," answers Tain a little puzzled. Food ale and sing root flow freely and soon laughter and merriment is coming from all around the room. Yarin whispers to Max, "May I asks you, how did your daughter know the old witch was coming and know she'd do that?"

Max shrugs. "I've no idea. How do you feel after taking her medicine?"

"Now you mention it," Yarin replies. "I, I actually do feel quite, well wonderful, what was that stuff. And what did she mean by the old woman's life taking another path."

"To answer both your questions," says Max politely. "I've no idea, but I do know she learns all about healing and medicine from the greenem, truly amazing little creatures. But as for what she said about the old lady, my daughter is rather special and she seems to know things. Things you would think impossible to know, and she is seldom wrong. We have come to trust her judgment completely." Yarin sits there open mouthed.

Everybody gets steadily more drunk as the evening continues, all except the old witch, as no one is quite sure if she's sober or drunk at the best of times. Later still the old crone gets up and starts to dance around the room singing all the time, "Ninginy nanginy noo."

Then after a few cart wheels and a handstand she shouts to all, "Who will challenge me to a drinking competition, and perhaps a small wager."

"Did I hear right?" asks Big Dan.

"For a moment there I thought Lane was here," he sighs.

"No my friend," replies Cin. "It's the old witch."

"Be careful," Tain tells them. "Do not let her looks deceive you, she has never been bettered in a drinking competition."

Big Dan running his fingers through his beard shouts to John, "Did you hear that, sounds like someone else I know, wouldn't you say."

John sits there deep in thought with his hand on his chin, until finally he stands up and shouts, "Yes old woman, I will challenge you."

"Tell your husband to sit down," Yarin tells Max. "He won't win."

Max smiles. "Don't worry he knows what he's doing."

"Excellent," cackles the old woman rubbing her hands together.

The table is then cleared and everyone gathers round as John and the old crone sit facing each other and ale is placed in front of each of them. "Are you ready?" she cackles.

"No," grins John. "Not quite, just to make it a bit fairer on you, you being so old and frail."

"What do you mean by that?" snaps the old witch putting her elbow on the table and her arm up. "Come on an arm wrestle, I bet I can take you."

"Quiet," shouts John. "I thought this was a drinking competition. Now I will drink the finest ale they have here, and just to make it fairer, as I said, can someone bring a drink for this old woman."

"That's old crone to you boy," snaps the woman.

Heaving a heavy sigh John continues, "Ok, if someone could get this old crooonne some sing root, she can do the competition drinking nothing but that, a sign of my goodwill you could say."

"John my friend," shouts Tain pulling him nearly off the chair. "What do you think you're doing, are you mad, this is lunacy?"

"No madder than her," replies John and he winks. "Hey trust me."

A look of horror then comes across the old crones face as she is handed a large mug of hot sing root. "What's the matter?" asks John with a sly wink. "Not frightened are you."

"I thought this was a drinking competition," shouts the old woman.

"It is," shrugs John. "But you didn't state what we should drink. I'm giving you a chance, there's no problem is there, there's nothing you want to tell us."

The old crone leans across the table. "You don't play fair," she tells him putting her tongue out. "I'm not doing it." She then jumps to her feet and starts to dance around the room again, making everyone rush back to their seats.

Trace scratches his head and turning to Cin and Big Dan asks, "What just happened there? That was the oddest thing I've ever seen, she would've won hands down. Well that just proves it, she's as mad as they come."

Both Cin and Big Dan just smile broadly as John shouts over to the old woman, "Come here and sit down please."

The old crone reluctantly dances over, "What do you want now?" she asks. "I'm not playing with you."

"Please," asks John softly. "Sit let's talk a while, just you and I. We'll have a mug of sing root together as friends. What do you say?"

"You are different," says the old crone sitting down cautiously. "I don't know why you want me to have sing root with you, it'll have no effect on me."

"No of course not," replies John with a cheeky wink. "Just as it won't have an effect on me."

The old woman gives out a wry chuckle. "You aren't like the people of these lands, where are you from?" she asks.

John smiles and nods. "I could say the same of you my dear."

"Huh, be like that," grumps the old crone before she pulls a face. "You ninginey, nanginey, noo."

"Hey," laughs John. "Anyway put them together and what have you got."

"You talk rubbish," complains the old witch.

"Again," replies John with a cheeky wink. "No more than you, now come on, let's have a drink and talk. What do you remember about your childhood and family? How long have you been in this land?"

"If I told you," she answers. "You would think I was madder than I already am."

"Please," continues John. "Humour me, I might surprise you."

"As I've told you," she tells him quietly. "I don't remember much of my family, just fragments as I was very young before I was lost. But young as I was I do remember my home being so much different than anything here."

John then sits quietly nodding as the old woman tells him the little bits she remember, but with her occasionally slipping into her usual mad ways and having to be coaxed back until finally. "I've had enough. I've had too much to drink, and now I must dance and sing," she announces screwing her face up.

John smiles, bows his head and as she dances away he shouts, "But I thought sing root would have no effect on you."

Loud cheers come up from around the hall as two drunken men shake arms in the middle and proceed to fight. John nudges Lord Tain. "Do you think we should stop them?"

Tain looks at him oddly. "Why, it's just some of my warriors blowing off a bit of steam, testing their prowess and fighting skills."

"Yes of course," answers John now a little puzzled himself. "But what happens if someone gets hurt or cut, burst nose, split lip and that, are they not bothered they might bleed too much."

Now Lord Tain is looking at him oddly as Max whispers in John's ear, "Thick skin remember dear, besides lips and noses never bleed that much."

John shakes his head muttering, "Nation of odd bods."

"What?" says Max frowning. John just smiles and pulls a face.

Big Dan nudges Cin. "Look entertainment my friend, do you think we might get a chance to fight later." "Yes let's hope so," replies Cin excitedly slapping his hands together.

Several fights and lots of drunken cheers later, and a large Tain warrior stands triumphant and proceeds over to them on the head table. "Obviously our turn," says Cin excitedly to Big Dan.

"Let's hope so," laughs Big Dan. "You warm them up for me, and I'll show them how to fight properly." Cin chuckles, "Let's leave it up to them. I can't wait, I haven't had a good fight in years."

"Yes," sighs Big Dan. "It's a pity Lane's not here, he loves a good fight, and there's none better in our whole province."

Cin bows his head in sadness. Then the large Tain warrior stops in front of the table and bows. "My Lords and Ladies," he slurs in a slow voice. Then he turns and looks back around at his drunken friends, who all snigger waving him on so he turns back round now sniggering himself. John still quite sober and a little suspicious nods to the warrior. "Go on then spit it out."

"What do you mean my Lord?" asks the warrior.

"Why have you come over?" asks John. "Your friends have obviously put you up to something."

"N, no my Lord," stutters the warrior. "It's just I've won all our warriors here and I thought, well, maybe yours might want to test themselves."

"Yes," Dan and Cin shout in unison.

Ignoring both the warrior sniggers, "My Lady would you care to."

Big Dan and Cin's cheers stop instantly and John gasps, "What. You, you want to fight my wife. Really, why."

He then turns to Lord Tain. "Is this how your people greet visitors, by wanting to beat up their wives."

The large slow warrior's face suddenly turns to horror as the stupidity of his drunken joke dawns on him. "I'm sorry my Lords and Ladies," he stutters. "It's just she wears the leathers of a warrior and well she's."

"Silence," shouts lord Tain. "You dare to insult Lady Taraten, on this evening of celebration. You can see she is a frail slip of a woman."

"What the hell do you mean by that?" explodes Max "I earned my leathers. I've been to battle, and I've battered many a so called warrior."

John shrinks down in his chair screwing his face up. "Keep me out of this," he mutters.

"Well my Lady," stutters Lord Tain. "I just thought."

"You just thought what," snaps Max. "I'd be too frightened to fight some drunken oaf."

"I've beaten bigger than him," she hollers before she gets up throwing off her shirt revealing a skimpy top and leathers.

John puts his hand over his eyes, "If you get hurt don't think I'm going to jump in and help you."

"Yeah my Lady," sniggers the warrior. "You should listen to your husband before you get hurt."

"No you muppet. I was talking to you," John shouts to the warrior. Max is so mad she doesn't even go around the table, but runs over it then she stands in the middle with her fists raised high. A loud cheer goes up around the room. Trace then starts to get up, "I'm going to stop this madness."

"No," shouts Cin and Dan in unison.

Trace looks at them oddly. "What is it?" he asks.

"Well," sighs Cin. "She looks, very, very mad."

Big Dan shakes his head. "We've learned when our Max gets that mad, the best thing to do is keep well out of the way, if you value your teeth that is." Trace looks at them both unsure whether to believe them or not.

"Well then," shouts Max. "Are you going to fight or just stand there looking stupid?"

The warrior turns to his friends. "Did you hear what she said to me?"

But they don't get the chance to answer as a loud yell comes from Max as she swings as hard as she can, catching the warrior clean in the mouth, as he turns back round. The warrior staggers back slightly before shaking his head. "You hit me," he splutters. "And look," he grunts, spitting out a tooth.

Max takes a loud gulp, and she suddenly thinks to herself, "Maybe this wasn't such a good idea."

"She's done it now," gasps Trace.

"What do you mean?" asks Big Dan.

"Well," continues Trace. "That large fellow she just slugged, let's say, he may not be the sharpest sword in the armoury. And that's maybe why, but he can take a blow to the head like no man. That's how he got his name, and that's why he always wins on nights like this."

"Oh I see, what is his name?" asks Big Dan.

Trace chuckles, "Stony, because he has a head like stone."

"Hmm, yes I see," nods Big Dan now deep in thought.

The warrior lunges forward swinging at Max but she ducks his swing and the warrior stumbles forwards slightly. Max counters with a left to the stomach and a right to the head. The warrior swings wildly and catches her in the left eye sending her flying backwards landing across the table between Cin and Big Dan. She shakes her head and lays there a little stunned. "Having fun Max," grins Cin.

Max just grunts shaking her head. Big Dan cups one hand over his mouth and silently mouths to her, "Ching Ching."

"What?" asks Max looking at him upside down.

"Captain Ching Ching," whispers Big Dan winking.

He then grabs her by the shoulders and throws her back up off the table and onto her feet. "You're a warrior of Luguvalio woman, get back over there and act like one, that's an order," he booms.

Max turns and bows to him. "Yes Sir."

She then marches back to the centre of the room and the warrior, raising her fists again. "Is that the best you've got," she shouts.

The large slow warrior scratches his head but replies, "No not really Miss, how's your eye. I take it you want a matching set."

"Huh," grunts Max. "Only if your arms are longer than my leg."

The warrior then looks at her confused, and takes a sudden jab. But Max takes a step back with her right leg, and quick as she can throws it forwards and up, as hard as she can, catching the warrior perfectly between the legs. A loud and unanimous, "Ooh" rings around the room and the warrior drops to his knees clutching his privates. Max then clenches both hands together and swings them as hard as she can at the man's unguarded chin, catching him perfectly, and the warrior is knocked onto his side. Now semi conscious and curled in a ball he gasps, "No more, please, I. I give up, no more."

A loud cheer goes up around the room from all there. Big Dan rushes over and throws Max up onto his shoulder, and proceeds to strut around the room shouting as excitedly as if he'd won himself. "Luguvalio's finest, unbeaten and undefeated, in all fights. Lord Luguvalio's personal guard, I give you my Lady Max," he booms. "Come on," he booms again.

Another loud cheer goes up. Trace shakes his head and nudges Cin. "And I thought you were joking."

Cin shakes his head. "What do you think they give her the leathers for, looking cute and being pretty?"

Trace sighs. "Obviously not."

With all the excitement and frivolity going on around the room no one but Woodnut notices the old crone dance and skip up to Lady Yarin who suddenly starts to get very nervous. "Please," she asks nicely. "Could you not talk to someone else please? Lord Taraten perhaps, he likes talking to you."

"Oh like that is it," cackles the old crone pulling out her pendant. "How about a little fun."

Woodnut runs over to Maxie who is busy giving her mum something to take the pain from her eye and reduce the swelling a little. "Maxie, Maxie," he shouts.

"Quickly over there," he shouts pointing to the old woman. "She's terrifying that nice lady."

"Right," shouts Maxie running over before she steps in front of the old crone and grabs her pendant. "Leave this lady alone. It's not funny, you know she's scared of you. Go and play with someone else."

"Let go of my necklace now," shouts the old woman.

"Or you'll be next," she cackles. "I'll put a hex on you."

But Maxie's eyes turn to fire as she let's go of the pendant. "I've warned you before," she tells her quietly but angrily. "Do not threaten me."

"Get out of my way silly girl, I'm only having a bit of fun," the old woman cackles.

Yarin sits there, too frightened to say a word. Maxie then grabs the old woman's wrists and turns her palms upwards. Cin noticing something going on nudges Trace and putting his fingers to his lips whispers, "Shush, watch."

"Look into my eyes," Maxie tells the old crone.

"Get off me," shouts the witch.

"I said," orders Maxie. "Look into my eyes, now, deeper, deeper."

Their eyes are now transfixed and neither of them speaks a word until the old woman manages to shake her wrists free of Maxie's grip, and grabs her head. "No, no, stop saying that," she shouts. "Get out, get out of my head."

Trace whispers to Cin, "But the child's not saying a word."

"Shush," replies Cin transfixed himself.

"No more, no more," begs the old crone.

"Do you agree?" asks Maxie.

"Yes, yes, I agree," squeals the old woman.

"That's better now isn't it," smiles Maxie breaking her gaze and turning to lady Yarin.

"Don't worry," she giggles. "She won't do that to you again."

Yarin just nods. The old crone puts her tongue out behind Maxie's back. "I hope you're not pulling faces back there," shouts Maxie.

The old woman quickly puts her tongue in. "No, no, not me dear," she splutters nervously.

"Good," replies Maxie. "Now go and play with someone else, and I'll be there in a minute."

Woodnut scratches his head. "How did she know that?" he asks himself. "I guess Lane was right, it must be a woman thing."

"Oh well," he giggles.

"Now if you'll excuse me my Lady," curtsies Maxie.

"Yes, yes of course my dear," answers a stunned Yarin.

So Maxie then skips off grabbing Woodnut's hand and the pair head over to the crone singing, "Ninginey nanginey noo."

The old woman is delighted and the three start to skip around the room together singing it over and over again. "What, how?" stutters Yarin turning to Cin and Big Dan.

Cin shrugs. "I've no idea my lady," he answers. "I've never seen her do that before. Well only to animals."

Yarin still dumfounded turns to her husband next to her, who's nodding off and gives him a shake. "What, what is it?" he splutters loudly waking with a start.

"Maybe I will take the child and her friend with me tomorrow," she tells him.

"Yes, as you wish dear," he yawns.

Max flops down beside John. "Tired?" he asks.

"Yes," she smiles. "I think it's that stuff Maxie gave me, shall we go to bed now?"

John smiles getting to his feet and takes her hand. "Goodnight everybody," he shouts to all.

"Can we stop up a little bit longer?" shouts Maxie.

"Yes a little bit," replies John smiling as he makes his way to the door.

So Maxie, Woodnut and the old crone skip off again singing loudly. And as he goes out John shouts back, "Put them together and what have you got ...?"

Maxie and Woodnut shout, "Ninginy nanginy noo."

The old woman stops dead in her tracks repeating the words in her head. Then giving out a shout that silences everybody she hollers, "He knows, he knows some of the magic words. Put them together and what have you got, ninginy nanginy noo."

John opens the doors and proceeds out, but before shutting them he shouts over, "That's bibbity, bobbity boo, you old goat, now goodnight."

The old crone is so shocked she collapses to the floor. "What's the matter?" asks Maxie.

"Your, your father," she stutters. "Help me up child, I've things to do. I've got to organise so much."

"So much to do, so much to do, no time to do it," she mutters over and over again.

Maxie gives her a hand up, the old woman then rushes over to Lord Tain and bows. "Please?" she asks.

"What is it witch?" gasps Tain stunned at her sudden change.

"I need to get home as quickly as possible," she tells him. "Could you take me on your verum verum please?"

"No I'm sorry," he answers. "It's dark and I'm very drunk. And the one rule John gave me when I got it, was that I was never ever to drink and drive."

"Yes, yes of course," she replies curtsies politely, and proceeds to rush out the room at high speed.

"What was all that about my Lord?" asks Trace.

Tain just shrugs. "I've absolutely no idea my friend," he answers.

Back at the room and getting into their bed Max asks, "So what was all that about then, are those really magic words? She said you know their real meaning. But you told me they were just nonsense."

"They are," yawns John. "They're just words from an old song from a child's film, they mean nothing. Well to her I suppose, as you've probably guessed she's originally from my earth, and however she got here, she was very young. And I think it's one of her last fading memories of her with her mum, sitting together watching this film and singing the songs together."

"Oh how sad," sighs Max. "The poor old stick, so what happens to her now?"

John lies down having just put the candles out. "Nothing," he answers. "She's made a pretty good life for herself here. And I bet she's got a pile of cash stashed somewhere."

Max yawns. "Yes you're probably right dear."

10

THE NEXT MORNING they are all awoken early by their personal maids. Max is gently shaken by one. "My Lady," says the maid softly.

Max wakes a little startled. "What's the matter?" she asks.

"Nothing my Lady," the maid answers smiling. "We were told to wake you early, something about an early start with Lord Tain."

"Oh yes, sorry," apologises Max.

"Oh, my Lady," gasps the maid. "What happened to your eye?"

"You must have taken an awful beating last night, men, hu," she grumps.

Max sits up. "Oh that, just a bit of fun at the celebration last night. Don't worry he'll be feeling a lot worse than I this morning."

"If you say so my Lady," says the maid bowing. "The last Lord Tain, a lovely man, but my Lady, well she was always, err, let's say having accidents Miss."

"Hmm, oh no," gasps Max. "It wasn't. No my husband would never, I mean we love each other very much."

"Yes of course Miss, if you say so," says the maid bowing before she goes around to the other side of the bed where she carefully leans over and places her hands on John shoulders.

"Wake up," she shouts shaking him vigorously.

John jumps up instantly. "What, what, is it?" he gasps. "Is there an emergency?"

"You're to get up early," she tells him gruffly.

"Yes thank you," replies a dazed John.

The maid bows. "I'll get you each some water to wash, unless you'd like me to do it for you."

"No thank you," replies Max. "Please call me Max. And what would your name be?"

The maid a little shocked smiles politely and bows. "You do have a name?" asks Max getting out of bed. "Yes my Lady," she answers. "It's just not normal to be asked by someone as noble as yourself my Lady." The maid then proceeds to pour her some water and pulls a screen around in the corner of the room. "There you go my Lady."

Max goes behind the screen with the woman. "Please call me Max. And where you see a noble woman, I see the cleaner from the tavern, and that was one of my better jobs around the town. You see it's the person inside that counts. Not the fancy title or clothes they adorn themselves with. The old maid smiles broadly and pats her hand. "My name is Lani. Now let me get Lord Taraten some water, and I'll bring you some breakfast."

"Yes thank you," smiles Max. "Would you care to take breakfast with us?"

"Oh you are one," laughs Lani. "I've never heard of such a thing. What would Lord Taraten say?"

Max smiles. "Please call him John. Have some breakfast with us, and you will make him very happy."

The two women then talk as if long lost friends, with John getting washed and dressed behind another screen in the other corner. He comes out and gives a shudder. "What's the matter dear?" asks Max.

"That water was freezing," he replies shuddering again.

"Oh, that's odd," answers Max. "Mine was lovely and warm."

"Hu," grumps Lani as she brushes past John. "I'll go and get your breakfasts."

John scratches his head. "What's her problem?"

Max shrugs, "She seems nice to me."

They then go out into the large communal room where the others are already sat around a large table talking. "Morning," shouts Cin and Big Dan, as their personal maids serve their breakfast.

John and Max sit down and soon Lani enters the room with theirs. "Well," splutters Cin stuffing his face. "I think it's going to be another fine day. Good food, good company, what more could you asks for."

Lani carefully serves Max some food, then goes around to serve John. "Hey Max, how's your eye?" asks Big Dan. "That's a beauty you've got there."

"No pain," she answers. "But I'm struggling to see out of it."

Lani then suddenly slaps a very small portion of something sloppy on John's plate. "Enjoy my Lord," she snaps before stamping back out the way.

Big Dan leans over and whispers, "John what have done to her."

"Nothing," he whispers. "She's been funny since I woke up."

"You must have said something," whispers Dan.

"No nothing honest," whispers John.

Max pulls a chair out from the other side of her. "Lani please come and sit down."

Lani nervously sits down beside her. Max then gets up and proceeds to bring the woman some breakfast, much to the gasps of the other maids standing around the room. "So what are your plans for the day Lani?" asks Max as she sits back down.

Lani gives out a wry laugh but replies, "The same as every other day I expect. I'll be cleaning the room, taking out the dirty water, and disposing of the buckets in the small room, if you'll pardon the expression."

John suddenly leans around Max and says, "No not really."

"JOHN," snaps Max.

"WHAT?" replies John in a heightened voice. "I was only asking?"

Big Dan whispers to him, "The little room where you use the clinker beetle."

"Oh, oh yes, oops sorry," apologises John going a little red.

Then a puzzled look comes across his face and he looks around to the maid again, "So where do you take it, I mean what happens to it."

"JOHN," snaps Max again. "We're eating here."

John shrugs. "I only asked we all do it."

"It's taken across town my Lord," she answers. "It goes to the tannery there. It is used to help produce the leather."

John nods. "Oh that's good, a bit of recycling aye."

"My lady, err Max," stutters Lani. "What will you be doing today, if I may be so bold."

Max smiles and nods. "We are going to take a trip back to the rainforest at the edge of your province."

Lani gasps, "Oh my Lady be careful. I've never actually been in a forest, but I hear they are very dangerous places."

"What," gasps Big Dan. "A woman your age and you've never been in a forest, not even as a child playing?"

"No Sir," she answers. "I was born into service, my whole life I've only left the town limits no more than thrice."

Max shakes her head shouting, "That's awful, and that settles it then. Today you shall accompany me, as my friend and companion."

"My Lady are you sure?" she asks excitedly. "I won't get in trouble will I?"

"No of course not," Max answers smiling. "Now go and get yourself some suitable clothes."

Lani scratches her head but replies, "What would those be Miss?"

Maxie and Woodnut jump down and take her hand. "Don't worry we'll help," says Maxie.

"Yes we will," says Woodnut.

So after breakfast they all start to gather in the courtyard with Max and Lani chatting constantly. John whispers to Woodnut and Maxie, "If they don't stop to take a breath soon I fear one of them may faint."

The three of them giggle but Max doesn't stop chattering and just turns her head slightly frowning.

"Ah Suelan my friend," shouts John as he sees Lord Tain making his way over with his wife Yarin, closely followed by Trace and Glendra.

Trace waves over to the stables, where the stable hands proceed to lead over the horses. Lord Tain then helps Yarin onto her horse having first given her a kiss farewell. Maxie and Woodnut are placed on a horse together and both are given a kiss by Max. "Now be good, and do as you're told," she tells them.

"Mother," shouts Maxie. "Stop fussing."

"Yes, sorry dear," apologises Max.

Yarin, Maxie and Woodnut then slowly proceed out the yard on their horses. "Try not to worry," Maxie shouts back. "I'll keep you informed."

"What did she mean by that?" asks Tain a little confused. "How by the green grass would, could, she do that?" John just shakes his head and shrugs.

"Oh my," shouts Max. "I nearly forgot."

"What's the matter?" asks Lani.

"Nothing," mutters Max. "If they're away on their own I just like Spot to keep an eye on them that's all." Lani completely baffled just nods. "Spot, Spot, come on girl," shouts Max.

Lani and the Tain men just stare at her baffled. "Spot," shouts Max again. "Oh that lazy animal. Spot if I have to find you."

"Max," says Big Dan pointing to an open window high up.

"Ah excellent," shouts Max. "Come here girl."

Gasps then come from the Tain friends as Spot proceeds to jump into Max's arms. "Now," she says smiling and giving Spot a kiss. "Go with Maxie and Woodnut. I'm trusting you to look after them for me, now go."

Spot makes a soft wittering noise and gently shakes, then springs out of her hands and takes off across the courtyard and out the gates.

Trace and Glendra just stare at each other speechless. "By my father's teeth," gasps Lord Tain. "Did my eyes deceive me? That, that was a yellow belly."

Now Max looks at him oddly. "Yes so."

"But," he stutters. "You've just sent, well, sent a dangerous animal after your daughter."

"Yes to look after them," sighs Max shaking her head. "Men."

Lord Tain still bewildered climbs on to his horse muttering, "Oh that's ok then."

Big Dan and Cin just chuckle as Trace climbs on his horse also muttering, "That's just not right."

The talking and banter flows freely as they all ride along, and the morning passes quickly. After a break for dinner they are on their way once again. "Tell me John," asks Lord Tain. "What would you say you'd miss most about being away from your own land?"

"Oh that's easy," grins John. "Indoor plumbing and loo roll."

Lord Tain stares back with a puzzled look. "You just can't be serious can you," says Max frowning.

John shrugs. "I am being serious."

"What is indoor plooming and loom roll?" asks Tain.

John then proceeds to explain all about plumbing and even loo roll, with Tain listening to his every word, mulling it all over as he does so. Then after John has finished explaining Lord Tain sits back in his saddle nodding. "You know John, this plumbing of yours sounds a marvellous idea. And when we get back I intend to discuss it with some of my people in the stronghold. Maybe we could work out a way to pipe all the waste from there, straight to the tannery. But this loom role stuff, it sounds very unhygienic. I think we'll stick with the clinker beetle there, after all that's its purpose in life isn't it?"

It's late in the afternoon when they first set eyes on the rainforest in the distance. "We should be there by evening," says Trace. "It looks like a night under the stars for us."

The light is starting to fade by the time they reach the forest and dismount. "What happens now?" asks Lord Tain. "Do we just go in?"

"No just wait here a moment," John tells him. "There are a few formalities first."

"There are," replies Tain in a raised voice. "Oh that's excellent, and always a sign of good breading I've thought."

Evening Thunder then proceeds to walk out of the forest alone, and slowly walks towards them, stopping a short distance away. John invites Tain to step forward with him to meet the old greenem. He then formally introduces himself and Lord Tain. Then waving the others over he introduces them all one by one. All bowing as they do so, with the old greenem bowing in return and introducing himself. He then invites them all to sit down in a semi circle before beckoning over the eager young greenem hiding at the edge of the forest. But all the Tain people suddenly start looking very apprehensive as hundreds of excited greenem rush over. Lani gives a little squeal but is calmed down by Max. Glendra starts to sweat profusely as they get near, and he tries to scramble to his feet. "Sit," bellows Big Dan pulling him back down.

"This is safe isn't it," whispers Lord Tain out the corner of his mouth.

"No, not really," whispers John. "We're probably all going to die."

"WHAT?" shouts Tain in a high pitched voice.

"Don't worry," replies Max. "He's only joking, you've never been safer."

Soon they are all surrounded by giggling chatting greenem, all as excited as excited can be. With the older wiser greenem congregating around John and Lord Tain, and the younger more child like all surrounding an exasperated Cin. Max starts to giggle as Lani whispers, "What's the matter with him, they seem to really like him."

"They do," whispers Max. "He's very popular with the young ones because he grumps a lot. They find it very funny, which makes him grump more. Don't worry he loves it really, he fights it but watch carefully every now and again you'll see him break into a smile."

Cin gives out a loud sigh, "Why me, what will it take to get rid of you?"

"Jump, jump," giggles some of the very young greenem.

Lani & Max then watch as Cin lies down, frowning, huffing and grumping as he does so. The young greenem then climb all over him, with some jumping up and down. "Why me?" he groans loudly. "What have I done to deserve this?" The young greenem laugh even louder.

"First things first," says Evening Thunder, as he sits down with John and Tain. "In a moment we will escort you to a small clearing where you may rest the night and take some nourishment. But before that, I have news for you my Lord from Woodnut and Maxie."

"You, you have," stutters Tain. "But how, that's impossible, we've just arrived here ourselves."

"Suelan my friend," interrupts John. "Are you not interested to hear what the news is?"

"Oh yes, yes of course sorry, continue," Tain apologises.

"Thank you," chuckles the old greenem. "Now where was I, oh yes, they've broken the old lady's fever and she is expected to make a full recovery in a few days. And they are presently treating the sores on her legs to prevent it happening again."

Lord Tain starts to stutter, "That's, that's, I mean, this is impossible, you lie, you must be."

John elbows him. "Hey less of that," he snaps. "Greenem never lie, only people lie."

"Err, yes sorry," stutters Tain. "Yes, yes of course, how rude of me."

He bows. "Please forgive me old one, it's just such a shock. I'm still bewildered how you got this news so quickly. But not to have just cured such a fever, but to be able to cure her sores. These two things sadly afflict many of my people, and are not thought to be curable. Although the sores do not kill, the fever often does."

The old greenem stands back up and bows slightly. "Come we will go to the clearing, and talk as we go. The particular fever the lady had, was directly caused by the sores on her legs."

"It was," gasps Lord Tain.

"Well yes," continues Evening Thunder. "There is a certain fly, normally quite harmless to oomans. They normally cannot penetrate your skin, and the fresh blood from your wounds does not interest them. They are normally found around sick or injured animals. But the sores that sometimes afflict your young and old, secrete a sweet obnoxious fluid, which these flies are attracted to. And although the flies themselves do not cause the fever, they often carry small organisms that do."

"I see yes," nods Tain. "This is fascinating, but it's so hard to believe something as small and insignificant as a fly could do this. Maybe we should try and eliminate these flies."

The old greenem gives out a wry laugh. "No my lad, that's not the key. You couldn't manage that if you tried, and if you did it wouldn't be a good thing. Every thing has a purpose."

"So is there nothing we can do?" asks Lord Tain.

"Let me think a moment," the old greenem tells him as they make their way to the clearing.

The old greenem then stops at the edge of the clearing. "Now my lad," he says turning to Lord Tain. "The sores themselves are easily treated. But if I give you the knowledge to treat them, you must promise to try and eradicate their cause. It's your duty as a leader, and will prove your worth to all."

"Yes, yes of course," Tain answers instantly. "You have my word I will do my best whatever the cause."

The old greenem smiles bowing his head a little. "Now my boy, it's quite simple, they are caused by a lack of nutrition. Have you never noticed it tends to be more prevalent in the neglected and the poor?"

Tain sighs deeply, slowly shaking his head. "Now you come to mention it, how stupid of us not to notice something so plainly obvious."

He then bows down low to the old greenem. "You are clearly much wiser than I, and I stand here as if a veil had just been removed from my eyes, humbled before you."

They all then proceed to sit down on the cushions that have been prepared for them. Max whispers to Big Dan and Cin, "Do you think it'll be safe to sleep here tonight?"

Nodding Big Dan whispers back, "Oh yes after what happened to Lane, I must admit, I'm more than just a little nervous myself. John could you come here please?"

John kneels down beside them. "Yeah, what is it?" he asks.

"Is this place safe?" asks Cin. "Remember last time we were here?"

"Evening Thunder," shouts John. "Could we borrow you a mo please?"

"Yes my lad of course. Now what is it my lad?" he asks coming over.

They all then quietly tell him their worries, not wanting to frighten their Tain friends. "I've pondered that very question myself," answers the old greenem. "And even taken council with Meadow Spirit. And we both think you will all be quite safe. After all, we have been here, well always, and it is the first time it has happened. To happen again in such a short period of time is most unlikely. But you are right not tell these people you are with, there is no point in worrying them over nothing."

"Yes thank you," whispers Max. "You are very wise."

The old greenem then gets back up and goes back to sit with Lord Tain. "Well I don't know about the rest of you," whispers Cin. "But I still won't sleep tonight."

John grins cheekily as he gets up and goes back over beside Lord Tain also. "Hmm," grumbles Big Dan raising one eyebrow. "Always up to something."

"Would you have him any other way," giggles Max as she sits back with Lani.

"No I guess not" chuckles Big Dan.

"Oh no, quickly run," screams Trace, jumping to his feet and drawing his sword.

Everybody looks round startled. "Quickly my Lords run," he continues. "There's a jackerbell. I'll keep it busy, while you escape, go now quickly."

There at the far side of the clearing thundering out the undergrowth, snarling and snorting is Fluff hurtling towards them. Lord Tain goes instantly white as he tries to scramble to his feet. John grabs his arm and pulls him back down. "Just sit still and be quiet," he tells him.

But Trace shaking like a leaf gulps and raises his sword high in the air. Fluff doesn't even slow down running straight over him as if he wasn't even there, and flattens him to the ground. Then jumping Fluff pounces on John knocking him backwards also and proceeds to lick his face madly. "Get of you big soft lump," laughs John. "Before you drown me in slobber."

Cin and Big Dan then go over to a still flattened Trace and standing either side of him stare down. "Do you think he's dead?" asks Cin scratching his head.

"I don't think so," chuckles Big Dan running his fingers through his beard. "I think he's still breathing. I tell you what though, that was one of the bravest things I have ever seen."

"Agreed truly," replies Cin nodding.

Trace gives out a loud groan and slowly opens one eye. "Am, am I dead," he stutters.

"No not dead," laughs Big Dan. "Just a little trampled."

"Oh," sighs Trace still a little dazed and winded. "Did, did I stop it?"

"No," laughs Cin. "I don't think you even slowed it down. But to sacrifice yourself like that, now that took true courage."

A look of horror then goes across Trace's face as he scrambles for his sword. As he grabs the hilt Big Dan puts his foot on the blade and shakes his head. "Just leave it there my friend," he tells him offering him a hand up.

"But my Lord," stutters Trace as he gets to his feet.

Cin smiles. Don't worry, he's alright, it's with John."

A loud gasp then comes from Trace as he slowly turns to see Lord Tain scrambling backwards and John flat on his back with Fluff standing over him. Trace goes white again and hardly able to catch his breath looks desperately back and forward at Cin and Dan. "We, we, must help surely," he says.

"Why?" Cin asks a little puzzled.

"Your friend," stammers Trace. "L, Lord Taraten, he's being eaten by that, that savage beast."

"Oh no," smiles Big Dan. "You've got it wrong, he's not attacking him, he's licking him."

"You, you what," squeals Trace in a heightened voice. "You, you mean that thing's a pet?"

"No, no pet," replies Cin. "Be in no doubt that is a true man eater in every sense of the word. But it does travel with us, err how can I explain it. Dan please can you."

"Hmm let me think," sighs Big Dan. "I suppose it sees us as friends, but more John and Hope. I tell you what let's get it off John, and I'll introduce you. Fluff, Fluff, come here boy."

Fluff turns and comes excitedly over then jumps up putting his enormous paws on Big Dan's shoulders and proceeds to lick his face and head. Big Dan's legs start to buckle. "Get down boy," gasps Dan through gritted teeth.

Trace stands there stunned, too scared to move. Suddenly there's a loud scream making even Fluff jump, so they all turn to see Glendra scrambling to his feet and shouting as he stumbles backwards, "You, you, people are mad, completely mad, you bring chaos and disorder everywhere you go. And you have no respect for etiquette or hierarchy, you are all insane."

Then he gives out another scream and takes off running. Evening Thunder scratches his head and turning to John asks, "What's the matter with him?"

John shrugs. "No idea."

Cin grins broadly, winks to Big Dan and says, "I've wanted to do this since I saw John do it."

Then patting Fluff on the head he asks, "Could you go and fetch him back please?"

Fluff wags his tail and takes off, soon rounding him up and chasing him back.

"That was cruel," splutters Big Dan laughing loudly.

All the greenem in the clearing are now laughing so hard they can no longer stand up. "Are you sure you can trust that beast?" asks Trace.

Big Dan nods. "Yes as long as you show him a little respect and talk to it properly. It's a very intelligent creature and understands nearly everything you say."

"Really," gasps Trace.

"Yes really," nods Big Dan.

Max takes Glendra's hand. "Come sit with me and Lani."

"And as for you," she tells Fluff frowning. "Sit down with John, and be good, or else."

Fluff sits down laughing as he does so. "I heard that," she shouts and Fluff stops instantly.

"Do you know," says Lord Tain excitedly. "Glendra's right, you people really do bring a kind of chaos in your wake. But I must also say, it's a wonderful kind of chaos as you people are a joy to be with. I never know what to expect next and if I were not the lord of this province I would love to travel with you all. I bet you have some truly wonderful adventures."

"Well it's never boring, that's for sure," mutters Big Dan.

"I mean," continues Tain. "Who could have ever guessed that that spikey was going to charge out of the wood? Then instead of savaging and killing, it would be a friend. I mean whatever next."

John smiles. "I'm pleased you're happy, and no more surprises, well none that I can think of anyway."

Evening Thunder waves to some young greenem who proceed over in two's carrying woven platters of food, placing them down in front of them. Some more then arrive with drinks for them. Glendra still very nervous is given some medicine by one of the older greenem to calm him down. "Lord Tain," shouts Cin. "Before you take a drink, think of your favourite beverage."

Tain looks at him oddly shrugs and takes a mouthful. His eyes shoot wide open and he gasps, "That's amazing."

Similar gasps then come from Trace, Lani and Glendra. "Now," chuckles Cin. "Think of another drink." More gasps come from all. "This is tr, truly amazing," stutters Trace. "How is this possible? Is it some sort of magic?"

"Good stuff aye," booms Big Dan.

"My Lady," says Lani excitedly turning to Max. "This tastes just like dring bush fruit syrup, here taste." Max smiles. "Its ok thank you, you drink it."

"No you've got to try it," Lani insists.

John hearing this calls over, "It doesn't make a difference."

But he is cut of in mid sentence by Lani. "I was offering it to Max, my Lord, not you," she snaps sharply. John puts his hands up. "Sorry," he apologises.

"John," whispers Big Dan. "What have you done to that woman? If it were another lord but you, she would be flogged for such an attitude."

"No nothing honest," whispers John in a semi heightened voice. "Well, nothing I can think of."

As the evening wears on laughter and merriment abound, with each of them getting a little tiddly. "Max my dear," says Evening Thunder. "May I ask, what happened to your eye, it's some lovely shades of black and purple. I've been meaning to ask you all evening."

"Oh this yes," she replies smiling proudly. "Good isn't it."

The old greenem just looks at her oddly. "Last night," she continues. "We were having a party, and their warriors were fighting by the end of the evening, and the winner thought it would be funny to challenge me to a fight."

"I take it he won then?" asks the old greenem.

"Are you joking?" replies Big Dan laughing. "She left him curled up in a ball on the floor, not knowing which end to nurse first. I've never been prouder."

"Really," gasps Lani.

"Yes," laughs Cin. "We may not make them all big in Voreda, but there are none tougher."

"Who did she beat? Trace?" asks Lani.

"Stony," answers Cin.

"Really," she squeals loudly. "Honestly, Stony, she can't have."

She then whispers to him, "He must have let her win. Did he?"

"No not at all," he answers loudly. "She beat him fair and square."

"But, but how," she gasps. "She's so, and well he's so, well big."

"Max it seems you've impressed your friend," laughs John. "But why do they call him Stony."

"Because," chuckles Trace. "He may be a little slow, but he has a chin like stone."

"Yes maybe," laughs Dan. "But a set of swingers as brittle as flurry eggs aye."

Everyone falls about laughing. John then wipes a tear from his eye. "Well one more cup of beelack juice and I'm turning in."

"Here have this one," replies Lani jumping to her feet and handing him hers.

"No it's alright," answers John.

"Please," she tells him in her nicest voice. "Mine tastes of dring bush syrup."

John cautiously tastes it and thanks her, as she fluffs his pillow up and sits him back down. He looks over to Big Dan and Cin and shrugs, they look at him equally as baffled and simply shrug back.

"My Lord Tain," says Evening Thunder. "I would like to introduce you to an old friend of mine, this cantankerous old greenem here is called Tall Tree. And is it true you like a good argument Sir."

"Yes I love a good argument," nods Tain.

"Well Tall Tree here has been known to argue for years, literally," replies Evening Thunder. "And he has never been beaten."

Lord Tain's eyes light up like beacons and he claps his hands excitedly. "Oh I love a challenge."

"You're just saying that," snaps Tall Tree.

"No I'm not," answers Tain.

The two then start to argue, mostly about nothing just stopping now and again to laugh or complement the other, which instantly starts another argument. Trace nudges Glendra. "He'll be happy now, they've found his weak spot there."

Max sits up looking all around the clearing from ground, to the tops of the tallest trees. "Are you looking for something?" asks both Lani and Glendra.

"Err yes," answers Max still looking around the clearing. "My little boy."

"You have a son," gasp the Tain people.

"Yes," she answers. "Well adopted, until we find his real parents. Fluff, Fluff, where's Hope?"

Fluff gives out a strange snarl and looks up. Everyone jumps as Hope then lands in front of Max, out of seemingly nowhere. "Did you mean it?" he asks excitedly with tears forming in his eyes.

"What dear?" asks Max.

"Y, your son," he stammers.

"Yes of course, until we find your real ones," she smiles lovingly.

The young boy lunges forward flinging his arms around her. "Hey it's ok," she reassures him. "Come on now get off."

"No really," she gasps. "You're hurting me."

"Oh sorry," apologises Hope letting go.

"My how strong you've got," says Max. "The only other person I've known with a grip like that is John."

The Tain friends just stare at the child in disbelief. "Ah Hope my lad," bellows Big Dan. "How are you my boy? Been having fun."

He nods excitedly. "Aha this place is wonderful, and the greenem have been so nice to Fluff and I."

"Where have you been all evening anyway?" asks John.

Hope points to a tall tree high above just behind them at the edge of the clearing. "And you jumped all the way from over there?" asks John.

"Aha," he answers.

"What, err I mean who is that?" gasps Lord Tain stopping in mid argument.

"Ah yes," replies John winking towards Hope. "Lord Tain this is Hope. Hope this is Lord Tain, and beside Max is Lani and Glendra and beside Cin and Dan is Trace."

Hope bows politely. "Nice to meet you."

"Likewise," they reply.

"John," whispers Tain. "You told me there were no more surprises. This, this, well child I suppose, I've never seen his like. From where does he hail, it must be your earth surely."

John shrugs, "No idea to be honest, we rescued him from a cage on a farm back in Taraten."

"Could I examine, err take a closer look at him?" asks Tain.

"I can ask him," replies John. "But if he agrees you will have to be careful, as our Fluff here is very protective over him."

"Hope," he continues. "Would you mind if my friend Suelan here has a closer look at you please."

"If you like," Hope answers.

"Your eyes," gasps Tain. "They're so large and nearly all black."

"Yes Sir," answers the boy. "That's because it's getting dark, they're not always like this."

Tain takes the boys hand. "You only have four fingers my lad. What are those round pads on your fingers and palms?"

"They are for gripping things Sir," Hope answers. "They also help me climb."

"Amazing," mutters Tain.

John yawns, "Now I don't know about the rest of you, but I think I'm going to try and get some sleep."

"Yes, yes of course," stutters Tain still a little shocked. He then turns back to Tall Tree.

Everyone finally settles down for the night all except Lord Tain and Tall Tree neither wanting to finish first and be thought of as losing the argument. John sits up smiling from ear to ear at Cin, Dan and Max. "Goodnight sleep well," he grins.

"About as well as you," frowns Cin.

"Yeah right, you wish," winks John popping half a small leaf on the end of his tongue and swallowing. Big Dan stares at him through one eye head cocked and the other closed. "I might have known, I knew he was up to something, always up to something."

"Why, what was that?" asks Max.

"It's one of those leaves we were taking the other day to get here. You know the one's that knocked him out," frowns Big Dan.

"OOH the," grumps Max.

Within a few minutes John is fast asleep. One of the other old greenem starts to laugh. "He got you there," he chuckles before he then goes around and hands them and the Suelan people something to help them sleep also. "Don't worry," he chuckles. "Just swallow, it will guarantee you all a good night."

11

THE NEXT MORNING they are all awoken bright and early by giggling greenem. All excited by the start of a new day and the prospect of showing John and the others around their home. As soon as they open their eyes there are greenem all around them with food and drink. "Eat, eat, drink, quickly," come the giggles.

"Guys, guys please," groans John. "I've literally just opened my eyes, at least give me a chance to sit up."

"Yes, yes sit up," they giggle trying hard to pull him up.

"Why, why me?" come the groans from Cin, who seems to have young greenem climbing all over him again.

"They seem very keen," chuckles Lord Tain. "And always such happy little fellows."

"Yes, yes, eat," says an excited greenem handing him a xenthem fruit. "There is so much to see, and we don't want you to miss anything, your lives are so fleeting."

Lord Tain looks at him oddly. "What a strange thing to say. What do you mean little fellow?"

The young greenem not sure how to answer just shrugs and looks hopefully to John.

"Ok," he smiles. "I think he means we don't live very long, well not compared to a greenem anyway. And I'm not sure myself, but I think they don't see time quite the same as we do either. Is that right little friend?"

The young greenem nods excitedly. Lord Tain sits there stunned for a moment before snapping out of it and asking, "Just how long do they live?"

John scratches his head. "Err, well I think Evening Thunder's, err somewhere around five to six hundred, but they don't consider that old, more coming up for middle aged. Oh and back in the fire forest we were talking to a couple of old greenem who were over eight hundred."

Tain's mouth falls open. "You jest surely John."

They then see the old greenem Evening Thunder enter the clearing and call him over. "There you go ask him," says John.

"Err yes of course," stutters Tain as he turns to Evening Thunder. "May I ask, how old you are?"

Evening Thunder rubs his chin. "In your years, err now, hmm, I think it would be around err, six hundred and ninety-seven. Why?"

Lord Tain is speechless again, then splutters, "The things you must have seen and experienced."

"Hey great minds think alike," agrees John. "I said that when I first found out."

They all sit there eating and talking until a very excited young greenem runs up to Evening Thunder. "Calm down young greenem," he chuckles. "Now take your time and tell me slowly. What is it?"

"It's the tunnel trees," puffs the young greenem. "The rainbow bugs are gathering in the trees, and the frogs and toads are calling in the stream below. We think the buds on the trees are about to burst."

"Really," gasps the old greenem now getting excited himself.

"Everyone listen," he then shouts jumping to his feet. "You must all come with me now, quickly, you can eat later."

Rather alarmed they all jump to their feet. "What is it?" asks John. "Is there trouble?"

"No my boy, come, I'll tell you all as we go," answers the old greenem.

The old greenem then takes off, and John quickly picks up his drink and a handful of fruit. "Here let me carry them for you," says Lani smiling. "You get yourself ahead dear, I'll catch up."

"Hu," gasps John.

"No it's alright I've got it. Get yourself away, I can go faster than you," he tells her, now feeling more than just a little puzzled.

"If you're sure," she answers curtsying.

Then as she walks away John puts the palms of his hands up and shrugs to Cin and Trace beside him. "Are all your women like this?" he whispers to Trace as they walk along.

"What do you mean?" asks Trace.

"Well," whispers John shaking his head. "The last day or so I got the distinct feeling she really, really didn't like me. But now she's the exact opposite, she can't do enough."

Trace shrugs his head. "She's always seemed quite pleasant to me. Although I'm led to believe she was a little funny with the previous Lord Tain, my lords' father. No one was quite sure why, or why he even put up with her."

"Keep up at the back there please," shouts the old greenem leading the way.

"Where are you taking us old friend?" asks Big Dan.

"Ah yes, yes pleased you asked my lad," answers the greenem. "There is a small stream that snakes its way through the forest, and is constantly filled by the daily life giving rains that fall here. And either side of the stream are tunnel trees, these trees line the stream exclusively throughout the forest. Their branches arch over the water hence their name, and you'll see for yourselves it looks like a large artery snaking its way through the forest feeding and nourishing as it travels. And it is actually known by a lot of my people as the artery of life, and are you in for a treat my boy, you'll see soon hopefully."

The old greenem then stops beside an endless line of trees disappearing into the undergrowth of the forest. "If you want to follow me through this gap," he says disappearing through. "Single file now."

They do so and find themselves walking onto the trunk of a large fallen tree spanning one side of the stream to the other. The old greenem stops on the far side and sits down. "Come on everyone," he shouts. "Sit down now, It'll be cramped but well worth it."

They then all sit there shoulder to shoulder along the tree trunk, with their feet dangling just above the water.

Fluff and Hope sit on the bank beside them. "What are you doing over there?" shouts Max.

Hope just shrugs. "Come and sit on my knee dear?" shouts Max.

Hope smiles broadly and jumps over onto Max's lap. "There now, that's better isn't it," she whispers putting her arms around him. The young boy nods.

Next giggling greenem make their way along sitting on everyone's knees and shoulders, all hoping for a better view.

"Hey, what are we waiting for anyway?" asks John. "Not that it really matters anyway, as this is one beautiful place, and well worth the journey on its own."

They all nod in agreement as they sit transfixed staring down the dimly lit tunnel, illuminated by the diffused light splintering through the branches above, and reflecting off large bulbous white flowers dripping and hanging from every tree and branch, as far as their eyes can see. This makes the water sparkle like a million diamonds, and further illuminating a multitude of iridescent rainbow colours, pulsing faster and faster between the large flowers. Excited frogs like living jewels start to call, and compete to nearly fever pitch in the water, and on the rocks below.

"Hopefully, if we are very very lucky," sighs the old greenem. "We will see the pollination of the tunnel trees. And then you will know exactly why we call this the artery of life. You will see those bulbous white flowers up there, pop open and expel huge amounts of pollen."

"So when will this happen?" asks John.

"Now that is the question," answers the old greenem. "We've never been able to predict it with that much accuracy, it's a bit of a mystery to us I'm afraid. They may pollinate once a year regularly, then they may not for several years."

"So why do you think they're going to now?" asks Lord Tain.

"Good question," nods Evening Thunder. "A few reasons, firstly, the size of the flowers they look ready to pop. But more importantly, it's the rainbow bugs you see smothering all the leaves and branches. Again we don't know how, but they only gather in huge numbers like this in the tunnel trees, when the flowers are about to pop. They feed on the pollen flying around and gather it up, which is the reason there are so many rainbow frogs also gathered. They seem to also know, hoping to feed on the rainbow bugs."

"Hang on, what rainbow bugs? Where?" interrupts John.

"John your eyesight," laughs Cin. "All around you, you see those little sparks of light with legs, those multi coloured shimmers above you. Tell me, could it be those bugs he's talking about."

"There's nothing wrong with my eyes," grumps John. "It's the light in here."

"Legs my eye," he mumbles straining to try and get a better look. "Anyway if those are bugs up there, I can understand their name, rainbow bugs. But why do you call those frogs the same, most are just brown."

The old greenem chuckles, "Some are at the moment my boy, but keep watching as they get more and more excited they start to change colour. The more excited they get the faster they change, and the more colours they go. Sometimes they do this to attract a mate, and sometimes it's to try and trick the bugs into coming down so they can eat them."

"Does that not make them more conspicuous to predators?" asks John.

"No my lad," answers the greenem. "They're quite toxic, there isn't much that eats them."

A gentle breeze slowly makes its way past, and the greenem all start to get very excited indeed. "You feel that," shouts the old greenem. "That's the start of it."

"Start of what? What are we meant to be feeling?" asks Max.

"The breeze," he answers excitedly. "It will get stronger and hopefully stimulate the flowers to pop. Which will then carry the pollen around the tunnel, pollinating all the other trees as it travels along. And not just that, it is a very important time for the whole forest, bringing vital nutrients and nourishment, to everything, from fish to fly and flower and fauna. Many animals even relying on it, feeding on it, storing it and breeding just after it."

The breeze starts to turn into a gentle wind, and a faint popping sound is heard in the distance behind them. "You hear that," shouts Evening Thunder excitedly. "It's started."

"Hear what?" asks John.

"John!" shout Cin and Dan.

"Ok, ok," he sighs. "Damn bat hearing weirdoes."

Soon the popping sounds start to get louder and louder, pulsing towards them and echoing back and forth as it continues past. And a fine red dust like pollen starts to fill the air, leaving it pungent and sticky as it wafts along the tunnel on the gentle breeze. It even turns the water below red as it travels along. Max nudges John and giggles, "Look it's sticking to you and you look like a red greenem from the fire forest."

"Oh yes you too," he sniggers back.

Trace shakes his head. "This is truly amazing," he gasps. "I now know why you call this the artery of the forest. I feel as if I'm inside someone's body watching the blood flow through their veins."

"My word," gasps Lani. "This is a sight I'll cherish until the day I die, and the taste in the air it's wonderful, but I can't help feeling it seems strangely familiar some how."

"Quick look up," shouts Big Dan.

They look up and see the multi coloured sparkles of light starting to descend, diving and swooping through the thick pollen. Hope still sitting on Max's knee shoots out his long tongue as one flies past. "Hmm lovely," he croaks as he sits crunching it.

Lord Tain and the others stare in disbelief at the boy, partly for eating a rainbow bug, and partly at how far he could put out his tongue to catch it in the first place, which makes the others and the greenem giggle. In and out the water the frogs and toads start to call at nearly fever pitch, their bodies changing from one colour to another getting faster and faster, jumping and hopping. Their tongues flicking wildly as they try to catch the equally excited bugs swooping and diving lower and lower. "I tell you what guys," sighs John. "If I never saw another thing, this alone was more than worth the journey. Everyone sighs, nodding in agreement.

Hope starts to giggle terribly. "What is it dear?" asks Max.

The young boy points to the water, now giggling uncontrollably. "What?" asks Max again. "The frogs, yes they're amazing aren't they, there like little explosions of colour?"

"No, no," he sniggers. "Listen."

Everyone listens to the excited frogs calling. "What is it my lad?" asks Evening Thunder. "They're just excited."

"Yes exactly," he sniggers. "They're very greedy, it's the first time I've heard them say anything apart from."

The young boy goes suddenly shy and quiet, now even the greenem are staring at him in disbelief. John looks to the old greenem, "What is it?" he asks, "Has he said something wrong?"

"No not at all," answers Evening Thunder. "It's just these frogs do not speak, they just have different calls for different things, you can't understand them."

Hope nods sheepishly. "Aha."

"You can honestly understand what they are saying?" asks the old greenem in disbelief.

Hope looks back equally as puzzled replying, "Why, do you mean you can't?"

The old greenem just shakes his head. "Why what are they saying dear?" asks Max.

Hope giggles. "Every time a sticky sweet goes near they all try to claim it."

"A what?" asks Evening Thunder.

"Sticky sweet," he answers. "That's what they call them."

"Well I'm dumb founded," gasps the old greenem, "What are they saying now exactly?"

Hope giggles again, "They just keep shouting every time a sticky sweet goes past, gerroff, gerroff."

The old greenem scratches his head. "Well I suppose it does sound a bit like that, but you also said it's the first time you've heard them say anything apart from, from what my boy."

The young boy just blushes. "Whisper in my ear dear?" Max tells him.

The boy cups his hands around Max's ear. Max then also goes instantly red. Big Dan starts to laugh nudging Cin. "I never thought I'd see the day, Max blushing, not even John's accomplished that feat."

"What did he say?" asks the old greenem.

"I, I can't repeat it," stutters Max. "I've only heard language like that, late at night from some of the drunks in the tavern."

"And, and that's all they talk about?" she asks.

Hope nods. "Aha, all the time."

"That's disgusting," shouts Max.

She then shouts down at the oblivious frogs, "Ooh you dirty little, how dare you talk like that in front of a child."

John starts to laugh but he laughs so hard he falls off into the water taking several greenem with him. "And what are you laughing at?" shouts Max.

"You, you crazy woman," laughs John. "They're frogs for goodness sake, you can't tell them off for talking dirty."

"Hu," grumps Max, then breaks into a laugh herself along with everyone else.

"May I ask you my lad?" asks Evening Thunder in a more serious voice. "I'm not sure how to put this, but just how do you understand them."

Hope shrugs. "I'm not sure, something's take longer than others to understand, but I can understand most things, given a little time."

"This is remarkable," gasps the old greenem. "Have you always been able to do this?"

The young boy just shrugs. "So why didn't you say anything my lad?" asks the greenem.

The young boy just shrugs again. "I thought everybody could do it?" he says.

They sit there for another hour, until the last of the pollen floats slowly past, and the wind settles back down to barely a breeze, and the stream turns back from red to blue. "You know my Lord," says Glendra. "The colour that water went and that taste in the air, is it just me, or does it remind you of Tain Pink."

"Oh yes," exclaims Lord Tain. "By my father's teeth, it's stronger, more pure so to say, but yes, it's Tain Pink definitely. May I ask where does this stream lead to?"

"It joins with a couple of other much smaller tributaries," answers the old greenem. "Which then goes on to become the river that flows past your town. Why?"

Lord Tain nods. "Now I have seen this, all is clear. You see there are times in the past when the river Tain has turned bright pink. Although very rare, it is thought of as a good omen, of prosperity, good health and good fortune to come. It is also collected and bottled by those lucky enough to hear about it and collect it in time. Its taste is unparalleled, and is thought to have many healing properties. Often taken in times of illness, or by couples struggling to conceive, if you are lucky enough, or rich enough to get some that is. But after what I've seen here today, I now understand where and how it comes to be. This is more than just a good omen, this was meant to be. And to think I nearly had all this destroyed."

"Yes, on that we can agree," nods Evening Thunder. "For us all to have been here on the very day, and at the very moment the tunnel trees pollinate, this was meant to be. To bring us together and to stop the death and destruction, and the great famine it would have brought."

Lord Tain smiles. "You make it all sound very dramatic."

The old greenem stare's him dead in the eye. "You really do have no idea what you nearly did, do you. If you had destroyed this forest, you would not have just lost the pink water. This place, as I said, is the main source for your river, you would no longer have a river, a trickle at best from the other two tributaries. Your weather would have also changed dramatically. The start of your seasons would be unpredictable, and proving quite often disastrous for planting your crops. The list of things is nearly endless. This isn't just a forest, or profitable commodity to be squandered, this place is a vital part of the earth itself. Loosing this would be like you loosing your right arm, you may live, but your life would never be the same again. This is why we pleaded and begged your people to save it. Why we offered to show you and explain, over and over again. But to no avail, until now. Saving this wasn't just for us, it was for all of us."

Lord Tain quietly nods. "I am humbled in your presence."

He then continues, "John you may have your verum back. I am not fit to own such a thing, but this forest is still yours, or should I say the greenem. I presume that's why you wanted it."

"Yes thank you," answers John. "But please keep the bike, it's of no use to me anyway."

"Thank you," says Lord Tain bowing. "You are most gracious."

He continues, "May I ask you old one, would it be possible, or, I mean, err, would you mind if I came back from time to time to visit you and this place, and talk more with you and your wise people."

The old greenem glows with pride. "It would be our honour and pleasure, this is what I've hoped for all along. And please bring friends with you, so that we may also show them some of the wonders that we will soon show you."

Lord Tain bows. "It would be my pleasure also, I see a new great and wonderful friendship forming here my friend."

"Yes as do I," replies the old greenem smiling. "Let's make our way back to the clearing, and you can finish your breakfast."

They then make their way back led by some of the young greenem. Evening Thunder is lingering at the back. "John my boy could I have a word please."

John waits for the old greenem. "Yes old fella, what can I do you for?"

The old greenem looks at him oddly. "What is it?" asks John.

"Oh yes," answers the old greenem. "I would just like a discrete word about young Hope, as he claims to understand other species language and within a relatively short study he understood the rainbow frogs. We didn't even know they could be understood, let alone speak to each other. I'm not sure what I'm trying to say, but for someone to be self taught this, let alone a child, it's not just unheard of, it's impossible. Keep this child safe, and keep a close eye on him. I will have to consult with Meadow Spirit and some of the elders as this child you've acquired is a true mystery."

"Don't worry old friend," answers John smiling. "He seems a kind and loving child, I'm sure everything will work out in the end."

Back at the clearing they all sit down to finish their breakfast and talk excitedly about what they've just seen. "I tell you this the only sad thing about is is Woodnut and Maxie weren't here to see it," says John sighing heavily. "They would have loved it."

"Yes you're right there," replies Cin. "But you know as well as I, if they were given the choice, they would have still chosen to help the lady."

John nods. "Yes of course, but its times like this I wish I had a camcorder with me."

"A what?" asks Max.

John shrugs. "Err doesn't matter."

"John my lad," asks the old greenem. "What is this I hear about you and a mastery mechanical beast, which can go nearly faster than a greenem can see?"

"Ah yes my bike," replies John with a big smile. "Or should I say my friend Suelan's bike. It's a humdinger isn't it?"

"A what my boy?" asks the old greenem. "You're telling me it's a... it's a small brightly coloured fruit beetle that vibrates when mad."

John heaves a heavy sigh as Max Dan and the others snigger. "Yes, yes, it's exactly that," he replies nodding.

"Really," says Evening Thunder scratching his head. "It's not exactly how I'd have pictured it."

"No it's nothing like that," replies John frowning. "I was being sarcastic. Humdinger, is just a saying where I come from, like err, really smart looking."

"So why didn't you just say that?" asks the old greenem a little confused.

"And you my Lord," he continues. "Is it true you have mastered this mechanical beast also?"

Lord Tain glows with pride and trying not to look too excited answers, "Yes it's true, and please call me Suelan. And you say you've heard of this all the way out here."

John gives the old greenem a sly wink. "Oh yes, of course," blusters the old greenem. "Everyone's talking about it, and how brave they thought you were for trying it."

Lord Tain sits a bit taller as proud as proud can be. "I must admit," chuckles the old greenem. "I would have loved to have seen it."

"Then you shall," answers Tain loudly. "When we return you can come with us, as my honoured guest, you and anyone else you may see fit to bring."

"I must admit it's very tempting," replies Evening Thunder with his hand on his chin. "But I don't know, to leave my forest."

"Oh come on," says Tain. "You will be treated with the honour and respect of any visiting dignitary. You have my word, I will even escort you back here afterwards myself."

"You also have my word no one will harm you," bellows Big Dan. "Or I will kill all involved."

"Ok, I'll do it," answers the old greenem excitedly. "I see the times are a changing, and I must learn to change with them also. But John may I ask where did this, err."

"Verum verum," helps Lord Tain.

"Yes thank you," continues the greenem. "Where did this thing come from? You did not have it with you."

"Now that is a good question," nods John. "It was Trace our friend there that found it, somewhere along their border."

"Yes," nods Trace. "It was found over at Desolation Border by my men."

"Desolation Border," mutters Cin. "I wonder."

"Owe," he then squeals suddenly feeling a sharp elbow in his side.

"What was that for?" he asks turning to Big Dan.

Dan puts his finger to his lips. "Shush."

"Why what is it?" whispers Cin.

"If you start asking about that place," whispers Big Dan. "And it's even half as bad as it sounds, there's one among us who won't be able to resist a visit there."

"Oh yes, I see what you mean," whispers Cin. "I just suppose we're lucky Maxie's not here, she's as bad as he is."

"Don't worry. I have an idea, watch this," replies Dan giving a wink. "John my friend could I possibly ask a favour of you?"

John shrugs. "Yeah anything."

"Excellent," says Dan with a big smile. "This may sound a bit bizarre, but could you put your hands over your ears please."

"Hu?" asks a confused John.

"Please," nods Big Dan. "Humour me please, just put your hands over your ears until I wave."

John shrugs and proceeds to as he is asked. "John," shouts Big Dan.

"Hu, did you say something," mumbles John taking his hands away.

"Hmm, no nothing," replies Dan with a big grin and winking to Cin. "Please put your hands back, and remember not until I wave, you promised."

As he does so Cin asks, "So what's all this about?"

"Yes what?" asks Max and the others.

"Well," says Big Dan, now very pleased with himself. "You know John, he's as deaf as a pill rat, I figure that with his hands over his ears, he won't hear a word we're saying."

Cin grabs his arm and shakes it. "Excellent idea."

"Now please Trace, tell us more of this Desolation Border," he continues.

Trace totally bewildered looks to John who's bopping from side to side as if listening to music. He then looks to lord Tain, who having no idea what they're up to simply shrugs. "Oh don't worry about John," smirks Big Dan. "Well fill him in later, if he asks."

"As you wish," answers Trace still very confused. "Desolation Border is just that, it is the border with an area of land known as the land of desolation. It's an area as best we can figure, that is about the size of a province. And as well as our province three others border it, two of whom we have trade with, and a third on the far side who shun contact with anyone. And I can assure you right here right now, there are some strange and weird tales that trickle through from that land."

He then heaves a sigh. "But the land of desolation itself, is also known as the dead lands, and for good reason, as nobody knows about it, as no one can enter it."

"Why? Is it guarded?" asks Cin.

Trace gives out a wry laugh. "No my friend it's not guarded."

"It doesn't have to be, nothing enters, because if they do they die," he tells them.

"What?" asks Max. "How? Are there traps? Who are the people that live there?"

Trace shakes his head. "Nobody lives there, nothing can live there as I told you."

Cin nudges Big Dan smiling broadly. "I'm so glad John can't hear this."

"Yeah," sniggers Big Dan. "I know what you mean, he wouldn't have been able to resist this."

"If you two have finished," interrupts Max.

"Sorry Max," they apologise still smiling pleased with themselves.

"What do you mean, nothing can?" asks Max.

Trace shrugs. "Just that, there is a line a single point so to say, that goes right around the entire area, and you will know it as soon as you reach it. As an awful fear will start to grip you as it does all, even animals. And if you dare to cross that line, then you die."

"Die of what?" asks Big Dan. "Do you just fall down dead?"

"No," answers Trace. "If it were only that humane. No you kind of fall apart as soon as you cross the line. Parts of your skin and flesh start to peel away, then your hair and eyes until there is nothing left of you." Cin, Big Dan and Max just stare at each other in disbelief. "I'm glad John's not listening to this," mutters Cin to Big Dan.

"As am I," puffs Big Dan.

"So how long has this land been like that?" asks Max.

"As long as anyone can remember," answers Trace.

"It hasn't always been like that," shouts Evening Thunder.

"I can remember a time, long, long ago when I was barely a sapling, that land was lush and fertile, and not the barren waste it is now," he tells them. "It just seemed to happen overnight, not to long after oomans started to appear. One day it was fertile, and the next desolation, what caused it we never found out. Even our greatest elders were at a loss. All but one, who is said to still be alive today, but he will not speak of it. He is said to be as old as the earth itself, living longer than another greenem."

"I met him once you know," he continues. "It was him who started all the legends, myths and predictions about John and his friends here. Before he left I asked him, did he not wish to return back to the earth and rest. He just smiled at me kindly, and said it is not his time yet, his wait is not yet over. There was one last thing he had to do, and that he had his destiny, and I had mine."

"What was it?" asks Max impatiently.

The old greenem just shrugs. "He did not say, he just bowed turned and slowly walked away."

"You know," says Big Dan. "We have heard of this ancient greenem also, Woodnut has mentioned him on occasion I think."

"Now if that's it," he continues winking to the others.

"John, John," he then shouts waving his hand in front of John's face.

"Is that it?" asks John putting his hands down.

"Yes thank you," smiles Big Dan still proud of himself.

"I tell you what guys," says John excitedly. "How scary does that place sound, skin peeling off, invisible lines. Now that has got to be worth a quick look. Oh and by the way, my hearing's not that bad you prune. Deaf as a pill rat indeed, cheeky git, whatever a pill rat is."

"Now look what you've done," shouts Big Dan nudging Cin.

"Me," shouts Cin. "It was your idea, you said he wouldn't hear."

"Yes, but it was you who wanted to know about this desolation place in the first place," shouts Big Dan.

"Quiet the pair of you," shouts Max. "Can you not hear yourselves, you sound like children? Now we have a few more days here in the jungle, then we head back to town to meet Maxie and Woodnut. And if after that we head that way for a look, well that's all it will be won't it John, we'll be going around through another province."

John shrugs. "Yeah I would have thought so."

"I don't really fancy my skin falling off, let alone death," he says winking to his to friends.

"Yeah right," mutters Cin under his breath. "It's never that simple."

"What was that, did you say something there?" asks Max.

"No not me Max," grumps Cin.

John grins from ear to ear. "Hey trust me." Big Dan scowls.

"Now listen up you two," shouts Lani making even Max jump. "If my Lord John says you should trust him, then you should, or you'll answer to me, you see if you don't."

Cin and Big Dan just stare at each other a little bewildered. "I tell you what," whispers Big Dan. "John was right about her, one extreme to the other."

Just then a few large raindrops start to slowly descend. Young greenem then rush up with large neatly woven leaves for each of them to shelter under. John kindly declines his, and as the rain gets heavier, he skips and dances around the clearing with the delighted young greenem and Hope, singing as he does so. This is to the further delight of the greenem as they learn a new song all about singing in the rain. Glendra turns to Lord Tain and says, "Do you think this is some sort of tradition of his?"

"I don't think so," shrugs Tain. "But it does look rather fun I must say."

He then proceeds to get up and join in. "That fellow's as bad as John is," laughs Cin.

Glendra smiles. "I don't know when I've seen my Lord Tain so happy. The pressures of being a lord have weighed heavy on him of late."

Max gets up and grabs Lani's hand. "Come on it does look fun."

"But, but," she stutters. "That is the strangest sound my Lord is making."

"Just have fun as you dance around, and try to copy the words," puffs Max as she dances off.

The rains fall heavily for the next hour, and they all at one point or another get up to join in with John, Hope and the young greenem, much to the laughter of Evening Thunder and some of the other elder greenem. Then over the next few days they are taken all over the rainforest and shown, sights sounds and smells to excite and amaze them all.

12

It is the morning of the third day and after a hearty breakfast they gather by their horses at the edge of the forest. "Will you be returning with us Evening Thunder?" asks Lord Tain.

"After your most gracious offer," bows the old greenem. "I think I will yes."

"Excellent," replies Lord Tain clapping his hands together. "Will there be anyone accompanying you."

"Yes," answers the old greenem. "My friend Shadow Drop, but first we have a little parting gift for each of you."

The old greenem then waves over to some greenem just in the line of trees before each are handed an oblong container about twelve inches long sealed at one end, with a plug in the other. "What is it?" asks Tain. "Have a look," replies the old greenem smiling broadly. "But open it carefully."

They all then carefully open the containers and see inside that there is a fine dry red powder. "Is this what I think it is?" asks Tain.

"Yes my lad," answers the greenem. "Pure dried tunnel tree pollen, you seemed so keen on it. Just put the slightest pinch in a bottle of water and shake well."

"One of them tubes should last you a few years aye," he chuckles.

"My word," sighs Lani aloud. "I'm not sure I should be accepting this. This is a truly lordly gift, if I were to sell this I would be rich."

The old greenem laughs. "Maybe to you, to us it is simply pollen, you may do with it as you please my dear."

"Oh thank you," she replies excitedly. "I'll treasure it always, and maybe treat my friends and I to a glass of it now and again." The old greenem smiles and bows.

"We have one extra thing for you Suelan my boy," chuckles the old greenem as he then holds out a neatly folded garment.

"What is it?" asks Lord Tain.

"It's a cape," answers Evening Thunder. "We saw you admiring Hope's clothes, you seemed quite taken with them, and we thought a cape would suit a man of your stature more."

Lord Tain gasps loudly as he carefully unfolds it. "This is truly magnificent," he says. "I mean, I saw the child's clothes, but I never thought for a moment, I would own such a splendid item. This will be my most treasured possession. The patterns and colours leave me aghast, and it's so delicate, I'm afraid to put it on."

"No you're ok my boy," replies Evening Thunder. "It may look delicate, but just like Hope's, it is amazingly strong, we made it to last."

"You, you made this," stutters Tain.

"Yes with the help of many other greenem," nods Evening Thunder.

Lord Tain bows. "The more I learn about you, the more humbled I feel."

He then proudly puts the cape on and climbs up onto his horse before he then leans over and offers his hand to the old greenem. "Please ride with me."

"What about me?" asks Hope tearfully. "Do I just stay here again?"

"Why, do you not want to come with us?" replies John with a wink.

Hope nods excitedly and John smiles. "Would you like to ride on one of the horses with us?" he asks.

"Yes please," Hope replies excitedly. "But what about Fluff."

John shakes his head. "No I don't think he'd like to ride on a horse, eat one maybe."

He then smiles. "But he'll be ok walking beside us, and he can probably run faster then these horses. If it's alright with my friend Suelan here that is."

"Yes of course," answers Tain. "As long as no one gets hurt that is."

John nods. "Don't worry I'll keep an eye on him."

"You listening over there," he shouts to Fluff.

Fluff makes a strange noise which makes Hope start to laugh. "He promises only to eat the sickly ones," he giggles.

Lord Tain suddenly looks very worried. "He's only joking," John reassures him. "He just has a wicked sense of humour."

"Yes of course," replies a still nervous Tain.

"Would you like to ride with me young Hope?" asks Big Dan.

Excitedly Hope then leaps up and the others then mount their horses with John picking up the other old greenem Shadow Drop placing him proudly in front of him. The trip back is full of laughter and conversation of the amazing things they have seen and done. And after another night under the stars they reach the outskirts of the town late the next day. They go through the slums at the edge of town with Lord Tain leading the way. He looks down as they do, to see the look of shock and horror on Evening Thunder's face. And as if seeing for the first time himself, he understands the look on the old greenem's face, and sighing heavily cannot help but hang his head in shame. "What's the matter?" asks John seeing his reaction.

"This, all of this," mutters Tain. "How could I have been so blind?"

"Do you know what I think makes the difference between a good man, and a truly great man," John tells him. "Knowing and admitting his mistakes, and doing their upmost to rectify them. Especially when it's for the betterment of others."

"You're a good man," he continues. "That is plain for all to see, and I'm in no doubt you'll do the right thing."

As they then come across more towns folk, instead of stopping and bowing their heads most turn and flee. Lord Tain and Trace now leading the way look around a little confused. "This is very odd behaviour," says Tain.

"Yes my Lord," agrees Trace. "Do you think something's happened while we were away?"

Cin behind then bellows out a loud laugh then shouts, "Could it possibly have something to do with our large and imposing jackerbell friend here, following closely behind."

"Oh yes," laughs Tain and Trace.

"Never thought of that," says Trace.

Then after nearly terrifying the guards to death at the gate, they dismount and enter the building. All are pleased to see their lord return, until they catch sight of Fluff close behind them, making the two old greenem giggle every time without fail. They then enter the main hall to a wave of gasps, except for one familiar voice. "Mum, Dad" shouts Maxie rushing over closely followed by Woodnut.

Max picks her up and swings her around. Woodnut greets the two old greenem with a gracious bow. Yarin makes her way over to Lord Tain and greets her husband appropriately, then whispers in his ear, "That beast behind you, it is tame isn't it."

"More or less," he whispers back.

"Hope, Fluff," shouts Maxie rushing over to them next and flinging her arms around them in turn.

"I never expected to see you two here," she tells them. "But I'm glad you are. I've so many things to show you."

"How is your mother dear?" asks Tain.

Yarin gasps, "Oh my, she's like a new woman, and she says she feels twenty years younger. And I tell you what she looks it. If I had not seen it with my own eyes, I would not have believed it."

"Ah yes," nods Tain. "I was told this back at the rainforest a few days ago?"

"Really," she gasps again. "Maxie told me she was going to get word to you, but how, that's impossible surely."

"Yes remarkable isn't it," nods Tain. "I've no idea how they do it, something to do with travelling on the wind or something. Some of the things I've seen and experienced in the last few days my dear, you could not begin to imagine. When I return with Evening Thunder here, you must come with us my dear, and see some of them yourself, if that's ok with you old one."

"Yes of course my lad," smiles Evening Thunder.

"Now do I get to see this verum verum of yours," he asks excitedly.

"Yes of course," smiles Tain equally as excited. "Shall we go now, and maybe Trace you could arrange some refreshment in the small hall."

"Maxie and Woodnut can you come with us?" asks Evening Thunder. "Help explain things to a couple of silly old greenem aye."

As they leave John claps his hands. "Right who's for a drink?"

"Excellent idea," reply Big Dan and Cin.

"Would you like something Hope dear?" asks Max.

"Yes water please," he answers. "Fluff would like some also."

They then stand at the side of the room with Glendra and Lani enjoying their drinks and chatting while waiting for Trace to come back. However before he does a nervous middle aged man cautiously enters the room and stands in the middle for several minutes silently staring at them. John starting to feel a little awkward nudges Glendra and says, "Hey what's his problem? Do you think I should ask him over?"

Glendra sighs deeply. "Leave it to me my Lord, he is a troubled soul."

Hope obstructed from view by Max and the others then goes to sit down on a nearby chair and is promptly followed by Fluff. The man stumbles back and pointing at Fluff starts to scream, "That beast, that beast, I know that beast. The trials, kill it, guards kill it now."

Glendra rushes over as several guards run in hearing the commotion. "Anilis please calm down," Glendra tells him. "It's alright, these are friends."

The man pushes him away. "That is the beast of Taraten," he screams. "It should die like my friends died, slowly. Guards kill it, kill it now."

The guards unsure what to do then draw their swords and Fluff stands up and starts to snarl. The man screams to the guards once again, but still unsure what to do they cautiously step forward. Big Dan and Cin nod to each other, and in unison they then draw their swords and proceed to stand in front of Fluff and Hope. "These are our friends," bellows Cin. "And if you wish to harm either of them, you will have to go through us first. And I warn you now, it will take a lot more than you."

John throws his drink down and stands between the two parties. "Right everyone calm down. Why has there always got to be some butt hole causing trouble."

"JOHN language," shouts Max.

"Sorry," replies John with shrug. "But really it seems like every five damn minutes. Right let's sort this out, like the decent people we are. Now I'm led to believe, Anilis is it, you were sent to Taraten as a peace envoy and witnessed some awful things, and for that I am truly sorry. But I cannot undo what has been done, but I can assure you, nothing like that will ever happen again."

"That I understand," shouts the man. "But that beast should die."

"Now listen," shouts John getting mad. "That beast as you call it, is an intelligent creature, and was as much a victim of that place as you were. More so in fact as he was captured, lost his mate and family, was poked, stabbed and starved, and constantly provoked. Left to go nearly mad in an open cage, with the only nourishment being the odd poor soul thrown into his area. And he was kept like that for around two years, and as I see it, he has a damn sight better reason to resent us, than we have him. Now we can all leave if that is what you want. But we are friends, and side by side we laugh together, and side by side we fight together, you want one of us, you take all of us."

Fluff suddenly starts to growl and snarl at Hope. "Uhu hmm, yes now," answers Hope. "Ok then."

John, Max, Cin and Big Dan look to Hope as Fluff stops growling and Hope turns to his friends. "Fluff told me to tell you, in his eyes you have all shown your worth, and he now considers you all part of his pack. Something he never thought any man person would ever be worthy of."

Big Dan bows his head. "We are truly honoured."

Fluff then starts to make further noises and Hope laughs. Cin looks over at Fluff curiously and says, "Hang on I know that noise, he's laughing isn't he."

Hope giggles, nods and replies, "Yes he is."

"So why is he laughing dear?" asks Max.

The boy suddenly looking more serious replies, "He says, if you would all now like to step aside, this will only take a moment."

Fluff then starts to slowly make his way forward. "Stop that now," shouts

John. "You Fluff get back over there with Hope, nobody is going to get anybody."

Just then Trace comes back in the room. "What by the moons and stars is going on here?" he hollers.

"Just a misunderstanding I'm sure," answers John.

Anilis then shouts in a nervous voice, "There's no misunderstanding, it's that beast it's a killer, it should be put to death. They're protecting it, and that abomination of a child with it."

"You what," screams Max. "How dare you?"

Then mad as mad can be she sprints towards the man. Shooting past John he puts out his left arm out and grabs her around the waist lifting her up, kicking swinging and screaming as he does so. "How dare you?" she shouts at Analis. "You threaten my friends, you insult my family."

"Let me go," she shouts at John still kicking.

"See you," she shouts again at Anilis. "When I get my hands on you, you dangle sack, I'm going to beat you black and blue."

"Dangle sack," says John in a heightened voice.

Then turning to Cin and Dan he asks them, "Does that mean what I think it means?"

Both men nod grinning like cheshire cats. "Corr," says John with a cheeky smile. "I've been dying to say this, Max language please."

"Let me go," she shouts again.

"Calm down now," John tells her.

"Now everyone quiet," shouts Trace. "And you Anilis, we have always pitied you, but on such an important occasion to insult not just visiting dignitaries, but friends of Lord Tain, and more importantly mine. This is inexcusable and you will be dealt with appropriately, now leave my sight."

Max calms down and John let's her go. "Please," says John looking over to Trace. "What this man went through was obviously very traumatic, and I feel he should be helped not punished."

Trace nods, bows and replies, "As you wish."

"Did you hear that," he calls to the man nearly at the door. "You have been shown leniency by the new Lord Taraten. This is a new era for all of us. Do you not wish to thank my Lord?"

However Anilis turns slowly around and points to Fluff, John, and the others and replies, "This isn't over you'll see."

Hearing this Fluff bolts forwards and in a couple of bounds pins the man to the door by his shoulders with his mighty paws. And he snarls as loudly and viciously as he can, his teeth no more than an inch from Anilis's face. The man stands terrified white with fear and can do nothing but whimper as Fluff's hot breath steams in his face. He would have fainted if not for being held up by Fluff's powerful paws. "Seems some people never learn." sighs John.

Trace stands there speechless looking over to John and the others for guidance. "Is, is it going to kill him?" he eventually stutters.

"If it wanted to kill him," answers Big Dan. "He'd be dead already."

"Quickly Hope dear," calls Max. "Go over and calm him down."

Hope nods and walks over and then stands close beside them. "Hmm yes, aha," he then says listening to Fluff's growls and snarls.

"Yes I'll tell him," he continues before he explains to the terrified man, "Now my friend has told me to tell you exactly what he's said. If you ever threaten him or his pack again, he will not hesitate, he will not pause, and he will not be stopped, and he will rip your head from your body. Now do you understand, if so blink." The man does so. "Very good," Hope continues. "He also tells me he knew what was happening to these people. And he did his best to kill them as quickly as possible. But he also has little respect for a species of creature who gets enjoyment out of such games of entrapment and torture. He will let you go now, so be good. Oh and on a more personal note from myself, you should maybe go and change, you seem to have soiled yourself."

Fluff then steps down and the man collapses, and has to be carried away. Fluff and Hope go back over to stand with the others. "Never mind him," sniggers Cin to Big Dan. "I nearly soiled myself."

"Yes," sniggers Big Dan. "Now that was impressive."

"Well if you are all ready," announces Trace. "We shall return to the small hall and have some supper." Max links arms with Lani and Yarin and follows Trace, closely followed by John and the others. In the hall Lord Tain, the three greenem and Maxie are sitting at a large table waiting for them. And soon they are all eating and drinking and laughter and merriment abound. Yarin whispers to her husband, "Where did you get the cape? I have never seen its like."

"Wonderful isn't it," smiles Tain proudly. "The greenem made it for me."

"Never really," she gasps.

"Anyway," asks Lord Tain. "What's this I've been hearing about Anilis my dear?"

Yarin not sure what to say just stutters, "Yes, yes, err it seems to be all sorted now my love."

Lord Tain then turns to John, Dan and the others and tells them, "You know when Anilis was younger, he was with us on a tour of the province. When camping one night he came down with the five minute madness. Do you remember Trace?"

Trace nods. "Oh yes, that was a long time ago. We thought at first he was just mucking about and my how we all laughed, it was very funny. Until we saw the fear in his eyes that is, and listening to his pleads we knew what it was."

The two girls, John and the greenem start to giggle, with Big Dan and Cin sitting growling and frowning at them. "Is there a problem?" asks Trace."

"No, no none at all," chuckles John. "Please carry on."

"Where was I," mutters Trace. "Ah yes, it is sometimes thought of as a bad omen you know. Other places I've heard it can be a sign of luck, you have heard of it haven't you."

"Hey trust me," grins John winking to Cin and Dan. "I hadn't until I came to these lands, but my friends there seem very familiar with it."

Big Dan frowns and leaning over says to John, "Don't think we've forgotten, we still owe you for that."

"Hmm yes," stammers John. "Moving swiftly on now. How about a trip to that Desolation place, we will be going roughly that direction anyway."

"Hmm," grumps Cin. "I think I'd rather have the five minute madness again."

"You've had it," gasps Lord Tain.

"You could say that," grumps Cin. "It seemed to hit half our party one day, isn't that right John."

John, Maxie and Woodnut are sniggering for all their worth. "Err yes," answers John trying not to giggle again. "And very mysterious it was."

A short time later after a few more drinks Lord Tain whispers to John, "Come on then, what was all that about."

"Hmm, err, I'm not sure I should say," winces John.

"Oh go on," says Tain. "I won't say anything, its something to do with the five minute madness isn't it." John looks to the three greenem. Evening Thunder smiles and nods. "Ok then," grins John. "Let me ask you Suelan my friend. What do you think causes the five minute madness?"

"Now that is the question isn't it," nods Tain. "Men have tried to work that out for generations, some say it's a disease that afflicts the simple of mind but others say it's a problem that runs in families."

He then suddenly stops in mid sentence to see the greenem creased up with laughter. "What are they laughing at John?" he asks.

John winks and replies, "Do you want to really know what causes it?"

Tain nods enthusiastically so John grinning whispers in his ear, "It's a practical joke played by the greenem."

"You what," yelps Tain excitedly.

"Shush," says John. "Yes honestly, it's like a berry pill like thing. Sometimes the odd mischievous greenem, given the chance, will slip one of thesm in someone's drink, and a short time later it kicks in."

Lord Tain throws his head back and laughs so hard it starts to hurt his sides. "That, that is the best, funniest, most insane thing I think I've ever heard, and I take it, it has no lasting effects."

"No, none at all," answers John.

Lord Tain slaps his hand on the table laughing again. "Absolutely marvellous, oh I wish I could get my hands on one of them."

"You mean one of these," giggles Woodnut handing him a small round object.

"Is that it," stutters Tain excitedly.

Woodnut nods enthusiastically. "May I?" asks Tain equally as enthusiastic.

He then looks around nearly bursting with excitement. "It's got to be Trace," he says. "I'll explain it to him later, he'll see the funny side I'm sure."

Five minutes later and Lord Tain sees his chance and drops it into Traces drink. Tain, John, Maxie and the three greenem sit there excitedly waiting with anticipation. "What's the matter?" asks Trace. "Why is everyone staring?"

"Oh no reason," grins Lord Tain. "Just carry on, please drink."

"How long does it take?" Lord Tain whispers to the greenem.

"There," says Woodnut excitedly. "Look at his foot."

They all then stare down at Trace's foot which seems to be tapping out a beat. Another few moments pass and his other foot starts to do the same. Trace a little worse for wear slowly stares down at his feet a little bewildered. John, Tain and the others are now finding it really hard to control themselves. When suddenly without warning Trace springs to his feet and proceeds to run around the room. The others look on in total confusion at Trace's odd behaviour and John and Lord Tain's belly laughs. "Help," screams Trace as his legs now seem to have taken on a life of their own, and proceed to jig and dance him around the room. Big Dan nudges Cin pointing to John and the others creased up and says, "Looks like someone's been up to their old tricks."

"Yes, but seeing it from this side, I must admit it does look very funny," laughs Cin.

Big Dan frowns. "Now we know it's nothing serious."

"A toast my friend," laughs Lord Tain raising his mug, "To good friends and good times."

John raises his mug. "I'll drink to that, and if you finish that I'd like to propose another."

Lord Tain then quickly finishes his drink and waves to a girl for another. "Well John my friend what's your toast?" he asks.

John grinning broadly winks, raises his drink and replies, "To more good times, and even more foot tapping madness."

"Yes, yes, that sounds good to me also," chuckles Tain a little confused, until he then notices John staring down towards his tapping foot. Then with a total look of horror he stutters, "You haven't."

John winks at him mischievously. "Hey trust me, now just sit back and enjoy the ride."

John, the girls, and the greenem all start to fall about laughing as Lord Tain's other foot starts to tap. "He will be alright won't he," whispers Yarin to Max.

"Yes of course," whispers Max. "It's just a bit of harmless fun."

Lord Tain suddenly then involuntarily jumps to his feet and starts to stammer, "I, I, I."

"Hey enjoy it," John tells him. "Remember it's harmless."

"Yes, yes," answers Tain excitedly. "You know I think I will."

He then starts to giggle and laugh like a school boy, as he feels his lower body take on a life of its own. "Can you see what I see," says Big Dan to Cin. "I can't believe they'd do that to Lord Tain."

"Hmm," frowns Cin staring at John and Woodnut. "I think you're starting to get naive in your old age my friend."

"Hey Woodnut," laughs John wiping his eyes. "Considering you don't have pockets, where on earth were you keeping those pill things?"

Woodnut starts to open his mouth. "No, I tell you what," chuckles John looking at him suspiciously. "Maybe you'd better not tell me." This makes Woodnut and the other two greenem laugh even more.

Lord Tain is now in mid flow and enjoying every moment of it, much to the shock of his subjects there but Trace has now stopped and is bent over with his hands on his knees panting and nervous. Hearing the gasps of shock from some, and laughs from others he looks up to see what's going on himself. A different look of shock and horror now adorns his face as he sees Lord Tain. Panicking a little he runs after Tain and tries to grab him. "My Lord," he shouts. "This cursed madness has struck us both, this is a bad omen, here let me help you."

"Nonsense," laughs Lord Tain.

"Let go, it's only a bit of fun," he splutters.

"W, what, what do you mean?" stutters Trace automatically letting go. "This madness has taken your mind Sire."

"No don't be silly man," laughs Tain, his legs springing him back round and running him past Trace once again. "It's just John and the greenem messing about."

"You, you what," shouts Trace.

"The five minute madness is their work," he gasps.

Lord Tain just nods. Flabbergasted Trace stumbles backwards falling onto someone's lap. "Oh sorry," he stutters getting back up, then still in a daze he stumbles over to John and the greenem. "Is, is this true?" he asks. "I mean, did you, err, the madness, was it?"

John grins then putting his finger to his lips says, "Shush, our secret."

Whether through excitement or just through sheer relief Trace slaps his thigh and shouts at the top of his voice, "Yes."

Everyone turns and stare. "I wondered why my Lord seemed in such good cheer, you people are insane, I mean how," explodes Trace happily.

"Shush later," replies John with a wink. "Come on, sit down here and have a drink.

Trace then sits down still very excited and whispers, "I still can't believe it, all this time, all these years, your honestly telling me. The five minute madness is nothing more than a practical joke."

John smiles and nods as Trace throws his head back and laughs loudly once again.

"Mum," asks Maxie. "Did I here Dad say we were moving on tomorrow?"

"I don't think so dear," answers Max. "But he did mention going for a look at the border, err you know, the one with that awful name. I think Trace said it's about a three day trip."

Maxie nods. "Maybe we should take our bags with us tomorrow Mum," she replies softly.

"Why dear?" asks her mum a little shocked.

Maxie sighs and replies, "I have an awful feeling we won't be returning here."

"What do you mean?" Max asks nervously. "Maybe we shouldn't go then."

Maxie seeing her mother's sudden fear changes her tone. "Don't worry Mum," she says smiling. "I'm sure it's meant to be, and that's a good thing I think."

"I'm probably wrong anyway, it's probably just something I ate," she answers a little nervously.

"My dear," replies her mum smiling. "I love you dearly and trust you implicitly. If you say that's what we should do, then that is what we will do. But something you ate, come on, surely you can do better than that."

Maxie puts her hand over her mouth and giggles making her mum giggle too. Lady Yarin sitting with them shakes her hand and says, "If you leave I think it will upset my husband greatly, he has grown very fond of you all, as have I. Your coming here has lifted him so. I've never seen him this happy since he was a child. Please can you not stay a little longer?"

Max shrugs sadly and looks to Maxie, who smiles kindly and simply looks away. "In that case," replies Yarin with a bow. "Please do not tell him tonight, it would only spoil his evening. My husband and I will accompany you to the border."

"If that is alright with our honoured guests," she continues smiling towards the two old greenem.

"Yes of course," they answer. "It would be our honour also."

Max nods in agreement and says, "I think that would be an excellent idea. I won't tell the boys until morning either, I think it will be hard for them also."

Lord Tain finally comes back over and slumps down on his chair exhausted and delighted. John slaps him on the back. "Well Suelan my friend, how was it."

"Most exhilarating," he pants. "You will have to get me some more of them."

Woodnut giggles to the old greenem, "He must be the first ooman to not only enjoy the madness, but want it to happen again."

"Maxie, please," Lord Tain then shouts.

Maxie smiles back and replies, "I suppose, but only a couple of goes."

"What does he want dear?" asks Max.

Maxie giggles. "Since I told him I can tell when people lie, he keeps trying to catch me out."

"What do you mean dear?" asks Max.

"He tells me something," replies Maxie. "And I have to say whether he's lying or telling the truth."

Yarin tilts her head to the side just staring at Maxie for a moment. "How odd," she says. "And have you ever got it wrong child."

Maxie shrugs. "No never," she answers.

"But how do you know?" asks Yarin.

Maxie just shrugs and turns to listen to Lord Tain's story. "Well?" he asks excitedly. "Was I telling the truth?

"No," she answers. "You lied from start to finish."

"Astonishing," replies Tain clapping his hands.

Yarin whispers to Max, "The more I learn about your daughter, the more I am astonished."

"As are we," replies Max. "As are we."

Yarin a little confused simply bows.

13

THE MORNING COMES as it always does with the rising of the sun and the tweeting of flurries. Maxie and the greenem are first up and sitting in the communal room, when John and Max come through and sit down with John chuckling to himself. "Morning," go the greetings back and forth.

"And what are you laughing at?" asks Max.

John chuckles shaking his head. "Outside our window, there was a flurry singing its heart out."

"So, what's funny about that?" shrugs Max.

"Well, it's just not right is it?" he chuckles again. "It still tickles me, they're like spiders that have been somehow crossed with birds. And singing away, it just doesn't look right does it, come on."

"Hu," grumps Max. "There's nothing wrong with them."

"It's you, you weirdo, with your burbs and spicers," she replies with a grin.

"Oh why do I bother?" groans John. "Anyway what's wrong with you lot, wet the bed or something?"

"Oh no of course not!" shout Max and Maxie in unison.

John shrugs and smiles. "It's just an old saying, it just means you're up much earlier than normal. Any who, why up so early?"

"We are going to pack our stuff, we'll be taking it with us," sighs Max.

"Oh ok," he replies yawning.

"Are you not going to asks why?" asks Max.

"Nah I trust you," he replies yawning again.

Not long later Big Dan tumbles through shortly followed by Cin. The two slump down. "Ooh my head," groans Big Dan. Cin feeling too rough to even speak half puts his hand up in a gesture of solidarity.

"We are packing our bags up boys and taking them with us," Max tells them.

Cin just groans but Big Dan mumbles, "Yeah sure, but can it wait till the widows root starts to work."

"Yes of course," giggles Max. "Although if you didn't drink so much, you wouldn't have to take that stuff to recover."

After breakfast they stand in the yard outside waiting for Lord Tain and

Trace. They give a loud cheer on their arrival. "I'm sorry for being so late," apologises Lord Tain. "But I felt so ill this morning, oh I can tell you."

"Yes as was I," groans Trace.

Big Dan and Cin give out a wry laugh. "Lightweights aye," laughs Big Dan nudging Cin cheekily, "Obviously not real men," agrees Cin.

"I'd like to argue," replies Trace. "But I still feel a little delicate, and you two, well, you look as if you haven't had a drop."

Max frowns. "Hmm."

"Err yes well," coughs Cin ratching in his pockets. "Here chew a piece of this each. And in a short time you'll be as right as rain."

But suddenly noticing their bags Lord Tain asks, "Why are you them there? You are not leaving are you?"

"Err yes, I think so" sighs John.

"No you can't," pleads Tain in a heightened voice. "Why didn't you say something last night?"

John, Cin and Big Dan all suddenly start to look sad. "Yes I know," sighs John. "We have become very fond of you all also, but we didn't know ourselves until we were informed this morning."

Yarin comes out of the building with a bag on her back. "Well it appears we are ready," sighs Lord Tain deeply. "Shall we go?"

"Don't look so sad my boy," says Evening Thunder looking up at him. "You'll meet again, I'm sure of it. And besides you have days left together, enjoy them."

"Yes, yes of course," smiles Lord Tain taking Yarin's hand.

Woodnut, Evening Thunder and Shadow Drop then climb onto Fluff's back, who then sets off walking beside Hope and the others. A short distance out of town and Trace shouts, "You know I feel, well pretty good."

"Yes me too," agrees Lord Tain. "I don't know what that stuff was you gave us, but it's worked marvellously."

"It's something called widow's root I think," answers John.

"You what," shout both men.

"That's deadly," says Trace.

John grins cheekily. "Our deadly plan has worked," he shouts.

The three Suelan people stare in horror. "No don't be silly," replies Maxie. "He's only having you on."

Max frowns at John, Cin and Dan all sniggering like kids. "And that wasn't even remotely funny" she snaps.

"So it wasn't widow's root," stutters Trace.

"Oh yes it was," says Maxie. "But it was the bark you chewed, only the inner flesh is deadly. As you can see the part given to you is a great remedy for hangovers."

"Yes, yes of course," puffs Lord Tain nervously relieved.

"Don't worry," laughs Big Dan. "It hasn't killed us yet."

As the day goes on they are all enjoying each others company in the mid day sun. Maxie is walking beside Hope, and both are giggling and humming together while sharing ear phones. The two old greenem and Woodnut are joining in with them. Yarin whispers to Max, "Are you sure they should be making them noises?"

"Yes of course," giggles Max. "Don't worry they're just happy."

"John my friend," asks Tain. "Why have the children got a piece of vine stuck to the side of their heads?"

"Why don't you go over and ask?" John replies smiling. "Don't worry its nothing bad, in fact it's quite fantastic."

"Some sort of drug or medicine?" asks Tain nodding.

John looks at him just a little oddly replying, "In some ways yes I suppose."

"Hey Maxie," he shouts. "Suelan wants to know why you have that in your ear."

Maxie giggles and takes it out of her and Hope's ear. "Come over here my Lord," she tells him.

Lord Tain comes over and kneels down. "This won't hurt will it?" he asks.

"No silly," answers Maxie. "Now I'm going to slip these in your ears ok. Then I'm going to switch it on ok, don't be alarmed just listen." She then switches the mp3 player on and Tain's eyes instantly shoot wide open, and after a few moments he takes the ear piece out. "What is this madness?" he shouts. "This is witchcraft."

"I'm glad you asked," replies a smiling Maxie. "I used my powers to once shrink an army of men, then trapped them inside this little box, and the sound you can hear is their tormented souls screaming out in terror."

Lord Tain flops down. "R, r, really," he gasps. "I must admit, it, it does sound like that."

The three greenem laugh so hard they fall off Fluff and have to climb back on. Maxie giggles also but replies, "No silly, it's just music, and this bit of music my Dad calls MCR. It's very good don't you think."

Cin nudges Big Dan. "You know that kids getting as bad as he is," he mutters nodding towards John.

"Yes," chuckles Big Dan. "But did you see the look on Tain's face, priceless."

"Let's stop and have something to eat," announces Max frowning at Maxie. "And maybe we can explain, and stop any confusion aye."

So as they eat they all try to explain music and the music player to the three Tain people, with both Cin and Big Dan telling them how popular it has become in their provinces, especially on an evening with ale. Then the two Tain men and Yarin all take turns at listening to some of the different songs and styles. With each having a different favourite and getting more impatient for their next go.

They then walk for the rest of the afternoon and into the early evening before settling down for the night with a bottle of ale each that Trace has brought. Lord and Lady Tain along with Trace join in with John and the others for a sing along. "Do you know?" shouts Tain as they finally settle down to sleep. "This singing lark, really does seem to go well with ale on an evening. And maybe it's just me, but it also kind of makes you feel good inside you know."

"Yes me too my dear," answers Yarin.

"Yes and I also Sire," mutters Trace yawning.

Finally John is nearly asleep himself, when he feels a tug on his ear and jumps up with a start, just to hear a faint familiar giggle. "Hey silly man," comes the whisper.

"Hey pretty lady," he answers looking around for the little mossy.

"So what do I owe the pleasure?" he asks.

"I just thought you ought to know," she tells him. "I think you are being followed."

"What?" gasps John. "By who? Where are they?"

"Shush," snaps Lilly. "I don't want them knowing about me."

"Oops sorry," apologises John. "But it was a bit of a shock."

"Who are they? Do you know?" he whispers.

"There's just one," answers Lilly. "An old woman, she's tracking you just out of sight, keeping her distance."

"Oh, how bizarre," whispers John. "What does she look like?"

"She's a little scruffy," answers Lilly. "Wild unkempt hair, and even for an ooman, she's very strange. If she's not talking and arguing with herself, she's singing the same few words over and over again. Stopping to do the odd cartwheel or hand stand. One thing though, for an old ooman she seems remarkably fit."

John scratches his head. "Ah," he sighs. "It's the old crone from the party, but what the hell is she following us for."

"You know her?" asks Lilly.

John shrugs. "Yeah kind of."

"What are you going to do?" asks Lilly.

John shrugs. "Nothing" he answers.

"Do you want me to do something?" she asks. "I can make her disappear if you like, return her to the earth."

"I hope you're joking about that," frowns John. "We'll just ignore her, she's harmless, and she'll soon get bored and stop."

"As you wish silly man," comes the muffled reply as she disappears back into the earth.

They all rise relatively early, and to the Tain people's surprise a small neat plate of food is placed beside each of them. "Where did this come from?" asks Yarin.

"Some of our people earlier," answers Shadow Drop.

"They thought you might be a little hungry when you woke up," he continues with a kindly smile.

"Oh yes, thank them kindly for us please," replies a curtsying Yarin.

They are then soon on their way, as a mist starts to rise from the suns gentle warmth. "I love this time of the morning," says Trace "I always feel, err, I don't know, a little fresher, a little cleaner you know, as if I'm walking on the clouds."

"We've been above the clouds," shouts Maxie excitedly.

Both Trace and Tain give out a wry laugh. "We have," snaps Maxie.

"And where was that?" asks Trace.

"At Cloud Falls, back in Luguvalio province," she answers.

"You know," says Lord Tain nodding. "I have heard of this place, they say for anyone brave enough to go there, its beauty is immeasurable."

"Yes," sighs Big Dan. "That is a perfect description of it, and one day perhaps we could take you there."

Tain nods. "Yes I would like that."

"Perhaps in the mean time my dear," he then says turning to Maxie. "You could tell us all about it."

Maxie's eyes light up, and with the help of Woodnut the pair tell them all about their journey from Luguvalio stronghold to Cloud Falls, and even on to Feather Fields.

Then in what seems like no time at all it's early afternoon and they are walking through meadow. A short distance slightly out of the way is a line of trees and bushes. "Right," says John. "You lot carry on without me, I'm away to feed Henry."

"You know what he's like when he doesn't get fed," he tells them.

He then takes off running towards the trees. Trace scratches his head. "How can he go that fast?"

"Believe me," answers Cin. "That's not fast."

"May I interrupt," asks Tain. "Who on earth is Henry?"

"Does she travel with us?" he asks.

Max sighs as Cin and Big Dan start to giggle like school boys. "No," sighs Max again. "I'm very sorry, how do I put this, it's err, well. It's what he's called his clinker beetle."

Lord Tain rubs the back of his head. "He's named his, err, clinker beetle," he asks going rather red in the process. "How does he know it's a girl?"

"It isn't, he says it's a boy," answers Dan.

"Oh," shrugs Tain a little unsure what to say next.

"That's nothing," laughs Cin. "You watch him late at night when he thinks no ones watching him, he often plays with it, he's been trying to teach it tricks you know."

"To be fair," chuckles Big Dan. "It seems to be working, it always fetches that little stick back."

"That's enough," snaps Max. "I know what he's up to, and I've given up telling him off. I just ignore him now."

"And what are you lot laughing at," she says turning to Maxie, Fluff, Hope and the greenem.

"Nothing," Maxie replies.

Lord Tain smiles. "My dear. And I mean this with no disrespect, but he is the strangest fellow I have ever met, but I do like him."

John slows down as he reaches the line of trees and makes his way in. He stops about halfway in and proceeds to do what he came to do. At first it is relatively silent where he is, with nothing but the odd twitter of a flurry, and gentle breeze rattling the leaves. But as his hearing starts to adjust to his surrounding environment, other sounds start to creep in. A faint whining noise appears on the breeze, and then faint giggles and mutters start to come from all around him. "It's him," he hears in a quiet giggling voice.

"Shall we go and see him," giggles another.

"No," giggles another. "They don't like it when you bother them."

John let's out a big sigh but replies, "Guys, guys, please, a little privacy here, please. I'll see you all in a minute or two."

"Where's a public toilet when you want one?" he mutters to himself.

Then as he stands back up sorting himself out a little voice calls, "Can we come out now?"

John now a lovely shade of red replies, "Why don't I come to you?"

Then he proceeds past a tree to where the voices are coming from and about a dozen young greenem are excitedly waiting for him. He sits down and they all excitedly crowd around him. "Hi guys," he says with a broad smile. "This is a nice place you've got here."

"It used to be," giggles one of the greenem.

"Yes well," stutters John going red again.

"Sorry, anyway," he then apologises trying to change the subject but going even redder making the young greenem giggle even more.

"We were so hoping you might come this way," one of the young greenem tells him. "Do you think we could possibly meet Woodnut, Maxie and the others please?"

"Well I don't see why not," says John smiling. "I think they'd like that too, I'll just go and get them shall I. But first what is that noise I keep hearing?"

"What noise?" asks a greenem.

"Hmm, like a faint whining, err high pitched, err noise," he answers.

"Oh that," replies one of the greenem nonchalantly. "It's a child just across from here, near the orchard crying."

"Oh ok," John says nonchalantly too. "Well I'll just go and get the others then."

"Curiously, do you know why he's crying?"

"Oh yes," answers a greenem.

After a few minutes John sighs, "Well then."

"Oh you want to know," giggles the greenem.

"Please," replies John shaking his head.

"The man who owns the orchard gave him a beating," answers the greenem.

"Fair enough," John shrugs. "I'll be back soon."

He then starts to walk away but after only a few steps he turns back again. "Any idea why he got a beating?" he asks. "I mean it must have been a heck of a welting, I can still hear the poor mite."

Most of the greenem just shrug but one little fellow answers, "I saw most of what happened. But it's just what you do, some do it to each other, and some do it to children. But even for an ooman, it did seem very bad."

John slowly nods. "Maybe I'll go and have a quick look then, just for a moment you know. Would you kindly show me the way please?"

"Yes of course," answers the little greenem proudly. "It would be my honour."

The little greenem then guides him the short distance to the other side of the wood. Stepping out he points a short distance ahead to a woven hedge, forming a boundary around a decent sized orchard of bubble berry trees. Just in front of the hedge there is a large tree running parallel with a small bank of earth. And sitting there on the bank with his head in his hands, is a young boy of scruffy appearance crying inconsolably.

"What are you going to do now?" asks the greenem.

"Hmm," thinks John aloud.

"What's your name by the way?" he asks.

"Sky Blue Sir," answers the little greenem proudly.

"Nice to meet you Sky Blue," John replies nodding. "I'll leave my bag here with you, if that's alright. I'll just go and have a quick word with lad I think. See what's going on, cheer him up a bit maybe."

"Don't worry," bows the little greenem. "I'll keep your bag safe for you."

John smiles and nods. "Thank you, I know you will." He then steps out of the line of trees and down a small bank. The young boy still with his head in his hands, crying on the small bank opposite doesn't notice John walk over. He stands there in front of the boy for a minute or two unsure what to say. But the boy raising his head for a moment sees him, and his head falls back into his hands. "I'm, I'm, I'm, s, sorry," he sobs. "I, I, won't do it again," he cries. "P, please don't hit me again."

"I'm afraid you've mistaken me for someone else young man," answers John. "I didn't hit you, and by the way my friends call me John. Do you mind if I sit down?"

"I, I, if, if you like," he sobs. "S, s, s, so, w, what do you want?"

"Shush, it's ok," John tells him softly. "So what do I want, nothing, it was sheer curiosity. I heard someone crying, and well, I thought I'd just come and have a look."

"You, you'd better go Sir" the boy sobs again. "The man who owns the orchard behind is still about somewhere. You'll get in trouble if he thinks you're with me Sir."

"Hey I told you my friends call me John, and just you let me worry about him, ok. Now what's your name?"

"V, V, Valantina Sir," he sobs.

"Here give me your hand," says John.

The boy lifts his head and cautiously and reluctantly prizes his hand from his eyes and gives it to John. John carefully takes it and shakes it. "Nice to meet you Valantina," he says.

The young lad nearly breaks into a smile and stutters, "M, my friends call me Val."

A faint giggling is heard coming from the trees as a loud angry voice shouts from further down the track, "Hey you there, is that your boy."

And just about in ear shot, one of the greenem is heard giggling to the others, now gathered around John's bag, "Let's watch, this should be fun, I bet this bully get's just what's coming to him now."

"Yeah let's," giggle the others.

"You there," shouts the angry man. "Does that thieving brat belong to you?"

"Is this him?" frowning John asks the boy.

"Y, yes Sir, err John," the boy sobs.

The man then stops a short distance away leaning on a thin walking stick. "Hey you there swifty. Are you ignoring me? I'll give you a taste of my stick if you don't answer me sharp."

John leans forward and glares. "You can try," he replies.

"Is that thief your son?" the man shouts. "Like father like son aye, you look as bigger thief as he does."

"Now listen up," growls John. "I am no thief, and I do not like being called one. And no, this child is no relation to me, in fact, this is the first time we've ever met. I heard crying and just came to see who it was."

"Liar," shouts the man. "So you honestly expect me to believe you just happened to be passing."

John jumps to his feet starting to get mad. "Now I don't know what the lad has done," he shouts. "But I'm sure he's very sorry and won't do it again. But if you keep talking to me like that you're going to seriously peeve me off."

"Err well," stutters the man. "I caught him stealing from me."

John turns back around and leans over putting his hand on the lads back and asks, "Is this true?"

But the boy suddenly reels in pain. "Ow, ow, ow," he screams.

"Oh sorry," apologises John. He then notices a few spots of blood on the back of the boy's shirt and cautiously takes the tail of it. "It's ok, I'll just have a quick peek," he tells the boy softly sitting back down. "I'll be as careful as I can, I promise." He then peels up the shirt as carefully as he can with the boy jumping and squealing the whole time. John cannot believe his eyes, as across the boys back are three thick lines from the man's stick, one so deep it's broken the skin, leaving a trickle of blood running down his back. He then lowers the lad's shirt and turns back around glaring at the man too mad to speak.

The man stands there brazen. "I did nothing wrong," he says. "I caught him stealing, I only hit him three times. That's law, I'm within my rights."

"What did you take son?" asks John.

"I, I, j, just took a couple of fallen bubble berry fruit, f, f, from the orchard. One for me and one for my mum." the boy replies. "They were bashed and bruised any, anyway," he sobs. "He couldn't have sold them."

John turns back around in disbelief once more and says, "So you did this simply because he scrumped a bit of fruit?"

"Err well yes," stutters the man. "You've got to nip this sort of thing in the bud you know."

"And that gives you the right to hit him that hard, you made him bleed," growls John.

"I'm quite within my rights," bellows the man. "If you catch a junior stealing, or showing disrespect the law says you can give him up to three hits. I thought I let him off quite lightly."

"Jesus I don't believe this," shouts John. "A clip around the lug or smacked bottom yes, but that, that's just cruel and sadistic. Would you like it if I did that to you?"

"I'd like to see you try swift," laughs the man.

John jumps up instantly and darts over. "Oh you would, would you," he snaps eyeballing the man.

"No please John," sobs the boy. "I don't want any trouble."

"John," laughs the man. "You have a woman's name. And if you don't like the law then I suggest you take it up with Lord Tain."

John then raises his hands up, cocks his head and slowly bows, then walks backwards until he comes across the bank and sits back down with the boy. He then whispers to the boy, "Don't be scared." Then covering the boy's ears firmly with his hands he gives out a loud whistle. It still makes the boy jump, but brings the man to his knees.

"What was that you cur?" shouts the man getting back to his feet.

"Just what you asked for," snaps John.

"I should beat you where you sit," shouts the man waving his stick.

Then a few minutes pass with the man still bellowing and posturing, until a faint rustling of leaves, and the odd cracking of branches is heard. And as the man turns to see what's coming it's too late, as Fluff has launched himself out of the woods, and is flying high through the air towards him. He doesn't even get the chance to turn, before the jackerbell has landed on him flattening him to the ground. Then he proceeds to pin him down, snarling no more than a few inches from his face. The boy is so stunned he forgets his pain for a moment, and falls backwards himself. John now grinning from ear to ear claps shouting, "Nice entrance, come here pal."

"What are you doing back there?" he asks the boy, suddenly noticing he's lying down.

"Err, I'm kind of stuck," the boy sobs.

John takes his hand and carefully pulls him back up. The boy then suddenly starts to shake as Fluff bounds over. "Are, are we going to be eaten now Sir?" he asks.

"No," laughs John. "Don't you worry, he's with me."

The man struggles back to his feet winded and bruised. "Oh you going to pay for this now, swifty, err John was it?"

"I'm only John to my friends," John snaps. "You may call me Lord Taraten."

"Oh that's a good one," laughs the man. "That nearly makes it all worth it."

Three moaning voices are then heard coming out of the line of trees and John turns to see Woodnut, Evening Thunder and Shadow Drop staggering towards him, with Woodnut rubbing his head and Shadow Drop rubbing his backside. "Well," groans Evening Thunder. "We managed to keep hold until that last bush."

John frowns at Fluff. "Could you not have let them off first?"

Fluff just sniggers. "What's the matter anyway John?" asks Woodnut. "Is there an emergency?"

"Kind of," replies John nodding.

The young boy's eyes are now like dinner plates and his mouth falls open. But John barely gets the chance to answer, when jumping out of the trees rush the others all with swords held high. Panting deeply Cin bellows, *"John, what is it?"*

The man cannot believe his eyes. "M, m, m, my Lord Tain," he stutters bowing his head.

"Ah John my friend, what's the emergency?" asks Lord Tain.

John points to the man. "Really," gasps Big Dan running his fingers through his beard before he then puts his sword back in its scabbard.

John calls to Maxie, the three greenem and Suelan to come over and then says, "Could you stand up and turn around please Val. I'm going to take your shirt off ok, I'll be as careful as I can."

The boy in great pain then grits his teeth trying hard not to cry anymore. Gasps of horror come from all there, as John pulls the boys' shirt off over his head. "By the stars lad," gasps Tain. "What happened?"

"Apparently," snaps John. "It's your law, and this man is quite within his rights to do this, and for what, picking up a couple of windfalls. And when he'd finished insulting, and threatening me, he said if I had a problem with it I had to ask you, so, I have, and I am. Go on then get on with it, justify yourself."

Lord Tain exasperatedly shakes his head. "I did, I never, I mean I would never condone such a thing" he gasps. "I mean, yes there are laws, and you are quite allowed to give a junior a spanking or even the belt in extreme cases. But this, no, no, not at all."

"Could you please kneel down young man?" asks Evening Thunder. "Let's take a good look at your wounds my boy."

"I, I, I don't know if I can Sir," answers Val. "It hurts too much."

"Could you please help Maxie?" asks the old greenem.

"Could you face me please?" Maxie asks the boy.

So the boy carefully turns round and Maxie places her hands flat out. "Now place your hands on mine," she tells him.

Val does as he is asked, but cannot help going a little red at being made to hold a girls' hands. She then tells him softly, "Close your eyes, and with your mind, push all the pain up your back and down your arms through your hands, and into mine."

"Can you do that for me?" she asks.

"I'll try," he sobs.

There is then silence all round apart from Max who stands muttering to herself with tears in her eyes. After a few minutes Maxie asks, "How's that, is it better now?"

"Yes, yes it is," Val answers excitedly.

"Good," replies Maxie smiling. "Now kneel down and let my friends take a look at your back. As what I have done will not last long."

Woodnut and the two old greenem then stand quietly looking at the boy's wounds, touching carefully and muttering to each other. "Max?" asks Hope. "Why did that man do that to that boy?"

"I don't know dear," she answers wiping a tear from her eye. "But I'm damn well sure I'm going to find out."

She then marches over to the man. Cin nudges Big Dan and points then Dan marches after her and just manages to catch her fist, as she swings it back to slug the man. "Get off me," she shouts.

"Here hold her," says Big Dan lifting her up and handing her to Trace.

"Get off me now," screams Max.

"Thank you," gasps the man just before he is then promptly slugged by Big Dan, knocking him to the ground.

Dan then turns back to Max and tells her, "I hit harder than you."

The greenem then finish examining the boy. "Right Woodnut my lad," says Evening Thunder. "You get some felem leaves and flowers. Shadow Drop you get some tangle root, and then mix it with the felem ingredients, that'll stop the bleeding. Maxie you need to deal with the swelling and infection, so if you could get."

"Yes, yes I know," she answers taking off. "Fengle fungus, cellam sap and pel bark."

"Yes excellent," answers the old greenem. "Quick as you can now."

"Will this stop the boy hurting?" asks Yarin.

The old greenem nods and replies, "Yes it should, with the stuff they're collecting, but it will take a few weeks for his short rib to repair."

"You what?" she gasps as well as everyone else.

"I thought you'd realised," answers Evening Thunder. "His lower rib is broken. It'll heal but will take a while and be very tender. As long as he takes what we give him everyday as prescribed, he'll be ok."

Woodnut and Maxie arrive back, shortly followed by the other old greenem Shadow Drop. The boy's pain starts to flair up again and they proceed to treat him overseen by Evening Thunder. "I don't mean this the wrong way," whispers Lord Tain to Yarin. "But this is rather amazing to watch, they seem to know exactly just what to do, and they're using, well, I don't know, weeds I suppose. It's astounding, would you ever have thought it."

"No truly dear, it's outstanding," whispers Yarin.

"Now," says Lord Tain loudly turning to the man. "What to do with you?"

"But my Lord," pleads the man. "I was just punishing the boy, he was thieving after all. It's not as if I was just doing it for the fun of it."

Lord Tain doesn't even get the chance to answer when Maxie shouts, "Say that again."

"N, no," stutters the man.

"Do as you are told," growls Trace. "Or you will feel more than a stick across your back as you'll feel my blade."

"Err yes Sir," he stutters. "I just said, it's not as if I was doing it for the fun of it."

"Liar," shouts Maxie.

"That is exactly why you did it, it's written across your face," she snaps.

"No I didn't," shouts the man. "Who are you to say otherwise, you're just a kid?"

"Please my Lord," he continues. "Who would you believe?"

"Quiet, now," shouts Tain, starting to get mad. "If this were any other child, I may doubt it. But this child I believe whole heartedly. You are obviously a man with no honour or integrity as you not only brutally beat this child, but you've also threatened and insulted Lord Taraten. And just to cap it all off, you are a liar Sir."

"L, L, Lord Taraten," stutters the man dropping back to his knees in fear.

"He said, I mean, but how could I know," stammers the man. "He doesn't even look like a lord, he, he just looks like a swifty, err I mean a normal person."

"By my fathers' teeth man," rages Tain. "You're doing it again man, you just can't help yourself can you. How dare you, this calls for the most severe of punishments."

"Yes I agree my Lord," snaps Trace. "Swift and rapid I'd say."

"Suelan my dear," whispers Yarin. "These insults were aimed at Lord Taraten. Why don't you let him choose his punishment?"

Nodding Tain replies, "Yes my dear, that's an excellent idea."

"John, My Lord Taraten, how do you want him punished?" he asks.

"Hmm," says John rubbing his chin and winking slyly to Cin and Dan. "Maybe we should take him back to Taraten with us, a good candidate for the trials I think. What do you say boys?"

The two men glaring at the man nod in agreement before the man suddenly gets to his feet and screaming in terror turns and bolts down the track. "Would you like me to go after him John?" asks Trace.

"No please allow me," replies Cin grinning.

"Err no, my turn," says Big Dan pushing him back. "Fluff, could you possibly go and drag him back please?"

So Fluff takes off like a bolt of lightning and is soon behind the man. "Why isn't he passing him?" asks Max.

"I've no idea," shrugs John.

The three greenem are now creased up laughing, "And what are you lot up to?" John asks them.

The greenem just shrug. "They know what it's going to do," answers Maxie. "He's letting the man get a good distance ahead first. Remember father this is not just a very literal creature, sometimes it has a mean sense of humour. In this case well deserved I think."

"Oh, yes of course," says John, not really having a clue what she's on about. But as the man gets a good distance down the track all becomes clear as Fluff pounces on him from behind, flattening the man. It then grabs him by the scruff of the neck, and proceeds to lop back with him, dangling from his mouth like an old rag. The man is then promptly dumped at Big Dan's feet, like a puppy fetching its favourite toy.

"Maybe I shouldn't have worded it quite like that" says Big Dan, nonchalantly running his fingers through his beard.

"No, no," booms Cin patting him on the back and laughing. "I think you worded it just right."

John grins and kneels down in front of the man. "Now, what to do with you?"

"Please," begs the man. "I did not know it was you my Lord. I'll do anything, but not the trials, I've heard such ghastly stories about them."

"And you know what," answers John in a serious voice. "They're all true, and ghastly is definitely the word."

The man then starts to beg, "Please my Lord Tain and Trace, do not let them take me. I would rather die now."

"Not a problem," grunts Cin drawing his sword.

"Put that away silly," Maxie tells him.

"Why?" Cin asks a little confused. "It's what he wants."

John not listening turns to the young boy Val. "Tell me young man, what do you think we should do with him?" he asks. The young boy too scared to answer just shrugs. John grins. "Oh I know, what about I tie him to a tree and give him a good flogging with a stick. A taste of his own medicine."

Trace nods. "Now that is a good idea."

Lord Tain also nods. "Yes quite that seems very fair to me also."

Cin and Big Dan smiling broadly also nod in agreement before John picks the man's stick up. "Use this did you?" he asks the man.

The man sobbing simply nods. "Hmm now, maybe I should have a practice first," growls John. "Were you just standing, or did you take a run at him."

"John my lad, you can't," shouts Evening Thunder.

Winking slyly John replies, "Oh yes I can, watch me."

The two old greenem smile and turn away. "I, I, was just standing there when I hit him," stutters the man.

"Maxie is that true?" asks John.

"No Dad he's lying again," she replies before she then stares the man in the face and asks, "Three paces, five paces, seven paces, eight paces?"

The man stays silent but Maxie shouts, "He ran from eight paces father."

"How, how did she kn, know," sobs the man.

"Eight paces was it," growls John.

"Sit up and watch," he then tells the man. "Because in a few minutes this is what I'm going to do with you."

He then measures out eight good paces from the large tree, and gripping the stick firmly in his right hand runs as fast as he can, and hits the tree as hard as he can. He hits the old tree so hard the stick cuts straight through the thick bark like a hot knife through butter, and still carries on another few inches before disintegrating. Loud gasps and sharp intakes of breath are heard from all there. Big Dan and Cin start to clap.

"Nice John, that'll do it," shouts Big Dan.

"Oops," says John shrugging. "It looks as if I need a new stick."

The man simply faints. "John my friend," says Tain. "I think if you hit him like that, and I'm not quite sure how you did it, but I think you will simply cut him in half."

John winks to the greenem again. "Yeah maybe you're right. Somebody wake him up."

Fluff gives out a strange noise and darts over to the unconscious man. "Oh this should be good," laughs Cin. "How do you think he's going to wake him?"

Big Dan shrugs. "Shake him I guess."

But to everyone's surprise and titters, Fluff promptly cocks his leg and pees on him. The three greenem laugh so hard they have to hold each other up, and all along the edges of the wood laughter is heard echoing from all the other greenem watching. John grinning shakes his head. "You just couldn't resist it could you."

The man splutters awake, now terrified at Fluff towering over him and begs, "Please my Lords and Ladies."

"What do you think I should do with him?" asks John looking to the two old greenem.

"Feed him to Fluff, it's what he deserves," shouts Woodnut cheekily.

John just frowns and looks back to the two old greenem. "I think," answers Shadow Drop. "He should promise to never be cruel again for a start."

"Yes, yes I will honest," begs the man.

Evening Thunder nods and says, "Some sort of compensation is maybe in order here I think."

"We will leave you to come up with a suitable offer," he tells the man. "Then go to the child's home and make this offer to them in a day or two, and if they think it's not a fair offer, or you threaten them in anyway. Then I think you will be showing your ignorance, and should be flogged as just seen."

John nods bowing. "Wise words my friend."

"How does that sound to you?" he asks the man.

The man nods terror still on his face. "Y, yes my Lord, I'll make them a brilliant offer. You'll see, the best offer ever, just please don't beat me like. And, and please don't make me do the trials Sire."

"Go on then," shouts Trace. "Be on your way man, before we change our minds."

So the man gets up bowing, and thanking all.

"You'd better hope we never meet again," shouts John as the man half runs down the track still shaking.

Lord Tain turns to the old greenem. "But why did you let him choose what he has to pay?"

The old greenem smiles. "Did you see how terrified he was after seeing John hit that tree? Whatever offer you told him, wouldn't be as good as the one he'll make himself, the fear will make him over compensate."

Lord Tain bows slightly. "As always you're very wise."

Yarin then kneels down in front of the boy. "Now dear, Val was it?" she asks.

He nods. "Yes my Lady."

She smiles. "Good where do you live dear? We will escort you home."

"Really my Lady," he replies he smiling broadly.

"Yes of course dear," she answers kindly.

"I'm from the village of Tellum my Lady. About half a day's walk from here," the boy then tells her.

"Then," she says softly taking his hand "We should set off promptly, or it may be dark before we get there, and your parents would be worried."

Val sighs. "Yes miss. But I only have a mum, my father left us when I was small."

14

THEY MAKE THEIR way back through the trees and set off towards the village. "What's this place like?" asks Big Dan.

"A very small place," answers Trace. "A dozen cottages maybe, very rundown, if memory serves."

As they walk along the young lad starts to look very tired, and Hope whispers in Fluff's ear. Fluff gives a grunt and proceeds over to walk behind a very nervous Yarin and Val. Then Val gives out a sudden squeal as Fluff darts forward lowering his head picking him up, and throwing him on his back.

"It's ok," Hope reassures him. "We just thought you were looking a little tired. He'll carry you for a while."

"Well I am a little," yawns the boy.

"Hey young Val," shouts Trace giving the young boy a wink. "Do you think your mum will be surprised when we turn up at the door?"

Val nods. "Yes Sir. I think she'll probably faint Sir."

The sun is nearly setting by the time they reach the small village. "This isn't a village," laughs Cin. "It's two rows of houses. Which one is yours son?"

"The last one on the right Sir," he answers.

Cin frowns. "It would be."

"What you whinging at now ya big lug," chuckles John. "It'll only take a couple of minutes to get there, and besides, maybe we came in the wrong way, and that's actually the first house."

"Oh yeah," replies Cin scratching his head. "I never thought of that."

Faces are pressed against windows as they walk down the small street, but quickly disappear again once noticed. "Well my lad," chuckles Trace. "I think you're going to be the talk of the place for quite a while to come aye."

Val giggles with excitement. "Yes I think so Sir."

In no time at all they are outside the boy's bungalow. "Shall we wait out here?" John asks him.

"No just come in," answers Val flinging the door open. "Mum, Mum, I'm home Mum."

"I'm in the bedroom dear," shouts his mother. "I'll be out in a few moments."

"Ok Mum, I've got friends with me," shouts Val. "Is it alright for them to stop the night?"

"Yes if you like," shouts his mother. "But try not to make too much noise, I'll be there in a mo."

They all then stand in the dimly lit room silently looking around. "Sit, sit," says Val excitedly pulling Cin and Trace by the hand to a long seat.

"Yes thank you," stammers Trace.

Big Dan nods. "Not bad, somewhere warm and dry for the night."

"Now listen all of you," says Max sternly. "When this lady comes in, I want all of you to comment on what a nice house she keeps ok. I know how hard it is for this woman, I've been there myself."

Just then a door opens and a medium sized woman of unkempt appearance comes in. She shuts the door and turns around. But to their surprise she steps back against the door squealing, "Please, don't hurt us, I beg you."

"Oh Mum," shouts Val running over and grabbing her. "They're friends."

John smiles bowing his head. "Nice place you have here,"

"Yes very neat and tidy," shout the others.

A voice is heard at the back by the door, "It's a little dull and rundown."

Everyone parts and turn to see who it is, and they find Lord Tain standing there, now as red as a beetroot with Max and Yarin glaring at him. Now feeling very uncomfortable indeed he stutters, "But I suppose it just needs a little restoration and decoration. I, I have men who do that for me. I'll send them here as soon as I get back, if, if you like. They'll do anything you wish, if, if you want that is."

The stunned lady just stammers, "Y, yes that would be very kind of you, err."

She then leans forward for a better look through the dim light. "L, L, Lord Tain," she gasps.

"Catch her," shouts John.

Big Dan nearest darts forwards and just manages to pick her up as she proceeds to faint. Evening Thunder a little bemused chuckles to Woodnut and Shadow Drop, "And I thought the boy was joking." Woodnut just giggles.

Cin and Trace stand up as Big Dan lays her out on the long seat. Fluff sitting by the door lopps over to where the woman is lying and bending his head down he proceeds to lick her face. Val suddenly starts to look worried. "Its not going to eat my Mum is it?" he asks.

"Yes, yes, I'm sorry, that is exactly what its going to do," sniggers Woodnut.

"Ow," he then shouts as he feels Max's hand clip him around the back of the head.

Max sighs and is about to say, "No dear, it's not going to eat your mum."

But she is interrupted by Hope who says, "He's just trying to help, and wake her up."

Max shakes her head. "Fluff, go and sit back down dear."

However Fluff turns looks at her then gives the woman another lick. Max sighs. "Fluff, I know you're just trying to help, but what do you think the lady's reaction is going to be when she comes round and sees your ugly mug there."

So Fluff grunts and lopps back to the door with Hope and the greenem. He curls his lip up as he sits down, and he shows his teeth to the back of Max's head. Woodnut seeing him do this franticly tries to stop him as quietly as he can.

"I hope that face you're making back there is because the floor is cold on your bottom," snaps Max.

Fluff stops instantly and mutters to Hope. "No, I don't know how she knew," whispers Hope.

Woodnut whispers to them, "Shush, she just does. It's a woman thing my friend Lane told me." Max just smiles to herself.

Val pats his mum's hand. "Mum, Mum. Wake up Mum."

"Huh yes dear," she mutters in a groggy voice. "You're back, I, I had the strangest dream, I dreamt."

She then sees everyone standing around the room, and panicking jumps to her feet. "Quick Valantina," she shouts. "Bow your head in respect, do not look at them. Please my Lords we meant no."

"Oh Mum," interrupts Val. "They're friends."

"Val don't be so stupid," shouts his mum.

"Yes it's true," bellows Big Dan. "Now put your head up woman."

The woman cautiously raises her head. Big Dan puts his arm out. "My friends call me Big Dan," he tells her.

He then proceeds to introduce the others. "And your name would be?" he asks.

"My name is Cade," she replies curtsying to them. "Have we, err. Has my son done something wrong? I'm sure he didn't mean it, I promise he won't do it again."

Max steps forwards. "Do not worry yourself, neither yourself nor your son have done anything wrong. We are here as friends, nothing more. My husband found your son hurt and injured, and after we treated his wounds, we decided it best we escorted him home."

Cade bows, and smiling a relieved smile to her son puts her arms around him. "What have you been up to aye?" she says.

Val still very tender gives out a loud, "Ow."

He then wriggles away. "What is it dear?" she asks.

Val turns and pulls up his shirt. The woman nearly faints again, then coming round shouts angrily, "Who did this, come on, who did this? Tell me now."

"It's ok Mum," Val reassures her.

"No," she shouts madly. "It's not. I, I, have never seen such wounds, you must be in agony."

"No it's not that bad now Mum," he answers sheepishly. "Not since Maxie and the greenem gave me something for it."

He then gets his mother to sit back down and starts to explain all that happened. It takes him quite a while to tell his mum the story. She sits there frowning the whole time. "Yes dear, now the truth," she tells him. "You had me all the way to the jackerbell. What have I told you about lying?"

"No it's true Mum honest," he pleads.

"Err yes its all true," interrupts John. "I think the man's due here in a couple of days, but don't be surprised if he turns up tomorrow. He'll be desperate to settle up."

"And if he threatens you," shouts Yarin. "Or treats you disrespectfully, or you don't think his offer is fair, you come and see me personally. And I will show him a woman's true wrath."

"M, m, my Lady Yarin," stutters Cade. "Yes, yes of course, thank you, but really a spiked jackerbell. I mean he is prone to the odd flight of fancy but."

"Fluff," shouts Maxie as she steps forward. "Come and meet the nice lady."

Fluff then jumps up and barges his way through and straight up to the woman. Sitting down he is still taller than she is sitting on the long seat. She starts to shake with fear as Fluff gives her a lick. "Come on dude," says John patting it on the back. "Go and sit back down."

"Well, I, I'm speechless," she stammers.

Trace steps forward. "It's starting to get dark may we stay the night."

"Yes, yes of course," splutters Cade. "But we have only two bedrooms, you may have mine of course."

"Nonsense," bellows Big Dan. "We'll not put you out of your own bed, we will make do here."

"No," replies Cade. "Val and I can sleep in his bed, and my Ladies can take the other room."

"Excellent," bellows Big Dan. "That's settled then."

"Maxie," says Woodnut stepping forward. "You'd better give her the medicine for the lad, and tell her how to use them."

Maxie smiles. "Oh yes good idea." Cade then stands there silently listening to Maxie's every word, all be it a little stunned once again.

"Now," says Lord Tain excitedly clapping his hands together. "How about a little something to eat? Perhaps something hot if I may be so bold as to ask the lady of the house."

Cade curtsies nervously. "I will try my Lord, but my house is a meagre one, and times are hard at the moment, and most of the time we don't have enough to feed ourselves.

Tears start to fill her eyes as Yarin steps forwards and puts her arm around her. "Don't worry my dear," she says. "We have plenty provisions with us."

"No, no, I'd like to try," insists Cade. "I won't have anyone think at least I didn't try."

Yarin bows. "As you wish my dear."

"Oh, ok, I tell you what then," interrupts Lord Tain. "When I was a child, sometimes I used to go down and help cook. She used to say I was quite the little wizard in the kitchen. Maybe I could help you come up with something."

Everyone turns and just stares at him in disbelief, before spontaneously bursting into laughter. Lord Tain stands there red faced and scratching his head. "What have I said? She did you know," he insists.

"Yes my love, I'm sure she did," chuckles Yarin. "But I think this is a little different."

Cade then goes into the kitchen closely followed by Yarin, Max and Maxie. They are through there quite a while before the men starting to get hungry poke their heads around the kitchen door. "Well?" asks Trace. Max just shrugs. "Very meagre pickings indeed."

"Now why don't we make something for you instead as we have plenty of provisions," Max tells Cade kindly.

"That would be very kind of you my Lady" she answers.

"Yes," shouts Cin cheekily from the door. "Maybe she could have some of John's baby food."

Cin, Dan and Woodnut then start to giggle, much to the frowns of John.

"Hey I'll have you know, I have excellent taste, and I'm quite a good cook," he tells them.

"Oh yes of course, how stupid of us," chuckles Big Dan. "How could we have thought anything else?"

"Right," grumps John. "Step back give me a look."

"John dear," sighs Max softly. "You can't make something out of nothing. There's only a few root vegetables, tough outer leaves, only fit for animals really. And a small pile of bones in the cold room, with barely a scrap of meat on them."

John then stands there rubbing the back of his head. "And that's all there is aye, give me a look at the bones."

Cade opens a door into a small darkened cold room. "Hmm, and what do you use these bones for, soup I presume?" he asks.

"Err what?" asks Cade. "No sometimes I do the odd job for a butcher in the nearby town. Just a bit of cleaning and that you know, and he gives me them."

"If we get enough we roast them, and sit on an evening picking the bits off," she tells them sighing deeply.

John nods then shrugs. "Can you not just make soup out of them then?" he asks again.

Cade looks at him baffled. "I'm not sure what sloop is Sir."

"Orr come on, soup," he gasps. "Max, tell her."

Max just looks at him equally as blank. "Yarin, you must know soup surely," groans John.

"Guys, come on help me out here," he pleads to the others but they also look at him blankly.

"Awe come on you heathens," he then exclaims exasperatedly. "Boil the bones up for stock, add a bit of veg and seasoning."

"Come on, bread and soup, stock of life," he shouts.

They all just simply shake their heads and John rubs his hands together and grins. "Oh, you are in for a treat then."

"May I use these bones please?" he then asks.

"Y, yes of course," stutters Cade. "If you think you can use them in some way."

John simply winks. "Hey trust me."

"Right you lot out," he then shouts at the others.

"How long will this sloop take John?" asks Tain.

John frowns. "That's soup, and err about an hour or so."

"Err John," stutter Cin and Big Dan. "Err, I think we'll just have something out of our bags."

"Orr come on guys," sighs John. "You've got to try me soup."

"I suppose, maybe just a little bit, but only a very little bit mind," stutters the pair.

"Can Val and I help Dad?" asks Maxie.

John smiles. "Please."

"Could I possibly help also Sir?" asks Cade.

"Yes please," nods John. "The rest of you go back into the other room."

"Now," he then shouts clapping his hands.

He then asks Cade. "Have you got a large pot or cauldron? Big enough to put all those bones in."

"Yes Sir," she answers.

"Please call me John," he replies. "Now we crack the bones and put them in and fill it with water. And the bits of meat and marrow from them will make great stock."

"Always important in a good soup you know," he explains.

"What's marrow?" asks Val.

John smiles. "Hmm good question young man. It's the fatty stuff inside bones, very nutritious and very good for you."

He then winks. "And tastes great ok."

"Now could you do that for me please Cade, and get that simmering away," he says. "Maxie you and Val carefully cut them leaves into smaller more mouth sized bits for me please."

"Those leaves are very leathery and tough John," says Cade.

"Don't worry," nods John. "They'll soften when we boil them."

"It's just a pity we haven't got any salt and pepper," he sighs.

Val starts to jump up and down excitedly and tells him, "There are pepper plants out the back John. But there not good for much, just weeds."

"They wouldn't have little green or black round seeds?" asks John hopefully.

Val nods excitedly. "Yes that's them."

"Fantastic, what's the chances of that," shouts John equally as excited. "Fetch me a good handful please dude."

"We have salt Sir," says Cade. "In the store room with the chuck food, we sometimes use it for the animals."

"But what on earth do you want that for?" she asks.

He simply smiles. "Hey trust me. Now let's have a look."

They then enter the small store room and after crumbling a little off and licking it he winks. "Spot on," he says. "A handful of that, yep, that'll do."

Then in the far corner he notices several large containers of grain. "Hang on," he shouts picking up a small handful.

"It's just chuck food Sir," shrugs Cade. "We have a few flurries out back."

"What are you doing?" she then gasps as John puts a bit in his mouth and bites it.

"Hang on," he gasps. "But unless I'm mistaken that's wheat."

The woman just shrugs. "It's just flurry food Sir."

"Please call me John ok," he replies. "Now tell me, do you not grind this and use it for flour."

Cade just stares at him blankly. John sighs, "I wish we had something to grind it up with, we could have made a bit of bread to dip in the soup."

However to his surprise Cade throws a sheet back to reveal a large set of grindstones. Seeing this with a braod smile John says, "This has got to be fate. Definitely meant to be. Surely you must have used this to make flour at one time or another."

"No," she answers. "It's used to grind fell berries and grim nuts.

"How much of this stuff would you like ground up?" she asks.

John nods. "Quite a lot."

"I'm afraid," she answers timidly. "It would take a stronger arm than mine to do that Sir."

"Well I think we have plenty of them in the house don't you," he says. "One of them big lugs can do it."

John then shouts on Big Dan to come through. "Yes my friend, what is it?" asks Dan.

John smiles. "Could you grind up that tub of grain please?"

"Really," answers Big Dan in a heightened voice, "You want me to grind up chuck food."

John simply winks. "Hey trust me."

Dan frowns. "Hmm."

It then takes him a along time to grind up the large amount of wheat wanted to make the flour, and when finished he is sent back through. "So what's going on in there Dan?" asks Cin. "I'm starved."

"Will, will, it be edible do you think?" he stutters.

Big Dan sighs deeply. "Well that's something to be seen," he grimaces.

"Why what's he doing through there?" ask Trace.

"You won't believe it," Big Dan tells them. "But he really is boiling bones. And get this, he's had me grinding up chuck food."

To this he sighs not quite believing it himself. "So," gasps Lord Tain. "Am I led to believe we are expected to eat boiled bones and flurry food? Hmm, do you people always eat like this?"

"No not usually my Lord," answers Cin. "And I was hopeing we weren't going to have to this time either."

Back in the kitchen the soup is about ready and John gives it a last taste. "Hey, you know," he says. "That's not bad, not bad at all."

Maxie and Val then have a taste. "What do you think then guys?" he asks.

"Lovely," answer both children enthusiastically.

He smiles and then says to Cade, "Now what about you Cade."

"Em, yes, I, I suppose Sir," she answers nervously. "Do we eat the bones as well?"

John laughs. "No ya prawn, they're no good now, we'll give them to Fluff, he'll like them. And please, it's not Sir, or Sire, or my Lord, or Lord Taraten, it's just John."

Cade's eyes go as wide as wide can be. "Y, y, your Lord Taraten," she stammers. "The Lord Taraten?"

"Yes Mum," answers Val. "That's what I've been trying tell you."

"I, I," stutters Cade flopping down on a chair.

John heaves a big sigh. "Now woman are you going to try this stuff or what?" he asks.

"Y, y, yes of course," she answers curtsying.

He sighs with his whole body going limp. "Oh I give up."

Cade then cautiously takes a mouthful of soup, then looks up in total bewilderment, and quickly takes another mouthful. "You know, this stuff is actually, really, really good," she exclaims.

"Hey at last," shouts John.

"No really," she gasps again. "And I'm not just saying that. It really is good, shall we serve it now."

"Another five minutes," answers John. "And the bread rolls should be ready."

Back in the other room and the smell of the soup and freshly baking bread starts to waft through. "Smell that," says Yarin.

"I don't know what your husband's food will taste like, but it smells wonderful," she exclaims.

"You know it does doesn't it," agrees Max.

Finally the kitchen door is flung open, and John, Cade, Maxie and Val all come through carrying bowls of soup and thick crusty rolls. All are then handed one of each and they sit cautiously staring and sniffing the food. Impatiently John sighs. "Well, err come on guys, its nice honest."

Yarin takes the first mouthful, and immediately her eyes light up and she tucks in. The others do so too but of them don't. So John shouts at Cin and Big Dan, "Come on lads don't let the side down."

"And what pray tell are we meant to do with this, this err," stutters Cin.

"It's called bread," answers John. "Eat it as it is, or dip it in your soup."

So begrudgingly they both try it also, all be it more cautiously. But just like the rest they are soon tucking in. Big Dan then splutters, "Hey John good sloop."

"Yeah John good sloop," slurps Cin.

"I must say," announces Lord Tain. "This is simply astounding. I mean, you honestly made all this from just the scraps in that kitchen, and flurry food?" he asks.

"Yes," replies John. "With the help of Cade and Val that is," he continues winking to Maxie.

"Remarkable," mutters Tain.

Going back into the kitchen John then shouts, "Hey Fluff, don't think we've forgotten about you pal."

He then comes back through with a large platter of bones and places them down in front of a drooling Fluff.

"Hey John," splutters Cin. "Any chance of another bowl of this sloop."

"That's sloop, err I mean soup," grumps John. "Now you've got me saying it."

"You cloth eared doughnuts," he mutters to himself.

"Yeah sloop, that's what I said," replies Cin slyly winking to the others.

"I tell you what," says Tain. "Seriously, you'll have to give cook this recipe, and this stuff you dip in it, simply magnificent."

"Now, I'm sorry if I can't offer you any ale," apologises Cade. "But who's for a nice mug of hot sing root?"

John grins. "Oh yes please, just what the doctor ordered."

"Hem yes of course," says Big Dan frowning at him. "Wouldn't mind a prescription from him myself."

Val sits on his mums knee and she whispers in his ear, "Look around you dear, and remember this moment forever."

"Why Mum?" he whispers back.

"Because in our house today," she whispers. "We are witnessing something truly unique and amazing, for anyone, let alone people like ourselves. In our house today we are eating, drinking and talking with the lords and ladies of at least four provinces. This will never happen in your lifetime again, and if I were not here witnessing it, I would not believe it myself."

Hearing this Max whispers to John, "My dear, I think Cade's feeling a little left out, say something nice to her."

"Like what?" he asks a little flummoxed.

"Oh I don't know," she whispers. "You're normally good at things like that."

So John shakes his head and shouts over to Cade, "So do you think you'll have a go at making the soup or bread again."

"Oh yes definitely," she answers. "That sloop is so easy to make, and from things most people would simply throw away. And that bread stuff also, if I have the energy to grind the grain that is."

"So truthfully guys," asks John. "If you were in town and come across a little place selling a bowl of soup and a roll, or even just soup, would you go in and buy a bowl?"

"Oh yes definitely," come the answers.

"I would pay a good price too for something so nutritious and tasty," agrees Lord Tain.

John winks and asks Cade. "What do you think?"

"But, I, I couldn't," she stutters.

John shrugs. "Why, what have you got to lose?" he asks.

"Err nothing I suppose," she answers somewhat puzzled.

John then nudges Lord Tain and whispers in his ear, "Makes you wonder doesn't it?"

"In what way?" asks Lord Tain.

"Well," whispers John. "If only all your poor and starving people knew how to make something so simple and nutritious. Or even just had somewhere to go, where they were always guaranteed a warm meal until they are back on there feet at least."

"Hum yes," Tain whispers back. "I see where you are going with this, there is a place in the middle of town we could use. Hum, and this sloop and bread of yours it would cost next to nothing to make."

"I tell you what," agrees John nodding. "Now that is an excellent idea you've got there, but who would you get to run it. I mean a normal person would be better I suppose, someone who knows what the people want. Someone who wouldn't come across as pompous and patronising."

"Gosh but who," he frowns shaking his head. "That's the dilemma, and it would have to be someone who already knew how to make it."

"Wow this is a dilemma," he continues nodding. "Especially with us moving on."

"Oh, oh, I have an idea," replies Tain excitedly. "Do you think Cade might be interested in running it?" John winks. "Hey now, that is a good idea. In fact that is a marvellous idea, I can see why you're lord of the province. You are obviously the wisest person in it."

"Really do you honestly think so?" asks Tain puffing his chest out a little further.

John nods. "Oh yes definitely."

"Should I ask her then?" Tain whispers.

"No time like the present," agrees John.

"Here let me," he continues." Everyone if you could all be quiet a moment please, my good friend Lord Suelan Tain here, has had an absolutely brilliant idea, Which he is about to tell you all about, and he would appreciate your thoughts and ideas on it also, my friend over to you."

Cade gets up. "While you all talk about your important business. I'll just go and make us some more sing root," she tells them.

"No, please sit down my dear," Tain tells her. "This involves you."

"What are you up to John Fox?" whispers Max.

John shrugs. "Mee darling, I'm not sure what you mean, it's his idea."

"Yes of course," she replies smiling lovingly.

Lord Tain then excitedly tells them all of his ideas. "Well what do you think?" he asks them. "Honest opinions now."

"That is not just a good idea," answers Cin. "It's inspired, in fact I'm going to get word back to my Lord Voreda, and put the same ideas to him."

"Yes I agree whole heartedly," booms Big Dan. "I think my Lord Luguvalio would also be very interested indeed. And I also think my Lord Tain, this is going to make you very famous, throughout many lands."

Lord Tain now glowing with pride gasps, "Really, do you think so."

"Yes my dear," Yarin tells him smiling kindly. "I'm very proud of you already."

The old greenem then shouts, "I would just like to say, I have never thought I would come across an ooman, with such goodness and compassion in him.

It's a privilege to know you Sir." Bowing he then steps aside.

Lord Tain is now nearly bursting with pride. He then turns to Cade and says, "But I suppose it all depends on you my dear."

"Would you be prepared to take this on?" he asks her.

"Well err, I don't know," she stammers. "It would be such a responsibility."

"I'm not sure if I could," she gasps.

"I could be wrong here," interrupts John. "But I would imagine you will be able to get people to work for you, if needed that is. And you would be given all the rights, privileges and payments that go with such a possession, although I could be wrong."

"Yes, yes of course she would," answers Yarin. "And she may hire as many people as she sees fit. To start with, obviously she'll need someone to get the provisions needed, and grind the grain. And any problems, any questions at all you come directly to me."

"If that's ok with my husband. As I would also like to be involved with this project," she tells him.

"Yes of course my dear," answers Tain excitedly.

"So it's settled then," he continues.

Yarin smiling gestures to Cade. "Yes of course she will," shouts Valantina. "And I'll help too."

"Marvellous," shouts Tain. "Now how about that mug of hot sing root mentioned."

Max turns to John and says to him, "Come here you."

"What?" he asks.

Max then kisses him tenderly on the lips. "Oh," he replies with a broad grin.

"What was that for?" he then asks her.

She smiles lovingly at him once more. "Just for being you."

John a little confused just shrugs. "Works for me."

Everyone then chats and talks throwing ideas about until the early hours. As usual John and the greenem are first up and sit on a bench just in front of the house taking in the fresh new morning air. "Well John my boy," says Evening Thunder. "If all goes well we will be parting company later today."

John nods. "I'll miss your company and your wisdom old friend."

The two old greenem laugh riley and one replies, "Yes thank you my lad, but I think you have enough wisdom of your own, without my friend or I to hinder you."

John smiles kindly and tells them, "You are never a hindrance, and you are always welcome."

Suddenly a voice comes from the doorway, "Where are you going from here?"

Valantina is standing there yawning and proceeds to sit down beside them. "Well," answers Shadow Drop. "Your Lord Tain, his party and I are going on around to the other side of the province, back to the rainforest. But John and his party will be continuing on over the border into Desolation."

"No," shouts Val. "You can't John, you'll die. Nothing can go there, nothing."

John shrugs and smiles. "We better be careful then aye."

Hope, Fluff and Maxie come out next, and sit together in the early morning sunshine, taking a little to eat and drink from their bags. Soon they are all out there, including Cade, who is still a little overwhelmed and graciously takes the food offered to her by Lord Tain and John. "Well it's another lovely morning," exclaims Trace. "Shall we be on our way my Lords?"

"Excellent idea," replies Tain grabbing his bag. "Now Cade my dear, my wife and I will be away about a week or so, then we expect to see you and your lad back at the stronghold. Ok."

"Yes my Lord," she replies curtsying.

Then as they set off down the street having said their goodbyes, John pauses a moment and discreetly slips a few coins into Val's pocket and whispers, "Give these to your mum when we've gone, just a little something for her kind hospitality."

He winks and continues, "Tide her over a week or two aye."

"Oh thank you very much" whispers Val who then proceeds to shout and wave until they are clean out of the village.

15

LORD TAIN IS still very excited and talks constantly throwing ideas to the others, barely giving them time to answer before he's onto his next. "If I can interrupt for a moment," asks John. "What's ahead of us then? And how far is the border now?"

"We should be there by tomorrow evening," answers Tain. "Trace you know this area better than I."

Trace nods. "Yes my Lord. There isn't much between us and the border now, a couple of farms and a few fields here and there, filled with domestic beasts."

He then sighs. "And beyond that just wilderness."

"What you call wilderness," says Woodnut. "We call unspoiled."

Soon they come across a large hedge encircling a large field, and as they walk along the outside, John and Fluff stop to look through a gap into the field. Fluff licks his lips and drools, with a curious Hope sitting on his back.

"What the heck are those?" asks John in a high pitched voice. "They look like, well, I don't know, there the oddest looking beasts. Hmm a bit like, big woolly giraffes I suppose."

Maxie squeezes her head through for a look. Fluff gives out a growl, and Hope asks, "Fluff wants to know if he can go and get one."

"No silly," giggles Maxie.

"They belong to someone" she tells him.

"Really John," gasps Woodnut. "Everybody's seen them before."

John shrugs then sighs. "Come on, it's only recently I learned you existed, never mind those things."

"Oh, yes, I see what you mean," chuckles Woodnut.

"John dear," says Max, "they're tessel, just domestic beasts, they're bred all over."

John shrugs again. "Nope never seen them before in my life."

"Me neither," says Hope.

"Oh come on John," laughs Cin. "Tessel, simply tessel, their wool is used to make clothes and the like. What do you think we're wearing right now? They're even eaten in some places, although their meat really isn't very good to say the least."

Again John shrugs. "Nope, not mine, mine all come from cotton back on my earth."

Woodnut who is now a little further ahead disappears into the hedge, reappearing a few moment's later with three greenem, two of whom are very young indeed. Then a little agitated he waves over Evening Thunder. Who after listening to the other greenem then turns and calls to the others, "Could I have your attention please. This is rather important."

"Yes what is it old one?" asks Cin.

The old greenem clears his throat. "My good friend here Diddlers Gulch, informs me we are being followed."

"What?" they gasp.

"By who?" growl Trace and Big Dan in unison.

"Diddelers Gulch," interrupts John. "Really, you're not related to the old greenem Diddler back at the fire forest are you?"

The young greenem bows low to John. "We're all related Sir," he answers.

"Not in the way you think though John," giggles Woodnut. "Diddler is a very popular name amongst greenem, and not just for greenem, places as well."

John nods. "Really, fascinating. Why?"

"Well," continues Woodnut. "Diddlers are quite reveered amongst our people, they are one of the most important things on the planet. Without them the soil itself would no longer be fertile, and everything would die."

John nods again. "Wow, well I'll be. We are talking worms now aren't we?"

"Yes," sniggers Woodnut. "Worms."

"As much as I hate to break up this most fascinating of conversations," frowns Cin. "We are being followed by a would be assassin. If we could get a little perspective here please John."

"Oh yes don't worry about it," replies John nonchalantly. "It's just that old crone from the stronghold."

"It is," Max shouts.

"How, how the heck do you know that John?" asks Trace.

"Oh come on," shouts Maxie. "It doesn't take that much working out."

They all stand there looking very confused. Maxie opens her mouth to answer, but sees her dad frowning and slowly shaking his head. "Oh well," she answers. "If you're all that silly I'm not telling you."

"So how long has she been following us John?" asks Big Dan.

"Since we left," he answers.

"And you've known all along," says Trace. "Why haven't you done anything?"

John shrugs. "No, not all along, but I figure she's just some dippy old woman. I hoped she'd soon get bored of following us."

"So what should we do?" asks Yarin nervously.

John just shrugs again. "What does everyone want to do?" he asks.

"I think we should confront her," growls Big Dan. "See what she's up to."

"Do, do, you think that's wise," stammers Yarin.

"Don't worry my Lady," Maxie reassures her. "When we go our separate ways, it's us she intends to be with, not you."

Yarin gasps, "Really, how do you know this child."

Maxie simply shrugs. "Why else would she be following us? She sees you everyday, but she knows we are leaving."

Yarin nods. "Oh yes I suppose, when you put it like that."

"What do you mean be with us?" bellows Big Dan.

"Oh no," growls Cin. "No chance, she's not coming with us."

Maxie just shrugs and giggles. Max chuckles cheekily and says, "Well I think it would be fun."

Cin just growls at her. John nods. "I've got to agree with you there lads."

"Well should we carry on then or what?" he asks.

"Yes lets," agrees Tain.

John then bows to the greenem. "Thank you for the information, Diddlers Gulch was it. And you two little gigglers. What would your names be anyway? You seem very young."

Diddlers Gulch bows in return. "Ah yes that is our other reason for being here. As you can see my two young greenem here are merely saplings, and this is their first venture out of the woods. And as yet they have not been named. Sometimes young greenem choose their own names, and other times names are given to them. And we, as they, would be honoured if you John, would choose their names."

John kneels down in front of the two young greenem. "Hmm, yes I would be honoured, now let me think." "Are you two brothers?" he asks them.

The little greenem just giggle and shrug. "They came from the same root," answers Diddlers Gulch. "So in a way you could say, they are I suppose. But as you can see for some reason the little fellow on the right here is a little smaller than normal. It's very rare, but it does happen from time to time."

"Oh well that settles it," John replies smiling broadly. "We'll call you Bob."

The young greenem is so excited he starts to jump up and down. "Me, me, me now." shouts the other little fellow excitedly.

"And you," John continues. "We'll call you Little Bob."

Max frowns. "John you can't do that, that's just silly."

But as the other greenem break into fits of laughter, it's too late and the two young have greenem disappeared back into the hedge. They are then heard shouting excitedly back and forth to each other right the way along the large hedge, until their voices fade into nothing. "Bob, Little Bob, Little Bob, Bob."

Woodnut and the three older greenem are now laughing uncontrollably. Then bowing down low to John, Diddlers Gulch wipes a tear of laughter from his eye, and as he also disappears into the hedge and shouts, "I knew you'd pick good names. I did you know, I just knew."

Big Dan throws his head back and roars out a deep booming laugh. "I guess they like it then, Bob and Little Bob."

"There'll be no parting them now," chuckles Shadow Drop. "Well done John my boy."

They carry on walking along the hedge chatting and laughing as they go, and it's not long before they pass the first farm. They carry on through the fields and meadows, and by mid afternoon they are past the last farm also. "There's no knowing what we'll come across now people," announces Trace. "So keep your eyes open, there could be anything lurking in the long grass, or behind bushes and trees."

The three greenem and Maxie just snigger a little but do not answer. "There's a small stream just ahead," says Evening Thunder. "And a circle of ring trees. May I suggest we camp early, and stay there tonight."

"Any particular reason?" asks Max.

"Yes my dear," he answers. "It would be easier if we followed the stream back up and around to the forest. But your path lies across and straight on, unless Lord Tain wishes to go with you right to the borders edge."

"I will leave that decision with you," answers Tain. "Whichever you think is best?"

The old greenem nods. "Then we will camp here overnight and say our goodbyes in the morning. Now Woodnut, Maxie I have a job for you both."

He then whispers something to them, and they take off running through the long grass towards some trees in the distance. "Will they be alright on their own?" asks Yarin. "I mean this is a wild place."

"Don't worry there's nothing that would hurt them," replies Max.

"Yes my dear," agrees Shadow Drop. "But if it makes you feel any better, Fluff, Hope would you like to go with them, make sure they're alright."

Hope gives out a big smile, then squeals as Fluff takes off suddenly, making him nearly fall off his back. "Is that better my dear?" asks Shadow Drop.

Yarin nods. "Yes thank you."

"Where are they going anyway?" asks Cin as they walk along.

"Just passing on a few messages for me," chuckles the old greenem. "A surprise for this evening."

They then carry on to a group of about a dozen trees, and as they get closer they see the trees are standing to form a perfect circle. With the sound of a nearby stream being heard softly making its way along. "We can make camp in here," the old greenem tells them.

John, Cin, Max and Big Dan make their way in and throw their stuff down. "What's the matter?" asks John seeing the others standing just outside nervously.

"It's, err, well," stutters Trace. "There are three such places as these in our province, perfect circles of twelve trees, and each holds many superstitions and warnings about them."

The two old greenem cannot help but chuckle. John frowns but says, "Superstition my eye, come on, they're just trees. I guarantee there will be a perfectly reasonable explanation for them."

"Evening Thunder, could you help please?" he continues.

"Certainly," he answers walking over. "They are in the same family as the yalam trees, but instead of growing in a straight line, they grow into an ever increasing circle. Again it is really only one tree not twelve, with their main tree, the tree of life we call it, being the constant mother of the other eleven. As the eleven mature they die off, but their work is done, nourishing the ground all around and making it easier for mother to send her next eleven offspring out a little further."

"That's amazing," gasps Lord Tain. "Is this all true, and why haven't we seen more of these trees? Well I mean, even bigger circles of these trees, you only ever see the odd one here and there."

"Yes it's all true," replies Shadow Drop. "And those odd ones you see are not actually odd ones at all. And if you could go high enough above the ground, and into the sky, you would see they still do actually form a very, very large circle indeed."

"Well I'll be," exclaim the three Tain people as they then promptly walk in the circle of trees now with no fear at all.

John stretches arching his back. "You know, I swear that our bags are getting heavier."

"Not the bag my friend," laughs Big Dan. "Just the occupant, it must be nearly twice the size of when it first moved in there."

"Oh yeah," groans John. "You're right there."

"Spot, Spot get out here now," he shouts.

Spot then lumbers out of the bag yawning as she does so. "By my father's teeth," gasps Tain.

Yarin sighs. "Well I'll be. I mean Maxie told me, but, once again, I thought, well a child's imagination. How by dimlocks tendrils can you let that dab live in your bag. They're poisonous, are you not scared."

John just shrugs and shakes his head. "Now you madam." he says sternly to Spot. "Do you not think you are getting a bit big to be carried around all the time? You're not light you know."

She ignores him jumps up and he catches her and holds her up in front of him, and she witters with pleasure. Then she shoots out her tongue and licks his face. "Hey, that's emotional blackmail," he frowns.

"He definitely has a way with animals my Lord," Trace whispers in Lord Tain's ear.

"And then some," Tain whispers back.

"Now listen little lady," John tells Spot. "Do you not think it's time you left home, found another of your own kind and settled down?"

Spot then makes a funny noise and licks him again. Shadow Drop start to laugh. "Go on then, what did it say," sighs John deeply.

Still chuckling Shadow Drop answers, "No, your bag is her home, she likes it there, she told me."

"You, you understand it," gasps Lord Tain.

Shadow Drop gives him the oddest look and simply nods. John sighs once again and looks Spot straight in the eye. "Now listen madam you're getting a big girl now, and I'm only a little fella."

Spot pauses for a moment, before making another strange noise and wriggles out of John's hands. The two old greenem are now in fits of laughter. "What?" sighs John.

But Shadow Drop cannot speak for laughter. "She, she has an idea," answers Evening Thunder, just about managing to blurt it out.

Everyone then looks on as Spot runs over to the bags, but right past John's and into Cin's. And then proceeds to run in and out excitedly, before finally disappearing in for the last time, and proceeds to curl up inside it. "Well works for me," says John grinning broadly to the others.

"Oh no," gasps Cin marching over to his bag, picking it up and opening it. Spot witters at him shaking her tail with excitement, and proceeds to lick his face. "No," says Cin sternly. "Out now, I've enough to carry without you."

Spot then makes another noise which is quite obviously a sad one, and slowly climbs out. "John stop being rotten," says Max.

"Come here girl," she shouts.

Spot then runs over to her excitedly and jumps up onto her shoulders. Max gives her a tickle under the chin. "Oh come on John, how can you resist that cute face."

John sighs. "Oh I suppose, but you've got to walk more little lady."

"Do you understand?" he asks.

She jumps excitedly off Max's shoulder, and onto John's licking his face as she does so. "Ok, ok," he grumps. "No one likes a crawler, go and get yourself something to eat."

"Are you sure it's safe to let that thing lick your face?" asks Yarin.

"Yes, yes it'll be ok," answers Shadow Drop. "As long as there are no open wounds, the poison is in the saliva, and tends to be more along the gum and teeth, the tongue is relatively dry." Spot then jumps off John's shoulder and disappears into the undergrowth.

The late afternoon passes into early evening, and as they sit chatting a familiar voice is heard calling. "Hello everybody we're back." They turn to see Maxie and Woodnut and the others coming towards them, with Maxie carrying two wooden tubes. "Ah excellent timing," chuckles Evening Thunder. "As a farewell treat I thought, it maybe appropriate for a farewell toast, and here it is now."

"Is that what I think it is?" grins Big Dan.

"Yes my lad," laughs the old greenem. "Beelack juice."

Cin slaps his hands together. "Yes, you are in for a treat now my friends," he booms.

"Just take a mouthful and think of your favourite drink," he tells them.

Maxie then hands one container to Lord Tain and the other to John. "Just one mouthful?" asks Tain.

John nods. "Yes just one then pass it on, you can have another later if you like."

However a little confused Tain shrugs and takes a swig and then hands it on to his wife. "You know, that was really quite good" he says. "But I'm not sure how effective one mouthful will be."

"Oh hang on," he suddenly gasps. "Woe, my head's spinning."

"This really is good stuff," he slurrs. "But how, I feel as if I've had several ales."

Yarin hiccups. "Oh my."

Trace gives a big grin as he takes a mouthful. Everyone then sits there very merry indeed laughing and chatting, all except Big Dan who sits there solemn and silent. "Hey what's the matter?" asks Max.

Big Dan just shrugs. "Come on," she whispers.

Dan shakes his head, then sighs heavily. "It's the beelack, it just reminds me of Lane that's all."

"Yes I know what you mean," whispers Max. "Why don't you make a toast, and we'll have another drink aye."

He sighs again. "Yes I suppose, why not."

"Everybody," he then shouts. "If you'd all like to take another mouthful, I would like to make a toast. To Lane, my best friend lost, and to my new friends found."

They all sit silently for a moment before Trace slurrs, "So how long does this stuff last, an hour or so."

"Oh no my boy," replies Evening Thunder. "This is beelack juice nothing like your ales. You will stay in the same condition you are now, for seven, eight hours easily, you will get no better or worse."

"Well unless you have another drink I suppose," he chuckles.

"Really," shouts Trace. "That's fantastic, and with just two mouthfuls, simply amazing."

"Yes," slurrs Tain. "I can see why you say only one mouthful. But John my friend you seem to have had several mouthfuls, yet you seem relatively sober."

John nods. "Yes, it doesn't have the same effect on me as it does others."

"Wouldn't you be good in a drinking competition," laughs Lord Tain.

Everyone then looks as Big Dan gives out a loud sigh as he slowly gets to his feet. "Well if no one minds, I think I'll get a little air." he tells them sadly.

"As you wish my friend," slurrs Tain as Big Dan walks away. "But we're outside."

"Have I said something wrong?" he asks the others.

"No," says Max softly. "He'll be alright, just let him go, he's missing his friend that's all. Woodnut could you go with him please, make sure nothing happens to him."

Woodnut nods and takes off after him then after a short walk Big Dan sits down silently by the riverbank, and is promptly joined by Woodnut who sits down beside him. "You been sent to keep an eye on me have you," mutters Dan.

Woodnut shrugs. "Just thought you might like the company."

"Hum, sure," grumbles Dan.

"Do you want to talk?" asks Woodnut.

Big Dan sighs heavily. "Nothing to say. I know it's not deliberate, but everything Lord Tain said just reminded me of Lane that's all. I'll be alright in a few minutes and you can tell them that."

"You know," says Woodnut, staring into the dark towards the gurgling of the stream. "There is a story amongst my people. A tale so old, told on an evening to the young. It's the story of an ooman, who helps the lost ones, he shall be taken deep into the black, and he shall face death many times in the fight against the unnameable beasts, before returning them back to the light."

"Hu, what," stutters Big Dan. "What, what does that even mean? And what by the green grass of blood meadow has that got to do with me. If it describes anyone, it's got to be John."

"Who said it was either of you," Woodnut replies in a more serious voice. "Anything I say beyond this point must never go any further, do you promise."

Nodding Big Dan replies, "Yes, and not only do you have my word as a warrior, but as a friend."

Woodnut bows his head. "There is a lot more to this story than I've told you, and it is open to wide interpretation. It was told only once by the ancient one, and he refuses to ever tell it again."

Dan nods. "Yes I have heard of this ancient greenem. He's the founder of most of your tales and legends."

"Yes that's him," says Woodnut softly. "But one thing is certain, this story he told was not about John, his destiny is set, even before he knew it himself. But the other ooman in this story was a warrior, a warrior who came from the heathen hordes to become friend and council to all."

Dan frowns. "Heathen hordes aye. Now let's just say for one moment, this story of yours was about Lane, what does it all mean anyway? And I thought that greenem, Meadow Spirit was it. He said we would never see him again anyway."

"Well I don't think it's all about Lane," answers Woodnut. "And I mean no offence, but to my people all oomans are heathens, killing and plundering."

Woodnut's voice then goes to barely a whisper as he continues, "But I must tell you, this story is the only reason my people have let oomans live."

"What?" gasps Big Dan. "What do you mean?"

"Well," continues Woodnut. "There has often been, let's say, many heated discussions between greenem and mossies over the subject. They would have happily, as they call it, err, returned you to the earth."

Big Dan gulps but asks, "Does that mean what I think it means? Suddenly I feel very sober."

Woodnut nods. "Yes you've seen Lilly Milk do it. They would have quite happily done this to all oomans, long, long ago, if we'd agreed with them. And with my people poisoning your water and destroying crops, your people would have been no more than a faded memory many years ago. Even now, as you may have noticed mossies still don't think much of oomans, and are not quite as peace loving as greenem are. And some disgruntled mossies do now and again return the odd ooman back to the earth, when they feel it fitting. So please do not mock our stories, for some of them, have come to pass, and have kept your people alive."

He continues more, "Now take heart in the fact, yes, we may not see our friend again. But he is most definitely alive, and fighting to help friends back to the light. And anyway, on rare occasion, Meadow Spirit has been known to be wrong."

Big Dan nods and runs his fingers through his beard. "You know your words though sometimes a little scary, do give me heart, and shall from this moment onwards, knowing he is somewhere helping those who need it. And if he is with those lost people of yours, it truly warms my heart to know he could not be with better people, or have better friends. But one thing does puzzle me though, what does all this into the dark, and back into the light stuff actually mean?"

Woodnut shrugs. "We are not quite sure ourselves, and there are often great debates about this on an evening."

Big Dan then gets up. "Well my friend," he says. "Shall we make our way back, and perhaps another drink aye? Although I'm surprised John's never mentioned it. I take it he knows all about these legends and stories of yours."

Woodnut shakes his head. "No, not at all, he knows they exist and most are about him and the rest of you. But he does not wish to know, it just upsets him, so we don't tell him."

Big Dan gives out a wry laugh as they walk along. "Yes that does sound like him, probably refuses to believe they're even about him aye."

"Yes," giggles Woodnut. "Although Maxie is the one for stories legends and the like, she probably knows as many as our elders."

His laughter then slowly subsides as he continues, "And she seems to have an understanding of them we do not. It, it's the oddest thing, it's, it's as if she knows the way in which they were meant to be interpreted. And if I didn't know better, I would say she knew the ancient one. And I would have said she understands how he thinks. She does seem to have that ability, but I haven't even been lucky enough to meet him yet."

Big Dan nods. "Yes she certainly is one remarkable young lady, but sometimes it just takes a fresh perspective on things."

"Shut up minky boy." "That's monkey boy to you shark girl." Are the shouts they then hear from a very tidily Max and John as they get back to their friends. Big Dan smiles down at Woodnut smiling back and says, "It's nice to see something's never change aye."

"Hey Big Dan ma man, how ya doing ya big old viking you," shouts John swaying a bit. "Tell this, this woman, she's being even more annoying than normal."

Big Dan smiles broadly. "Thanks John that was a nice compliment."

John too tidily to ask or argue simply frowns. "Hu, yeah right."

"Oh annoying am I," shouts Max jumping on John and showering him in kisses.

"See, see," he shouts. "Get off woman, not in front of the guys."

"Everything alright?" asks Cin handing Big Dan the beelack juice as he sits back down.

"Yes thanks," answers Dan. "Couldn't be better, just needed to get my head right."

He then takes a large gulp and is soon back joining in with all the fun and banter. Cin leans over and whispers to Woodnut, "I don't know what you said to him my friend, but it's certainly worked."

Woodnut just smiles politely and shrugs. The laughter and merriment then goes on well into the night and nearly into the morning, and its mid morning before they all start to rise and eat a little breakfast.

"Well," sighs Lord Tain. "I don't know when I've had so such a good evening. It's odd isn't it, I've only known you all for such a short time, but I will miss you all terribly."

John nods. "Yes I know what you mean. Sometimes you just seem to hit it off with people, you know. Who knows why, but I can assure you we'll miss you all just as equally."

"Nonsense," shouts the old greenem. "You are all talking as if you will never meet again, for all you know you will see each other in a few days. And if not, it's not the end of the world is it. You'll meet again one day I'm sure of it, and besides when new friends are made, the world becomes just a little bit brighter, that's what greenem think anyway."

John bows his head slightly. "Yes of course, you are very wise as always."

But the mood is still sad as they all pack up their things and stand talking in the mid day sun. Putting off there fare wells as long as they can, until finally they run out of things to say to each other.

John sighs. "Well I suppose it's time to part my friend. And I'd just like to say, I feel a better person for knowing you Suelan my friend."

Lord Tain gives out a wry laugh. "You are very modest my friend," he says grabbing Johns arm. "I can assure you, it is I that is the better for meeting all of you. You have opened my eyes and warmed my heart, and given me a new world to explore. And for that I will be eternally grateful."

The two old greenem and Woodnut bow to each other politely then give each other a hug before turning their separate ways. Finally all the goodbyes are said and Lord Tain and the others are led down the stream by the two old greenem, while John and the friends paddle across it.

16

THEY STOP TO rest under the shade of two large trees in the afternoon sun, and as they sit there quietly having a little to eat John hears a little voice come from the ground beside him. "Hey silly man."

"Hey cutie pie," he answers. "Why don't you come up and sit beside us?"

The little mossy does so. "Hi Lilly," the others shout.

"And to what do we owe the pleasure?" asks John.

"You do know that mad woman is still following you don't you," answers Lilly.

John sighs. "She is, I was hoping she might have got bored and gone back home by now."

"Well I think we should find out what she's up to," says Big Dan.

Cin nods. "Agreed."

"Oh she's harmless," giggles Maxie.

"You're not scared of an old woman are you," she teases them.

"No of course not," bites Cin.

Big Dan just frowns at her. "Scaredy flumps," she teases.

"Hmm, maybe we should see what she's up to," mutters John. "How far away is she Lilly?"

"You see those bushes in the distance, she's resting behind them," answers Lilly.

John grins John. "Hmm that's not a bad distance away. I bet she can't make us all out at that distance."

"Oh John," sighs Max. "Not everybody has your bad eyesight," she giggles.

"Why can you honestly make her out from here?" he asks.

"Well just about, maybe if she was in plain sight," she stutters.

"Exactly," replies John. "And remember she's not from around here, she's from my earth. And at her age her eyesight won't be as good as mine."

They all start to snigger. "You can go off folk you know," grumps John.

"John never mind them," says Max. "Get on with it. What does it matter anyway?" she asks.

"Well," grins John winking. "I think we should put on a little show for the old coot. Put the frighteners on her a bit, if needed that is." He grins broadly.

"Play her at her own game."

"Do tell," says Max excitedly.

John winks. "Firstly it all depends on our friend Lilly Milk here. Is there any way you could, err, let's say, bury her up to her ankles or knees say, and then fetch her here to us like that?"

"Hmm," ponders Lilly thinking aloud to herself. "That is a very long way, I would need help. Give me a minute, I'll go and see if I can get help."

She then disappears down, and a few minutes pass before she appears again. "Yes," she tells them excitedly. "Just say when."

John smiles clapping his hands. "Oh very good."

"Now Fluff," he continues. "Could you hide please, just behind that tree there? Hope you hide up it, and if I call on either of you, come out as quickly as possible and right up to the old goat."

"Oh that does sound fun," laughs Max.

"You know that does sound quite a good idea," chuckles Big Dan.

"Well I think you're all being rotten," snaps Maxie.

John winks. "Noted, now shall we begin? Lilly would you do the honours please."

She gives a cheeky wave and disappears down. "What should we do now?" asks Cin. "Just sit here."

"No we should all stand up," says Big Dan. "Arms folded, make it look as if we've summoned her here."

"She's an old woman you know," snaps Maxie. "Mad or not, I think this is cruel. What if she's got a bad heart, you could kill her."

"Oh yes," exclaims John. "I never thought of that."

He then shrugs trying hard not to grin. "Oh well too late now."

"Do you know what she's on about Dan?" asks Cin.

Big Dan just shrugs not quite sure. "Some bit inside you or something I think," he answers.

"Men," grumps Maxie stamping her foot.

"Oh Maxie," says her mum. "It's just a bit of fun, and besides who knows what she's up to."

"You're as bad as them," grumps Maxie again.

Max looks at her more seriously. "My little girl, I nearly lost you once. I never want to be put in that position again."

She then smiles lovingly. "She's brought it on herself, and if she had nothing to hide, she would have declared herself by now. She's here now anyway."

"How do you know that? You can't see her surely," asks John a little puzzled.

Max simply smiles. "No not yet, but I can definitely hear her. Oh wait, yes I see her now."

Big Dan nudges Cin and points ahead. "Yes I see her," he answers.

"Where?" gasps John.

"John your eyesight," grumps Cin shaking his head.

"She's there," he continues pointing.

John nods. "Oh yeah, I see her now. And there's nothing wrong with my eyesight."

"Damn freaky, weird, hex vision sharks," he mutters to himself.

"We heard that," frowning the others shout.

"Yeah, yeah," shouts back John cheekily.

"You were meant to, damn bat eared swines," he mutters again.

"John are you sure you mean bat ears?" asks Big Dan.

John sighs deeply. "Yes, yes I meant bat ears, and no I don't want to know what it is."

"Oh thank you," replies Dan smiling broadly, and slyly winking to the others.

The screams get louder as the old crone gets nearer. John grins broadly as he sees her getting closer still, now buried nearly up to the knees. Her arms are flailing like the blades of a broken windmill, and her screams like a demented fire engine. Finally she comes to a stop about ten feet in front of them, and slowly her screams subside. "You, you," she stutters pointing at John. "You did this, didn't you, come on admit it." "I, I, should turn you into a glimbit," she shouts.

"A what?" asks John. "Never heard of them."

Big Dan whispers in his ear. "Really," mutters John. "Now that does sound interesting, you'll have to show me one sometime. Right where was I, ah yes, go on then you old witch turn me into one then."

"No, shan't, changed my mind," she replies putting her tongue out.

"Be quiet woman," bellows Cin.

"You don't frighten me, you, you big bully," she shouts.

"I said be quiet," shouts Cin. "Or we'll have to bury you up to your neck."

"Oh sure," cackles the old crone. "I'd like to see you do that."

Suddenly and sharply she is then buried up to her chin and is now silent and terrified. "Now that's better," growls Cin.

"That's enough," calls John. "Get her out completely please."

The old woman is then thrust out the ground as quickly as she was thrust down. With the shock making her go a little wobbly and she flops back down on to her bottom. Maxie steps forwards and puts out her hand and smiles. "Come on I'll help you up, no ones going to harm you, I promise."

However the old crone gives out a loud squeal and jumps to her feet rubbing her bottom. "I said no one," shouts Maxie.

"Don't you dare cross me Lilly Milk," shouts Maxie angrily.

"Now everyone calm down," says John softly.

"Now would you like a drink Harry?" he asks the old crone.

"That's witch to you," she replies putting her tongue out again.

John frowns at her. "Yes thank you," she answers bowing her head slightly.

So John hands her his flask of water. "Now tell me please, why were you following us?" he asks.

"It's a free land," she cackles. "I can go where I choose."

John sighs. "Yes "But why are you choosing to go the same way as us."

"Who says I am?" she snaps.

John sighs again exasperatedly. "We are saying you are, because, because you are. Why do you have to be so contradictory all the time?"

"I say be done with it and feed her to Fluff," booms Big Dan.

"You hear that?" John asks her. "My friends aren't as patient as I."

"I don't know what a Fluff is, but it doesn't scare me anyway," she tells them.

"As you wish," John says bowing and stepping back. "Fluff, Fluff, come on dude."

Fluff then shoots out from behind the tree like a bolt of lightening, growling and snarling fiercely as he does so, straight up to the old crone. Slightly shocked she steps back a little then as Fluff puts his snarling face right up to hers she grabs his muzzle with both hands closing his mouth. Fluff now shocked and startled himself gives a muffled yelp and tries to back away, but to no avail. Shake as he might, he cannot seem to get loose.

Big Dan's mouth falls open as he stutters, "Hey Cin, do, do, do you see what I'm seeing?"

"I'm, I'm not sure," he stutters back. "I'm not sure how she's managing to keep hold of him. But, but that is either very, very brave, or complete insanity."

"Well considering who's doing it," stutters Big Dan. "I know which I'd go for."

"Hey Cin," he then suddenly sniggers.

"Yeah what?" Cin asks.

"What do you think Fluff's going to do when she finally let's go?" sniggers Dan.

"Oh yeah, this should be good," Cin chuckles back.

John stands there shaking his head, then steps forward and is about to say something, when to everyone's surprise there is a loud thud, as Hope lands right beside Fluff and the old crone. And in a loud croaking angry voice he shouts as loud as he can, "Let my friend go now, you horrid old woman."

The old woman is absolutely shocked and astounded and dropping to her knees starts to plead, "Please forgive me. I, I didn't know that was your pet. Err, I mean how could I?" She then turns her head back around slightly, and after putting her tongue out at John and the others, shouts in a muffled voice, "You never told me you had a servant with you."

"Our *what*?" shouts Max. "How dare you insult my son like that! Old, mad whatever, you insult him again and I won't be accountable for my actions."

The old crone with a completely puzzled look on her face then gets to her feet. "That's impossible, you're not even the same species."

"He's my adopted son," growls Max. "Until we find his parents anyway."

The old woman puts her hand on her chin, deep in thought for a moment. "Yes, ok I see, yes," she cackles. "Now if someone could go and get my bag, we'll be on our way then."

Fluff stands round the back of Hope poking his head around and growling. "Oh be quiet," she tells it growling back. Then a sudden look of horror comes across her face as she catches sight of Hope frowning at her.

"What do you mean we'll be on our way?" asks John.

"I'm coming with you," she tells them.

"Oh no," shouts Cin. "No chance."

"You are going nowhere with us, you, you old witch," he flounders.

"Flattery will get you nowhere, wooden top," she mutters.

"What did you call me?" growls Cin.

"Wash your lugs out, cloth ears," she cackles.

Max, Maxie and Woodnut all start to giggle. Big Dan nods. "I must agree with my friend here. All she'll bring is arguments and annoyance."

"And you can be quiet too, you, you big monkey turd," snaps the old crone.

John suddenly bursts into fits of laughter, but stops instantly seeing Big Dan frowning. "I don't know what a monkey turd is," grumps Big Dan. "But I presume it's got something to do with John, I've heard Max calling him that monkey thing."

"It better be something good," he then growls.

"Yes, yes," cackles the old woman. "You're right, he's a big monkey turd too."

John just bursts into laughter again. "I take it, it's a good thing then?" asks Big Dan suspiciously.

"No not really," laughs John.

"So why are you laughing?" asks a puzzled Dan.

John shrugs. "Err, it just kind of tickled me that's all. Hey what can I say, funny is funny."

"Anyway you old goat," he continues. "Congratulations, I now think you've upset or insulted nearly everyone here. What chance do you honestly think you have of coming with us now?"

The old woman suddenly starts to get upset. "You must," she sobs. "You must, it's meant to be. I know it, I've been waiting for you."

"Come on now don't get upset," John tells her. "It's not that bad, I'm sorry if we've been, err, hem been a bit abrupt so to say. The truth is we've had people following us before, and they did have bad intentions, and did try to do bad things. But you have a good life here in this province, money, respect, well kind of. You can play your mind games with the locals, and they're all terrified of you. Besides we're on our way to Desolation Border, and by all accounts it's very dangerous and we might die."

Cin and Big Dan grumble behind him. "But I'm telling you," she begs. "I'm meant to go with you, and besides, I've been there. I, I could help. Yes that's it, that's maybe the reason, I'm meant to go with you."

She then smiles. "You see, that's it then, all settled."

"No chance," growls Cin.

John turns to Woodnut. "What do you think?" he asks.

But Woodnut is still creased up laughing. "Woodnut," shouts John exasperatedly.

"Oh yes she's very funny I like her," he giggles.

Big Dan turns to Woodnut and scowls. But Woodnut just puts his tongue out, then bursts into fits of laughter again. John frowns at him. "Well you're no help."

"Maxie, please seriously," continues John. "What are your thoughts?"

Big Dan and Cin suddenly turn to each other and start to look very worried. "Quickly Cin," says Big Dan nudging him.

Cin then nods shooting forward and grabs Maxie putting his hand over her mouth stopping her from answering. Max gives out a wry laugh and says, "And what are you going to do now, you can't hold her like that forever."

"Yes we can, we'll take turns," grumps Big Dan.

However Cin gives out a loud yell letting go instantly and shaking his hand vigorously. "Ow," he shouts. "She bit me. There was no need for that."

"Think yourself lucky I just bit you," snaps Maxie.

She then stands silently staring at the old woman, who stands silently and nervously staring back. No one says a word as Maxie then slowly walks over to her then whispers in the old woman's ear, "You may fool them with your false tears, but you cannot fool me old woman. I do not believe for a moment you were meant to come with us, or I would have known about it. But you honestly do believe it, and that leaves me with a problem. Do I give you the benefit of the doubt, or not? Tell me why I should."

The old crone smiles at her kindly. "If you truly can tell if I speak the truth or not. Know that when I say the voices tell me I'm meant to help, and although sometimes a little deceiving, they are never wrong. And besides I am not just the only person to have ever crossed Desolation Border. I am the only one to have ever done so and been allowed to live."

"What do you mean by that?" asks Maxie.

The old crone begins to cackle tapping the side of her head with her finger. "You have your ways and I have mine."

She then proceeds to dance and jig around. Maxie turns back round to the others. "Well?" asks John.

"She comes," answers Maxie.

Grumbles and moans come from all but Woodnut, who simply giggles. The old witch is so excited she instantly does a handstand, and holds it long enough for her skirt to fall down over her face baring her all. "No god please," yelps John. Max simply giggles at the three men's reaction.

However Maxie turns back around bends down pulling the old witch's skirt up just enough to reveal her face. She tells her, "You travel with us on a probationary period only, and then we shall vote, so be good. This is a warning, I will only give you it once. Now apologise to everyone you've just insulted."

The old woman tipples over and stands back up. "Even wooden top and monkey turd?" she asks.

"Especially wooden top and monkey turd," replies Maxie winking and smiling.

"Ok, I suppose," she cackles. "I'm sorry ok, now can we go. Oh, oh my bag, we'll have to go and get it."

All then turn and look as Fluff rushes forward making a strange noise. "What is it?" she asks.

Woodnut listens to Fluffs snarls. "He says as a gesture of good will, he'll go and get it for you."

"Oh that's very kind of you," she cackles. "No hard feelings aye."

With that Fluff takes off running. He isn't away long before they see him running back excitedly, with the large pack hanging from his mouth. He drops the pack at the old crone's feet but doesn't stop running until he gets to Hope, where he stands around the back of his friend. "Thank your pet for me dear," the old witch says to Hope bowing slightly.

"He's not my pet," replies Hope. "He's my friend."

Fluff suddenly starts to laugh in his own unique way. Big Dan turns to Cin and John and says, "What do you think he's laughing at? I thought being called a pet would have upset him."

John shrugs. "No idea, who knows what goes through its mind."

"Well shall we go," he then says picking up his bag and throwing it on his back.

The rest all collect theirs also and get ready to go. The old crone is dancing about singing to herself. "Well," grumps Cin. "Please tell me you've changed your mind?"

"You should be so lucky cloth ears," she cackles picking up her bag and putting it on her back.

"Hang on," she shouts quickly taking it back off again. "This, this bag is soaking wet."

Sniffing it she then shrieks, "Oh my word, what the heck, it stinks."

Fluff starts to laugh again and struts off proudly ahead. "You, you flea bitten mutt," she shouts. "Wait till I get my hands on you, I'll get my own back you see if I don't."

Laughter abounds at the old woman's outburst. "I guess we now know why Fluff was so happy," booms Big Dan.

"You all knew," shouts the crone. "I bet you told it to do that, I bet you taught it to do that some how."

John smiles. "No honest, it was nothing to do with us. Something you have to understand is Fluff is no one's pet. He is truly a wild creature, and chooses to travel with us as a friend of his own volition, and he is free to come and go as he pleases. Upset him too much he could kill you. So here's a friendly warning, do not take him as a fool, he is very intelligent, with a wicked sense of humour. But you embarrassed him earlier, you really should apologise."

"Intelligent, sense of humour," she cackles. "Next you'll be saying you can understand it."

John nods. "No don't be silly. I wish, but Hope and Woodnut can."

"Really," she gasps as they walk away. "That plant can understand it."

"Yes," answers John irately. "And that plant is called Woodnut, and happens to be my best friend. So mind your manners, old woman. And yes, before you ask Hope also understands it."

The old crone looks at him oddly answering, "Well of course the slave can, he's male."

"Look your doing it again," snaps John. "His name is Hope."

The old woman shakes her head totally puzzled. "As you wish," she shrugs. "But it wasn't meant as an insult. And anyway how did you do that thing to me.

"I mean how for goodness sake did you manage to drag me through the earth all that way," she asks.

John simply frowns. "Just get going."

Maxie trails at the back and signals to Big Dan when he happens to look round. "Yes what is it?" he asks. "Hang back a bit," she whispers.

Then as the others get a little further ahead Dan asks again, "What is it? There's no problem is there."

She sighs quietly. "No not really, well I hope not. I would like you to do something for me, if you will that is."

"Anything just ask," he answers. "But why me."

She answers in a more serious voice, "I trust your judgement more than the others. You think before you act, then you do what is necessary. Cin is a little too hot headed, to say the least, and my father's too, err, easy going."

"I'm flattered," he interrupts. "But what is it?"

"I want you to keep a close eye on the old woman," she tells him. "There is something she is not telling us. I feel she is keeping secrets, and I don't know why."

"So why did you let her come then?" he asks, a little puzzled.

Nodding she answers, "I feel she has a part to play, I'm just not sure if it's for good or bad. I once heard my Dad say, keep your friends close, but your enemies closer. And besides she does know about this desolation place. Which is where

I fear you will have to watch her most. And if she shows any sign of deceit or betrayal, I want you to."

"Err, how can I put it?" she stutters. "There's a saying the mossies have, you won't have heard of it, err."

Slightly taken aback he says, "You don't mean return her to the earth do you?"

"Y, yes exactly," she stutters equally as taken aback that he'd heard of the mossy phrase. "W, would, could, no sorry I should never have."

"Maxie," he interrupts. "Say no more, if it is called for, I will do what needs to be done, you have my word. I know you would never condone such an act normally."

He winks. "And do not worry little one this conversation shall go no further."

She smiles. "Thank you."

"Now shall we catch up with the others, before Cin beats you to it with the old woman," she giggles.

Cin shouts to the old woman, "Do you have to keep doing that, it's, it's well disgusting."

"You're just jealous," she cackles. "Just because you can't do cartwheels or handstands."

"Why would I want to?" he shouts.

"Can you not just act your age, or at least wear undergarments," he booms.

"Shan't wooden top, and you can't make me," she cackles.

"Do you wanna bet?" he growls.

"What's the matter with you anyway?" she laughs. "Do you not like women's bodies?"

"You don't like boys do you?" she asks sarcastically.

"No, no, of course not, you, you, old gimlock," he shouts. "No I, I, I just don't like looking at a wrinkly naked old woman."

"Old gimlock am I," she shouts.

"Will you two just knock it off please," shouts John. "Gees Louise, I'm missing the peace and quiet already."

"Why don't you tell us a little about yourself then Harriet?" he then asks trying to quieten everyone down and start a conversation.

"Harriet," laughs Cin. "I should have known you would have a man's name."

"What do you know, potato head," shouts the woman. "It's you freaks in this world that all have the wrong names not I."

John blurts out a sudden laugh and grins from ear to ear. "Sorry guys I've got to agree with her there."

"Oh you would say that," booms Cin. "Hu! I might have expected a man called John, to side with a woman called Harriet."

Big Dan starts to boom out a loud laugh. "He's got you there John."

"All of you quiet now," shouts Max. "I don't know, it's like being with a class full of children. Now come on dear, we can't keep calling you old crone or witch, so what would you like us to call you? Come on, let's get to know each other a bit."

"Why?" she asks stubbornly. "I like being called old crone and witch." She then frowns. "Harriet just doesn't seem right to me. Well for my personality in this province anyway."

"She's not lying there," mutters Big Dan.

"I heard that," she shouts putting her tongue out.

"Well what about a compromise then?" asks John. "I used to work with a girl called Harriet, but everyone just called her Hettie for short. What about that?"

"Hmm," she mutters to herself, as a sudden memory floods back and her lips start to quiver. "My mummy used to call me that you know. I remember now. Just, yes, but not in front of anyone though please."

John smiles kindly at her. "Hettie it is then. Now come on then tell us a little about yourself," he coaxes.

"OH you'd like that wouldn't you?" she cackles ominously.

He frowns, "Yes, that's why I asked."

She sighs. "Oh ok there's nothing much to tell you really, nothing more than I've told you already anyway. I've been in this province most of my life, since getting here anyway. I've been over the borders exploring with my adopted father, well except Taraten obviously. But when he died I did struggle a bit, until I started to hang around Lord Tain's stronghold that is. And when I saw how superstitious they all were, and how, err, hem, easily influenced they were. Well the rest is history as they say, well where John and I come from they do anyway."

"Oh great story," says Cin frowning. "Please, ramble a little more, I now feel as if I've known you for years." Suddenly he then shouts, "Ow!" and rubs the back of his head and turns to see an angry Max standing just behind scowling. "Sorry Max," he mutters.

"Don't blame her, when you're just as bad for starting arguments," snaps Max. "The poor old thing, she's obviously had a hard life, and had to live on her wits. Ripped away from her parents at a young age, left lost and alone in a strange land."

"Yes that's right you big brute," cackles Hettie. "You leave me alone, no in fact get over here and give me a cuddle, make me feel better." With that she gives a wry laugh and does a handstand.

"You have got to be joking," Cin replies frowning again. "I'll come over and club you. I don't know about cuddle you, and stop doing that."

Things settle down and the day wears on, and as the early evening approaches the old woman announces, "I think we should camp early, and stay here tonight."

"Why?" asks John. "There's a wood not far ahead, we would be better there."

"Oh no," she answers. "Some of these woods are dangerous places, full of all all sorts of creatures."

John looks at her puzzled. "You mean like jackerbells and greenem, that type of thing."

"Yes, yes that's it," she answers, then looking around at everyone smiling, and Woodnut and Fluff frowning she goes bright red. "Oh ok, maybe it wouldn't be so bad in the woods."

John smiles and puts his arm around her. "No maybe it won't. How far is this Desolation Border place from here?"

She nods. "Not far at all, a little more than an hours walk from the far side of the wood."

"Fantastic," replies John excitedly. "I can't wait until morning."

Big Dan and Cin both groan and frown at him and Max asks, "Are you sure this is a good idea John?"

He shrugs. "We're just going for a look."

"Hmm," groan both Cin and Dan again.

They then get to the wood and they are met by hundreds of excited greenem, all along the length of the wood. The old crone for the first time starts to look nervous.

"Don't worry," whispers John. "They're our friends."

"Worried," she snaps. "Who's worried? Not me. I'll, I'll, turn them all into, err, something anyway," she stutters.

He grins broadly. "It's ok, calm down."

"But I must admit," she whispers. "I never knew there was so many of them."

He nods. "Oh yeah, you'd be surprised. Although it's been a while since I've seen this many together in a wood."

"So why are they so excited?" she asks.

"Hmm good question," he answers. "Just pleased to see us I suppose. But really, it's my good friend Woodnut here," he whispers. "He's a bit of a legend amongst his people."

The old woman looks at him oddly. "How is it you travel with greenem anyway?" she asks curiously.

He shrugs. "Why not, he's my friend."

"You're weird," she answers cackling, before promptly doing a cartwheel.

"By heck you've got a cheek," he chuckles in a bemused voice.

Several old greenem are there to meet them, and after a few formalities they are all promptly surrounded by hundreds of excited greenem, all trying to ask them questions, all at the same time. Once calmed down the old crone is nearly as excited as the young greenem. And with all her strange ways, and sudden spontaneous acts, and ramblings, and singing of "nigginy nangginy noo," she goes down a storm, making them all go in into constant fits of laughter. Some of the younger greenem even copy her doing handstands and cartwheels while singing her song, which sends her into fits of laughter also.

Cin whispers to the others, "For the first time I'm actually glad the old witch is as mad as she is. I was expecting to be overrun. This many bugging me, I can nearly put up with."

ז7

THE DAY BREAKS after a night of frivolity and laughter, with John, Maxie and Hettie all excited about the on coming day, but the others are less so, with waves of apprehension coursing through not just Big Dan and Cin but Max also. John sighs deeply. "Aw come on guys. We're just going for a look, that's all."

Cin frowns. "Hmm, we know you. Just looking John yeah,"

"Oh you don't have to worry," says Hettie. "Crossing the border is no problem. As long as you use your heart, and not your eyes. I'll even go first if you like."

Cin nods slowly. "I've been told some truly awful stories about people and animals that have crossed the border there.

"And you are willing to go first and possibly die?" he asks.

"Yes, that's what I said cloth ears," she cackles.

He grins. "Works for me."

Max just frowns at him. "What?" he exclaims. "I was just agreeing."

Maxie looks to Woodnut. "Have your people been over the border?" she asks.

"No not really," he answers. "We tend to keep clear of going close, we've seen what has happened to some animals and the odd ooman that has tried to cross."

"Really," she gasps now not sure herself. Woodnut just nods his head solemnly.

Then all too soon, and even after Cin and Dan have drawn out breakfast as long as possible, it's time to go. But they both then insist on saying goodbye to nearly each and every greenem there and it takes a while before they set off. When they do conversation is mixed as they walk along for the next hour or so. Which seems to take forever for John and Hettie, but comes all too quickly for the others. "Are you sure about this John?" asks Max.

"There does seem to be an awful lot of superstitions about this place," she says nervously.

He sighs but replies, "What have I told you about superstitions. And besides my love, I would never deliberately put you in danger, you know that."

She smiles. "Yes of course."

"How far now Hettie?" he asks.

"We are there, more or less," Hettie answers. "You'll see it when we get to the top of this rise."

"So how do you see a border?" asks Cin. "Is there a fence or wall or something?"

"Oh you'll know it when you see it, you can be sure of that," she cackles.

Big Dan nods. "Hmm, there must be a distinct difference in the land appearance," he says running his fingers through his beard.

"Yes you could say that," she answers.

"Woodnut," shouts Maxie.

"Shall we run ahead and be the first to look?" she giggles.

"Yes let's," giggles Woodnut. "I bet we can beat Fluff and Hope."

"Go," shouts Maxie taking off. All four then run after each other laughing and giggling as they go. On reaching the top the laughter stops instantly. Looking ahead Maxie drops to her knees in shock and horror, at what lies ahead of them, even hitting John when he reaches the top. On seeing this Big Dan turns to Cin. "I know my friend," mutters Cin, "This must be pretty bad."

They all then silently go from a slow walk to a fast canter, partly through dread and partly through anticipation. But their mouths fall open and their bodies go limp as they also reach the top. Then their bags slip slowly from their backs as they all flop down in turn beside Maxie and the others. Not daring to go any further or even knowing what to say. The only one left standing is the old crone, Hettie. She looks at them all oddly. "What's the matter with you lot?" she asks, looking at them a little puzzled.

John shakes his head snapping out of it. "You have got to be taking the mick, are you blind or just senile." "Take a look around you," he gasps.

"Oh you mean the land ahead," she answers nonchalantly. "Well named Desolation Border isn't it, but it's not as bad as it looks."

"Not as bad as it looks," squeals John exasperated. "Are you mad, well, I guess you must be. Anyway, look around you old woman, as far as the eye can see there's nothing, but, but desolation. I can't even begin to describe it, I can only imagine this is what it looks like after a nuclear bomb has gone off, or, or, what it's like on the moon. But what the heck could have caused such a thing?"

"Hey Woodnut," he continues. "Has it always been like this?"

Woodnut shrugs. "All I know is what I've told you. This is the first time

I've seen it myself, but what I do know is, it appeared not long after oomans started to appear here themselves, and just seemed to appear overnight. One day it was a normal, quite a beautiful land, covered in lush virgin forest, and when the dawn broke on another day it was like this." He then sighs.

"So," asks John completely baffled. "It just happened overnight, and, and no one saw a thing? There must have been an almighty explosion surely, or, or, a blinding flash of light at least," he gasps.

Woodnut shakes his head. "No that's the odd thing about it," he replies. "As far as we are aware, not one ooman, not one greenem, not even one animal saw or heard a thing."

Maxie deep in thought then says, "Could it be, there was an explosion, but it was so loud it disorientated people, or made them unconscious? We have seen how much sound can affect us sometimes without even realising it. Thanks to Dad that is."

John nods. "Now that does kind of make sense."

Everybody then jumps as the old crone suddenly gives out a loud cackle. Big Dan frowns at her. "Do you have to do that?"

"Oh be quiet butter ball," she answers pulling faces at him.

"Shall we go down for a closer look then, it's quite safe," she cackles.

"Buller ball," exclaims Big Dan. "I'll buller ball you, you witch."

"That's butter ball, cloth ears," she snaps.

"Well sounds like a good idea to me," nods John.

They then head down the rise towards the border line, but as they get to the bottom of the rise, an awful fear starts to come over them, even Fluff. All but John, Woodnut, Hettie and Hope that is, who don't seem bothered at all. "I, I, I, don't, th, think w, we should go any further," stutters Max.

"Oh don't worry," answers John nonchalantly. "It'll be alright. There's nothing there but rocks and dead land. Oh no, hang on there's bleached sticks along its length."

"N, no John, I think she's right, this feels all wrong," stutters Cin.

"Your eyes John, look closer," stammers Big Dan. "Those aren't sticks, they're, they're bones."

"Never," gasps John. "That would have to be an awful lot of dead bodies."

"Awe poor things," cackles Hettie. "Are the big hard warriors scared? Are they?"

"Awe come here to crone, I'll give you both a big cuddle aye, make you feel better," she then says sarcastically with a deep grin.

"Th, this isn't the time to joke," shouts Cin nearly tempted to take her up on her offer. "This place is evil, I can feel it coursing through my body."

"Y, yes, as do I," agrees Big Dan.

"M, me also," answers Max now nearly too scared to speak.

Then she just about stammers, "M, M, Maxie what do you think?"

"I, I, agree mum," she stutters in return. "B, but it's strange, I, I can't explain it. W, whatever is affecting us, doesn't seem to bother Dad, Woodnut and Hettie or Hope. I, I, can clearly see that."

"Oh yes, how strange," agrees Woodnut casually. "The last time I saw you all in this state, it was through the effects of the remyoull mud. But there is none in this province, let alone around here. And you are all immune to its effects anyway, I just can't explain it."

"J, John look," stutters Max pointing to a dilapidated sign.

"What is it?" asks John a little puzzled.

Groans come from all. The old woman gives out a loud cackle, "You mean you can't read."

He sighs exasperatedly but replies, "Yes, god yes I can read."

"I thought you'd understand at least," he puffs.

"So what does it say then?" she asks him.

His body goes limp. "I can read, honest I can. I just can't read this language that's all."

"John," stutters Cin. "When we get through this, I'm going to sit you down and teach you how to read."

John sighs again. "God no, please I can, honest I can."

"That's enough," snaps Cin. "I'll have no argument on the subject. As soon as we are away from this evil place, we will sit down together and I will show you, ok."

John sighs exasperated and defeated. "Oh why do I bother, so are you going to tell me what it says then or not."

"It says," mutters Big Dan. "Beyond this point lies only despair and death."

"Now are you sure it says that?" asks John. "I mean, to me it looks more like a few funny shapes, err, a bit like hieroglyphics. Yeah that's what they look like."

"Like what?" asks Woodnut.

"Err doesn't matter," mutters John.

"So shall we take a closer look then?" asks Hettie.

"Oh, I, I don't think so," stammers Max.

"Y, yes it does seem a little silly," stutters Maxie.

"I, I think this is far enough," splutter both Cin and Dan.

John nods. "Well I'm up for it."

"I'll come with you if you like," croaks Hope.

Fluff makes a strange noise. "What?" asks Hope turning back to him,
He then nods. "U, hu! Ok."

"I must stay here with Fluff," he tells them. "He is very frightened, and will not go any further. This is a feeling he has never experienced before, so I must stay with him, I'm sorry."

"That's ok dude, we understand," answers John.

Woodnut then shouts, "I'll go, not that there's anything to see. It's just a barren waste land, although it might be fun trying to match the bones to the animals."

Big Dan shakes his head. "This really isn't right."

"Why do you want to go nearer?" ask Cin. "It's not as if there's anything more to see here."

"So stay here then you scaredy dooflers," cackles the old woman. "All on your own, in this scary place." Then still cackling she skips ahead. John gives a wry laugh and walks slowly after her closely followed by Woodnut. The others watch them walk away, which seems to make their fear grow.

"Th, th, this is insane," stutters Big Dan. "It, it's totally irrational. I'm, I'm truly scared, and, and I don't know why."

"It, it, it's that evil place," stutters Max.

"I, I agree," stammers Cin. "But, but there's nothing ahead to be scared of, but a barren waste land."

"Do, do you think it's safe to stay here?" stammers Maxie. "Maybe it would be safer to be with Dad and Woodnut."

Max nods in agreement. "Y, yes I, I always feel safer with John."

Cin nods also. "Y, yes I agree."

Max then starts to run after John shouting as she goes, "Wait, wait there."

She is closely followed by Cin, Big Dan and Maxie. "I'll stay here with Fluff," shouts Hope.

"Y, yes dear," calls Max. "You two stay here safe, we won't be long."

"I hope," she mutters under her breath.

It's only a several yard walk until John, Hettie and Woodnut are standing at the border line. John then stands there scratching his head looking up and down the border line. "It's the oddest thing," he mutters aloud. "But as I stand here looking up and down this place, the line between these two provinces, it's, it's as straight as a die."

Woodnut squats down closing one eye, also looking along the border line. "Amazing, what could have caused such a thing John?" he asks.

John shrugs. "Absolutely no idea pal. Err; I couldn't even hazard a guess, a natural disaster perhaps. But I doubt it. A weapon possibly, but why, who would have such technology, and why use it here. Was there a people here somebody didn't like. No, I'm not sure, even if it was a weapon, no it couldn't have been, to do such devastation on such a grand scale without an almighty blast, or at least a blinding flash. Sorry I'm stumped, I have absolutely no idea."

"As far as I am lead to believe John," answers Woodnut. "There was no oomans at all on this land at the time, and not many even bordering it. This was just lush unspoiled forest."

The old crone looks at them both oddly. "You are a pair of silly sausages," she cackles. "It still is."

"What did she call me?" asks a baffled Woodnut. "John what's a pair of snilly sorcieges."

"Hang on pal, I'm just looking for Harriet," replies John sarcastically. "I can't seem to see her through all these trees between us."

Woodnut starts to giggle. "Yeah, come out, come out wherever you are," he sniggers.

"Oh you two think you're so clever don't you," she snaps. "I know more about this place than anyone alive. I'll show you, I'll show you all, see if I don't." And with that she storms over the border line stopping and turning around a short distance in.

"What, what are you doing?" shouts Big Dan. "It's not safe, come back you old fool."

John laughs. "How can it not be safe? It's just a bit of scrubland."

"John," stutters Max. "Look around her, them bleached bones are not just animals, they're human also. Do not tell me it's safe."

"Oh no *look*," shouts Cin alarmed and scared.

They all then stare speechless at the old woman as the skin starts to peel from her hands and face. And as a soft breeze brushes by, it gently takes the skin like autumn leaves, and floating away it simply turns to dust. Then to everyone's further surprise she starts to cackle, "Remember, if you are afraid keep your eyes closed and your hearts strong, and no harm will come to you."

Snapping out of it Cin calls, "Get back here woman, quickly we can help."

John is about to make a run for her but is held back by Big Dan. "Leave her my friend." he says. "There's nothing you can do, even if you got her back here without the same awful fate happening to you."

"But, but," stutters John. "We've, I mean, *I've* got to help."

The old witch starts to cackle again. And then as the flesh starts to peel from around one of her eyes, she simply plucks it out, and after juggling it from one hand to another. She simply throws it up into the air, and catching it in her mouth she spits it back up into the air once again. But as it comes back down, and about to land back in its socket, the wind simply turns it to dust. And still cackling she simply turns her back to them, and walks further in.

"I, I, I think I'm going to be sick," shouts Max turning away.

"Mum," shouts Maxie as she turns and sees her mum swaying from side to side, before promptly fainting. "Mum, Mum," she shouts again rushing over.

"Y, yes dear," mutters Max, then remembering what she'd just witnessed she tries to scuttle backwards.

"Look, look," John then shouts pointing to the old woman. Then as they all turn back their eyes are transfixed, as all that is left of the old crone is her feet taking their last few steps, before turning to dust themselves.

"I, I just can't believe it," stutters John. "What, what could do such a thing?" He then flops to the ground. "Why didn't she try and come back. I mean, we weren't that bad to her surely, the poor old stick."

They all then stand there in total shock, unsure what to say or do next.

"You know I do feel a little guilty," mumbles Cin. "I suppose she wasn't that bad, just a little eccentric. But, but she told us she'd been across the border."

"You better believe it wooden top," comes a cackle. They spin round instantly to see the old woman standing where she had just previously disappeared.

"But, but, how?" stammers John. "We, we saw you turn to nothing."

"I told you to keep your heart strong," she shouts. "And don't believe your eyes, they will just deceive you. Now, are you coming or what?" And as the skin starts to peel from her once more, she walks off again disappearing in a puff of dust.

"Did, did, did anyone else just see that?" asks Cin.

"I, I, I think so" stammers Big Dan.

"Well if you're hallucinating, then so am I," replies John.

Her head then appears floating on its own. "Well," she calls once more. "Are you coming or not?"

"What?" exclaims John.

"Well, what the heck," he sighs. "Nothing ventured nothing gained."

The others then shout desperately as John steps over the border. But he is now committed and his heart starts to beat a little faster as he looks down at his hands. "Oh my god," he thinks to himself as the skin starts to peel away. "What the hell am I doing?"

He then starts to panic. "That's it," comes the old crone's voice. "Just a little further now."

"Here take my hand," she calls and a hand suddenly appears from nowhere floating on its own.

Cautiously John takes it, the hand grasps his firmly, and with a jolt pulls him forward making him stumble and fall at the same time. The hand then lets go and John looks up panting, and he sees the old woman staring down at him and smiling.

"Well?" she asks enthusiastically.

John looks around totally astounded. "What the...?" he mutters aloud getting to his feet.

As he looks round all he can see is thick lush forest. "But, but, how?" he stutters.

"Good isn't it?" she cackles.

"Now turn around and look at the others," she tells him.

So John turns back to see the others staring over in horror and disbelief. "It's like looking through a window," he stutters. "I, I can see a small patch of scrubland in front of me, then the others."

"But, how, why," he stammers.

The old woman grins. "Yes that's right." "I think its some sort of visual barrier," she tells him. "Most people and animals of these lands would not even get as far as the others have. As you saw an awful fear seems to take over them, and they loose all sense of reason before they even get close. And if they do manage to step over the border line, as you also saw. It then appears you are being stripped of skin and flesh, and that's enough to make anyone flee, or die of heart failure. But for some reason it doesn't seem to affect us, why I don't know. But I suggest you go and get the others before the fear gets the better of them and they flee."

John then steps back out the line of trees and into the scrubland, much to the further shock of the others. Then as he walks quickly back over to them they stutter, "John, John, you're, you're alive."

"But, but how?" asks Big Dan. "We saw you die."

"Your body turned to dust," he gasps.

"Are you ok?" asks Max panicking and checking John's body.

"Yes of course, stop faffing woman," he answers.

"Are you sure Dad?" asks Maxie.

"Yes honestly, I'm ok," John reassures them. "All this is just some sort of illusion, it's not real. Once you get twenty or thirty feet, it all stops. It's like going through a bubble, even your fear, I would guess."

"Then," he tells them. "And I know it's hard to believe, but you are in forest."

"John surely not," answers Cin.

John gasps, "No honestly, I can hardly believe it myself. You have got to come and see this."

"John, I, I would love to honest," stutters Big Dan. "But I'm not sure I can, this fear is nearly over powering."

"I, I'll try," stutters Maxie.

John smiles. "Ok."

"No Maxie you can't," shouts her mother.

"Mum please," answers Maxie. "I'll be ok."

John smiles again. "Take my hand. Now remember it's only a short walk, and what appears to be happening to you really isn't, it's all just an illusion. When you get out the other side, you'll see no harm has come to you, and I'm guessing your fear will end there also."

"What do you mean guess?" asks Maxie.

John shrugs. "Well this fear that has come over you all, doesn't seem to be affecting me or Hettie, or even Woodnut.

Maxie then nervously takes John's hand. "Wait," shouts Woodnut as he runs over and takes Maxie's other hand. "We shall go together, and we will face it together," he tells her.

"Oh I never thought," says John aloud. "That's what she meant."

"Remember," he says. "If it starts to bother you, just close your eyes, and I'll guide you ok."

Slowly they then start across the border line, but they only get about a third of the way across when Maxie starts to shake with fear. John stops and kneels down beside her. "Close your eyes Maxie, you're ok," he says. "The fear will go and we'll be there soon. I'll guide you." He then notices Woodnut, also starting to look very nervous, staring at his own little stick like hands dissolving and tells him, "Woodnut why don't you close your eyes as well, and keep tight hold of Maxie. I'll guide us all, don't worry my friend."

Woodnut nervously bows and in no time at all they are through the invisible barrier and into the trees. "Right you can open your eyes now," says John.

They then both open their eyes. "This, this is amazing, how could this be?" exclaims Woodnut.

Maxie looks around in awe. "It's, it's ok," she stutters. "The fear, you're right it's gone."

Hettie gives out a cackle and ruffles her hair. "I told you, sometimes the old witch isn't as daft as she seems aye," she cackles again.

John goes back over to the others. "My baby," stutters Max. "Is she ok?"

John nods smiling kindly. "Yes of course."

"Hi Mum," comes a shout and they all turn to see Maxie's head and arm floating and waving, as it sticks through the invisible barrier.

"Come on, it's ok over here honest," she hollers.

Max gives a defiant grunt and puts out her hand. "Take me to my baby, now," she tells John firmly.

John takes hold of her hand and guides her. "Close your eyes my love," he says. "I'll tell you when you can open them."

Soon Max is also over and after a little more explaining and coercion he finally gets Big Dan and Cin across. "What is this place?" asks Cin.

"How can this be possible?" asks a flabbergasted Big Dan.

John shrugs. "I've no idea, but all this deception has been to keep people out. And that suddenly makes me feel very, very nervous. Who or what has the capability to do such a thing. And why go to such lengths to do so. What the hell could they be hiding here?"

Big Dan nods. "Now you put it like that John. If all this is beyond your knowledge, then maybe we should once again be scared."

John shrugs. "Well to be honest, it doesn't take much to be beyond me."

"Maybe we should go back then," sighs Cin.

"Why, we're here now," says Maxie, "And as long as we are, it could do no harm to have a little look around."

"Famous last words," gulps John.

"I don't know," answers her mum. "We've been lucky so far, why push it."

"John, what do you think?" she asks.

John sighs deeply. "Well I must admit, the curiosity's nearly killing me. But this is way above my head, and I have an awful foreboding about this place. But we are forgetting something. Come on you old goat, what do you know, you've obviously been here before."

"Why all of a sudden so quiet, no handstands cartwheels or niggity naggity noo," he continues.

"Good question, come on," booms Big Dan. "Speak now or else."

"Or else what," she cackles "I'm not scared of you, you big gawk."

Big Dan growls drawing his sword. "What are you doing?" snaps Max. "Put that away."

"Another thing," growls Cin. "Could you not have just told us all about this illusion, and the fear, instead of letting us think our friends were dead."

"Be careful old woman," growls Big Dan. "If you cross us, I promise you, you will not live to regret it, you have my word on that."

The old crone just puts her tongue out. "I'm not telling you anything. But I will tell you John, we real earthers have to stick together, not like these, these, inferior bleeders."

John sighs turning to the others and says, "Give us a minute please."

He then turns back round and puts his arm around the old woman. "Right let's walk a little," he says. "You have to stop calling people names and upsetting folk, even if it is very funny. A word of warning though, be careful with Big Dan, he is a good man, but he us also a man of his word. And if you upset him too much, or cross him, he will not think twice about killing you, you can be sure of that. Now you say you've been here before, so what is this place. Who created it and why?"

"Yes," she answers. "Over the years I've been here several times, and it's always been here just like the plant said. Unspoiled and never desecrated, until now that is. That's the way they wanted it."

"Who, who wants it," gasps John.

The old crone then looks at him oddly. "The sky gods of course," she tells him as if he should already know.

"The what," he gasps again.

"Sky gods" repeats Hettie. "This place reminds them of their own home, some like to rest here. They are good creatures, mostly, explorers they say. I think this is a very important world to them. Oh what was it I heard once, err, I didn't really know its full meaning, but now, I think I do"

"Now what was it again? They have travelled to many different earths and planets in many different, err, now what was the word, it was a long strange word," she mutters.

"Realities?" asks John.

"Yes, yes, that's it," she answers excitedly. "Many different realities, looking for others like themselves, and as yet, I do not think they have found one. But this earth I think is a, con, con, convergence of them all, err, a jumping point to others, so they say, to them other, re, re."

"Realities," prompts John.

"Yes, yes that's it." she cackles.

John shakes his head. "This is mind blowing," he gasps. "A revelation, I can hardly believe it. So, so why didn't you tell me all this sooner."

The old woman just shrugs. "You never asked."

John frowns. "Ok, ok," she mutters. "I figured if you knew all I knew, you would have no reason to take me with you."

John winks. "Ah well. Don't worry about it; we probably wouldn't have believed you anyway. So you say you have been here many times before."

"A handful," she answers.

"And they just let you come and go?" asks John.

"Yes," she cackles. "They think I'm mad you know."

"NO really," replies John in a sarcastic voice. "How on earth could they think that?"

"Yes I know," she answers in a serious voice.

John just shakes his head. "So if these people are peaceful explorers," he says. "Surely they wouldn't mind us meeting them then, as fellow explorers like themselves so to say."

"Ah now," stutters Hettie. "I wouldn't say they are altogether peaceful."

"But I thought you said—?" asks John.

"No, no," she interrupts. "I just said they are explorers. They say they all know about me."

"They think I'm funny, I don't know why." she says suddenly going quiet. "I'm not funny what a cheek, hu. How can they say that, I've never even seen or heard one of them laugh? I don't even think they have the capability to laugh."

"Your rambling woman," interrupts John. "Now come on let's get back to the others."

"Well anything useful, or was she just rambling as usual?" asks Big Dan.

"Oh no," replies John in a heightened voice. "You are not going to believe this, I can hardly myself."

He then proceeds to report all that the old woman has told him word for word. The old woman stands back singing to herself with the odd handstand thrown in for good measure. They all stand silently mesmerised by Johns every word until he's finished. "This is, I, I don't have the words," gasps Max. "M, Maxie."

"I, I'm as speechless as you mother," she answers. "But wouldn't it be fun to meet them."

"I don't know about that dear," stammers Max.

"As do I," agrees Cin. "John what do you think?"

John slowly shakes his head. "Err, I'm more confused now, than I was before to be honest, although I must admit, I'd love to meet these, err, explorers. Corr so many questions, but."

"Then it's settled," interrupts Big Dan. "We continue, for a look if nothing else. As long as we are careful and not seen that is, what harm could it do? And if they seem friendly then we approach."

"Sounds good to me," agrees John enthusiastically.

Cin simply frowns. "As you said earlier, famous last words."

18

THEY SLOWLY CARRY on. "So," asks John, "if all we see from the outside is an illusion, how big roughly is this area, is it all forest or what?"

"Ninginy nanginy noo, ninginy nanginy noo," sings Hettie skipping ahead.

"Quiet woman," shouts Cin. "Can you not be serious for once, this is not the time to mess about. Just answer the question."

"Don't you speak to me like that," snaps the crone. "Or I'll wipe the smile right of your big fizzgog."

"You'll, you'll do what?" asks Cin.

"Please," asks John.

The old crone curtsies. "See, now that wasn't so hard now was it?" she says.

Cin just grunts. "Hem, now let me think," she says. "It's hard to judge the size of the place. But I would hazard a guess at roughly, the size of a province. And in the middle there is a large structure of unusual form, where they run things from. Around it is a large area of open ground, and although I've never seen one. I think that is where their sky chariots rest sometimes."

"So," asks Woodnut excitedly. "It's all forest apart from the middle?"

"Y...yes mostly," she answers. "There are large clearings here and there for basking and such, some with large areas of water, and some without."

"How long before we come across these people then?" asks John. "And how many are there likely to be?" The old woman just shrugs but replies, "It changes all the time, in the main structure there's always a minimum complement of seven. But if on rest here between journeys, oh, anywhere up to several hundred easily I would guess. Plus some seem to like their aides and servants with them."

"Servants," gasps John.

They all look at him oddly. "Why so surprised John?" asks Cin.

"HU, err," he stutters. "I just presumed, anyone so intelligent, and enlightened enough to explore different dimensions, and the cultures and the creatures there in. Would have, err, learned, err no, have evolved more to live in peace, and be beyond things like that, that's all."

The old woman bursts into fits of laughter, shortly followed by the others. "What?" gasps John. "Come on ya bunch of gits, what have I said."

"Sorry John," apologises Big Dan. "But that was some pile of nonsense you spouted there. The higher you get the more stature you have, the more servants and aides you will need. You just have to look at the lord of any province to see that John. So if these people can do all you say, it just stands to reason they would all have loads, you see."

John shakes his head. "Heathens," he mutters to himself.

Then looking decidedly more serious he says aloud, "I tell you what does make me worry though, and I mean this with no disrespect my friends. But you people are, err, how can I put it. Err, more medieval in your thoughts actions and ways. And theoretically, these people are more evolved than me, and should think in a different way again. But to have servants, well that just makes me wonder that's all."

The old woman raises her arms and wafts them down, instantly bursting into fits of laughter as she turns and walks on. "You people really have a lot to learn, come on then," she cackles. "If you're lucky we may come across some tomorrow or the day after perhaps. But we must not make too much noise, although their hearing isn't good, we can't take chances. Their reactions to me I know, but to you I can't guess, it could go either way. But I think they will find you all very interesting, as you are a rather unusual group."

"This forest is so unchanged," Woodnut gasps. "Some of these trees and plants have evolved so much outside this place, I barely recognise them in here. This place is a miracle, this has made everything worth it."

"I feel so privileged," he sighs smiling broadly to himself.

"I tell you what I find unusual," announces John. "It's got to be the first wooded area we've ever been to, were I've never seen a greenem."

"Oh yes," the others mutter.

"Hem, yes very unusual," replies Woodnut. "Now you mention it, neither have I, they are obviously not present in this forest for some reason."

"I've seen one," answers Maxie. "Briefly for a moment, I'm sure of it."

Woodnut gasps, "You have, I must go, I must go now, I'll catch you up later. Maxie I'm sorry, you'll have to stay here or."

"Yes yes," interrupts Maxie. "I understand, now go."

As Woodnut takes off into the undergrowth Max turns to Maxie and tells her, "I'm pleased you didn't go dear, but I'm also surprised you didn't."

"Well it kind of makes sense," interrupts Big Dan. "This is probably the only place anywhere that greenem don't just know who we are, but what we are, so it stands to reason they will be very cautious."

John nods in agreement. But Cin suddenly grins broadly and says, "You mean, this will be the first time I may not be awoken to the sounds of giggling young greenem, checking to see if I am awake yet."

"Yes," he jubilantly shouts.

John grins. "Well at least somebody's happy."

As they then slowly walk through the forest John and Maxie's heads are spinning like tops, much to the chuckles of the others, and the frustration of Hettie keen to guide the way. They all stop suddenly on hearing a loud howl just above their heads, and a gasp comes from all but John. "What by all that's good and green is that?" asks Cin.

Big Dan shakes his head. "I have absolutely no idea my friend. Maxie?"

"I've never seen anything like it either," she answers.

"These are not the people we are looking for are they?" she asks.

The old crone just cackles. "I know what it is," announces John.

"You do," the others call.

He nods. "Yes I've never seen them in the forests here though. But it's some sort of primate, err, a monkey of some sort. And often a very curious creature, it's probably never seen anything like us before either, and has just come to check us out."

"Yes," cackles Hettie. "The sky gods introduced them here a long time ago, they often like to hunt them."

"John," squeals Max in a heightened voice. "You must feel awful, did you hear that, they're, they're eating your relatives."

He sighs. "Hu, oh very funny, everyone's a comedian."

Cin nods in agreement. Then he grins and says, "You know, now I look at this creature a bit closer. Yes, I can see a resemblance with you, you old witch, I think it's all the body hair."

"OH insult me would you," shouts Hettie. "You big ugly goose gob. I'll put a hex on you if you're not careful."

"You know," says Big Dan. "If that thing gets any closer, I should be able to get it, if you think it might be good eating."

He then grins. "Unless you and the old woman would see that as cannibalism that is."

"Get away you bunch of sharks," shouts John smiling. "Go on Hettie, turn them into frogs or something, teach them a lesson."

Cin simply grins. "Well I'm scared, I don't know about the rest of you."

"Yeah you should be butter ball," cackles the crone. "A frog would be a good thing to turn you into. They like frogs, and not just to eat, but probably in your case, you're not that intelligent."

Cin frowns but replies, "You're weird."

"Tell you what guys," says John. "Maybe we should find somewhere to sit, I'm starting to get a bit peckish."

"Now that is a good idea," agree the others.

"I tell you what everybody," says John taking a bite of xenthem fruit. "This is one truly amazing place, and I'm starting to get a very good feeling about it."

"Hang on," squawks Hettie. "Where's the sla..., err, I mean the boy."

Max frowning at her answers, "He's waiting back on the other side of the border."

The old woman stares at them all in disbelief. "Are you people mad?" she shouts.

Maxie smiling reassures her, "You don't need to worry about him, he's with Fluff. The fear was too much for Fluff, and he wanted to keep him company. But you needn't worry, Fluff will guard him with his life if something happens."

Cin chuckles, "Now there's a turnaround, her calling us mad."

"Oh like that is it," grumps Hettie. "Suit yourselves then, see if I care why don't you."

John sighs deeply and tells her, "If you have something to tell us, or say, can you not just spit it out."

"Here's Woodnut back," shouts Maxie excitedly.

Woodnut skids to a halt. "Well dude?" asks John. "Had fun?"

"Oh yes," he replies excitedly. "This is one truly amazing place, everything here is so different. Like err, from an older time so to say. Even the greenem themselves, they are like an evolutionary step behind me. I wish some of the elders were here to see this and meet them."

Big Dan nods. "Maybe we could go and get some, fetch them back here. If you like that is."

Woodnut nods back excitedly. "Yes please," he says. "When we've finished our business here that is. The greenem here can't even speak yet you know, they can greenem obviously, but not the language you know anyway. They've never even seen an ooman before you lot, only the old woman."

"And I'm not sure if she counts," he giggles.

"What do you mean by that you silly plant?" snaps Hettie.

Woodnut just pulls a funny face and whispers something to Maxie, and the pair both start to giggle.

"Well if everyone's ready," announces John. "Shall we?"

Nobody gets to answer as John's bag starts to ruffle as he picks it up, and a yawning Spot appears out the top. He opens his hands and Spot jumps into them. He then grins and says as Spot stretches out across his shoulders, "I take it that fear back at the border line didn't bother you then."

Spot simply gives out a little witter and gently shakes. Big Dan frowns. "Lazy animal. Never awake enough to notice."

"Aww don't you listen to the nasty man," replies John tickling her under the chin.

"That's, that's, that's," is all the old crone can say.

John nods. "Yes I know it is."

"But, but, but," is all she can stutter again.

John nods once again. "Yes we know it is' poisonous, and no it won't hurt us, although you maybe, so be careful."

She cackles loudly, "You people are the oddest people I've ever known."

Cin sighs. "I can't believe it. Twice in two minutes I've been insulted by a mad woman."

"Oh you be quiet you big potato head," cackles Hettie.

"Right let's go," shouts John. "Spot why don't you go and get yourself something to eat pal, you can catch up with us later ok."

Spot gives a witter and jumps off his shoulder and into the nearest tree. "Oh and be careful," John shouts after it. "This isn't like the other forests we've been in."

Spot doesn't even pause to stop, and is soon out of sight. "Ha har," cackles Hettie riley. "Well that's the last you'll see of that."

"You'll have to get yourself another pet now," she laughs.

"I should be so lucky," mutters John, much to the titters of the others.

They walk all day taking in the sights and sounds of this new forest. All are interested in the different types of monkeys pointed out by John. But with Woodnut and Maxie being especially interested asking question after question. They sit talking together at the end of the day, and Max cannot resist saying to both John and Hettie, "I didn't know you had so many relations, this must be a real homecoming for you too."

"What does she mean by that?" asks Hettie.

Frowning at Max, John answers, "I once tried to explain evolution to these damn sharks here, I wish I'd never bothered."

"We'll have to take a trip to the ocean sometime, and maybe see some of your relatives' aye," he continues.

"Can we honestly?" asks Max. "I've heard all about it, I'd really love to see it, please?"

"What's an ocean Mum?" asks Maxie.

"You don't know what an ocean is child," gasps Cin. "Did your mother teach you nothing?"

"What do you mean by that?" snaps Max angrily. "We can't all be brought up in fancy strongholds, with servants and teachers. Some of us had to beg, fight, and scrape a meagre living. Education wasn't exactly the top of my list you know, some of us spent most of our time wondering if we had enough for a next meal."

"Max please, I'm sorry," apologises Cin. "It was very thoughtless of me, I should have known better."

Max smiles softly calming down. "Yes its ok. I'm sorry also. But can we go John, can we please?"

John smiles clapping his hands together. "Yeah why not. If that's alright with the rest of you that is. I suppose you would all like to see the old ancestral stomping ground again aye."

"Maxie, Woodnut, get him," shouts Max.

Maxie and Woodnut then instantly jump on him trying to pin him down. "Oh yeah," squeals John. "Just because you're not hard enough to do it yourself woman."

"*OH* is that so," exclaims Max instantly jumping on him. "We'll see about that."

Hettie leans over to Cin and Big Dan. "Are they always like this?" she asks.

Big Dan nods. "Yes pretty much."

"I'm curious," she then asks. "If you're not bringing the boy in here with us. Which I may say, I think is a terrible mistake. Are you just planning on leaving him out there all alone all night?"

"He's not alone," answers Dan. "He's with Fluff, and besides as the sun goes down they'll have made their way back to the woods for the night. The greenem will take care of them both."

"You have great faith in that beast and those plants," she tells him. "And for the life of me I cannot fathom out why."

Big Dan gives out one solitary wry grunt, "Then maybe if you stay with us long enough, and you keep your eyes and heart open, you may also be lucky enough to realise why. I would trust them with my life, and have done, and likewise, I would not hesitate to lay my life down for them."

The old crone just scratches her head, then gives out a cackle, "Dying for plants indeed."

Then she puts out her tongue and turns her back. "Big weird butter ball, goose gob head," she cackles.

"Why do I bother?" grumbles Big Dan to himself.

Finally they all settle down for the night and are soon fast asleep but they are all woken up at the crack of dawn by a loud scream nearby. "What by the two moons above was that?" shouts Max in alarm.

Hettie gasps, "I've no idea."

Another scream is heard high above, Big Dan and Cin put their hands on the hilts of their swords. "John any idea?" asks Big Dan.

Woodnut and Maxie sit there with their hands clamped over their mouths trying to hide their laughter. Cin frowns at them and says, "If this is something to do with you to."

"No nothing to do with us," they giggle.

John yawns and tells them, "It's the monkeys above, they must have just awoken themselves, and are bringing on the new day."

"And you say these things are found a lot on your earth John," grumps Big Dan. "I think I'd be hunting them if it was like this every morning."

John shrugs. "It's just their way, you don't get them in my country anyway, but I'm quite pleased to see them myself."

Max giggles. "Yeah, catch up with your friends and relatives," she sniggers.

"You just can't leave it alone can you, you annoying woman you," jokes John.

Soon they are on the move, making their way through the ancient trees and fauna. With defused light just about making it to the ground, and warming the forest floor. Just enough to make the moisture turn into a light mist, with the odd clear shaft of light screaming to the ground like a bolt of lightning, and turning other patches into relative saunas. Woodnut and Maxie skip ahead hand in hand, as if dancing in perfect partnership with the forest and nature itself. A tear silently runs down Maxie's face, and she wipes it quickly away, hoping Woodnut hasn't noticed. "What's the matter?" he asks.

She smiles back at him lovingly and in the quietest whisper quivers, "Shush, let's just enjoy this moment together in silence."

Woodnut smiles back broadly and the two skip on silently. John sighs and says, "You can't blame them can you. This must be the best time of the day."

"We shouldn't let them get too far ahead," warns Hettie. "You never know."

Big Dan nods. "She has a point there, this is a strange forest, even for Woodnut. And you are better safe than sorry."

John agrees, "Yes agreed, stay in sight guys."

"Back this way a little please," he then shouts.

But the pair have stopped anyway, and are excitedly examining something. "Come and have a look at these?" shouts Woodnut.

They make their way over to where they are. "What is it?" asks Cin.

"Ants," replies Maxie.

Cin shrugs as they all gather around. "So."

"Look at the size of this ant hill, and the ants guarding the entrances," says Woodnut excitedly.

"Oh my, yes," gasps Max. "They're massive, I've never seen ants as big as that ever, and look at those pincers."

"Corr blimey," sighs John. "You wouldn't want a nip off one of them, not with heads and pincers like that. It would go through your skin like a hot knife through butter. Although, I've seen something similar, if not the same on the natural history channel."

Everybody starts to laugh. "What?" gasps John. "I have honest, in the South American jungles."

"No it's not that," chuckles Cin. "They're big ants with big mouths yes, but to bite through skin. John please maybe your parchment like skin."

Then still laughing he bends down to pick up one of the large soldiers guarding the mound. But everyone jumps as he shoots back up hollering loudly, and shaking his hand vigorously. "Get it off, get it off, get it off, get it off," he shouts still shaking his hand and dancing from side to side.

"What's the matter?" laughs John. "Aww that little ant hasn't bitten the big warrior's little pinkie has it. Aww now who's got thin skin aye."

"Ok, ok," winces Cin grabbing the insect's body with his other hand and trying to yank it off.

"Come here silly," says Maxie.

"Oh my look," she then says taking his hand.

They all look at Cin's hand to see the large ants pincers have gone clean through the skin on Cin's index finger, and have even crossed over each other. "Now that's a powerful bite," says Big Dan.

"Yes it is," agrees Cin. "Now, can someone please get it of me?"

So Maxie grips the ant's body and gives a good hard pull and twist, but to no avail as its body simply comes clean away, leaving its head still well clamped on his finger like a staple. "Wow," exclaims John. "When those things clamp on, they really do clamp on."

"Knife please," asks Maxie turning to Dan.

She then takes the knife and slipping the tip between the jaws finally prises it out. "There we go," she says smiling. "Now I think we should get away from this ant hill before someone else gets bitten."

As the morning wears on they see the bright light of a clearing a short distance ahead. "Right single file behind Hettie," announces John. "And everyone be quiet until we take a look. Any trouble, and we throw the old crone in the way, while we make a clean getaway, everybody got that."

"Yes works for us," agree both Cin and Big Dan.

"Well I can live with that," sniggers Max.

"Yeah us too," giggles Woodnut and Maxie.

"What do you mean by that?" squeals Hettie. "You bunch of rotters, you wouldn't do that to me would you."

John smiles putting his arm around her. "No we're just having a bit of fun, you can probably run faster than these slow coaches anyway. Now let's have a look aye, everyone quiet."

"Well I couldn't go any slower," she laughs. "Not unless I go backwards."

"But you don't have to be that quiet," she announces. "Their hearing isn't very good anyway, but you will have to try and be light of foot, they are all quite good at seeing vibrations."

"Never," exclaims John. "Wow how bizarre, I can't wait to meet these people."

They then creep up the last part of the way in silence, taking no chances. The old woman and John carefully peer through into the large clearing, and the others fan out either side and proceed to peer through also. They look out onto a small expanse of water filling most of the clearing.

"All clear," announces Hettie.

John sighs. "Aww now that's a pity."

"Although, if we leave the bags here, who's up for a paddle?" he asks.

"Me, me, me," shouts Maxie excitedly.

They all then fling their bags off and are soon paddling around the clearing, with Woodnut bobbing about on top and giggling like mad. Maxie sneaks up behind him and quickly pulls him down, but he pops back up like cork from a bottle laughing and giggling more than ever. "Isn't this wonderful?" exclaims Max submerging herself in the water.

Cin sighs deeply. "Yes I must admit, this is the life."

They all lthen ook up as a whooshing sound is heard just overhead, and see a flock of aquatic flurries coming into land on the other side of the water. "A couple of them roasted over an open fire would go down a treat," says Big Dan.

John chuckles to himself, "Hmm, I wonder if they taste like duck or spider, In fact I wonder what a giant spider tastes like anyway, prawn perhaps."

After an hour or mores paddle and swim they make their way back to their bags, and after a bite to eat they make their way around the small lake in the clearing. They then walk for hours hearing the occasional giggle and wave of the hand from one of the ancestral greenem, with Woodnut and Maxie waving enthusiastically back. After another few hours walk they come across another smaller clearing with dry land this time. "Now be careful this time," whispers Hettie. "I met one of them here the first time I ever came."

Once again they approach in silence, but all that is there are a small heard of vilock dribnels, which take cover on them entering. "What the heck are those?" gasps John.

"Vilock dribnels," answers Woodnut.

"They're what," squeals John. "Oh come on, vilock dribnels indeed, you're making that up."

"Now why would we do that," answers Cin. "You can see them right there. What did you think they were?" John shrugs. "I don't know, some sort of, weird flockey, skinny, stumpy headed, ratty bear like things."

"Oh yes," laughs Big Dan. "Because that makes perfect sense now doesn't it. Just rolls of the tongue like civit grease."

John nods. "They're quite bonny though, very unusual."

John now a little bored as the others take a break, wanders about the clearing. Then noticing something hop into the line of trees, he makes his way in for a look, but try as he might he cannot see it anywhere. "Well better not go too far," he thinks to himself. "Or I might get lost." He is about to turn back when he notices a thin silk like thread running across the ground in front of him. He bends down for a closer look, the trail of fine silk is fresh and whatever it was must have just passed by. "Why does this seem so familiar?" he thinks to himself. He carefully touches it with his index finger and a sudden voice screams out, "Leave me alone." He let's go instantly a little shocked. "Hang on," he then says aloud. "I know that voice."

So he touches the silk again. And instantly he hears a scream of, "Leave me alone, you, you, stupid, stupid backward inferior plants."

A little puzzled he stands back up and decides to follow the trail of silk further into the wood. "I hope I'm going the right way," he thinks to himself. A few minutes walk and he hears familiar giggles, it's the giggles of mischievous young greenem. He proceeds to peek around the side of a large tree. And there just in front of the tree are a group of young greenem encircling a boing boing. They pull faces at the trapped boing boing, with one even poking it with a small stick to stop it from passing. John slowly and quietly steps out, then crouching down he puts his hand out to display the mark of the greenem on his hand, given to him by the old greenem king. "I don't know if this will be recognised by these greenem here," he thinks to himself. So he shouts, "Guys, guys, come on, you should know better than that."

The young greenem stop instantly and all turn silently towards him, unsure whether to stay or run. John speaks to them softly, "Its ok I'm not going to hurt you."

"Do you understand me? Can you understand what I'm saying?" he asks.

The young greenem turn and look at each other then back at John and nod. "That's very good," he says smiling and bowing his head slightly. "And may I say it's a privilege to meet you all for the first time. Now it's nice to have fun I know, and very good to see you all laughing and playing. But what you are doing to this creature is very wrong, do you understand that?"

The young greenem slowly nod. "Good," continues John still smiling. "Now I would like you to stop teasing it, and go and play somewhere else ok, and no teasing it in future now alright."

The young greenem giggle and nod. "Go on then," he says smiling. "On your way then." The young greenem take off sniggering.

John kneels down near the boing boing and places his finger on its silk. "Are you ok?" he asks. "They didn't hurt you did they?"

"Hu," comes a disgruntled grunt. "Leave me alone, we don't talk to inferiors, especially oomans."

"No of course not," replies John. "You just shout frantically at young greenem."

"Err well, that was different," stutters the boing boing.

John nods. "Yes of course, how stupid of me."

He then pauses a moment in thought, "So you have heard of humans then?" he asks.

"Yes of course," answers the boing boing arrogantly. "Now I'll have to go I'm not meant to communicate with inferior life forms."

"Before you go" asks John a little irately. "How have you heard of us? I take it you haven't always been in this forest then."

"Unlike you inferior life forms," announces the boing boing arrogantly, "We can come and go from this place as we choose, the trickery does not work on superior minds."

John sighs. "Wow, I guess Woodnut was right about you lot, talk about stuck up your own backside. And if we are so inferior, how is it my friends and I are here now then."

The boing boing does not answer, but instead makes a strange gesture to him before taking a few hops away. "By the way, my name is John," shouts John. "And it was, err, kind of a pleasure to help, I think."

The boing boing turns back round. "I know who you are, John Fox," it says. "That is the only reason I allowed you to talk."

Then to John's surprise the boing boing takes a couple of large hops, and bounces off the root of the tree, and onto John's shoulder back onto the trunk of the tree and onto a low lying branch. "Catch me," calls the creature as it proceeds to spin twice around the branch letting go.

John catches it in both hands. "Very impressive. Would you like me to let you down now?" he asks.

"No," snaps the creature. "Now be quiet and listen before my spinners start to produce again, and I am connected back to the collective. Do not go any further, for the masters of this place lie just a short distance ahead, just beyond the trees in front of you there. And if you think we are arrogant, these creatures make us look humble in comparison."

Then the boing boing suddenly gives a squeak, "I have to go now." So it jumps down and hops swiftly away shouting, "Now leave me alone ooman."

John stands back up and just before the creature is out of sight, it stops turns around and does the funny gesture again. John gives a wave and it carries on. "I guess that's a friendly gesture then," he mutters to himself. "What an odd little creature." He then stands there looking back and forth, unsure whether to go straight back for his friends, or creep ahead for a quick look to see if he can get a sneaky peek at these people before the others. He spins back and forward until he cannot resist the temptation any longer, and he races quickly and quietly ahead. "A quick peek," he thinks to himself. "What harm could it do? And if there's any trouble at least the others will be ok."

The light gets more intense as he gets closer, and he soon comes to the last line of trees, and is faced with a perfect wall of sunshine, and he slows to a stop. Cautiously he approaches a thick piece of undergrowth surrounding a small tree. Carefully he parts the branches and peeks through, his heart now beating so fast he can hardly breathe. Then to his utter shock and horror he feels something viciously grab him from behind. He tries to spin around but the sudden shock makes him stumble, even winding himself in the process.

"Hi John, what's happening?" comes a voice.

It's Cin with the others standing just behind sniggering like crazy.

"Gees Louise yu big lug," gasps John, still trying to catch his breath. "What are you trying to do, kill me? What an utter swine, could you not have just said boo? Or a gentle prod or something, god, that's got to have knocked a good ten years off me life."

Cin half frowning and half grinning replies, "Call it payback for the five minute madness, remember."

"Come on," stutters John still gasping. "There's a time and a place."

Cin just gives him a cheeky wink. Big Dan puts his hand out to help him up. We got a bit worried when you didn't come back," he says. "Did you manage to get a look?"

Getting back to his feet and brushing himself down John answers, "Not much, I barely got the chance to take a look, before I was interrupted."

Both John and Big Dan then turn and take a look together carefully parting the foliage. "Well?" asks Max excitedly.

"I'm not sure," stammers Big Dan. "Grass ahead for a good distance, a large pond to the left. But, but, there's a handful of the oddest looking trees I've ever seen, scattered here and there. And ahead of that I, I'm at a loss."

"John what are they?" he asks.

"I don't think they're trees," whispers John. "A row of satellite dishes perhaps, some sort of communication dishes maybe."

"I'm not quite sure," he stutters.

The old crone standing behind starts to cackle. "They're sun pads," she tells them.

"They're what?" asks Cin.

"Sun pads, pads for sunbathing," she repeats. "Now listen cloth ears, they climb up the central shaft, then curl up in the dish and sunbathe. The dish rotates, following the sun around the sky all day."

Both Maxie and Woodnut burst into fits of laughter. "That's just silly," says Maxie between the laughs.

Big Dan just frowns at her. Hettie shrugs. "Suit yourselves." Then she says,

"Why bring me along if you're not going to listen to what I tell you?"

Cin frowns and tells her, "We didn't, you followed us remember."

"Oh now you're just nit picking," she flusters.

"Is there anything else?" asks Cin.

"Yes," stutters John. "A distance from them there's some sort of runway, or platform, err a landing strip perhaps."

"A what?" asks Max.

"Err doesn't matter," gasps John.

Hettie then tries to quickly explain a runway to them.

"Is there anything on it John?" asks Hettie.

"N, no," he stutters.

"Dad what's the matter?" asks Maxie.

"In the distance," replies John. "I'm not sure, err, a structure, I, I think, I'm not quite sure a large hill perhaps, a small mountain. But, but."

"This is what you would call their stronghold," the old woman tells them.

"Here John give me a look," says Cin pulling him back.

"By the golden ocean," he then exclaims. "I've never seen anything like it."

They each then take their turn staring at the large ominous structure in the distance, all equally transfixed and having to be pulled away so the next can take their turn, even Hettie even though she's seen it before. Finally they all step back. "Well what do you think John?" asks Max.

"I'm not sure," he answers. "I thought I'd seen it all, no offence but where I come from the diversity of buildings, and the materials they're made from is nearly never ending. But this, this is something else, the size of it, it's immense, and it's maybe just that ominous matt black colour but."

"John your eyesight," interrupts Big Dan. "It's grey."

"No, no, you're both wrong," says Cin. "It's definitely silver."

"Well I've the best eyesight out of the lot of you," Max tells them. "And I don't know where you're getting it from, but it's more of an orangey colour."

"Well I can see in two light spectrums," announces Maxie. "And I can definitely tell you all its red."

Hettie starts to cackle again. John ssighs but says, "Go on then, what is it?"

"You're all right," she replies.

"How can we all be right?" asks Max.

John nods. "It changes colour doesn't it?"

"Yes, yes, that's right," she answers excitedly. "It changes colour depending on the heat inside, and absorbs or reflects the light accordingly. To keep the temperature inside a constant, err now, what was it they said, err, oh, oh, that's it, to keep it a constant 88.5 degrees, if that means anything to you that is."

They all sit there amazed. "Now that's clever," says John. "And it means to me, they obviously like it hot then."

"Some more than others," answers Hettie. "It all depends on which cast they are from, but this is suitable for most I am lead to believe."

Big Dan frowns. "You seem to know an awful lot about these people."

"Yes of course I do, I am a person of learning, just like my father," she answers. "I strive to learn as much as I can, as should all people of good intellect and culture. But I don't suppose you'd know anything about that now would you."

Big Dan squints his eyes and growls. The old woman just cackles and growls back.

"What now?" asks Cin.

John shrugs. "I'm not sure, maybe we should stay here a few days, suss things out before we let our presence be known."

Big Dan nods. "Makes sense to me."

"Yes I agree," says Max.

19

"OH COME ON you scaredy flumps," comes a little voice.

They all turn to see were Maxie is. "I'm here," she calls.

They look to see her and Woodnut standing a little way ahead out in the open. "What are you doing?" calls Max. "Get back here now."

"Oh come on you silly things, we go forward there's nothing to be scared of," shouts Maxie.

"Are you sure about this?" asks Big Dan as they all step out.

Maxie nods. "Aha, mostly I think."

Big Dan frowns. "Hmm, mostly aye."

John gives a chuckle, "Come on then, who am I to argue with a little girl and a plant anyway?"

Woodnut starts to giggle. "We'll see soon enough I suppose," replies Cin frowning just a little. "At least it's exciting. Who knows, we might even get to have a bit of fun yet Dan my friend. Perhaps they like a good fight. After all they like to hunt, they can't be all that bad. I think we might have a lot in common with these people."

"Is that all you two think about?" snaps Max.

"No don't be silly," answers Big Dan, slyly winking to the others. "We like to drink as well, and at a push, maybe, and I mean maybe, even eat a bite of your cooking once in a while."

Max stamps her foot and shakes her fist at them. "Men."

"Don't worry Mum," sniggers Maxie. "Next time they're hungry, we'll get Dad to cook them something out of his bag perhaps."

"Oh well," blusters Big Dan. "I meant it in a completely complementary way Max. You know there's no need for that now."

"What do you mean by that?" asks John a little miffed. "What's wrong with my stuff?"

Cin sniggers, "Nothing if you're about three"

It's not long before they reach the first of the sun pads standing tall and proud high above the short grass, like some strange inverted mutant black mushroom. The structure itself stands about fifteen feet off the ground, and consisting of a central black column with a large black circular dish on top.

And a spiral staircase of about two foot wide runs around the outside base of the column, leading up to the top centre of the dish, and ending at a small hatch, with the dish itself roughly having a ten foot circumference. They stand there beside it wondering and pondering.

"Hello up there," calls John.

Max gasps, "John what are you doing?"

"Hello," calls John again but there's no answer.

"I'm seeing if anyone's there, and trying to introduce myself," he mutters out one side of his mouth.

"Hello up top," he shouts again, but again there's no answer.

He then shrugs. "I guess there's no one there then."

Then he takes a few steps more to inspect the pad from underneath. "How odd," he exclaims.

"What is it?" asks Big Dan.

Maxie and Woodnut rush forward. "Oh yes," answers Maxie. "You'd think these would have been steps spiralling up, it's more like a slide with grooves across its base. It must be a little tricky to get up there, but I bet its great fun sliding down, maybe a little hard on the bum though."

The others come over for a closer look. "Can I go up Mum?" asks Maxie excitedly.

"No, no way, no chance," answers her mum. "You'll stay down here in my sight and out of trouble."

Maxie sighs. "Aw Mum."

Hettie starts to cackle, "I've said it before and I'll say it again, you people are strange, what other way would you have them get up."

John shrugs. "Well, stairs spring to mind. I tell you what though guys, maybe I'll go up there, get a better lay of the land, so to say. See if I can see anything from up there."

"See Mum, Dad's going" twines Maxie.

Max sighs. "No please stay here with me, this all makes me very nervous dear."

John shinnies up and around the central column until he gets to the hatch, which as he puts his hand up opens automatically. He makes his way through, and as he does so the hatch closes shut automatically behind him again, and he proceeds to stand up. He then put's his hands on his hips and does a full 360 of the area. "Well it's definitely a lovely place," he shouts down. "You definitely get a good view from up here that's for sure."

"We should have maybe sent someone up there with decent eyesight," says Big Dan.

"I heard that," comes the shout from above as John sits down hanging his legs over the side. "I tell you what guys, its damn warm up here, I'm getting a queer sweaty ar."

"JOHN," shouts Max.

"I was going to say armpit," replies John grinning to himself.

"Yes of course," snaps Max. "That's why you're grinning so hard."

"How does she do that?" mutters John. "Oops, hang on, there's a bit of activity over there in that small lake. There must be some large fish in there or something."

"Why's that?" asks Woodnut.

"Something's just pulled one of them duck, err flurry things under," he shouts down.

"That could be anything," answers Woodnut. "Spot for all you know."

"Here hang on," gasps John suddenly.

"What the hells that?" he hollers.

"What?" the others shout.

"I, I, I'm not sure," stutters John. "Something's coming out of the water, Jesus, look at the size of that thing. Oh well, I guess that explains what took the flurry."

"What?" the others shout again.

"Oh don't tell me you can't see from there," replies John sarcastically. "I thought you lot had good eyesight."

"John please," grumps Cin.

"There," John says as he points. "It's some sort of large serpent."

"Oh yes," gasps Max.

"Yeah me too," says Maxie standing with Woodnut on her shoulders.

"Oh yes," say the others in turn.

John sighs. "I tell you what everybody, I've seen quite a few in my time, but that's one big assed snake."

"Yes it does seem quite big," mutters Cin. "I didn't think you got them that big."

"Oh yes it's not that unusual," Maxie tells them excitedly. "Especially in rainforest anyway, and a forest as old, large and unspoiled as this one, there will be many species, of many different sizes and colours."

"Now that is strange," shouts John. "It's standing more or less upright.

There must be something there causing a threat. Corr blimey, there must be some queer power in its tail to hold it up like that."

"That thing must be standing as tall as a man," gasps Big Dan.

"Taller I would say," stutters Cin. "But it's hard to tell from here."

"No they always stand like that," the old woman tells them. "They are only rarely on their bellies."

"You've seen these things before?" asks John.

The old crone just looks up at him oddly. "Yes of co," is all she gets to answer as John jumps down with a thud. "What are you doing you fool?" she squawks.

"Getting down," says John.

"Look quickly" shout both girls in unison.

The serpent is now running back across the grass towards the runway at a tremendous speed. "By the hand of fell knar," gasps Cin. "That thing can run nearly as fast as you John."

"Here hang on," shouts John in a curious voice. "I could have sworn that thing didn't have legs a moment ago, and now they're twirling around like windmills in a storm."

Big Dan nods. "For once John that's not your bad eyesight, you're right, it didn't."

"Now that is no ordinary snake," says Woodnut excitedly.

"They do not like using their legs," Hettie tells them. "They are kept hidden internally, and are only excreted if needed, in times of emergency or shock and the like."

"You seem to know an awful lot about these beasts," replies Big Dan suspiciously.

The old woman now looks at him oddly and says, "Well it's why you brought me wasn't it. I told you all to be light of foot, but no, you scared him away. I could have gone over, explained and introduced you. This has made it a lot more problematic."

"You, you, don't mean," stammers John, the only one now able to speak.

"Yes, yes," she answers nonchalantly. "One of the sky gods you came to meet."

"Well slap me backwards," stutters John, "Never in a thousand years would I have guessed that."

Cin now getting his voice back growls, "I thought you said they were people."

"Oh, no, no," she answers. "You lot said that, not I. I just called them creatures, which is what they are."

John shakes his head. "So what's your advice now then? What do you think we should do?"

The old woman ponders a moment before she says, "Hem, everything from this moment on must be done slowly, no sharp movements. Sharp movements may upset them, make them trust us a little less. They are the most intelligent creatures in the universe, so they say. But at close quarters especially, it can make them feel very threatened, it's an automatic response I think. An evolutionary habit they haven't quite managed to shake yet I think. We should slowly make our way down to the runway. Then when we get there, you lot stop back a little and I will go forwards and do the talking, introductions and the like."

"Come on then, and remember," she repeats as they set off. "No sharp movements from this point on, they now know we are here."

"They must have really good eyes, to see us here from that building," says Maxie.

John ruffles her hair. "Let's do as she says. Think about it though, if they have things that can fly them into space, they will no doubt have things that can monitor our movements. In fact for all we know, they could be watching and listening to everything we are saying and doing right now, as we speak."

Woodnut and Maxie start waving franticly. "Hello, hello," they shout. "We come as friends."

John smiles to himself, "Wish I'd never said out," which makes both Maxie and Woodnut giggle terribly.

As they walk along past more of the sun pads Cin frowning asks, "Are you sure they should be doing that?"

John smiles. "They're just enjoying themselves. And besides what harm could it do?"

"Yes, yes, they may think its funny," cackles Hettie excitedly.

As they get closer still they can't help but be in awe of the building. "It seems very err, what's the word" says Max. "Round, tubular, yes that's it."

John nods. "Hmm yes I know what you mean, there doesn't seem to be a corner or sharp edge on it."

"No, no there isn't," cackles Hettie. "Even the doors, you can't see them from here, but even they are round. And if they are travelling a long way from one end of the complex to the other, there are two ways you can go, corridors with serrated steps and floors similar to the sun pads, and the other one. They allowed me a go once you know, it was a little frightening at first but what fun, I felt like a little girl again."

Cin gives a sarcastic chuckle, "I didn't think it was possible for anyone to remember that long ago."

"Oh you be quiet you big dogs butt," snaps the old woman. "Do you want me to tell you or not? Oh now look what you've done, I've lost where I was now."

"A little frightening but great fun," prompts Maxie.

The woman smiles excitedly. "Oh yes dear, thank you. You go up to the appropriate hatch as signed, which opens automatically when close enough. You then position yourself correctly, and it sucks you in, which then propels you all the way to where you are going."

"It's wonderful, you've never experienced anything like it," she cackles smiling her broadest smile.

"Oh yes that was the most fun," says both Maxie and Woodnut excitedly.

"Can we do it again sometime?" they ask.

"Hey," laughs Cin putting his hand on Big Dans shoulder. "Do you remember the look on John's face when he saw Lane flying towards him, and realised he had to catch him, then got a slap off Max for dropping her first."

Big Dan throws his head back and laughs, "Oh yes, and Lane was so relieved to still be alive he nearly kissed him."

"What are you lot talking about?" asks Hettie a little irately. "You've never done that before, you've never even been here before."

"Yes we have," answers Max. "Just not here, it was back at the whistling mountains in Voreda. We spent a day there once, and oh my, it really was good fun."

"Hu, I don't believe you," grumps the crone.

"Max shrugs. "Suite yourself, I'm not defending myself when I'm in the right."

The old woman then turns as something dawns on her. "So these tubes, holes you were pulled through, they went from one side of this mountain to the other yes."

John nods. "Yes that's right."

"I know not where," she answers. "But I do know there is a mountain somewhere on this earth. And it is the only one anywhere in any universe, which they can collect a certain mineral, err stone thing from. And I know they've taken many a core from this mountain over many years. Although now I think they have learned to, err, sin, sin."

"Synthesize," prompts John.

She smiles. "Yes that's it thank you."

"You mean," asks Big Dan. "You're honestly trying to tell us, that those things cut the tunnels through that mountain? And each tunnel is only one sample taken in, in one go by, by them things, with, with some weapon?"

"Yes of course," she answers. "But it's not a weapon, it's a tool."

"Yes of course," mutters Big Dan blowing out deeply. "How stupid of me."

"Look, look," shouts Maxie and Woodnut excitedly pointing to the top of the building.

"They must be pleased to see us now," she shouts excitedly. "They're going to shower us in pretty lights to celebrate our arrival."

"Oh yes," smiles Max. "That is lovely."

"At last a good sign," bellows Cin.

But John's mouth falls open as he squints his eyes for a better look. "Get down now," he screams pushing both Max and Maxie to the ground. He then throws himself to the ground. "Cover your heads," he shouts.

Big Dan and Cin are not long in following and the only one left standing is Hettie. "Oh get up you silly things," she cackles.

The brightly coloured lights then land all around them, spectacularly banging, popping and fizzing like some sort of macabre fireworks display. Not long and there is silence once again and cautiously they all start to get back up.

"What the heck was that?" asks Cin angrily. "Was that some sort of attack?"

"Well if not," replies John. "It was a damn good impersonation, or a practical joke in very poor taste."

"No you silly things," laughs Hettie. "I think it was just to mark our arrival, you know in a special way, you just took it all the wrong, you should have looked it was very pretty."

Big Dan frowns. "Could they not just have waved and said hello."

"What was that?" asks John.

"I think they call them fizzes," she answers. "I know they use them sometimes to deter some of the larger wild animals from straying too far from the forest. It simply scares them back without hurting them."

"OH, so now we're wild animals to be played with and scared are we," growls Cin.

"No silly," she answers. "You've just taken it all the wrong way. Come on lets carry on to where we planned."

The old woman walks on as the others just stand there. "John, what do you think?" asks Max.

John just shrugs. "She's the expert I suppose, but everyone keep your eyes open and your wits about you, and that includes you also my love."

Max smiles kindly. "Yes dear." smiles Max.

"Hang on what do you mean by that," she then snaps.

John smiles winking to the boys. "Oh nothing dear."

"We'll see about that," she says rushing over to him.

"MAX," shouts John. "No sharp movements remember."

Max stamps her foot. "Just wait till we get out of here John Fox."

Big Dan and Cin try to hide their titters but one slips out anyway. She frowns. "And you two needn't start." "Hey Max, would we," replies Big Dan grinning.

They then set off following the old woman but don't get very far before Max points up to the top of the building and something sticking out. "Look," she shouts a little alarmed.

"What is that?" asks Cin.

"I, I have no idea my friend. But it doesn't look good," answers Big Dan. "John what do you think?"

"I'm guessing," stutters John. "Well it looks like some sort of weapon to me. Hettie, have you seen this before."

The old woman just silently shakes her head. "Oh my god," shouts John. "It's just shot at us, quickly run, under that dish there."

They just get there in time as they hear something whistle past, and there is a loud explosion a short distance behind them. Both Max and Maxie give out a loud scream as they are all hit by flying earth. "I, I think I'm deaf," shouts Max. "John help please, there's just a whistling, that's all I can hear."

Big Dan gets up and rubs his eyes in disbelief." L, look," he stutters.

They all then look to a large crater where the blast had come from. "I, I, can't believe it," stammers Cin. "What type of weapon could do such a thing? If that had hit us, there wouldn't have even been parts left to recognise. What type of evil beasts are these?"

John ratches through Max's pockets and finds the bungs for her ears, and puts them in for her, and Maxie quickly does the same. "So much for peaceful intelligent creatures," he snaps.

"I. I don't understand," stutters the old woman. "I just don't, they're, they're explorers just like yourselves. This must be some sort of joke, yes that's it, it must be, it's some sort of joke, you'll see."

"Everybody down," shouts Cin.

There is then another explosion, this time just ahead of them, and they are covered in earth once again. "Let me go out," says Hettie franticly. "I'll talk to them, and it'll be alright."

But Big Dan grabs her arm and pulls her down and replies, "Stay here you old fool, or there won't be enough of you left for us to bury."

"John we have to get out of here," says Cin.

John nods. "Agreed we're just sitting ducks here. Woodnut get in my bag and Maxie I'll carry you. On three we make a dash back towards the woods. Stay close to the pads, we go from one to another. We can use them for cover, is everybody set, lets go."

They make a run to the last pad. "I tell you what," shouts Cin as they run along. "If I manage to get my hands on one of them things, I promise you now, I'm going to have myself a nice shinny new pair of snake skin boots, that's for sure."

"Down," shouts John.

They all instantly duck for cover and there is a loud bang in front of them then one behind. "Right go," shouts Big Dan as the earth settles.

"Do you know?" shouts John as they run along. "I think we're being played with here."

"What do you mean?" shouts Cin and Max simultaneously.

"These explosions are always the same distance away from us, whether it be in front or behind," shouts John. "Not enough to hurt anyone, but just enough to cover us in dirt and terrify the life out of us. Surely by now with their technology they should have got us."

"Hey don't complain," shouts Big Dan.

Cin nods. "You know I think you have a point there, but what do you think they're playing at."

"I've no idea," answers John. "Putting the frighteners on us perhaps, making sure we don't return in a hurry."

"Well I hope they're congratulating themselves," replies Cin. "It's worked."

"Hettie, any idea why they are doing this?" asks John.

"No I am at a loss myself," she stutters. "They can be a little unpredictable I know, but they are good creatures for the most part, explorers like I said."

"I'd like to explore the inside of their body's with my sword," growls Big Dan.

"Maybe so," replies the old woman. "But as big as you are, you would be no match for their strength and speed, two of you maybe, but even then."

They collapse with exhaustion a few hundred yards short of the forest. "A moment's breather," pants Cin. "Well unless I'm mistaken," pants Big Dan. "They seem to have stopped trying to kill us with them, them, explosions."

"Yes," agrees John. "Maybe they think we are no longer a threat. Now they can clearly see we are heading back to the forest. Now let's get back into the forest where we know we'll be safe."

"Yes please," pants" Maxie.

"Woodnut, you alright back there?" shouts John tapping the back of his bag.

"Yes," comes a muffled shout.

"It'll be alright Dad," shouts Maxie. "I'll run the rest of the way myself."

John nods. "Ok let's go."

They only get half way to the woods when they hear a loud high pitched scream, "Stop."

So they all stop instantly. "Lilly," shouts John. "Is that you? Are you ok?"

Two little eyes then appear from just under a clump of grass in front of them. John steps forward and kneels down. "What is it?" he asks.

"It's a trap," pants Lilly, now very shaken herself.

"What do you mean?" asks John.

"There are at least five of them creatures waiting for you," she pants. "Just inside the line of trees there."

"Are they armed? Do they have weapons?" he asks in an alarmed voice.

"It's strange John," stutters Lilly. "As they do not appear to have arms, but they do appear to have weapons. As leaning against a tree next to each of them is a long staff with a ball like structure on one end and spikes on the other. Be careful silly man I have a bad feeling about this, I will help you where I can."

He winks. "Thank you, it's just good to see you alive pretty lady."

Lilly lifts her head a little, just enough to give him a slight smile before disappearing.

He gets back up and turns to the others. "What is it John?" asks Cin.

"Who were you talking to?" asks Hettie.

"Quiet woman let him talk," snaps Big Dan.

John shaking his head answers, "It appears there are at least five of them things waiting for us in ambush, just in the trees there."

"Weapons?" asks Dan.

John nods. "Yes some sort of staff, barbed at one end, and some sort of club at the other end. Which explains why they've stopped shelling us."

"Thoughts anybody," he asks.

"This is good," shouts the old crone excitedly. "They're ceremonial staffs, they probably want to greet us now."

"Are you deluded woman," bellows Cin. "The only thing they're going to do with them, is ceremoniously beat us to death with them."

"No, no, let me go and talk to them. Please, let me make peace," she begs.

"I think that's a very bad idea," answers Big Dan running his fingers through his beard. "There is strength in numbers. You cannot trust these beasts, this is plain to see, and they obviously have no honour. You should stay here where we can protect each other. And if we face them, we face them together, on a ground of our choosing, not theirs."

Cin nods. "Agreed, never give the enemy the advantage if you can manage it. And in that's where they hunt and kill regularly for sport, they would have the advantage. I say we stand here, where we can see all around us, and can swing our swords without fear of burying them into a tree trunk. And we can also maybe make use of those sun pads of theirs if necessary."

"Yes," continues Big Dan. "Even those blast holes maybe of some use as shelters if needed."

Both Cin and Big Dan then draw their swords and stick them in the earth in front of them, then drawing their daggers hand they one each to Max and Maxie. "Stand together," Dan tells them. "If attacked do not let them part you. One go high the other low, hopefully it won't be able to defend both simultaneously."

The old woman suddenly takes off like a rocket towards the trees. "Hettie," shouts Max taking off after her. "Come back."

John grabs Max's arm and tells her, "Stay here, she's made her choice, and hopefully she can do some good and end this madness before it begins. But I don't mind telling you, I don't think I've ever been as scared in my life. And as strange as it would have seemed to me not so long ago, not for myself."

He then kisses her tenderly on the lips. "Do not fear my love," whispers Max. "For I would not change one moment together, and neither would Maxie. And I do not fear, for whatever happens, I am where I want to be, by your side my love, and that brings me happiness even now. And if the worse were to happen to us, I would still die happy, knowing we would still be together in death."

John tries to raise a smile. "I wish I'd never seen this damn place. But I tell you what, if I do go down, I'm going to take as many of them things with me as I can."

"John," calls Cin nodding ahead.

"Max stand behind us with Maxie," mutters Big Dan.

The three men then stand there side by side, defiant, resolute and focused, like the head of a conquering army. Max and Maxie are whispering to each other behind them, then standing up as tall and straight as they can, they take a position one either side of the boys. "What are you doing woman?" growls Cin.

"Don't even think about arguing," snaps Max. "We've decided. We are family, and in times of trouble we stand together, side by side, and unflinching."

"Do not cross us," snaps Maxie joining in. "Or your first fight will be with us."

Big Dan gives out a sigh. "You know what this means Cin my friend," he says giving him a sly wink.

Cin sighs also. "Yes unfortunately I do," he says winking back. "It means when all this is over, we're going to have to get this young lady some leathers of her own."

Maxie suddenly starts to smile, beaming from ear to ear and now feeling ten foot tall. They see the old woman stop at the forests edge and curtsy down low. "Can you hear what she's saying Max?" asks Big Dan. "Err, just about, the breeze is helping a little," mutters Max squinting and turning her head. "She, err, she begs their audience as she is saying please, err, something, magnificence, err, something, something sky gods."

"Oh my word," she then gasps.

"What is it?" asks John.

"Err," stutters Max. "She's still praising them, err, rulers of worlds, destroyers of planets."

"Just what are we fighting here," gasps Big Dan.

John shakes his head. "I wouldn't read too much into all the rubbish she's spouting," he mutters. "She's just kissing their butts, and trying to flatter them as much as possible, buttering them up you know But I'm guessing."

They then stand there silently, gazes fixed ahead, as one of the serpents appears from behind a tree, striding out proudly using its staff as just that, marching directly up to the old woman, like the lord mayor on ceremonial duties. "Is, is this a different one?" asks Cin. "That thing has both arms and legs."

"As far as I can gather," whispers John. "It's like the old goat told us before.

They all have both arms and legs, but most of the time they prefer to leave them retracted internally."

Max shakes her head. "How strange," she whispers. "It must be easier to use your arms and legs surely, to lift and carry things, operate their machinery, the list is endless."

"Can't argue with you there," chuckles Big Dan. "How would you pick up your ale?"

"Shush," says Max suddenly cocking her head to the side. "I think she's arguing with them."

"What do they sound like?" asks John.

"I've no idea," whispers Max. "I've only heard her speak, she's now saying. Err, it's not true, no, no I didn't, it's not true, they're, they're good people. Explorers, explorers like yourselves, they came here as friends. No, no I'm no traitor, and neither are the. You, you. err, something something, err ugly, something something bellied reptiles."

A sudden gasp comes from them all, as they see the serpent suddenly go into a rage striking the old woman with its club. The old crone is knocked flying backwards, the serpent follows straight over to where she lays striking her viciously once again. Both Max and Maxie give out a loud squeal. "There was no need for that," growls Cin, with a sly grin just managing to escape.

Max frowns angrily. "Don't you worry Max," he blusters. "They'll pay for that you'll see."

Maxie suddenly gives out another squeal. "What is it?" asks Big Dan.

"That, that thing," she stutters. "It just, err, I don't know, spat something at her. Two long sharp objects. I, I, can see them sticking out of her body."

"I think they've killed her" she gasps.

The serpent looks back around to the wood gesturing with its staff. Out of the trees come four others, staffs in hand. "Excellent," bellows Cin grabbing the hilt of his sword. "One each."

"Remember everybody," booms Big Dan. "As well as the staff weapon they carry, they possibly have some sort of weapon in their mouths."

"What happens now?" asks John. "Do we make a run for them or what?"

Big Dan slowly shakes his head. "No that's what they want us to do, to get us of foot, exhaust us, and split us up. No, we stand here together, on our terms, where we can look out for each other. Let them make the first move," he growls.

"Woodnut, what are you doing here?" squeals Maxie. "Go and hide, quickly."

He doesn't but stands silently beside her, head fixed firmly forward trying to glare his meanest glare at the reptiles. She puts her hand down and grabs his. "I'm pleased you're here" she whispers.

The lead serpent first gestures to one of the others who instantly takes off running towards them, its legs spinning like windmills. "Do you know," chuckles Big Dan. "Any other time watching that thing run would be very funny."

They all then brace themselves as it hurtles towards them. Woodnut lets go of Maxie's hand and rushes out in front of them plunging his hands and feet deep into the ground. He is so deep there is barely even his little head left sticking out the ground, as the serpent is nearly upon them. A sudden shaft of earth is then thrust up from the ground in front of it nearly skewering the beast. And it runs straight into the column nearly knocking itself out. It lays there for a moment slightly stunned and confused as to what had just happened. Suddenly to its further surprise the weapon in its hand gets pulled down into the earth.

Woodnut gets back up now looking physically exhausted. The beast stumbles back to its feet, as its tail is then suddenly thrust down into the earth. The creature's body starts to flail and wriggle with shock, but slowly it is drawn down into the earth. Cin looks down at Woodnut and winks. "All this time my friend and you are still full of surprises."

"Gees Woodnut," shouts John. "I didn't know you could do that, dude."

Woodnut giggles, "No neither did I, but you can thank Lilly Milk for it being sucked down, that wasn't me."

"Excellent," bellows Big Dan. "Now that evens things up."

John nods. "Now that's rattled them. Look, I think they're trying to work out how we did it, and what to do next."

"What do you think they'll do now?" asks Max.

"It's hard to say," answers Cin.

"It'll be one of three things, I'd have thought," answers Big Dan. "They will either make a sudden hasty retreat, which will mean they will try and blow us up again. Or they may try to negotiate with us, or they will simply attack."

He sighs. "It's hard to tell with creatures I know little of."

"I hope it's negotiating," sighs Max. "But I would rather fight than face those explosions again."

"Fight it is, get ready everybody," bellows Cin.

"Right," shouts John. "You boys take the two on the left, I'll try and get the two on the right."

"Agreed," shouts Big Dan.

"What about us?" hollers Max.

"Mother," shouts Maxie. "Dad gets them down, we stab them."

Max now breathless just nods. "Be strong and stand fast everybody," booms Big Dan. "They want us to panic and run, they're trying to intimidate us with their size and speed."

"Two can play at that game," screams John. "Let's see if they like it."

He then takes off running, head down as fast as he can. "What's he doing?" squeals Max.

"Stand fast Max," shouts Cin. "He's trying to give us a better chance as he's playing them at their own game. He's going to try and slow them down and split them up."

Big Dan nudges Cin and tells him, "Get ready my friend, as soon as he hits them we go."

John's heart beats faster and faster as he gets closer, now making great distance between each bound. "What a way to end my days," he thinks to himself. "Who'd have ever believed it, I think I'd rather be on permanent back shift than this. How surreal, at one time I'd have been keeping things like these in cages as pets."

The serpents slow down a little on seeing John hurtle towards them even faster than them themselves, and unsure how. Now nearly on top of them, he aims for the middle two. He clenches his fists and braces himself for the on coming impact. He sees the reptile to the right of him raising its staff high. But the one to the left holds its staff to the side and putting its head back opens its mouth wide. This reveals two long large teeth angled at the back of its mouth. "Oh my god," he thinks to himself. "That's what those projectiles must be; it's going to spit them at me. They're like small daggers." For one moment he nearly panics, but now upon them it's too late and he pulls himself together. And instead of hitting the two serpents on the head he throws himself backwards for a flying kick. His two feet are now guiding the way, and aimed for their bellies. The serpent on the left shoots the projectiles from its mouth and they whistle straight for his face.

As his feet make contact with its belly, he feels a searing pain burn his cheek and he throws his head back a little more, missing the full on blow of the other tooth, which slides along his forehead cutting it neatly open. He knocks the serpent flying backwards with himself still propelled along behind it. But it's all he can do to miss the blow from the other serpent's staff, and he shoots clean past it. But as he continues to slide along, the beast stumbles a little after missing him with the staff, and he just manages to grab the tip of its tail. Not expecting this and still running forward the beast comes to a sudden and ungracious stop with its momentum still propelling its slinky body forward, and its chin is the last thing to hit the ground coming down hard. The staff once in its hand is flung forwards cart wheeling several times before stopping. The serpent stunned and in pain writhes and wriggles around the ground like a salted worm. Big Dan and Cin seeing John take the centre two creatures out, raise their swords high and take off running as fast as they can, screaming and hollering as hard and loud as they can. With Cin aiming for the one on the right, and Big Dan the one on the left. The two girls stand there shocked and stunned for a moment, before turning to each other, then nodding they take off screaming also.

Cin and Dan come upon their adversaries nearly simultaneously with their swords both crashing down heavily with the serpents staffs. With the power and momentum of each pair spinning them around past the other. Quick as a flash the serpent spins back round to face Cin, but Cin not being as fast takes a moment longer to turn ,and is caught hard in the side by the cubed end of the staff. Nearly knocked off balance, he stumbles to the side going down on one knee. Still in great pain he thrusts his sword hard at the creature's belly as it swings its staff once again, for another blow. The sword skims across one of its belly scales cutting it open. But the beast seems oblivious and swings the staff around and up above its head, to bring the spiked end down on him. His eyes go wide as he sees the staff crashing down towards him, and he instantly throws himself on to his back. And grabbing either end of his sword firmly with both hands, he just manages to block the blow. The blow is so hard it sends shockwaves down his arms and he grimaces with the pain.

Big Dan and the other serpent are also spun around. And the serpent again is the first to turn, swinging its staff down hard on the back of Big Dan. Big Dan does not attempt to turn, but instead he instantly brings his sword back above his head, grabbing the other end and blocking the blow, stopping the staff just inches from his head. The blow is still hard bringing him to his knees. But the spiked end of the staff which he'd just blocked is severed on his blade, and thunders past him, cutting his cheek open before sticking firmly in the ground just in front of him. He does not even attempt to stand up, instead he spins around on his knees, swinging his sword around with him hard and fast. The serpent itself now caught off guard stumbles back, and as its leg kicks up, Big Dan's sword catches it perfectly, taking its foot clean off just above the ankle. The reptile reels back even further, and clearly in pain proceeds to retract both its severed leg and its good one also as Big Dan jumps to his feet.

Max and Maxie rush between the fighting Cin and Dan, trying to get to the stunned serpent writhing on the ground, after being pulled down by John. The reptile just about comes to its senses as they get to it. Maxie is no more than a moment before her mum and grabbing the hilt of the dagger with both hands she dives like an Olympic swimmer, for the rear end of it. The dagger sticks between two of the beasts vertebra, and is instantly drove in deep as she lands down hard on top of it, winding herself in the process. The serpent is sent spinning in agony, parting Maxie from her dagger and throwing her out of the way. Now dragging its crippled back end it makes its way towards her. Maxie scrambles backwards gasping for air as the reptile opens its blood socked mouth. Her eyes go wide as the creature is now nearly upon her. But both she and the serpent start to look round, as they hear a deafening scream just behind them. And as the serpent starts to turn, its head is forced down, as a panting screaming Max drives her blade through the top of its skull, pinning its now lifeless body to the ground. Panting she screams, "Leave my baby along you damn slimy cur."

John and the serpent finally come to a stop heaped together. The serpent starts to wriggle trying to get its coils around him. John panics slightly now struggling to see from the blood running into his eyes. But he just about makes out which end is its head, and he wraps his arms around it, as high up its body as he can get them, closely followed by his legs. "Constrict me you bastard," he screams. "Let's see how you damn well like it."

He holds fast, and the serpent starts to panic, and now unable to extend its arms it starts to roll.

A short distance from them all the earth starts to shake, and a crack starts to appear in the ground. Making all the fighting stop, and as the rumble turns into a crash, the serpent buried earlier powers out the ground like a geezer, with a terrified Lilly Milk still holding franticly on to its tail. As the beast crashes back onto the ground Lilly is thrown clear of it, but the serpent turns instantly back towards her with death in its eyes. Getting close to her it opens its mouth wide, and the fighting starts once again. Lilly lays there terrified beaten and exhausted, barely able to move. "You parasite," hisses the serpent. "How dare you, you inferior." The creature opening its mouth wide aiming its projectile teeth straight at her.

Cin shakes his head with the shock at seeing the other reptile reappear, as is his opponent on seeing its comrade. Coming back to his senses a moment before the serpent, he rolls back curling up his legs and kicking as hard as he can, at the point where its body meets the ground. The serpent is taken by surprise and its lower half is taken from under it, making its upper half crash down towards him. Cin thrusts his sword up, and as it falls his blade pierces the reptile's side. The sword skims around the beast's ribs and clean out the other side. He then rolls over, and kicking it off he scrambles to his feet raising his sword high to finish off the squirming beast. And he is about to bring it down, until he sees Lilly's terrified face staring up at her on coming death. He takes off running in her direction hoping to reach the serpent in time. Lilly starts to whimper and closes her eyes as she hears a loud hissing then feels an awful crushing around her middle. Her head starts to spin around and around, as she feels her on coming death. Then to her utter surprise she hears a familiar voice. "Are you ok little one?" comes an agonised voice.

She opens her eyes to see Cin lying on the ground with her in his large bear like hand. "Are you alright little one?" he repeats.

"Y, yes," she stutters. "You, you saved me."

Cin lets go of her instantly turning back around to where the serpent is stood. "Go now," he shouts desperately trying to scramble to his feet, and now deeply in pain.

Lilly gasps seeing two of the serpent's teeth buried between his shoulder blades. "You, you did that for me," she stutters.

She then gives a squeal as she feels something grab her, its Woodnut. "Come on," he shouts.

"Hold me tightly," he tells her, then burrows down into the earth as fast as he can pulling Lilly behind him.

Cin getting up slashes at the serpents throat. The serpent he first fought finally gets to its feet and looks to Cin then around to Big Dan still fighting its companion. Then it sees his fellow companion dead with the two girls trying to pull their weapons from its lifeless body. The serpent flies into an instant rage and throwing its head back makes an awful unearthly noise, before taking off towards Max and Maxie. The two girls hearing the noise look around. "Run," shouts Max, just managing to get her dagger out.

Both girls take off running. "Where are we going?" gasps Maxie.

"Err, I don't know," gasps Max. "There, head for that crater."

They then run as fast as their legs can carry them, with the serpent in hot pursuit and catching up quickly. They get to the crater and do not pause to stop, jumping down into the deep hole. They come down with a clatter but manage to scramble back round. The two girls huddle together, both panting deeply. "I love you," whispers Max shakily holding her dagger out in front of them.

"And I love you" Maxie whispers, grabbing her mum's hand and helping to steady the blade.

Cin sees the beast take off after the girls as he slashes at the serpent's throat. The reptile just wriggles its body sending a wave upwards putting a loop where Cin's sword should have hit, and instead it just flies past. Now feeling physically exhausted it hits the ground throwing him off balance, and he lays there on his side panting unable to get away or help the girls. The serpent raises its staff high for the final blow and brings it down hard. Cin grabs the hilt of his sword with both hands and swings up and round, with the last bit of energy he can possibly muster. The reptile not expecting this tries to step back, but the force of its swing stops it. Cin's blade hits the staff at an angle and carries on down until it hits resistance. Which comes in the form of the beasts hand, it cuts clean through and carries on up its lower arm, stopping just short of severing it completely. The serpent drops the staff instantly screaming in pain. Now with a new hope and a second wind Cin scrambles to his feet, as the serpent pulls off what's left of its arm with its other, then retracts it instantly. Cin panting heavily shouts at the serpent as he swings again, "Take that you overgrown salamander." The serpent dives for its staff with its good arm and the fight continues.

Big Dan starts to breathe heavily as he blocks blow after blow from the spinning serpent. "Come on," booms Big Dan defiantly. "Is that the best you can do? When I'm finished playing, I'm gonna make your arms match your leg."

The serpent wound up now more than ever, stops for a moment and throws its head back, and opening its mouth wide spits its two large teeth at him. Big Dan tries to turn but they still catch him, one driving deep into his shoulder and the other just below his collarbone and into his chest. Dan stumbles back in pain then defiantly shouts, "Is that it? Is that all you've got? You must be the female of the species, because you fight like a girl."

"I'm gonna have your hide for a belt," he hollers switching his sword to his good arm.

The light in the crater starts to darken, as the serpent raises itself up as high as it can, high on the rim above the two girls. And all they can make out is its silhouette as the sun beats down hard behind it. "You will pay for this," comes a loud hissing noise. "Killing my brethren and declaring war on us, you humans make me sick, in whatever form you come. You infest planets like a plague, and this is our thanks for letting you live here. Your friends will soon be dead. And you two, I am going to kill very, very..."

"Agh," it suddenly screams as a pain cuts it of in mid sentence.

The reptile throws itself to the ground, instantly retracting all its limbs and rolling round and around, like a hungry crocodile trying to get its chunk of a carcase. "What was that?" gasps Max.

"I've no idea," shouts Maxie scrambling up to take a look.

"Mum," she then shouts. "Quickly, it's Spot."

"Spot," squeals Max now scrambling up herself. "That's impossible. What on earth could it do to that terrible giant beast?"

Both stare in disbelief as they see the serpent still spinning in agony. And as their eyes follow its large slinky body down, they see there firmly clamped on the end of the reptile's tail is Spot. Its arms and legs tucked well in, and its eyes tightly closed like the headlights on a sports car, looking as if it is clamped on for the duration. "Well," stutters Max scrambling to her feet. "I guess they have sensitive tails then. Stay here." Then as the serpent rolls back towards her oblivious to everything, Max swings her dagger wildly at its neck. But the writhing beast is quick and she misses. She lunges again this time hitting it, but not square on, and the dagger slices into the scales on the side of its neck. The reptile is pinned down for a moment, but its spinning motion rips its body away from the dagger. Max lunges again pinning it slightly more squarely this time, but doing little damage internally. Then as a dark shadow passes her eye line a scream is heard. And she sees Maxie run alongside her, smashing a large rock down on the serpents head. She repeats the action several times, with both hands firmly clamped on the rock, as her mother then throws herself onto the back of the beast, in an attempt to hold it down. It takes several more blows and a few more stabs from Max's dagger before the beast finally lays there lifeless. "Yes," shouts Maxie now completely exhausted, and the two girls hug before retiring back into the crater panting heavily.

John is still rolling around with the other reptile, each trying to dominate and constrict the other. Still struggling to see he manages to wipe his face on his shoulder. Neither side wining the fight and the serpent now tiring slightly, it decides to take another strategy and stops rolling letting its body go limp. "Yes," screams John. "Constrict me would you, you over grown corn snake."

But to his surprise then horror, its body tenses again as its head spins back around and it bites down on him, its mouth nearly engulfing his whole shoulder. John lets go in pain and shock, and the beast throws its coils around him. Coming to his senses and realising his predicament he manages to free his good arm. "Want to play dirty do we," he shouts breathlessly. "Let's see how you like this then."

Quick as a flash he buries his thumb as hard and deep as he can into the serpents eye. Harder and harder he pushes it in. The reptile lets go spinning and reeling in agony. John stumbles to his feet and looks around to the others, there is no sign of the girls and both Cin and Dan are battling for all their worth. He hears Big Dan's defiant shouts then sees him being struck by the serpent's teeth. "Oh no," he gasps. "Got to do something."

Again as quick as a flash he grabs the still writhing reptile by the tail, and starts to swing it around and around, spinning it faster and faster. Try as it might the beast can do nothing. "See how you like this," he grunts as he aims it.

He then let's go, trying to hit the serpent about to come down on Big Dan, with the one he has just flung. The serpent wriggles and spins as it is flies through the air. "Orr crap," gasps John as he sees his aim is a mile off, and is instead hurtling towards Cin and the other serpent.

"Cin duck," he shouts.

Cin a little surprised turns his head only slightly, not daring to take his eyes of the fight. But catching something hurtling towards him out the corner of his eye instantly ducks. The two serpents smash together heavily, and are knocked several feet backwards. Cin gets back up somewhat relieved and waves to John. John points to Big Dan as he also takes off running towards him. Cin nods taking off instantly towards Dan. He is first there and swings hard at the reptile. The serpent is caught off guard and just manages to block his blow. Big Dan gets back to his feet and joins back in. But the serpent manages to fend off both swords from the two exhausted men. John is running over, but being in pain and exhausted himself, his speed is far from normal. Nearly on it himself he pauses briefly to pick up a fallen staff, to use as a weapon himself. The reptile seeing John screaming over with a staff in hand, swings as hard as it can across Cin and Big Dan, catching both their swords hard and making them both stumble. The serpent then surprisingly drops to its belly and speeds off towards its two comrades. "Are, are, you two alright?" pants John.

"Just about," groans Cin. "Although I think I may have to stay off the ale for awhile, as I appear to be too full of holes to keep it in."

Big Dan gives out a single laugh, and then winces with the pain in his chest. "Not funny," he pants. "Not funny."

"Where are the girls?" gasps John.

"I think they're in that first crater," puffs Cin. "But John, it doesn't look good, there was one of them things in hot pursuit the last I saw. I tried to get to them, honest I did, but."

"Shush, quiet my friend," replies John softly. "Anything else would have never cross my mind. I'll see you both there."

As those last few words slip from his mouth he takes off running towards the crater faster than ever. Willing himself to get there, but terrified on what he might find. As he gets close he jumps the last short distance into the hole.

In the crater the two girls still terrified get their breaths back somewhat. "I, I'll see how the boys are doing," stutters Maxie scrambling up the side and cautiously peeking over. She gives a squeal as she sees a dark figure fly over her head and into the crater behind her. Max as equally taken by surprise, squeals also lashing out with her dagger. John groans deeply grabbing the searing pain in his right side. "Mother," screams Maxie. "You've just stabbed Dad."

"Oh no what have I done," cries Max.

"John, John. Are you ok?" she panics.

"You mean apart from this bloody big knife sticking out my side," he groans. "I've felt better."

Panicking she pulls it back out making him cry out in pain once more. "John please don't die," she sobs "Mother get out of my way," shouts Maxie. "Let me look."

John pulls up his shirt. "I don't think this is as bad as it looks," says Maxie, cleaning some of the blood away with a cloth from her pocket.

She sighs deeply. "It looks to have only penetrated some of the fatty tissue on his side. I'll bandage it later."

"Hey you're alive," come the shouts from Cin and Dan as they peer down into the crater.

Both then jump down in and collapse beside the others. "Are you alright?" gasps Max, "You both look awful. Dan your face."

"This is the hardest fight I've ever had," pants Cin. "These things are so powerful."

"Hey John," groans Big Dan. "That looks a painful wound on you side, I hope you made that beast pay for that."

"No not yet," frowns John glaring at Max.

"I'm sorry ok," she snaps,

"You just surprised me ok" she continues going bright red.

"Max," says Cin in a heightened voice. "You, you, stabbed him."

"It was an accident," she squeals. "I didn't do it deliberately if that's what you think."

"Could you not just have slapped him?" chuckles Big Dan, then grabbing his chest and regretting it.

"Dan stop your chest," she shouts. "You've been stabbed with, with them teeth."

She takes a closer look. "And your poor face," she says. "W, would you like me to pull them out?"

Big Dan nods. "No leave them in," interrupts John.

"Leave them in," stutters Max.

"Why?" she gasps.

"They're plugging holes mother," answers Maxie. "I'll try and sort them out later."

"But, but they're causing the holes," stammers Max.

"Yes," answers John. "And if you pull them out, what do you think will happen?"

Max nods. "Oh yes I see."

"Cin," she then squeals. "You, you've got two sticking in your back."

"Oh really, I hadn't noticed," he answers nonchalantly. "Well that stopped an itch."

"Be like that then," grumps Max stamping her foot.

"Max," whispers Cin softly. "It doesn't matter, for soon these beasts will regroup, and be on us once more, and I'm afraid we're about spent. We are all exhausted and wounded, the only one that wasn't was John. Although he must be struggling to see through the cut on his head, that is a pretty bad cut even for him."

"Yeah just a bit," groans John.

"I cut that things foot clean off," Big Dan tells then wincing in pain. "And it still kept going, I couldn't believe it."

"Yes," moans Cin. "I slashed one across the belly, it didn't even wince, another I left its arm hanging by a thread. It simply ripped the rest off with it's other, grabbed its staff and kept on going."

"Oh stop your whining," snaps Max. "You are all speaking as if we've lost."

Big Dan sighs. "Max they're nearly unbeatable."

"Unbeatable aye," snarls Max. "If that's so, how come Maxie and I have killed two of them?"

"You, you've what," reply all three men in unison.

"Yes it's true," says Maxie nodding and smiling. "We've killed two of them, although the last one we had help from Spot though."

"Yes of course," puffs a bemused Big Dan. "How stupid of us."

"Oh, oh," Max shouts excitedly. "Their weak point, it's their tails, they have very sensitive tails, so go for the tails."

"Their tails woman, are you sure?" asks Cin.

"Yes, yes of course," replies Max irately. "That's how we killed the last one, Spot grabbed its tail, and it was in so much pain it was nearly helpless. All it could do was roll around. I managed to stab it and hold it down, while Maxie beat it over the head with a boulder."

"Corr there'll be no living with them now," chuckles John grimacing.

Cin nods. "Yes, the next battle we have they can lead."

"Sounds good to me," agrees Big Dan again wincing in pain.

"How can you joke at a time like this?" asks Max.

"Who's joking?" groans Cin.

"Well," interrupts John. "I say its time to take the battle to them. And if we go out, let's go out kicking screaming and fighting, every damn inch of the way, agreed?"

A unanimous "Yes," comes up loudly from them all.

20

THEY TAKE THEIR weapons and prepare to climb out, but several large shadows are cast over them, from around the rim above. They sink back down in a semi circle against the wall of the crater. "For once," gasps John. "I really am struggling to see, and all I can make out are tall black fuzzy silhouettes. Please tell me my eyes are deceiving me, and there are only three of them."

"Sorry John," wheezes Cin. "As far as I can tell there's at least eight of them."

Big Dan grips the hilt of his sword with both hands ignoring the pain. "Brace yourselves, go for their eyes, if they can't see they can't fight," he growls.

"John, John, is that you down there John?" comes a voice from the rim.

John who is swaying back and forward, and from side to side splutters, "I, I think I'm hallucinating."

"John, it is you," calls the voice. "By the silver sands, you look terrible my lad, somebody give me some water quickly."

The figure in the centre then jumps down in front of them. "Leave my husband alone," growls Max.

"My John, you have been busy since we last met my friend," the figure says.

John clears the blood sweat and dirt from his eyes, and squinting leans forward for a better look. But rubs his eyes in disbelief. "Nas, Nas, is that you," he says as he lunges forward throwing his arms around the man, hugging him so hard the man can hardly breath.

"John my friend," the man gasps. "Please."

"Oh sorry," apologises John. "I never thought I'd see you again."

"Hello there John," comes another voice. "For a moment there we thought we were too late, you are not an easy man to find."

"Diss, Diss, is that you," shouts John.

"Yes my friend," comes the answer. "We are all here."

"Yarrhoo," shouts John.

"These are my friends from the desert," he tells the others.

"It's nice to meet you," calls Cin. "You are an awful long way from home. But truly, I have never been as pleased to meet anyone before in my life."

Another desert man jumps down and puts his arm out. "Come my friends, I will help you get out," he says. "And if it's of interest we have got plenty provisions just in the woods there." He then smiles and continues, "Including desert ale, the finest there is."

"What are we waiting for?" bellows Cin. "For a mug of that, I would fight them things again."

"What of them?" asks Big Dan.

"We have killed two of them, well I say us," answers Nas. "And one we have surrounded. A mad one eyed beast swinging wildly, it won't be long. The men are just having a little fun with it first. And to be perfectly honest, are more than just a little anxious. We have never been keen on snakes as you know."

"How on earth did you find us in here?" asks John.

"Ah now, there we had help my friend," answers Geyri helping John up.

As his words stop a sudden gasp comes from the friends as a dead serpent is flung down at them. Both girls give a squeal. Big Dan frowns. "Now that wasn't funny."

A strange noise is heard and they look up. "Well I recognise that laugh," wheezes Dan. "Fluff, that's got to be you up there."

Standing there is Fluff and Hope. "I might have known," Cin says with a broad grin. "It's good to see you both."

"Yes," chuckles Diss. "Your jackerbell here made short work of that beast. It was who killed them, and it's the first time he's dropped that one. He's had a great time with it."

Hope jumps down throwing his arms around both girls. Max kisses him on the cheek. "It's wonderful to see you my dear," she says. "I thought for a moment there, I never would."

He then scoops Max up in his arms and jumps back out, standing her up, then returning for Maxie. There are gasps all around. "Now that is one strong child," mutters Diss. "You will have to tell me all about him sometime. Now let's get the rest of you out."

Soon they are all out and walking back over to the surrounded serpent. Fluff walks with them snarling loudly at the beast, then looks to John, then looking back at the reptile. "He wants to know if he can go and get it." says Hope.

John nods. "Yes I guessed that. But let's see what it's got to say for itself first though. That's if it can speak I suppose."

"Oh they can speak," answers Maxie. "The one we killed back at the hole there spoke to us, just before it planned to kill us."

"Really, amazing," gasps Nas.

"You two managed to kill it. How?" he asks.

"With Spot's help," answers Maxie smiling. "That's my friend, she's a dab you know."

"Yes of course," replies Nas shaking his head. "Truly, amazing."

"They have very sensitive tails, them serpent things," Maxie then tells him.

"Really?" gasps Naz.

"That doesn't surprise me," says John.

"Not if they've got the same biology as other snakes. All their sexual organs are kept inverted in the base of their tails," he tells them.

Cin bursts into an agonised laugh, "And you say Spot grabbed it by them. Well now, that would certainly bring me to my knees, that's for sure."

"Maxie," asks Big Dan. "What did that, that thing say to you exactly?"

Both Max and Maxie then repeat every word it spoke up to the point it was grabbed. Much to the sheer shock horror and amazement of all there. "War," shouts John. "Are these things insane? They attacked us, we came in peace."

Diss gasps loudly, "And they, and you, say these things travel to other worlds."

John nods. "Yes."

Diss shakes his head. "John, surely you jest. How is this possible?"

John just shrugs. "I've no idea, let's find out."

So they join the circle of desert men surrounding the serpent. "Hey there, scaly," shouts John. "Stand down you've lost. Answer our questions and we may let you go."

The reptile just gives out a large hiss and strikes in their direction. The desert men raise their swords. But all are knocked out the way, as Fluff barges between them jumping at the beast, making the serpent recoil back.

"That is the first one of them beasts I've seen visibly scared," says Cin.

John nods. "Yeah but to be fair, you can't blame it."

Fluff grabs the serpent just under the chin getting a firm grip around its throat. It shakes the serpent about like an old rag doll. "Fluff," shouts John. "Just hold it down pal."

Fluff stops and pins it firmly to the ground, but not before giving it one last shake. "He just couldn't resist it could he," says John frowning.

Big Dan grins. "John it's just having a bit of fun. I'd like to do the same to it myself."

Geyri nudges Nas and whispers, "Have you ever seen anything like it? He commands that jackerbell like some sort of pet."

"Well," whispers Nas. "I think any of our people who were still unsure about John, and coming here, this should have just eradicated all their fears."

Geyri nods. "Time to go and have a little chat me thinks," says John.

"Maxie, is there anyway you can tell if it's lying or not?" he asks.

"I can try," answers Maxie.

"May I come with you John?" asks Diss.

John nods. "Yes certainly. But if you and Maxie wait here a mo, I'll shout when it's safe."

He then makes his way over to the pinned serpent in the centre. Diss turns and bows to Max while waiting. "Could you possibly ease an old man's curiosity?" he asks kindly.

"Yes of course, if I can," she answers.

"You're very kind," he says bowing again. "Your child, how could she possibly tell if that serpent were to lie or not. And what did he mean safe? Surely your jackerbell has it well pinned."

"Hem, how can I put it," ponders Max. "Err let's say our daughter has been given a gift by the greenem, and although this will be a first for her on such a beast. On people, she doesn't even have to hear what they are saying to know if they are lying. And John is just being cautious when it comes to your safety. These creatures are able to fire their teeth at you, two at a time. But we are not sure how many times they can repeat this."

Diss stands there speechless. Nas and Geyri behind gasp and Nas stutters, "Surely you are making with the fun there my lady."

Hearing his words Big Dan turns slightly taking his hand from his chest and shoulder. "Does this look as if she's joking?" he wheezes.

The desert men gasp. "Quickly," shouts Geyri. "Come with me, I will take you to our healer."

Big Dan turns back around clutching his wounds again. "When this is over," he grimaces. "And I mean no disrespect, but it will be Maxie and my friend Woodnut that will be treating me."

Geyri and Nas just look at each other in disbelief and shrug. "As you wish," says Nas.

Cin looks over to more and more of the desert people piling out of the wood. "You are the leader of all these people?" he asks Diss.

"Yes," answers the old man. "That is my honour."

"Then tell them to get back in the woods and hide, as quickly as they can," Cin tells him.

"Why?" asks Diss. "We have this creature beat."

Cin shakes his head. "No, you don't understand. In that building they have a weapon that shoots projectiles, and their effect can be devastating. And we don't know how many are left in there."

"That's, that's a building," stammers the old desert man.

"Yes of course," answers Max.

"What did you think it was?" she asks.

"We weren't sure what it was, a small mountain, or perhaps a large hill," he answers. "But that is a good distance away, surely there is nothing that could reach us here from that distance."

"You see that big hole in the ground we were sheltering in," barks Big Dan. "What do you think caused it?" Diss's mouth falls open and he turns to Nas and Geyri behind and tells them, "Go and tell everyone not needed to get back into the trees, as quickly as you can."

John stands in front of the serpent with arms folded. "Are you ready to talk yet?" he asks.

The beast just gives a muffled hiss. John sighs. "It really doesn't have to be like this you know. We came here in peace, you have brought all this upon yourselves."

"Let me go now, and we will talk alright," comes an angry muffled hiss.

John sighs again and kneels down beside it. "Why? Do you honestly think that kind of attitude is going to persuade me to let you go? Come on, work with me here. At least open your mouth and let me see you have no more of them teeth, you seem to like to use as weapons hidden in there."

The reptile tries to give a loud hiss, but is stopped instantly as Fluff tightens his grip. John stands back up, turns round and shouts, "Max, throw me that dagger please."

Watching him Big Dan nudges Cin and says, "Hey John's brave isn't he, she's already given him that blade once today."

Both men start to snigger. Max frowns spinning around towards them. "I heard that and I've told you, it was an accident right. I already feel bad enough without you two joining in."

Dan simply winks. "Come on Max, you wouldn't hit an injured man now would you?"

"Hu," grumps Max.

"No," whispers Cin. "But she'd stab one."

"Right that's it," snaps Max marching towards them.

"MAX dagger," shouts John loudly.

"Think yourself lucky," she grumps waving it at Cin and Dan.

She then throws throws the dagger and it lands just by John's foot. "Out the way, coming through, mind your feet," comes a little voice behind her.

They all turn to see who's trying to get through. The desert people all stand there totally bewildered, at the sight of a little greenem trying to barge its way between them. "Woodnut my friend," wheezes Big Dan. "It's good to see your ok."

Woodnut bows. "And you."

"How's Lilly?" asks Cin.

"A little ruffled," answers Woodnut. "But recovering nicely."

"Excellent," booms Cin.

"She says she is indebted to you," replies Woodnut.

Cin just frowns. "Yes I know," giggles Woodnut. "But she won't listen, you know how she is."

Woodnut then marches proudly over to John and the serpent. The old desert man Diss scratching his head turns to Max and says, "So am I picking this up right. Not only are you people friends with a greenem, but your large friends there want their wounds treated by your little girl and this, this, err, plant I suppose."

Max nods. "Yes that's correct, and his name is Woodnut, and we are friends with all greenem. Now surely someone as old and wise as yourself, should know to never judge on appearances."

Smiling politely she continues, "I myself, if have learned nothing else, have learned that."

Diss bows his head. "Yes of course, forgive me."

Then squinting his eyes deep in thought he mutters, "Woodnut you say. Is, is that Woodnut, Green, err, Greenfern."

Max nods. "Yes that's right. Have you heard of him?"

Lost for words the old desert man simply smiles, then bows his lowest bow.

"Hi John," greets Woodnut as he reaches him.

"Hi Dude," greets John in return. "It's good to see you."

"I'm just about to take a look in its mouth," he says picking up the dagger.

"You open it, I'll look," replies Woodnut.

"Easy way or hard way?" John asks the serpent.

But the beast clamps its mouth tight shut. "Suit yourself," says John with a sigh and prising the hilt of the dagger into the corner of its mouth.

The reptile opens wide all be it reluctantly. "Be careful pal," shouts John.

Woodnut cautiously peeks in its mouth from the side, quickly pulling himself back. He does this several times before walking around in front of it, then kneels down for a close inspection. "Fascinating John," he announces. "You should see this, I've never seen so many teeth in one mouth."

"Tell me about it," groans John looking to his own shoulder.

"Hu?" asks Woodnut.

John nods his head to the uniform spots of blood running from his shoulder to his chest. Woodnut nods. "Oh yes I see."

"Stand back dude, just in case," says John as he lets go pulling the dagger out."

He then waves Maxie and Diss over. "Right Fluff loosen your grip a bit please, let it speak" he says.

"Are you sure you don't want to sit together like civilised folk?" he asks the serpent.

But it just gives another hiss. John just shakes his head. "Fluff loosen off a little more please. Oh and if it tries anything, kill it."

Hearing him say that Fluff's strange tail starts to spin round like helicopter rotors.

"Is it safe to take a closer look?" asks Diss.

John nods. "Yes it should be, but still, be on your guard."

Diss squats down staring hard at the serpent. "This is so strange," he says." I just find it so hard to believe this, this serpent can speak, let alone have intelligence. Are you sure about this John?"

John shrugs. "To be honest, I used to find everything in this world hard to believe, but now." He just shrugs once again. "Well that is another story."

Hope takes Max's hand. Max looks down and smiles. "Come on Mum," he croaks. "We will stand over there. You shouldn't have to put up with these obscenities."

"Obscenities dear?" asks Max. "What do you mean obscenities?"

The young boy points to the serpent. Max stares at him oddly. "But, but, it's not saying anything dear," she replies rather confused.

"U hu," mutters Hope. "It's saying awful things, things that will now happen for this murderous outrage."

"Are you sure dear?" stutters Max. "How are you hearing it?"

"Is, is it whispering?" she asks.

"I can taste it through my skin," giggles Hope. "It's a strange tingle feeling."

Max gasps. "You can what?" she asks in a heightened voice. "Are you sure?"

Now Hope looks up at her oddly. "Yes of course," he answers. "Why, can't you?"

"Come with me quickly," she replies before she takes him over to John, Maxie and Diss.

On seeing her John winks. "Hi honey."

Then he smiles to Hope placing his hand on the lad's shoulder. "It's nice to see you young man"

"John," gasps Max. "You won't believe this, but Hope can understand what that things saying."

Now John looks at them both oddly and shrugs. "But it's not saying anything."

Max nods. "Oh yes it is. Tell him son."

"It talks in scent," answers Hope. "I can taste its words, even now, and I can hear its screams through every pore on my body. It's demanding to know what treacherous beast is translating the divine language, into the treacherous tongue of the vermin."

"Wow, well flabber my gast," puffs John heaving a big sigh. "Really?"

Hope nods "Uh hu."

Even Woodnut stands speechless staring at the child. "It now tells me," continues Hope. "We will soon all die, every male and female, young and old alike. His people will show no mercy."

"Maxie can you make anything out?" asks John.

Maxie crouches down sliding her sunglasses up on to her forehead with her index finger. She shrugs. "I'm not sure Dad. If I had time to study these things, but no father sorry, I can't tell."

"You are a very arrogant creature," says John. "Especially for one in your predicament. Please help me understand you, we came here in peace to talk. To what we were lead to believe were fellow peaceful explorers. We did not come to fight, or make war. I can't believe you'd even think that. You people, err reptiles, must be a really insecure bunch. All we came to do was talk, and what did you do. Just to show how intelligent and superior you really were, was to beat a helpless old woman to death. And well I'm sorry, any respect I may have had for you before that, went right out the window at that very moment pal."

"It is now laughing at you," says Hope.

"It is?" asks Diss.

Hope nods. "Uh hu. It says, back at the shadow complex, a small army is preparing to charge over here and kill you all."

"It's lying," interrupts Maxie. "If it means that large building over there, there's no army there."

"Are you sure now?" asks John. "I thought you couldn't tell."

Maxie shrugs. "I couldn't, it appears this is the first time it has lied to us, but now I know it can."

"Fantastic," says John clapping his hands together.

"Go on then scaley," he says. "What ya got to say about that then?"

"I will not repeat the word it has just spoken," answers Hope. "Not in front of my mum. But it is saying that, no vermin could possibly tell if he tells the truth or not."

"Wanna bet," squeals Maxie getting mad. "And I am no vermin."

"It is now telling me," continues Hope. "That they were sent as a diversion, so the others may get into place. And that he isn't as strong as some of the other casts of his people."

"Lies again Dad," says Maxie. "This was no diversion. But he was telling the truth about not being as strong as the other casts. Although I'm not really sure what that means."

"It appears you have surprised him," Hope tells them. "It's stuttering, saying that it's impossible, no one can do such a thing."

"Hu," grunts Maxie sliding her glasses back down. "You're so easy to read, I don't even have to raise my glasses. So who's the superior one now ay?"

The serpent suddenly starts to squirm, but is promptly pinned back down by Fluff. John winks to Maxie. "I guess that upset it."

"Yes," croaks Hope. "Between the bad words. It says there is one in the shadow complex watching us right now, as you spew your verminous words. And it is under order, in the event of such a travesty possibly happening, to contact the cleanser. A ship so big, so vast, so powerful, your tiny minds could not dare to comprehend it. It is a vessel filled with, with a..."

"I'm not sure what this word is," he croaks. "I'm maybe hearing it wrong, it insists it's a number."

"What is it dear?" asks Max.

Still looking a little confused the boy continues, "Yes, yes that's it, a million. A million of its people, who are all dedicated to, err, cleansing planets of vermin, and other unsavoury creatures. Whenever and wherever needed, and when they hear of this, every stinking two legged upright, shall be wiped off the face of this planet, one way or another. He then says, the cleansers are very, very good at what they do. And if you believe in a divine, you should start to pray to it, as in less than two of your, err, err, solar days the giant eye will open above the shadow complex, and your extermination shall begin, and there will be no hiding place." "Now it's just laughing" croaks Hope.

"M, Maxie," splutters John.

A tear silently runs from beneath Maxie's glasses, and she quietly nods. "Sshhhit," mutters John to himself.

"John what are we to do?" stammers Max.

John a little bewildered just shrugs. Diss does not react he simply turns to Hope. "Let go of your mother's hand child," he asks. "Now please, put yourself in the serpent's line of sight, if you don't mind that is."

The young boy looks up to Max, who nods him on. He then walks around to the front of the reptile. The serpent instantly explodes with anger, "How dare you, you treacherous slave," it screams out loud. "You and the old woman, after all we have done for your people. I will see to it personally you shall die a thousand deaths for this."

A sudden snarl and crunching noise is heard, as the beast falls silent, and they are sprayed with its blood, and the reptile's body is flung round as Fluff rips its throat out. A great cheer goes up from all around on seeing the beast dead, unaware of just what has been said. "How did you know it would act like that on seeing the boy?" asks John.

"I didn't," answers Diss. "It was just a hunch, to be able to speak to something so easily, that does not speak, well."

"I'm, I'm, nothing to do with those horrible things am I," cries Hope.

Max pulls him in and gives him a cuddle. "I do not know my dear," she tells him softly. "But one thing is plain for all to see, you are nothing like these horrible beasts. You are good, and you are kind, and no one can take that away from you, no one."

"Don't worry," John tells him. "You are not even the same species as them."

Diss shakes his head in despair. "Maybe it would have been better to have kept that thing alive, and reasoned with it. Tell it that we had made a terrible mistake. Persuade it not to take such actions."

John shakes his head. "I, I don't think it would have made a blind bit of difference. The only mistake we made was coming here In the first place. Friends or not, I don't believe these things are explorers for one minute. Whatever their reasons for travelling to other planets, their motives may not be clear, but it is not in the search for peace and friendship that's for certain."

He then sighs deeply. "W, what do we do now Dad?" asks Maxie.

"We retreat to the woods, and we treat the injured," Woodnut tells them.

"And you will assemble your leaders," he tells Diss. "And we will tell them what has just been said here. And from there, we can make plans."

"Now has everybody got that?" he asks.

Diss stares down at him and smiling broadly, and bows his lowest bow. "You are very wise little one, it is clear the stories about you are all true. I just never thought you existed, let alone, be lucky enough to ever meet you."

Woodnut glares at him. "What stories? Are you making fun of me?"

Diss graciously bows again. "No on the contrary. There are many stories of your courage in our culture. But until now, that's all I thought they were. I didn't even know you were a greenem, I'd just presumed, because there was a name you were a person, until now that is."

"John tell him," whines Woodnut. "This isn't funny, or the time and place."

John grins from ear to ear. "What's the matter, not like it when the shoes on the other foot ay."

Then winking he chuckles, "Now you know how I feel."

"Hu," grumps Woodnut really not impressed.

"Everybody listen," shouts Diss. "We must make our way back into the forest as quickly as possible."

John goes back over to help Cin and Big Dan. "Come on boys, let's get you sorted" he tells them.

"Did that slimy reptile say anything then?" asks Cin.

John sighs deeply but tells him, "Diss is getting all their leaders together, and we'll hopefully get you two sorted, and I'll tell you then."

Big Dan sighs deeply too. "It must have been pretty bad, but these wounds are pretty bad, and even if you manage to stem them John. You will have to pull these teeth from Cin and I. And then I fear our time is spent."

"In two days my friend," mutters John quietly. "I fear that everyone's time is spent."

Big Dan and Cin do not answer just stare at each other in disbelief and carry on walking. Then as they get closer to the line of trees they see the body of the old witch lying there, blood covering half her face, with two of the snake's teeth sticking out the side of her chest. They pause a moment over her body, staring down in disbelief.

"Poor old thing," mutters Big Dan. "She never stood a chance."

John sighs. "Maybe we should say something."

Cin grins. "You mean like good riddance." grins Cin.

Both Big Dan and John just frown. "I'm joking," replies Cin putting his hands up.

"Honest" he smirks slyly.

"You'd better be, you big gawk" comes a moan.

"Oh my god," shouts John. "She's still alive."

"Maxie and Woodnut quickly please," he continues.

Cin winks to Big Dan who just looks at him oddly. So Cin winks again, nodding down to the old woman. "Ah yes," blusters Big Dan. "Maybe we should do something to try and ease her pain."

"Yes I agree," replies Cin solemnly, slyly winking again.

He then draws his sword. "I'll put the poor old crone out of her misery," he says. "And stop her suffering, it's the least I can do."

"Agh,agh," screams the old woman trying to scuttle backwards.

"You leave me alone you big monkey turd," she squeals again.

"Wow she got better quickly," gasps John.

Cin gives out a sudden scream himself, as he feels the two projectiles in his back being flicked. "Now leave her alone," snaps Maxie. "Or I'll do that again."

Cin groans deeply. "There was no need for that," he whines. "Just like her mother."

"It's too late for flattery," growls Maxie as she then kneels down beside the old woman.

"Lay still, let me look," she tells her before she wipes the blood from the old crone's head, and parts her hair.

"That is a bad blow," she tells her. "We will have to seal it somehow. But first we will have to take you into the forest and get those serpent teeth out of your chest."

"Here let me see how deep they are," she says but she suddenly gasps loudly.

"What is it?" asks John.

"She really is a witch," shouts Maxie. "They are stuck deep in her chest, but there is no blood, none at all." "Just a black powder," she gasps.

"No, no, no," answers Cin shaking his head. "That's not powder, its dust, she's just so damn old."

Both John and Big Dan start to laugh but stop instantly, both grabbing different parts of their body's.

"Oh very funny yu big fuzz ball," shouts the old woman.

"Come here give me a look," groans John bending down.

He puts a bit on his finger and licks it. "I thought I told you to get rid of this stuff," he says. "You're lucky it didn't ignite."

"Leave me alone," she grumps getting up. "It's my last bit, I was keeping it safe."

"Anyway it saved me didn't it?" she shouts.

John pulls the teeth out and hands them back to her. And a small waterfall of black powder pours from the two projectile holes in her chest. "What is that?" asks Big Dan.

"It's called gunpowder," answers John. "She was meant to be getting rid of it."

With a frown he then asks the old woman, "You've got no other secret stashes, in secret pockets have you?"

"Why want to check?" she cackles, pulling her top right up above her head.

"No god no, put it down, we believe you," he moans.

"I definitely think I should have put her out of her misery now," growls Cin.

He doesn't get the chance as Maxie shouts, "Quickly you lot with me."

Just in the trees a large mat has been placed on the forest floor for them. Carefully with a few moans and groans they all sit down. "John," says Woodnut. "How much of that glue have you got left?"

John sighs. "No more than a drop I'm afraid,"

"That's a pity," replies Woodnut sighing too.

"Hang on," shouts John. "I've got an idea."

"First though," he continues as he puts the last few drops of glue along the large gash on Big Dan's face. "Right hold that tight a minute," he tells him.

"If that's finished," asks Woodnut, "may we have it?"

John shrugs. "Yes of course."

"Excellent," giggles Woodnut. "Maybe in the future my people can copy it."

"Oh the fun we could have with this," he mutters.

John just frowns, "Now Fluff, Fluff come here pal," he shouts.

Fluff bounds over. "Has anyone got a container?" shouts John.

"An empty water bottle? Anything?" he asks.

A lady comes over and hands him a bottle. John smiles. "Sturie, it's good to see you."

She smiles and kisses him on the cheek. "Not as good as it is to see you."

John hands the container to Woodnut. "Now get on Fluff's back, and direct him to where we saw those large ferocious ants," John tells him. "And see if you can get several dozen live ones in the bottle for me please. We only want the soldiers, and they must be alive ok."

Woodnut a little puzzled does as he is told and takes off with Fluff. "Now Maxie," he says turning to her. "Could you possibly get medicines to either stop or—?"

"Yes, yes, I know," she shouts taking off.

"John what on earth are you going to do with insects?" asks Cin.

John winks. "Hey trust me."

Big Dan frowns. "I hate it when he says that."

Nas walks over to them with another elderly desert man. "This is our finest healer," he tells them. "I thought you might need him."

"Thank you, but we have everything in hand," wheezes Big Dan.

"Yes it looks like it," answers the old healer kneeling down beside him.

The man then cautiously inspects both Big Dan and Cin's wounds. "Most should heal," he says. "Even the broken ribs in this one. But those, those things in your chest and back."

"They're teeth," John tells him.

The old man just looks at him oddly and bows. "Quite, but seriously they're quite deep. And although my instincts tell me they have punctured nothing vital. Open wounds of this magnitude, I'm truly sorry."

"Yes thank you for your optimism," replies John. "Now if you'll just keep out of our way, here's my daughter back."

She hands both Cin and Big Dan two bundles of leaves and herbs each. "Chew one of the poultices I gave you," she tells them. "And do not try to talk, as this stuff will make your mouths go a little numb ok."

Both men pop in one of the handfuls and start to slowly chew. "Corr Maxie, this stuff's vile," they both

"Be quiet and chew," she tells them sternly before she carefully takes Big Dan's top off, and with a little water and a clean cloth cleans around the projectile.

"Are you honestly going to let a child play with that warrior's wounds?" asks the desert healer.

"Ridiculous," he snaps.

"Be quiet, watch and learn," John tells him.

"Lie down and give me your hands," Maxie tells Big Dan softly.

Dan does as he is told and Maxie takes hold of his wrists. "Tell me when you feel no pain," she tells him.

A few moments pass and Big Dan nods his head. Maxie smiles. "Good, now spit the poultice into my hand, and start to chew the next."

She then turns to the old desert healer and asks, "Could you take this tooth out for me please?"

"Why so you can shove chewed up weeds in his wounds," he answers. "I shall have no part in this."

Cin leans over and grabs the projectile, and pulls it clean out of his friend. Maxie smiles and carefully puts on her mix. "Thank you."

She then does the same to the other projectile. "At some point Dad, these wounds will need to be closed, preferably sooner rather than later," she tells him.

"Ah here we go," he replies with a wink as he sees Woodnut jump down off Fluff. He smiles taking the container off him. "Good timing dude." He then carefully opens the lid and let's one of the ants out. He grabs it quickly by the body leaving only its head free. "Maxie," he says. "Could you hold one of Dan's wounds tightly together please?" Maxie nods.

Carefully John places the soldier ants head at the edge of Big Dan's wound. The ant instinctively bites down hard with its enormous pincers. This clamps the edge of the wound tightly shut and John then simply twists the ant's body, to see it come off leaving the head alone, like a perfect stitch. He repeats this several times, until both of Big Dan's wounds are tightly sealed together perfectly. As he finishes the last one everyone watching gives out a large sigh. Woodnut pats him on the back. "It looks like I'm not the only one full of surprises John" he says smiling.

"That, that," stutters the old desert healer. "That was amazing."

"Where by the Golden Ocean did you learn to do that?" he asks.

John simply winks. "National Geographic on SKY."

"Wh, what, what's that?" asks the healer.

John replies shrugging, "Err doesn't matter."

The same procedure is repeated on Cin, with a large crowd now gathered to watch. "Now your cheek and forehead Father," says Maxie.

"Oh no, no, no, no. I'll be alright," he protests.

"Oh don't be a big baby," snaps Maxie.

"Nooooo," blusters John. "I just thought we should do the old goat first."

"No you," snaps Maxie.

The old woman starts to cackle putting her tongue out. "No you Dad," insists Maxie. "Now sit still. I'll have to do her last; I've got her head to shave first."

"What?" screams Hettie.

"You are not," she shouts.

"Someone grab her before she takes off," shouts Maxie.

The old crone jumps to her feet raising her fists and shouts back, "Go on then, you just try it, I'm stronger than all of you."

She then feels arms grab around her body from behind, and she is totally immobilised. "This is impossible," she squeals. "No one can keep hold of me like this."

"Well I wouldn't say that," comes a croaky voice and the old crone looks down to see Hope's hands holding her fast.

The old desert warrior bows while taking a small sharp blade from his bag. "I know when I'm wrong."

He then proceeds to shave a small patch of hair from the front of the old crone's head, around the wound, despite the constant barrage of abuse and insults from the old woman. Meanwhile John squeals like a baby as Maxie stitches his cheek and forehead together using the soldier ants. "Now then," she says smiling. "All done."

"It wasn't that bad now was it?" she asks frowning at him.

"Yeah," puffs John.

"It hurt like hell," he twines.

"It can't have," she replies. "I numbed your body first, you won't have felt a...Oops!" She then gasps going red. "I thought I'd forgotten something... *SORRY DAD.*"

The old woman starts to laugh. "That's what you get you see," she cackles.

John shouts frowning, "Get for what you old goat. We're helping you here."

Soon the old woman is treated as well, and Max and Maxie sit with them making sure the boys rest, while the elders gather in a small clearing nearby. A few hours later and Maxie begrudgingly lets them go to the assembly, but they can't help but grumble as they go. "Will you stop complaining." shouts Maxie. "I'm only here you know, and you shouldn't even be up yet. You should be resting for several weeks yet you know"

"But Maxie we feel fine," whines Cin.

"Yes only because I've numbed your body," says Maxie exasperatedly. "It'll wear off soon, then you'll know about it. I won't do it again if you don't stop twinning. I could have just as easily made you sleep you know, for as long as I wanted. It only takes one touch."

"Sorry Maxie," mutters Cin closely followed by the other two.

When they get to the clearing all the desert men are there sitting in a large circle waiting for them. And as they all sit down on the cushions provided, mutters go all around. There is even a smaller cushion provided for Woodnut, and a slightly larger one for Hope to share with Fluff. Diss is placed beside John and the others. "Well John my friend," he whispers. "Shall we begin, would you like me to start my friend?"

John nods and whispers back, "Yes I suppose. But I must admit, I'm just more than a little nervous."

"Do not worry," whispers Diss. "We are all friends, and everyone here is with you, and for you, reunited and rejoined in a common cause, and to fulfil history and destiny. Just tell them what happened here today and I will help."

John smiles. "I have missed your wise council. I just wish I was as eloquent as you."

"If everybody would like to be quiet," he then shouts. "We shall begin."

He then starts by thanking them all for coming and saving their lives. Then he continues to tell them everything from the moment they entered the forest, until the moment of the last fight and even getting their wounds treated. Everyone there sits silently spellbound even Hettie, having been knocked out most of the time, with only the odd gasp here and there. He then hands over to Cin, Dan and the girls to each tell them the details of their battles. But the biggest gasp comes at the end when John and Diss tell them of the last serpents warning. "Now you know what has unfolded here," says Diss sitting back down. "We must now work out what our next actions are."

Directly opposite is an elderly distinguished looking desert man with a long beard, he slowly gets to his feet. "I can't speak for the others," he says. "But even though I have seen these beasts with my own eyes, and know they exist, and know their power is undeniable. But are we truly to believe this creature's threat. Translated, supposedly, by this, this child of unknown origin, and another child that can again, supposedly tell when a person lies, by no more than a mere glance."

"Please," he continues. "And I mean no disrespect here. But you do not get to my age by listening to over exaggerations and acting rashly."

Nas then stands up. "Why are we here?" he shouts. "Why did we come here at all? I'll tell you why, because our whole lives, and those of generations past, and generations before them have led to this point. To fulfil the prophecies handed down to us by our fathers, and our fathers fathers. You must have believed John was the one we were looking for. Or why did you bother to come here at all. And after coming so far and seeing what you've seen. How can you not continue? We must fulfil our destiny, and not just for ourselves, but for the future survival of generations everywhere. Or would you just have us sit here waiting to be slaughtered like ailing desert cows."

"Even if we are to believe," shouts another. "What would you have us do against such powerful serpents, of such unimaginable numbers? They are to come here in giant sky ships. We would appear no more than mere insects to them."

Cin jumps to his feet drawing his sword. "Yes I agree with you totally," he growls. "And now if you would all like to line up, I will humanly dispatch you all, right here, right now. Just so you don't have to suffer at their hands. Because suffer you will if we let them. But I am a warrior, and if I die, I die fighting, for my family, and for my friends, and for my freedom, and for what I believe in. And I have no time for babysitting cowards. You stand with us, or you crawl back to your desert and hide until they find you, and find you they will!"

Big Dan then stands. "I know your fears," he tells them. "I have fought army's that were not as hard to beat as those five beasts. And I thought they were nigh on unbeatable. Then I saw a little girl and her mother kill two of them, with nothing more than a dagger and rocks. United we stand, divided we fall. Where will you hide that they won't find you? You are just avoiding the inevitable. There is only one chance for all of us, and this is it. Then they have the advantage."

Woodnut then stands up and walks into the middle. "I have given much thought to what that creature said," he tells them.

Wry laughs start to come from around the circle, "Oh so now we are to take advice from a greenem," shouts one.

John jumps to his feet mad as mad can be and shouts back, "Now you'll all damn well be quiet, this is my best friend and wisest council. And you will listen to him. And anyone that insults my friends is insulting me. And the first fight you'll be having will be with me."

"Do we have an understanding," he snarls.

There is silence. "Good," he continues. "Woodnut please continue my friend."

Woodnut smiles and bows. "It would be easy to say nothing, or just to tell you to hide and wait until they have exterminated you," he tells them nonchalantly shrugging. "Even if they scorch the earth of all life. My people will survive, we shall just bury down until it's safe to come out once more. It would be a much better world for us without you. I can assure you of that."

"So why don't you?" asks a desert man sarcastically.

"Why," repeats Woodnut. "Because these people here, are my friends. And I stand with them to do whatever I can. And you ask why, because it's the right thing to do. And now as I was about to say, before I was so rudely interrupted. I've been giving great thought about what that creature said, and I think the time to act is now. For according to that serpent, within the next day or two, a great eye will open above their stronghold. And, and that must be the way in which they travel here. Like the opening of some great stronghold gates."

"So," shouts another man.

"Yes I see where you are going with this," shouts John jumping up excitedly, "Whatever this eye is, if we can penetrate that building of theirs, and stop it from opening somehow."

"Yes," continues Woodnut. "And according to that reptile, there is only one of its kind left in there on guard. And it would be easier to overpower one of them, than kill a million."

Max gets up and says, "It appears to me we have a plan, and the best chance we will ever have to defeat these things, once and for all. Now will you show your bravery once again and join us, or will you let my daughter and I fight them alone."

"I will stand with you," shouts Geyri.

"As will I," shouts Nas.

Diss stands up looking around at the others, giving a strange sign out with his right hand. All there then nod in reply, signalling back. He then turns back to John and the others and tells them, "It appears unanimous, we fight."

"Excellent," bellows Cin. "We go now, show no hesitation."

"No not now," comes Hettie's cackling voice.

"At first light," she tells them. "If there's any left in there, that's the time. They are always more sluggish at that time, their senses and reactions will be duller."

"I thought it was a constant temperature in there?" asks John.

"No not at night, it is allowed to drop," she answers. "To simulate their natural cycles."

"So maybe we should attack at night then," says Big Dan.

"No better not," answers John. "If that big gun of theirs is triggered by sensors, or works automatically some how. It would be impossible to see where the missiles are coming down. At least in the daylight we stand a chance of avoiding them."

"First light it is then," shouts Big Dan. "But what then, we all make a mad dash or—?"

"No," says Diss cutting him off. "My people will act as a diversion. Then John you sprint down the side and around the long way. It will not take you long at your speed, and we will make a full on assault straight for them. And hopefully they will be too focused on us to notice you."

Big Dan nods. "Yes good plan." nods Big Dan,

Then with a wink he says. "And we'll be with you John. No pressure my friend, but then it's all up to you to get to that place and somehow stop that, that."

"Cannon," says John.

He then sighs. "I'll do my best, or die trying. Now everybody, the only thing left to do is eat drink and rest. Max you have the best eyesight, could you come with me please. I want you to tell me every nook and cranny you can see on that building, ledges, balconies, handholds. Anything I can jump up to, to get me to that gun ok."

21

THE DAWN COMES all too soon for most, and everyone gathers just inside the line of trees. Diss, Geyri and Nas are standing at the front when John and the others make their way out. "Are you ready John?" asks Diss. John sighs. "As I'll ever be."

"Make your way along the trees," Nas tells him. "When you get to the edge signal us, and we will start our run."

John then looks around at some of the older desert people standing there. Some even standing with their grandchildren, "Before we start," he tells them. "We should have enough younger people to do this. So get all the old and children, back into the woods out of danger."

"But John, they all want to do there bit," replies Diss.

"Yes of course," says John. "And they have already done so by being here. And now maybe they could help even more, by staying here, and preparing to take care of any hurt or injured there maybe."

"Now Nas," he continues. "Tell everybody who is to make the run to keep a close eye on the top of that building. The missiles that thing shoots out aren't that fast, and you should, with a bit of luck be able to judge roughly where they are going to hit, and get out the way of the main blast. And any woman will have to plug their ears with something, to dull the noise of the explosions."

All the young and old are moved back, all but Sturie who stands by her husband Diss. John puts his hand on her shoulder and says, "Come on my dear."

Sturie shakes her head defiantly. "No, I go where my husband goes," she tells him.

John then looks to Diss and says, "Looks like you're staying here then."

Diss shakes his head and replies, "I must lead my people out."

"Sturie my love, please why don't you stay here?" he begs. "I'll be ok."

Sturie just shakes her head staring defiantly on.

John then turns to Maxie and smiles. "Doesn't she look tired Maxie?" he asks her slyly winking.

"Oh yes," replies Maxie smiling kindly at her.

"Tired?" laughs Sturie. "Are you joking?"

349

"Here why don't you take Maxie's hand," John tells her. "She'll take you back."

"I'm not moving," she tells him frowning. "And you can't make me."

Maxie takes the old woman's hands in hers. "You are feeling tired aren't you." Maxie tells her softly.

To everyone's surprise the old woman immediately starts yawning and answers, "Y, yes I am a bit. How strange, I felt fine a moment ago."

She yawns again and Maxie whispers softly, "Why don't you sit a moment, just lean against this tree here." Sturie sits down leaning back. "Maybe for just a moment," she says yawning loudly and closing her eyes. "She'll be asleep now for a good hour," says Maxie turning back to the others.

"How? How?" stutters Diss.

Maxie just shrugs and smiles. "Just a little trick I know."

Diss bows low. "I truly thank you little one that was very kind of you."

The old healer whispers to Max, "How did she do that?"

Max shakes her head and replies, "I've no idea, she just can."

John turns to Maxie and Woodnut and tells them, "Now I want you two, to stay here with their healer and help treat the wounded."

"That's not fair," grumps Maxie.

"Maxie do as you're told for once," Dan tells her sternly. "There are enough of us, and you are more valuable here."

"I suppose," grumps Maxie.

"Come on," says Woodnut taking her hand. "Let's go and gather medicine."

The old healer hearing him starts to stutter, "Would, would it be too presumptuous of me, to be allowed to come with you. And perhaps learn a little of your medicines."

Woodnut bows to him. "It would be our pleasure."

"Max you can stay here if you want," says John winking whilst kicking some large rocks out of the moss covered ground in front of him.

"No chance, you go, I go," snaps Max. "And don't even think of shouting Maxie back."

"That's my girl" he replies winking again, picking up two or three of the rocks and inspecting them before putting them in his pockets.

"John what are you doing with them?" asks Cin with a puzzled look.

John grins. "Maybe they'll slow me down a bit, I don't want to get there too fast now do I."

"What?" he then gasps seeing his three friends just glaring at him.

"Right I'm off," he shouts.

"Where are you going?" snaps Max.

"Hu?" he asks in surprise.

"Kiss first," replies Max in a girly voice.

"Max, not in front of the boys," whines John reluctantly giving her a kiss.

"Oh John do we not get one?" shouts Big Dan through the laughs.

"Maybe later," John shouts going red and taking off.

He then gets into place and signals back to the others. Cin signals back, then booms, "Right men, keep your eyes to the sky. Now let's make our presence known."

He then takes off running with Big Dan, screaming and hollering as they go, closely followed by Max. Then like a tidal wave, a screaming mass of desert people pile out the line of trees just behind them. Seeing them John takes off running, sprinting as fast as he can, he overtakes the others in no time, and is half way there before the large gun even appears out the top of the shadow complex. As soon as it is out it starts to fire, the projectiles whistle over head as he gets to the landing strip. And he hears the first explosion a good distance behind him, and the awful screams of torment and pain that go with it. "Must go faster," he thinks to himself, now pushing himself harder and harder.

The building is now only a hundred yards away and the enormity of its size nearly takes his breath away. In no time at all he is nearly up to the front of the building. "Oh no," he gasps. "I don't think I'm going to be able to stop in time." He braces himself for the impact. But then notices not too far above an unusual looking balcony. More like a shoe horn lying on its side. "What the hay?" he thinks to himself and makes a mad leap for it. He lands on it perfectly, but still cannot stop in time to prevent himself from hitting the wall behind it.

"You took your time," comes a familiar cackle.

John looks down to see Hettie, the old crone standing on the ground below. "How did you get here so quickly?" he shouts down.

"I just ran straight across," she shouts back up. "Now stop talking and get up there, you've a gun to stop." "Then get your scrawny backside back down here, and then you can pass the time of day," she cackles.

John doesn't answer, but looks up to where he can get to next. Just above is a black tubular rim, which runs gently upwards across and round the building. "That'll do me," he says to himself. It's a small jump to reach it, and as he starts to make his way up, but he cannot help but jump every time the large gun above goes off. Now three quarters of the way up, he pauses for a moment to catch his breath as the gun goes off once more. He looks out to where all his friends are making their run towards him, and with the bomb just missing them, a nervous sweat forms on his brow. "I've got to get up there quicker," he pants.

"But this is a heck of a height," he thinks to himself. "If I jump and slip."

The gun goes off again, and frowning he grits his teeth and crouches down, placing the flat of his hands on the floor, and springs up as hard as he can. He shoots straight up to the top, but instead of landing at the edge by the gun, he carries on upwards landing on the top of a large dome towards the middle of the building. "Oops," he mutters aloud, and looks down at where he's standing. "Well whatever this is it must open, there's a seam running right along the centre of it. This must be where this eye thing comes out, I hope this is a good sign. Agh well, at least we know where to look," he mutters to himself. He quickly makes his way back to the edge. The barrel of the gun sticks out about seven feet from a sealed port, and measures about four to five inches in diameter. "Got to time this just right," he thinks to himself mopping his brow. He takes the three rocks from his pocket and carefully measures them up along side the barrel discarding two. He then counts the seconds between the blasts. "That's got to be about twenty seconds surely," he thinks to himself.

With his heart now beating like a steam train he waits for the next bang, with rock firmly clasped in hand. Then as it goes off once again, he crams the rock into the end of the barrel as far as he can, and starts to sprint down the tubular rim jumping down lower, from one to another. "Gees Louise, please don't let me slip," he mutters with a tremble in his voice. "A little lower and I can jump off," he thinks to himself. A mighty boom then sounds from the gun above, and he sees shrapnel and flames flying. He throws himself down flat onto the rim, as some of the red hot shards of metal screams past him.

In the distance he hears a mighty cheer go up from his friends. So he stands back up and waves to them as they get ever closer. He then sees all the other desert people pile out of the forest towards them. And he starts to make his way back down again, a little more cautiously now. He jumps down the last section to where Hettie is standing. She smiles and nods. "Not bad, not bad at all," she cackles. "Well that was the easy part over with, shall we?" she cackles again, kicking open two large round double doors.

"No let's wait on the others," says John cautiously peering in. "We don't know what's to come; you're better safe than sorry. There is safety in numbers." With a wink he continues, "And besides if we have all the fun, Cin and Big Dan would never forgive us."

She shrugs. "As you wish, but I know what's in there. I've been here before remember."

John nods and sighs. "Please, humour me. You were lucky before, you may not be so again."

A few minutes pass before a breathless Max is first to reach them, doing a flying leap into his arms. He swings her around and kisses her before putting her back down. "I thought my time had come," she pants. "How did you get here so quickly?" she asks the old woman.

"I ran," cackles the old crone. "You had your head in the clouds, I ran straight past you and those other too fuzz balls."

Cin and Big Dan then grind to a halt, sweat poring off them and groaning with pain, and seriously struggling to breathe. John makes them sit down and catch their breath. "But John," they both pant.

"Don't worry," he tells them. "We will not go in without you ok, I promise."

So the two large warriors lean back against each other and smiling broadly nod.

"And you call me old," laughs Hettie. "At least I can go for a short run without having to lie down after it."

Nas and Geyri are the next to arrive shortly followed by Diss, all collapsing on arrival. Max cannot help but laugh and walks over to Diss. "You should be so fit, and get here as quickly at my age," he pants.

Max gives another giggle and takes a large clump of grassy earth from the top of his head then shows him it. "Oh I see," he chuckles. "That was rather a close one."

More and more reach John and the others and finally they all stand there puffing and panting. An awful snarling noise is then heard behind the crowd. And as gasps flood to the front like a wave, the crowd part and they see Fluff and Hope making their way through the parting crowd.

"Hi guys," greets John as Fluff promptly licks his face. "Right everybody," he then shouts. "Listen up only a handful of us will be going in, for safety's sake. The rest of you wait out here, unless you hear an almighty whistle that is."

Hearing him Big Dan and Cin get to their feet along with Max.

John smiles. "Nas and Geyri, if you would."

"As will I," says Diss getting back up.

John nods putting his hand out to help him back up and says to him, "Your help and wisdom is always welcome." He continues, "Fluff and Hope you too please, but Hope stay close to Fluff."

"What about us?" shouts Maxie and Woodnut just running up.

John frowns. "You two should be helping the injured."

They suddenly both look very sad, "There was two dead John," replies Woodnut. "We think it's only two anyway, it's hard to tell. There are several with minor injuries which we have treated, and are now sleeping." Woodnut then looks to Maxie.

"There was one older man," she says softly. "His wounds are beyond help. We made sure he will feel no pain, and I made him sleep, he shall not wake up."

"There are a couple of others," continues Woodnut. "But their healer is taking care of them."

John shakes his head solemnly and turns back round. "Come on trouble," he says to the old woman. "Lead the way then."

Cin frowns down at Maxie and Woodnut and says, "I don't suppose there's any way of stopping you."

Maxie simply stares ahead. "No none, we have to," she replies.

"Yeah," sniggers Woodnut. "We do."

Maxie stares down at him solemnly, sadness filling her heart and she nearly cracks a smile. Cin just shakes his head.

The heat hits them as soon as they go through the large doors. "What strange looking doors?" mutters Max. "Now this is more like it," mutters Diss as he enters. "A bit of warmth at last, oh how I've missed it."

"Yes," whispers Nas. "Doesn't it make you long for the desert?"

"Makes me long not to be in the desert," jokes Big Dan.

The floor is an orangey coloured stone, with a texture not dissimilar to sandstone. The room is a large oval shape with several tall narrow circular doors scattered about, and they all stand in ore looking around the room. Adorning the walls are battle staffs similar to what they had just been attacked with, two crossed over with a small shield above and below. "Hettie is this their armoury?" asks John.

"No," she answers. "These are more ceremonial, from their past, err, their history I think. And don't call me that in front of strangers," she moans in a loud whisper.

John heaves a heavy sigh. "Ok you old goat, is that better," he puffs.

"Now that wasn't so hard now was it," she mutters out the corner of her mouth.

John just frowns. "Right everyone, go and get one of those shields, and a weapon if you wish," he tells them.

"Why?" asks Max smiling. "What use are those small shields things anyway?"

"They're small agile and manoeuvrable," answers John. "And might just save you from two large teeth, if any are fired at you."

Everybody realising the sense in it, rushes over to grab one. Big Dan gives it a good inspection. "This isn't just a small shield," he tells them. "My guess is, it's a weapon in its own right also, look at the edge of it. It's serrated, and sharper than any blade I've ever seen, and the lightest strongest metal that I have ever known. A good blow from the edge of this would go straight through flesh bone leather most things in fact, with ease I would say, no two functions in one.

He nods running his fingers through his beard. "Hem, yes, very impressive, and will fit in my bag nicely." "Good idea," says Cin.

"Yes," agrees Max. "A nice memento, I think I'll keep mine also. You never know, it may come in handy again one day."

"If you are ever in a battle," Big Dan tells her. "I can assure you, a blade this sharp, and a shield also. Yes it wouldn't just be very handy, in close combat situations it would be invaluable."

"This way," shouts Hettie, heading towards a large corridor, the only one not to have a door.

"So why is this place so big, if there is only a few of them serpents things here anyway?" asks Maxie.

"If a large sky ship comes in," answers the old woman. "I am led to believe there can be thousands of them staying here. And if you think it looks big from the front, wait until you see how far it goes back. This place is vast, there are warehouses here nearly the size of large towns, filled with various supplies, and enough parts to build a new sky ship."

"You're joking," gasps John. "That means we could be searching this place for days, weeks, before we find what we're looking for, a lifetime in fact. And I'm still not quite sure what we're looking for anyway. Maybe we should just make our way to the roof I suppose, I think I've found where that eye thing will come out."

"No, first we should try down here," the old crone tells them.

"Why?" asks Cin.

"Because," she continues. "There is a section down here, which was the only place in this entire province of there's, I was not allowed. And I mean not allowed, under pain of death, and these creatures normally treated me well."

"More as a curiosity piece I think, a novelty you know," she says getting angry. "They thought me mad you know. How dare they?"

Big Dan frowns but replies. "Yes we know, you told us."

"Oh yes, yes," she stutters.

"At least there's one thing we have in common," chuckles Cin. "So," continues John. "Whatever's in this section you're taking us to, must be very important to them."

The old woman nods. "I asked them a few times you know, but they would never answer. Only once, the last time I asked, a guard, guarding it from me I think. He hissed, down here lies the beating heart, and the bleeding eye of the universe. And apart from now, it's the only time I've seen them show violence. There was another there, its superior I think. It attacked the other with a staff. It was awful, I thought he was going to kill it. I never came down here again."

Diss nods. "We must be on the right track then surely. Why else would you do that to your own, for something so trivial."

Further along and the old woman stops. "From this point on," she tells them. "You know as much as I."

"Right then," says John. "From here on we check every door, half this side, half the other."

Cin goes to open the first door with Nas and Max. He grabs the handle of the door and slowly opens it, then with a shout he jumps in raising his sword high, but nothing.

"It just seems to be filled with steam," shouts Max. "It's so humid in here I can hardly breathe," she says coughing.

John opens the next door, and peers in to a darkened room. Cautiously he steps in keeping his shield high, then nearly jumps out of his skin when the room is suddenly illuminated. "Corr blimey me heart," he squeals making Geyri and Diss behind jump also. "The lights must be activated by movement," he says patting his chest.

The room is quite large, and in the centre is a large stainless steel table, with tools and equipment all around it. And along either side of the room are solid stone benches. Each measuring about nine foot in length, four foot high to the seat with a backrest that carries on up another four feet. "What is this place John?" asks Geyri.

John shrugs. "At a guess," he replies. "An operating theatre."

"It is yes," comes a voice.

They turn to see Hettie sitting on one of the stone benches dangling her feet down. "I take it you've seen something similar before?" asks Diss.

"Yes," she replies with a sigh. "But this is slightly different, this is not for them. This table is far too small, and not long enough, and there aren't cold stones in the other ones I've seen."

"Cold stones?" asks Geyri.

"Yes," she answers. "These benches, come sit. I'm not quite sure what type of stone they're made from, but they are carved from one solid block. You will find them everywhere. They are always cooler than whatever temperature they reside in. They use them to regulate their body temperature. But these are here I would say, for observers."

"Or spectators," replies John.

Big Dan's head appears around the door. "Hey everybody, if you like that, you're gonna love this," he gasps.

They all pile out following Big Dan down the corridor past a few more open doors. There is an open door to the right, and all follow him in and come to a sudden stop, pilling into each other as John and Cin at the front suddenly stop dead. "What the hell is this?" gasps John.

"This room is enormous," stutters Cin.

"Not bad is it," booms Big Dan. "It seems to be some sort of trophy room."

Diss shakes his head. "This is no room; there are small provinces that could move in here."

Each gasps in turn as they look down the rows and rows of glass cases nearly as far as the eye can see, each containing a different species of creature. All perfectly preserved in their own natural setting. Some singularly, and some in groups, and others in what appear to be family groups with children.

"We, we should get out of here," stutters Max. "I, I really don't like this, it's not right, not right at all, it's just sick."

"You stay here then," John tells her. "We'll just have a quick look about."

He walks down the first aisle with Cin, Dan and the others. Cin gasps, "Why would someone do this? I really don't understand, there must be hundreds of displays here."

John slowly nods. "I would say it's more like thousands, and it's a museum of sorts, I would say," he mutters. "Does anyone recognise any of the creatures? Err, hem, species, any at all."

"Not I," come the answers.

"Woodnut," shouts John.

"Yes John," shouts Woodnut as he runs up.

"So do you recognise any of the creatures here, any at all?" John asks.

Woodnut walks ahead, slowly studying them all as he goes.

Big Dan in a shaky voice stammers, "Some of these creatures, unusual as they are, must have been intelligent I think"

John shrugs. "Why?"

"Look," stutters Cin. "All of these creatures are either clothed, or are standing with some sort of, of, fancy technology as you call it. The like of which I've never seen before."

"Oh my god yes, you're right," gasps John. "I, I think I know what this is. I could be wrong, but it's either a museum, or more likely a trophy room. Celebrating everywhere they've ever been."

Woodnut stops dead gasping, "John quickly, here's one you'll wish you didn't know."

They all rush over to Woodnut, and stare disbelievingly into the case at a father and mother of similar stature to John. The man is dressed in similar attire to him, and the woman in a long flowing dress with a pushchair and baby in hand. "By the two moons above," gasps Big Dan. "This place is an abomination, I've seen enough."

"No wonder they wouldn't let me down here," stutters Hettie in despair. "The poor things."

"Let's have a look up the next aisle" mutters John. "But I'll tell you one thing that is interesting though. If none of these things are from this earth. There is an awful lot of intelligent life out there. And it comes in more shapes, sizes and forms than we could ever have imagined. A lot look humanoid, well kind of, but there are an awful lot that look more like, I don't know, err, some sort of insects or, or amphibians I suppose."

"John you look as if you are enjoying this," says Cin a little disgusted.

John shrugs. "No, not enjoying it. But it is fascinating though, wouldn't you say. The world I come from has museums of stuffed creatures, none of them intelligent I hasten to add, well relatively anyway."

"So let me get this right," says Big Dan. "Your people like to go to large rooms like this, and stare at dead bodies in cases."

"Hunting to eat I have no problem with John, but this," he says solemnly shaking his head.

John starts to stutter going a little red and replies, "Hem, I, I, suppose. They don't do it anymore, though. Orr, come on guys, you must admit it's a little interesting, this is life from other planets."

"And so are you John," answers Cin. "But I would rather know you as you are, or have never known you at all. Than, than, have seen you stuffed and mounted in a jar for the first time. And what if you saw your family in one of them cases John, would you still be saying that."

John sighs. "No I suppose not. But that's different."

Big Dan shakes his head and answers, "No John, it isn't, now let's get out of here and do what we came to do. Before we become an exhibit."

Max and Maxie are waiting back at the door for them with Hope and Fluff. "Well?" asks Max. "Did you find anything interesting?"

Cin shakes his head and simply tells her, "You don't want to know."

22

"RIGHT NEXT DOOR," booms Big Dan as he bows to John. "Would you like to do the honours?"

John smiles as he cautiously opens the door. "Ah yes, it would be a pleasure kind Sir."

He then peeks around, then flings it open and walks in. In front of him and to the left are control panels raising from the floor to nearly five feet in height, with other panels flat against the wall behind it rising up even higher. "Gees Louise, you'd have to be pretty damn tall to work here me thinks," says John. The others follow him in staring at the same panels.

To his and their shock and surprise, they hear a sudden loud hiss behind them. John spins around instantly to see to the right of the doorway, the large room giving way to an even larger room. Filled on both sides with technical panels' buttons and switches, with each button and switch having two small holes directly underneath them. The serpent then hisses once more before extending its legs and making a run to the other side of the room and one of the doors there. "Nas quickly, throw me your staff," shouts John.

As soon as he get's it he throws it as hard as he can at the door the reptile is headed for. It whistles through the air and hits the door with tremendous power, just missing the serpent. The power and shock sends it reeling backwards. Fluff shoots past snarling wildly, and John just manages to catch it by the tail. "Fluff stay here," he tells it, but Fluff doesn't listen and still tries to get to it.

"Fluff," shouts John now flinging his arms around its powerful shoulders and neck.

"It's not safe yet, please, trust me," he tells it softly.

It calms down but only a little. "Nas, Geyri, hold it," shouts John.

Both men go white. "You have got to be joking," stutters Naz.

Hope hops forward and takes over whispering in its ear and calming it down a little more.

John cautiously edges forward into the room closely followed by Big Dan and Cin. "Stay here Maxie," orders Max following closely behind with dagger clasped firmly in one hand, and shield in the other. John edges forwards again, carefully going around an opaque square of crystals on the floor in the centre of the room. With a circumference of nine foot by nine foot square rising to a height of nine inches tall. He slowly puts his hands up and shouts to the nervous serpent, "It's ok, we aren't here to hurt you. Not unless you give us no other option that is."

The beast opens its mouth and hisses loudly. John stands ready with his shield. "Calm down," he tells it softly. "It doesn't have to be like this."

Hope rushes over to stand with Cin. "I can taste her screaming," croaks Hope.

"What are you doing boy?" shouts Cin. "Get behind me."

"Don't worry," answers Hope. "I'm faster than you are."

Cin just looks down, frowns and says, "Kids who'd have them."

"What's it, err, she screaming?" asks John. "She certainly is one big mother."

"The females are always bigger," shouts Hettie. "Be careful though John, they are also much more aggressive, and also more intelligent."

"She is screaming," continues Hope. "Liars, blasphemers, defilers."

"Really," replies John in a surprised voice. "Liars never, defilers and blasphemers, well now maybe, it all depends on what she means by it."

"She's now shouting, you should be bowing before your gods, and begging for forgiveness," Hope tells them.

"Now I know she's taking the mick," says a frowning John. "You're no god."

Hope starts to cringe a little. "She's now screaming, murderers defilers, you will pay for this, you will all pay for this," he says.

"Now listen scaley," shouts John getting mad. "We came here in peace, and your people attacked us, and we simply defended ourselves as best we could. And we gave them chance after chance, they brought it upon themselves right. We still want peace."

"Come on then, so why are we defilers and blasphemers anyway?" he asks.

"She, she says," stutters Hope. "Because you carry the relics of the ancient ones. And it is I that blasphemes, by translating their ancient pure language, into the tongue of the vermin. She, she says, I will die last, along with all my treacherous people."

"Gees Louise," gasps John. "What's with all this vermin crap? Who the hell do you think you are anyway, you over grown handbag."

"She's now shouting, she could kill us, she could kill us all," Hope tells them nervously. "And that I will make a tasty treat."

"Do not worry little man," booms Big Dan. "It's bluffing, if it thought that, it would have tried already, be sure of it."

The serpent gives out a nearly deafening hiss and shoots forwards striking at John. John steps to the side and strikes it across the back of the head with his shield. The serpent recoils slightly shaken, spitting her two large projectile teeth at him. John manages to deflect one, but the other shoots right past him and is stopped by a shocked Geyri standing between Big Dan and Cin, pinging off his shield and sticking in a nearby wall. "Come on," screams John. "Is that the best you've got?"

The serpent now as mad as mad can be starts coiling back quickly for the next attack. Then suddenly exploding from behind them comes Fluff, skidding to a halt by John's side. The reptile stops its attack slithering backwards. "What's the matter?" shouts John. "Not scared now are we, oh divine one. I thought you could kill us all."

John and Fluff step forward in unison with the serpent slithering back all the time. "Please," shouts the serpent nervously. "It appears, maybe we have got off on the wrong scale."

"That wouldn't be you sullying your tongue with our verminous words now would it," snaps John.

"Please, let us start again," she hisses nervously.

John puts his hands on Fluffs back. "Calm down pal," he says. "Let's see what it's got to say, it appears you make our scaly friend here, feel very nervous indeed."

"Well I wouldn't quite say that," hisses the serpent. "I just like to think myself intelligent enough to realise when I may have."

"Err, been a little, err quick to judge," she hisses.

"She's lying Dad," shouts Maxie. "She's so scared she's nearly glowing."

John nods. "It makes no difference, it's just good we are talking and not fighting. Now as a sign of good faith on my part, Fluff, could you go back and sit back over there with Hope please."

Fluff gives a defiant snarl. "Right dude, I tell you what then," says John. "You go back over there with Hope, and if this creature turns violent again, it's all yours ok."

Fluff gives him a lick before walking away with his tail spinning like a child's top. John then turns to the serpent. "You have no problem with that have you?" he asks her.

The serpent just shakes her head nervously. "You talk to that savage beast as if it has intelligence," she hisses.

"Shush," says John quickly. "You really don't want to upset him. And yes, he has more intelligence than a lot I've met lately, who claim to be. Know what I mean."

"Now my name is John," he continues. "John Fox, and what would yours be my dear."

The reptile shakes her head. "My name does not really translate into your tongue. It is more a series of sounds," she answers.

John shakes his head, shrugs and tells her, "All names are a series of sounds, in one form or another aren't they. Try saying it to the boy there in your own language."

Hope listens intently. "Could you say it again please?" he asks.

Then he nods and says, "It kind of sounds in human like Sesst, ssoor, larr."

"Wow now that is a tongue twister," mutters John.

"Although it does sound like Sesstor," continues Hope.

"Would that do, or—?" says John.

"No," she answers cutting him off. "That is expectable, yes."

John nods. "Brilliant, now Sesstor please. What of this place, tell me about it, and yourself, let us get to know one another a little."

He winks and continues, "Oh and I'll warn you in advance, if you lie my daughter will know instantly ok"

"She is maybe nodding," croaks Hope. "But she's laughing terribly."

"Really," gasps John. "You should take up poker, you'd win a fortune. Anyway its up to you, believe it or not, it's your funeral."

"This place is known by my people as the shadow complex," she tells them. "A resting point and supply station for my people sometimes. It is a place of little consequence, and not many ever use it."

"She lies," shouts Maxie. "This place is of great consequence."

The serpent turns its head towards Maxie giving a loud hiss. "She says," croaks Hope. "That is impossible, you can't know that, you lying verminous vermin filth."

"What did you call my daughter?" screams Max rushing forwards.

Big Dan grabs her around the waist holding her back. "Come her and say that bitch," screams Max.

"Max calm down," bellows Big Dan.

Geyri shakes his head. "Your friend is very brave," he whispers to Cin. "But I bet she wouldn't last more than a few moments with that thing."

"I'll take that bet, a barrel of ale she can," whispers Cin.

"You can't bet on such a thing," whispers Diss. "That's awful, and unfair."

Cin nods and grins. "A little I suppose, but I promise to share the ale with you when I win."

"You don't fancy making that two barrels do you," whispers Big Dan turning his head, and still struggling with Max.

"Geyri my friend," whispers Nas. "Before you answer, do not forget, this little lady and her daughter you may bet against, have already killed two of these beasts."

Geyri shakes his head and stutters, "She, she, they did, I, I, thought that was these two large warriors here. I just thought they were trying to wind us up by saying it was the two girls."

Cin just shakes his head.

John frowns and looks the serpent straight in the eye. "You really shouldn't upset my wife like that, be in no doubt, she really is the wildest beast in here. I warned you my daughter would know, so I take it this place of yours is important then."

"Yes, yes I suppose," hisses Sesstor. "I could try to explain, but you would not understand. This culture of yours is too primitive, you could not comprehend. It is the other reason we chose it, it was more or less uninhabited."

John frowns again. "Humour me."

"As you wish, I will try to explain in words you may understand a little easier," she hisses.

"No she won't," shouts Maxie.

"Ok, ok," hisses Sesstor frustratedly. "This place, this planet of yours, in itself is of little consequence. Although it does possess certain minerals and metals of value, a crystal in particular. I think your people call them jump stones. One place on your planet, a mountain has a particular high concentration and very rich deposits. We took core samples, it ran clean through the mountain."

"There's more Dad," shouts Maxie.

"Ok ok," snaps Sesstor. "It is, well was, very important, it is used for the propulsion drives in some of our ships."

John excitedly turns to the others grinning smugly. "I told you them holes in the whistling mountain must have been caused by something didn't I."

"Yeah, yeah, you're very clever," shouts a frowning Big Dan, "Now let her speak."

John nods. "Oh yes sorry, continue."

Sesstor gives a sudden hiss before continuing, "But our main interest is in this world itself and in its overall make up, and its position in the convergences in relevance to the lines of all other universes. It, err, how can I put it. It pulls them in, overlapping them in layers, in relative time and space. Making it easier to travel from here to other dimensions, more than anywhere else. And in some cases even back in time, although that is not advised, as it can have serious consequences. But you see. Sorry, I warned you."

John stands eyes squinted concentrating deeply before he says, "Err, so is this kind of like, hem, err string theory, unified M theory then, eleven different realities around us at any one time, just out of reach ."

The serpent's body slumps, and she flops down a little with shock. "That is an old and rather antiquated theory, there are countless other dimensions," she answers. "But its fundamentals are more or less right yes. But, but, this kind of knowledge is far beyond this world, most of these vermin, err I mean beings still think their world is flat."

John turns around to his friends, winks and tells them, "I think she's insulting you over here you know."

"You are not of this world," she hisses.

"You can't be, how did you get here tell me now," she hisses again.

"Now that is the question," answers John. "I thought you might have known."

The serpent leans forward slightly looking John up and down intently, and mumbles to him in barely a hiss, "You know there was talk of a creature, err human, not so long ago, a hero to the vermin, said to have come from the stars. Unfolding their stupid superstitions and myths as he went, and bringing peace to their primitive tribes. Superstitious nonsense I know, but we had our best operative take care of him. Just in case, you know."

"I am led to believe he died in an avalanche in a ravine somewhere," she hisses.

"Oh, that was you was it," says John rubbing the back of his head and frowning.

Big Dan nudges Cin and Max. "Well that answers that question."

"Impossible. That, that was you," stutters Sesstor.

John winks, smiles and says, "The one and only."

"That stinking verminus scum," screams Sesstor.

"Calls himself our best operative, he will pay for this dearly, you see if he doesn't," she hisses angrily.

"Maybe," snaps John. "But not as much as you will."

"Father," shouts Maxie. "I'm not sure why, but your friend there suddenly looks very, very happy."

John winks. "Yes, I have that effect."

The serpent then nods towards Maxie and says, "You do not wish to trade her do you. I could have great uses for a creature with such abilities."

"No sorry," apologises John with a cheeky grin. "Although I must admit, I'm tempted, but there'd be no living with her mother after it."

Big Dan, Cin, Woodnut and Fluff all give a snigger but stop dead on seeing both Max and Maxie's scowls.

"Now tell me," asks John. "One of your comrades out there told us, you would be contacting some great ship. A cleanser, or the cleanser, and it would kill us all. Is this true?"

"Maybe, maybe not," she hisses. "If I were to tell you, you would just kill me anyway."

"Two things," answers John. "Firstly, too late you've just told me what I wanted to know. And secondly, do not judge us by your own low standards."

She gives a loud hiss before answering, "Yes of course I did, what did you expect. And in one and a half rotations of your sun, my people will be here, and you will all die. And there is nothing you can do about it. We have travelled the universe and stars for millennia, in search of intelligent creatures of our own kind. And what do we find more often than not, humanoid creatures of various types similar to you. Infesting planets like a plague, killing and destroying each other and their planets with them. You repulse and disgust me, all of your kind does. But what we have learned is, there are many other civilisations out there, from types of amphibian, like your slave there, to insects of superior intelligence. But we have found we are the only one, which proves we are the pinicle of evolution. The one and only, the true race, the one race, the first race, to some planets we bring life, and to others death. We are your masters, we are the masters, we are your gods, we are the gods, you should drop to your knees and worship at our feet, so we may let you and your planet live."

Fluff suddenly comes bounding over snarling as it goes. "Hey, what are you doing?" shouts John as Fluff snarls past.

He winks slyly. "Get back over there, what have I told you about playing with your food."

Fluff goes back snarling as it does, much to the reptile's relief. John frowns. "That was one heck of a speech. On your high horse there weren't we."

Sesstor just gives out a loud hiss. "So there's nothing we can do?" asks John.

"Nothing at all. What about this eye it comes through? Can we not stop that?"

The serpent gives out another loud hiss. "She lies father," shouts Maxie. "There is something?"

Sesstor hisses again and shouts, "You could spend your whole lives trying to work out the controls in this complex, and still know nothing."

John shrugs and nods. "Yeah you're probably right."

"Hey witch, by any chance, you wouldn't have any of that flash bang on you, would you," he shouts.

There is a sudden flash of light and puff of smoke as the old woman gives out a cackle.

John winks. "Gun powder. I bet you know what that is don't you. There is wagon loads of the stuff back in the forest there, with my desert friends."

"Who needs buttons, come on boys," he says turning to walk away. "Let's blow the whole damn place up. Let's see just how tough those scales of yours really are."

"No, you can't, please," begs Sesstor.

"Watch me," snaps John.

"No please," she begs again. "Let us compromise, if this place were to be destroyed, my people would be stuck, trapped in whatever dimension they where in. Even in this one they would be light years away. Please I have an idea which should be most agreeable to us both."

John slyly winks to the others and turns back around. "Yeah I'm listening, for now that is."

"What if I contact my people, and tell them we have come to an accord," she hisses. "And neither you nor your friends here, are to be hurt. And in exchange you promise to go from here and never come back."

John heaves a big sigh. "Well, it kind of sounds alright, but, that's not much of a deal. How would we know you, or those above you, wouldn't change their minds?" he asks suspiciously.

"May I go to the panel over there?" asks Sesstor.

John nods, and she goes to a nearby panel and flicks her tongue into two holes, and a drawer slowly opens. She puts her head in and takes out an oblong instrument. "Do not worry this isn't a weapon," she tells them. "Some species we have, err, hem, err catalogued so to say," she stutters.

John frowns. "Catalogued or experimented on."

"Take your pick," snaps Sesstor. "I like yourself, am just a very small part in the grander scheme of things."

John raises his hands bowing his head. "Please carry on."

She bows in return. "I must place this device close to your temple," she tells him. "It will not hurt. May I approach?"

"Slowly," he answers.

The serpent cautiously comes over waving the device across his left temple. She then goes back over to the control panel. "Come," she tells him showing him a small screen on the device.

"You are very lucky, you have been catalogued," she tells him. "These letters and numbers represent you, and where you come from. I will enter them into the computer, it should tell me all about you, and exactly where you are from."

"N4003862198HS," she hisses. "My, my, you are a long way from home, in fact, three full dimensional jumps from home."

"But how is that possible. What is the last thing you remember?" she asks.

"Hem, let me think," mutters John. "Err, rushing down stairs I suppose. Hem, opening the door, and a blinding white light. I remember thinking I was dead, then just waking up in the desert here."

"You must have been caught in gravity wake, sucked in and pulled through," she hisses. "You should have been left in your dwelling, unconscious for hours, but obviously not."

"I have heard of this happening before on rare occasion," she tells him. "But it scrambles their brains. That is the ones that were lucky enough to be with a ship that jumped to an atmosphere, and did not just end up in space."

Big Dan nudges Cin, sighs deeply and says, "Why can I hear Lane's voice in my head now, shouting, it did."

Cin quietly chuckles, "Yes they were quite the pair, one as bad as the other I would say."

Sesstor then presses another button and writing comes up on the panel in front of her. "Hmm very interesting," she hisses to herself.

"Is that it?" stutters John. "That writing, it's all about me isn't it. Experiments or something, tell ME."

She quickly presses another button and different writing comes up. "No, nothing like that," she hisses. "Just general info, your height weight and that, you wouldn't understand our writing anyway."

"I, I wouldn't," he stutters. "Why?"

"Because you're just err," she stutters stopping dead.

"Ignorant vermin," continues John.

"Err, well I wasn't going to put it quite like that," she answers nervously.

"Now this is interesting," she tells him. "It says here your culture is very materialistic, and wealth orientated. And by the middle of this century your culture will crash."

"What do you mean by that?" snaps John.

"It is not our doing," she quickly tells him. "It's just what happens, you do it yourselves."

"And you know this for certain do you?" asks John gruffly.

"Not for certain," she hisses. "There's always the chance the right person, with the right information could change things. Maybe even you perhaps."

"Me," gasps John. "What do you mean by that?"

The serpent then turns around and tells them, "Stand back everybody, keep well away from the plinth in the middle there. I should not be showing you what I'm about to show you. But as you said, a gesture of good will, if my people found out they would kill me, now look."

They all stare at the opaque square in the middle of the room, as purple and blue crackles start to appear from it. The noise gets louder and the girls have to cover their ears. They all stand there mesmerised as slowly a red arc starts to rise from it. The minutes pass as it continues to rise, and form a large oval shape standing about nine feet tall. The crackling stops and the noise fades, and all that is left standing is a red oval shaped bubble. "Keep watching," hisses Sesstor as she presses more buttons.

A red line forms a crack in the middle of the bubble, which then slowly starts to part like two great bloodshot eyelids, forming a picture as it opens. Now fully open, drops of liquid red light drip slowly down from the top to the bottom, and back around again. "Do you recognise the image?" asks Sesstor turning to John.

John rubs his eyes in disbelief and stagers over to the oval picture. He tries to touch it still speechless. But his fingers are like stones on water, just causing a ripple to wash across the picture as he puts his hand through it. "John," shouts Cin. "What is it? Do you know this place?"

"It's his home," says the old woman. "As he saw it last."

"H, how," stammers John. "Where did you get this? How is it possible? That is my house, my, my doorstep."

"A simple monitor from the last time one of our vessels, err, visited you," she hisses.

"I have the power to send you back through this eye and home," she tells him softly.

"Y, you do, r, really," gasps John.

"Yes," nods the serpent. "I can even make it no more than a moment after you left."

John gasps again shaking his head in disbelief. "You, you can, e, even with that little problem."

"There will be no problems," she answers.

"No there is one little problem," he stammers his eyes filling up.

Sesstor nods. "You mean it may scramble your brain, no, not this way," she tells him.

"S, so this isn't how your large ships come through then?" he asks.

"No," answers the reptile. "They have their own on board each ship, and there is another larger one that opens out onto the roof above. We get the signal down here, but it has to be activated above to connect with theirs on board. So they can make the jump, and it depends on where they are coming from, on where they come out. It is impossible to be that exact, and may appear in the sky as no more than a flash of light."

"S, so," stutters an emotional John. "All you have to do is press a few buttons here, and I can go home. Y, you wouldn't be having me on now would you? Please tell me you're not," he asks as his eyes start to fill with tears.

"It's as simple as that," hisses Sesstor. "All you will have to do then, is step through the eye, and you are home."

"This is wonderful," shouts John. "I, I can go home, and my wife and daughter, they can come too?"

The serpent slowly shakes her head. "I'm sorry no," she says. "Your planet is much the same as ours, and our gravities are much heavier than here. Their bodies would be so heavy, there is a good chance their lungs would collapse, and they would die in minutes. And even if they didn't, they would be too exhausted to do anything. I'm so sorry, it's just they way it is. But I can promise you, if you do go, they will be safe. They will all leave here and no harm will come to them."

John looks back over to the others with tears in his eyes. "John," bellows Big Dan. "You can't honestly be considering this. You can't trust these things, surely you know that."

John stands there nearly in a trance and simply shrugs. Max's mouth falls open and her eyes start to fill also. "Please John," she begs. "This is madness."

"What about us?" she gulps.

"I, I, don't know what to think," he stammers. "I, I, feel so torn. I love you so much, all of you, and I do not want to be parted from you for a moment. But, but, if these things, creatures, come here in numbers, I, I might lose you anyway, it might be the end of us all."

"John," growls Cin. "This isn't funny."

"The choice is yours," hisses Sesstor. "If you go back, your life can go on as before, and you will be happy in the knowledge, you did the right thing. Or in just over a day the cleanser will be here, and all that will be left on this earth is the shadow complex and the woods surrounding it."

John collapses onto a nearby console sobbing with his arm around his head. "John," screams Max trying to get to him.

Big Dan grabs her around the waist once again. "No never," screams Max. "I won't accept it."

Sesstor grabs John's shoulder and pulls him up, "Get off that," she hisses. "You are leaking fluids all over it."

John stumbles back, landing on another console and is promptly pulled of that one also. "Max. Guys please," he begs.

"All that I do," he splutters wiping his eyes. "I'm doing for you, please trust me, it's, it's for the best. I know it in my heart, I must consider this, even with that problem."

"John NO," screams Max again.

"Max," snaps Big Dan. "Let this cur go, we are your real family now. And we will be alive at least, if this snake has any honour that is."

"It shall be as I said," hisses Sesstor angrily. "We aren't like you, we do as we say."

"Now what is your answer?" she asks turning to John. "Your comfortable world, your old life, your home back, no more hardships living like these savages here. You could be with your family."

She reaches high above one of the tall panels and grabs an object throwing it to him. "Here," she tells him. "It tells me on my screen, your culture may have some special value in this. Take it, it's of no consequence to me. They are only here for the children, they like to look at the light through them."

"They are of no real value to us," she tells him casually.

John catches the melon size object in both hands. "What is it?" he asks.

"Err in your language," she hisses and looks over to Hope.

Hope nods. "She says it's called a diamond," he answers.

John's mouth falls open and his eyes go wide. "This, this is a real diamond," he gasps. "An uncut diamond, it's, it's enormous. M, Maxie is she."

"No father," answers Maxie tearfully. "It is what she said."

"Here," she says throwing him another. "This is a cut one of similiar size, a touch bigger maybe. No matter, as I said, simply a child's play thing to us."

John places the uncut one carefully down, and gazes in amazement and awe at the other, holding it up to the light. He looks to the others then back at the diamond. "This would make such a difference to my life," he says. "And maybe with this sort of wealth. I, I, I could make a change on my world. Perhaps even stop my people and my culture from crashing.

"Damn it, yes!" he screams slamming his hand down on a nearby panel.

"Dad NO," screams Maxie running forward.

Cin grabs her and picks her up. "Let him go," he snarls. "Any person valuing a see through stone over friends, is not worth the tears."

"Please trust me," begs John. "This will make such a difference to me. To, to, us all, I'm, I'm sure of it."

He then nods solemnly to the serpent now standing between him and the eye. "I'm ready, damn the problem," he sighs softly.

"What is this problem?" she frustratingly hisses.

John lowers his head and mutters with a quiver in his voice. "What? I can't hear you," hisses Sesstor.

"Oh sorry," apologises John sombrely and stepping closer.

"I said," he mutters softly lowering his head.

The serpent cocks her head to the side straining to hear. "I am home," screams John suddenly shoving her as hard as he can into the bleeding eye.

The serpent screams loudly as she is engulfed by a blinding flash from the bleeding eye, as the final part of her flailing tail is sucked in. "Good riddance you overgrown handbag," shouts John triumphantly as the others stare over in total disbelief.

He turns to his friends throwing his fists in the air and shouts, "Who's the Man."

Big Dan and Cin rush over, Cin throws his arms around him lifting him up. Big Dan shakes his head and chuckles. "I knew you were up to something, but I wasn't sure what" he bellows.

"You, you did," stutters Max coming over. "How?"

"Oh come on Max," laughs Cin. "You didn't honestly take him seriously now did you? I mean. I had to bite my tongue at one point to stop myself from laughing."

"No, no, you didn't know at all," gulps Max.

"Max," laughs Dan. "You didn't honestly think, oh come on. Did you not hear him say trust me, and you know he's always up to something when he says that."

John frowns. "What do you mean by that?"

He winks grinning broadly. "I resent that remark I'll have you know."

Max spins round glaring at them all in turn. "Oh, you, you," she squeals. "You've done it again haven't you?" she screams. "Ooh, you're all nothing but a bunch of dangle berries."

"Does that mean what I think it means?" asks John.

Cin nods and John shouts, "Max, language please."

Now filled with a mixture of relief and embarrassment, Max simply starts to slap and punch each of them in turn. "Max. Max stop it," shouts John. "Look quickly."

They all turn to see what he's pointing at. He grins like a cheshire cat and wiggles his fingers cheekily at the bleeding eye. They all crowd around the eye with even Fluff getting his nose through. There in the centre they see Sesstor, staring up from John's doorstep in the dim cold morning light, hissing and screaming wildly. "I don't know what it's saying," chuckles Diss. "But it doesn't look very happy down there."

"Right everybody give a wave," says John.

"Do you think she'll be able to see us?" giggles Woodnut.

John shrugs and grins. "Who knows? But I'd like to think so."

"Oh quickly, out the way a moment everybody," he shouts. "I nearly forgot something."

He then looks round and quickly picks up the diamonds, turns and throws them through the eye to Sesstor. "We wouldn't want her to be without here valuables now would we," says winking to the others. "We know how materialistic they are on that earth."

Both Big Dan and Cin burst into fits of laughter as one of the diamonds bounces off her head. Now laughing so hard there's tears rolling down their cheeks, with Big Dan gasping, "Them, them, things, creatures can do all this."

"But, but," he gasps seriously trying to catch his breath.

"How intelligent are they, when they think a person would, would, not just sell out, but leave his friends, for, for, a see through rock," he squeals through the laughter.

"No, no," laughs Cin now bent double. "Get it right my friend, two stones. Oh, oh, but let's not forget, one's, a, a..."

"Yes, yes I know," splutters Big Dan. "A fancy shape."

"John?" asks Nas. "What does puzzle me though, is when you touched that eye, it was no more than an empty image, like the reflection in a pool. Yet when you pushed her in, she was somehow transported through."

"Oh yeah," replies John nonchalantly. "I had to calibrate the settings between here and there, and convert the heat from the beating heart, into energy. Then it was a simple task of pressing the on button, you see."

He nods shrugging. They all stare at him a gasp. "Surely John you are funning with us," gasps Geyri. "How by the Golden Ocean, could you know to do such a thing? And, and."

"Oh sorry yes," answers John a little puzzled by their reaction. "I read the instructions on a panel over there."

He shrugs again. "You? You did what?" gasps Nas.

"Yeah before when I was lent over the panel pretending to cry," he replies. "I then just had to get to the other side to make the settings. And as luck would have it, when she pulled me away it was with such force, it gave me the excuse to stumble over and on to the other controls, you see. Then a few minutes later, and when her back was to the eye, I simply belted the on button down. She just thought I was excited, and had decided to go back."

"But, but," splutters Cin. "You, you can't read."

John takes him over to a panel points and says, "There, what do you call that."

"That's not writing," Cin tells him. "They're just squiggly lines."

John gasps loudly and grinning sarcastically shouts, "Oh no, please god, don't tell me you can't read. See when we get out of here, I'm going to sit you down and teach you how."

"Ok, ok," grumps Cin. "So you can read snake, big deal."

"Oh, he's never going to let me forget this," he mutters to himself.

"No not snake," answers John. "They can write in, err, read in, they know err, whatever. It's English not snake ok."

"Can you teach me this English Dad?" asks Maxie.

John smiles. "Yeah sure why not. We'll teach each other, you can teach me you're writing too."

"What now John?" asks Max. "Can we stop these things from coming here?"

John nods. "I think so yes," he answers slowly.

"You don't seem so sure John," asks Woodnut.

"I just have to work some more of these panels out," replies John. "And read some more of the monitors. If you could all be quiet for a mo please, give me a little chance to read and think. Right let's get rid of that eye first, well the view in it. This, this, and that, two fingers in there, and there we go blank again."

23

THEY TURN TO see the serpent and John's doorstep slowly fade, leaving the eye blank and dripping red once again. "These creatures," says John. "Must be either really absent minded, or a bit stupid."

"Why?" asks Diss.

"Well look around," he tells them. "Every bit of panel, computer, work place everywhere. You see they all have these small glass monitors, every one of them, they're all instruction panels. Simply touch one and it brings up a complete idiot guide. How could something that not just travels to other stars, but other dimensions be so stupid? Surely not, there must be another explanation."

"John you shouldn't complain," says Big Dan. "It's better than having none."

John then goes around every work station and panel, reading them all with time ticking slowly by. "Right," he announces. "I think I've got it sussed, well more or less. I've stopped the signal from here, so none of their ships can triangulate with the beacon here. That should give us a bit more time. But they will eventually still get here. Now it appears there is a master system down by the beating heart, which is an automatic fail safe, in the event of emergences. If we can find and destroy that, then they are stuck wherever they are, they should never get here."

"So what is this beating heart you mentioned?" asks Max.

"I think it's a power source of some sort," he answers. "There's two of them I know that much."

Diss hand on chin and deep in thought nods. "So you say you have given us more time, before these serpents get here in their sky ships?" he asks.

John nods. "Yes but I'm not sure how much though, hours, days, weeks perhaps, who knows."

"And this eye here," asks Diss. "You could open this again to travel through?"

John shrugs. "Well, I suppose. Err yes it might take a little to work out, but, theoretically I could open an eye on planets anywhere."

Diss looks to his friends Nas and Geyri. "And so it comes to pass. John," he asks in barely a whisper. "Do you think you could set it to open on this earth?"

John gives out a puzzled look. "I'm not sure, where would you want to go.

Err yes, how stupid of me, back to the desert I suppose. Hem, I'm not sure if I could get it that accurate."

Diss sighs. "Not where, my friend, when. My friends and I are to go back in time to the beginning."

"What?" come the gasps.

"Hu what," stutters John. "I, I don't understand, you, found me, you, you, came here, and saved me. I really don't understand. What's the point? What do you even mean by it, the beginning? Err, what is the beginning anyway and why? I really don't understand this. I mean, this makes about as much sense to me as golf. As soon as you've found what you're looking for, you try you're best to lose the damn thing again. Why?"

Diss gives out a wry laugh but says, "I am so glad I met you my brother. You have the strangest ways of putting things, it does make me laugh so."

"It is what we were destined to do John," Nas tells him kindly. "It is what the ancient ones said must happen if the day should come, it was foretold. We were not sure ourselves what it meant, until now that is, and the explanation of the eye. It is the last sign we have been waiting for John. Just like the first signs on your arms. You see, it starts with the eyes, it finishes with the eyes."

Diss smiles. "Do not worry John,"he says. "This is a good thing, it was meant to be, it means the circle is unbroken. But first we will help you find the beating heart, so you may stop the heart from beating, and prevent the evil coming."

"Hu what," gasps John totally bewildered.

He sighs deeply. "Yeah ok then I suppose," he says. "Through the door there on the right, turn left, down the stairs, along the corridor. Big double doors at the end there, you can't miss it. Oh and mind the step when you go in."

"What?" shouts Cin. "You can't possibly know that?"

"Hum," mutters John casually. "Err yes I can."

Cin frowns. "But? But how?"

John points with a broad grin. "It says so on the door over there. Oh sorry yes, that's right, you can't read can you."

Cin groans, "He's going to be a nightmare to live with now."

Diss smiles. "You see John," he says. "It is as it is meant to be."

"So how far back do you want to go?" asks John and smiles. "At least you'll get to meet your ancestors I suppose, now that might be interesting. Here hang on, that means you'll actually be your own ancestors. Wow now that is bizarre, and a little hard to get my head around."

Nas stares at him oddly shaking his head then answers, "Around 1000 years please John, or there abouts anyway, before there were desert people. We will make our way there, and be the first to start the journey, and the long search. After all we wouldn't want to miss you my friend."

Max sighs. "Oh this, this is hurting my head. That would mean, you will be the ancient people of which your people talk of, and come from."

Diss smiles. "Yes it would appear so. And I am not just named after the ancient elder who originally lead the desert people. I actually am he, most peculiar."

The old crone suddenly gives out a loud cackle making them all jump. "You are your own ancestors," she cackles. "That's just silly. But at least you'll know the stories and legends you will tell will be correct."

Diss bows. "Yes, and that is another reason why we must go. Now if you'll excuse me, I will assemble our people and tell them of the good news."

"Maybe a few of our people should stay here," says Geyri. "As caretakers of this place. We would not want this place falling into the wrong hands, or even scales again, now would we."

Diss nods in agreement. "Now that my friend is a very good idea. I will ask for volunteers."

Geyri sighs deeply. "It was my idea, and I should be the first volunteer, although it seems to sadden me so."

"John," shouts Woodnut. "You must try and keep the barrier around this province. The forest, the creatures, and even the greenem here are unique and relatively unspoiled. It should stay so."

John smiles and nods. "I don't see why not. These two beating hearts seem to be the power sources. There's one that runs everything, from the complex, the barriers and such, and everything else here for that matter. And the other one, which is used solely for the bleeding eyes, one as you saw, and the other one above used for transporting their massive ships around the universe. Universes, I suppose, err, yeah. I presume they both need a power source all of their own, makes sense. So we just have to destroy that one really."

He smiles turning to Geyri. "There is one good thing though," he continues. "You see that panel over there."

Geyri nods. "Yes."

John winks. "Environmental controls. I'll show you how to use them later, and you can live here in whatever temperature and relative humidity you prefer. And one things for sure, you won't get bored in a hurry here. You could spend generations studying this place and everything in it, and still not have a clue. Heck by all accounts there's enough parts here, you could even build your own spaceship."

Geyri smiles bowing. "Yes, yes you are right," he says. "I was focusing on the negative, but now you put it like that. It fills me with pride and excitement, and I now know, this was meant to be also. We will learn, we will adapt, and my people shall have a new understanding. No longer shall we think the stars mere embers from the eternal fire of life. We shall study their place and ours in the universe itself. Now knowing there is more life out there, than we could ever have known or imagined."

John spends the next few hours working out how to set up the bleeding eye for the desert people, to travel back safely in time as asked. "Is that it?" asks Nas. "Could we go through now if we wished?"

John shrugs. "Err yes I suppose. I just have to press this button here, but I'm not quite sure where you'll come out. I think it's around here somewhere, but after 1000 years or so, give or take a few hundred. The landscape's changed somewhat, so you might struggle to find the right way to go, let alone the desert."

"Do not worry John my friend," says Diss coming back into the room with his wife Sturie. "We will find our way. After all, when you think about it, we already have, or we wouldn't be here now, and we will once again."

"Yes," shouts Nas. "But according to the stories, last time we had a guide."

Diss does not answer, he simply smiles and bows and turns to John. "Our people are ready when you are John," he says.

John nods and sighs deeply as he presses a large button, "I don't know," he says. "Whether I should be celebrating or commiserating."

Sturie steps forward and strokes his face and smiles. "Celebrating surely John. When the danger is over, you celebrate here, and we shall celebrate there, and we will still be together, in heart and thought."

She then bends down beside Maxie and Woodnut. "And you little lady," she says smiling kindly. "You made me miss all the fun and adventure."

"No," answers Maxie softly. "I was just making sure you didn't. The real adventure is still to come, and you have to look after my friend."

Sturie kisses her on the forehead and gets back up. "I will lead the way with Nas," she tells them.

"Do, do I just step through?" she asks. "It won't hurt will it?"

"It shouldn't do no," mutters John choking a little. "You may just feel a little disorientated for a moment or two that's all."

There are hugs, tears, and the shaking of arms all round, until finally bowing Nas and Sturie step through, one closely followed by the other. The flash of light fades and they quickly look to the eye to see if they have arrived there safely. And to everyone's relief they see their two friends standing there waving, in a green plush unspoiled meadow. "I shall go through last," Diss tells them. "And reassure my people they will be safe, before they go through."

It is then nearly three hours before the last of the desert people that are going file through, and Diss is left standing there alone by the eye. "Once again," a tearful Diss says and bows. "I must thank you all, you are such good people, and as one journey finishes another must begin. Take heart in that and thanks to you, life on this world will go on as before. And as our journeys take different paths, smile my friends, for we learn and grow as we travel along, and the road ahead may be even brighter. Only the sands of time will tell."

He then bows to Woodnut. "Until we meet again," he says and without another word he turns and steps through the eye.

"Woodnut," gasps John slowly turning. "What did he mean by that?"

For the first time ever Woodnut suddenly looks sad and sighs deeply. "I must go with them John."

"What?" come the gasps and shouts from his friends.

"It's true John, I'm sorry," apologises Woodnut. "I realised just before, just like the old desert man said, it all suddenly came together. My whole life, all of our travels and adventures, and all of the legends and prophecies, it all hit me at once, just like being struck by lightning. That's what Meadow Spirit meant, somehow, somehow he knew. The ancient greenem who told all the stories, who passed down all the legends, I was not named after him John, I am him. Who else could it be, who else is to lead them back to the desert, no one?"

Everyone stares silently at Woodnut too stunned to speak, all but Maxie that is, who picks him up and gives him a kiss. "I'll miss you, you know," she tells him.

Woodnut smiles back broadly and says, "And I you."

His face then suddenly screws up. "You knew, somehow, you knew didn't you?" he asks.

Maxie just grins cheekily and puts her tongue out. "But how? When?" he squeals.

Maxie shrugs. "I kind of guessed it was you, quite a long time ago," she answers. "I just didn't know how, but I knew it was you."

"H, how," stutters Woodnut.

"Oh come on silly," giggles Maxie. "Who else knows you better than me? Some of those stories and legends passed down, could only have come from you. And besides, some of them weren't meant for your people to understand you know, they were meant for me." She then gives him a cheeky wink. "You in the past will leave them for me, see. And besides, what other greenem has travelled with oomans and has your sense of humour?"

"And now," she giggles. "You'll know something no other greenem has ever been able to work out."

"What? What?" he asks excitedly.

She gives him another kiss and puts him back down. "How the desert people, could actually be the desert people if they hadn't got there yet. Remember, Knock Knock and Diddler."

Woodnut giggles, "Oh yes, just think of all the old greenem I will now get to meet, as, as barely saplings."

"Oh the fun I'm going to have," he sniggers.

Then a sudden sadness washes over him again, as he goes around all his friends saying his goodbyes and farewells, ending with John standing by the eye. "I, I don't know what to say," stutters John choking. "For once I'm, I'm lost for words."

"Do not be sad John," Woodnut reasuures him smiling. "I'm looking forward to the future, and so should you be. Oh but we did have fun didn't we."

John nods and sighs. "We still can my friend. You don't have to go, they'll find their way there sooner or later."

"John, I must, you know that," he answers. "Besides, I must go now and prepare for your coming. Or we would not have met in the first place, and that would be a tragedy now wouldn't it. For all the fun and adventures we've had together, we would then miss."

John steps back from the eye a little, and with tears silently rolling down his cheeks and bows. "I will never forget you my friend, and wherever you go, there will always be a little part of me with you."

Woodnut steps up to the eye as Max and Maxie rush over to John, both cuddling into him barely able to look. Woodnut slowly steps into the eye. "Oh Woodnut," shouts Maxie as he does so.

He just manages to turn and proceeds to fall in, just to see Maxie rush over to him. "See ya soon," she giggles waving cheekily.

"What? What? How?" are the last things heard as he is sucked completely into the eye.

Maxie turns back around giggling terribly to herself. But stops instantly on seeing everyone silently staring at her. "What's the matter?" she asks.

"Come on then?" says John. "What did you mean by that then?"

Maxie just shrugs. "Nothing really. I was just having a little fun before he went, that's all." Big Dan closes one eye staring wildly out of the other and says, "You must think we're stupid."

"No silly," she answers.

"Well maybe a little," she giggles cheekily.

She then sighs sadly. "Remember him fondly as you saw him there. It will be the last time."

They then all gather around the eye staring into it, and their friends, so close, yet so far away. All waving madly unsure if they'll even be seen as John precedes to closes the eye. Geyri sighs and turns to the other desert people standing with him. "Well that's that I suppose."

"Aye you old goat," shouts John to Hettie. He winks as he does so.

"Let's try this thing on you," he tells her holding up the reptiles scanning device. "Let's see if you're chipped, there's maybe a chance I can send you back. What do you say?"

The old woman does not answer, she just turns silently away. "What's the matter?" shouts John.

"Just leave her," whispers Max.

"What?" asks John a little puzzled.

"John," whispers Max. "What would be the point of an old woman going back to the moment when a young child was taken? Who'd believe her, would you?"

John nods. "Oh yes I see. I hope she doesn't think I was being nasty."

"Shush, just leave her my dear," whispers Max softly. "She knows your intentions were good."

They all suddenly look over to the door on the right as it slowly opens, and a large serpent slithers slowly in closing the door behind it. There is a sudden look of horror all around. Even from the serpent itself as it realises its mistake, desperately trying to get back through the door. "I told you there was a minimum complement of seven," shouts Hettie.

"Well are you lot just going to stand there like dead fish, or are you going to get it," she cackles.

Suddenly snapping out of it they all head to the door screaming and waving their weapons. The serpent just gets through in time. Stumbling with the handle Cin opens the door and they all pile through. They see the serpent sprinting down a long corridor and nearly disappear down some stairs. "It's going for the master system by the power supply," shouts John. "Fluff go get it boy."

Fluff ploughs through them so fast it knocks several of the desert people over. The serpent looks round at the snarling jackerbell screaming towards it. And it gives a hiss as it disappears down the stairs and through a large set of double doors, leaving Fluff hurtling down after it and running into the closed doors. Fluff gets back up, clawing and snarling wildly at the doors. "Out the way pal," shouts John as he gets there.

John throws the doors wide open and rushes in with Fluff, just to hear a whooshing sound over towards the wall on the left. Everyone else piles in behind them having just caught up. "Where's it gone?" pants Big Dan.

"There was a funny noise," answers John shaking his head.

"I think it went into, err, through that hole thing over there," he tells them.

The old woman ignores where the reptile went and instead runs straight across the room. The wall there does not go from floor to ceiling like most other rooms, but instead is only four and a half feet high, and goes round in a semi circle, from one side of the room to the other. The old crone looks over the wall and down, then with a gasp shouts on the others. They all rush to where she is leaning over for a look themselves. With all but John, Maxie and Hope instantly throwing themselves back and away from it. "By the sparkling stars," gasps Max. "I think I'm going to be sick, you, you could have warned us."

"Yes that would have been nice," pants Geyri. "That is one heck of a hole."

"Oh come on guys," shouts John. "I know this looks as if it goes clean down to the bowels of the earth. But we've looked down from higher, Cloud Falls remember."

Cin frowns. "Yes, but a little warning next time please."

"Will you all just stop whining on for a moment and look, you big bunch of fairies," shouts Hettie. Cautiously they all lean back over the wall and stare across the thirty foot circular abyss. Then even more cautiously they start to look down into the chasm. "It's a perfect hole straight down," puffs John. "I've never seen anything man made as deep, or snake made I suppose. There's something at the bottom, but I can't quite make it out."

"Hold my feet," says Maxie leaning further over.

"There's a large round orange thing down there," she shouts. "It takes up nearly all the space, there is a kind of pulsing glow coming from it. Like a beat, and there are some sort of tubes or cables coming out the side of it, leading to some panels similar to those in the other room.

Then she shouts, "Right you can pull me back up now."

"Wow, now there's a kid with gahonies," mutters Geyri.

"You have no idea," replies Big Dan.

"What do you think John?" he then asks.

"Oh come on you big muppet," cackles the old woman. "It's the master system, and it's wired directly into the power main supply. That pulsing, it must be why they call it the beating heart. But look around the edges at those tubes running around and around and down."

John nods. "It's like a giant helter skelter,"he exclaims. "How much fun does that look? Although I think by the time you got to the bottom, you would have no skin left on you."

"You don't get it do you," snaps Hettie. "That's what I was telling you about earlier. You are pulled or pushed through by a cushion of air. But look closely, nearly half way down, you should be able to see. All the tubes and walls are transparent. There look, the serpent."

She sighs deeply. "Even going through the tubes after it right now, it would still beat us down by twenty minutes, easily," she says. "And even then, it could pick us off one by one as we came out." She sighs again. "All is lost I think."

"John, what are we going to do?" asks Max. "If it gets to that thing, who knows. It could maybe get that ship thing back, or, or, who knows."

John sighs. "Err, yes, let me think a mo."

He then takes a deep breath and flops down hard on one of the nearby long cool stone seats. Then he shouts, "Hey guys, come and have a sit on this. It's fantastic, a little hard on the butt though."

Big Dan and Cin flop down. "Oh yes," agrees Dan. "It's solid."

"John please, never mind admiring the furniture, we have to do something," shouts Max.

"She's right John," agrees Hettie.

John frowns. "I'm thinking ok,"

"I could probably get down there," croaks Hope. "With my sticky pads I could jump from side to side, until I got to the bottom."

"And if you slip," answers John. "No it's too risky, and besides you couldn't fight that thing. And I wouldn't ask you to."

"John we can't just sit here," replies a nervous Geyri but John suddenly starts to grin, folds his arms and closes his eyes. "Max tell me when it's just about at the bottom please," he says.

"What are you up to?" asks Cin.

John smiles not even bothering to open his eyes. "Hey trust me," he replies.

"I hate it when he says that," mutters Big Dan.

Everybody then stands there nervously waiting as the minutes slowly pass. Maxie is leaning right over the wall trying to spit. "What are you doing child?" asks one of the desert woman.

"If I time it just right," she giggles. "When it comes out, I can spit on its head."

The woman turns to Max. "Are you not going to do something?" she asks. Max nods. "Oh yes. Move over dear, let me have a go."

"Damn stinking slimy reptiles" she mutters walking over.

"John," she then shouts. "Another few moments and it will be there."

"Ooh, excellent," shouts John getting back up.

He then spits on his hands rubbing them together. "Right lads you get that end of the seat and I'll get this end."

"Now that is a good idea," chuckles the two men gripping it firmly.

"Gees Louise," groans John. "This thing's even heavier than it looks."

Geyri sighs. "No John I wouldn't say that," he says. "It looks nearly immovable to me."

"Well of course it is, if you're just going to stand there whining," shouts John.

"Everybody grab a bit," shouts Geyri.

Slowly but surely they make there way over to the wall with the large stone bench. And after a lot of heaving and shoving they manage to get it up and balanced on the top. "I'll hold it," shouts John. "The rest of you gather around the wall and look down. Right hold your ears, Maxie give a whistle."

As she does so the serpent now just about reaching the bottom of the tube looks up. John lets go, and the large heavy solid stone bench silently makes its way down, getting faster and faster all the time. John grins cheekily and says, "Now everyone give a wave."

They all wave to the horrified reptile, as it stares back up in disbelief at the large solid object now hurtling down like an exocet missile.

The serpent is finally shot out the last tube and into its final destination.

Pulling itself together it tries to scramble back to the air lock. But to no avail, and realising its impending doom it simply curls in a ball, and places its hands over its head. "Yes I'm sure that'll help," cackles the old woman as the stone bench crashes through the power supply.

"Well that's stop that beating," she cackles again. "Call it a heart attack."

There's a nearly deafening explosion as a mushroom cloud of flames and shrapnel slowly makes its way up. "Time for a hasty retreat me thinks," shouts John.

They pile back out the doors closing them firmly behind them. The whole place shakes as they sprint down the last corridor and out the building. They all lthen ook up as the blast blows a small part of the roof above clean off. "Well that's the end of that," says John nodding his head. "I don't know where those damn things are right now. But one things for sure, they ain't coming back here in a hurry. And you can take that to the bank."

A loud cheer rings out from all, and John is reluctantly hoisted on to their shoulders. "Now my friend," shouts Geyri beaming from ear to ear. "Now we celebrate, to battles won and new friends made, and old friends parted."

They all make their way back over to the desert peoples' supplies. "So what now?" asks Max as they walk along. "What do we do? Do we stay here or—?"

"Nonsense woman," booms Big Dan. "I want to see the ocean. Didn't you?"

John grins. "Yeah sounds good to me. Maxie what do you think."

"Yeah," she shouts, excitedly clapping her hands.

The celebrations go on for days, and they stay on for a further several weeks helping the desert people settle in. Until finally their friends escort them to the border, Geyri waving them off turns to his wife and says with a heavy sigh, "It seems lately, all we are doing is saying goodbye."

"Yes it seems that way," she replies softly. "But it also means when we meet again, it will be all the more pleasant."

And as the friends turn and walk away Maxie whispers to John asking, "So how long did it take you to decide not to go back? You know, when that serpent tried to tempt you with those diamond things?"

"No more than a few moments," he whispers back. "After all, what is the point in money and wealth, without your loved ones to share it with? And I would not swap a moment without any of you, not for any amount."

Maxie sighs, folds her arms and whispers, "But Dad, they were just two silly bits of see through crystal. I mean, how much could they have been worth anyway?"

"P-lease," she giggles folding her arms again and cocking her head to the side.

"Put it this way," he whispers back. "In your money, probably enough to buy several provinces, easily." Maxie's mouth falls open, and they walk along together in silence smiling to each other. Their thoughts now set on their next adventure. But this time, untold and unforeseen by all.

Lightning Source UK Ltd.
Milton Keynes UK
UKOW07f1846071214

242753UK00002B/23/P